A
M... ...DE

For Betty Taylor

From Marcus with compliments and best wishes

[illegible signature]

11 Dec 1996

TO KILL A MAN'S PRIDE

and other short stories from South Africa

Second Edition

Edited by Marcus Ramogale

RAVAN

Published by Ravan Press (Pty) Ltd
PO Box 145
Randburg 2125
South Africa

First edition 1984
Second edition 1996

ISBN 0 86975 460 2

Cover design: Monica Seeber and
Centre Court Studio

Typesetting: Maxwell Avenue Design
Bembo 11/12

Printed by: Clyson Printers 11th Avenue
Maitland Cape

CONTENTS

ACKNOWLEDGEMENTS

We are grateful to the following for permission to reproduce copyright material:
Human and Rousseau Publishers, for 'Unto Dust' by H.C. Bosman from *Unto Dust;* A.P. Watt Ltd on behalf of The Society to Help Civilian Blind, for 'A Sack of Ninepence' by Sarah Gertrude Millin; Heinemann Educational Books Ltd, for 'The Suit' by Can Themba from *The Will to Die,* 'The Wind and a Boy' by Bessie Head from *The Collector of Treasures* and 'Six Feet of the Country' by Nadine Gordimer from *Some Monday for Sure*; Johnathan Cape Ltd, for 'Ha'Penny' by Alan Paton from *Debbie go Home*; Weidenfeld and Nicolson Ltd for 'Beggar my Neighbour' by Dan Jacobson from *Through the Wilderness;* Ad Donker Publisher, for 'The Visits' by Richard Rive from *Selected Writings*; Curtis Brown Ltd for 'No Witchcraft for Sale' copyright Doris Lessing 1951; Ahmed Essop for 'The Hajji' from *The Hajji and Other Stories*; Mbulelo Mzamane, for 'My Cousin, Sitha' from *Mzala*; Mtutuzeli Matshoba, for 'To Kill a Man's Pride' from *Forced Landing*; Njabulo Ndebele, for 'The Music of the Violin' from *Fools and Other Stories*; Miriam Tlali, for 'Devil at a Dead End' from *Soweto Stories*; Gcina Mhlope, for 'The Toilet' and Maud Motanyane, for 'Two Minutes' both from *Sometimes When it Rains*; COSAW Publishing for 'The Finishing Touch' by Deena Padayachee from *What's Love Got to do with it? and Other Stories* and 'The Wedding' by Bheki Maseko from *Mamlambo and Other Stories*; Es'kia Mphahlele, for 'Crossing Over'.

PREFACE

This anthology is meant to be used by senior high school pupils, and by tertiary education students at college, technikon or university in the early years of their studies. The accessibility and narrative styles of the short stories anthologized here vary. The teacher has the latitude to choose stories that are appropriate for his or her own group.

The anthology offers the reader stories that are unmistakably modern and South African in terms of perspective. Twenty writers present portrayals of the experiences of South Africans from excitingly varied angles. Even the story *Mr Nakasa Goes to Harlem* is, despite its concern with the African-American experience, arguably South African in that Nat Nakasa looks at the African-American experience through South African eyes.

As in the first edition of the anthology, the present stories have no idiom or style of writing that is alien to this country. The milieu reflected in these stories, with the exception of Nat Nakasa's story, is also unambiguously South African. There are stories set in rural areas such as the village, the farm, the veld or the dorp;

others are set in urban centres such as the big city, the suburb or the township.

The present edition demonstrates again the success with which the short story form has been naturalized in South Africa, and features more women writers and a new male voice to make it more representative. Four stories from the first edition have been taken out and seven new stories added: Sarah Gertrude Millin's *A Sack for Ninepence*, Miriam Tlali's *Devil at a Dead End*, Gcina Mhlophe's *The Toilet*, Maud Motanyane's *Two Minutes*, Deena Padayachee's *The Finishing Touch*, Bheki Maseko's *The Wedding* and Es'kia Mphahlele's *Crossing Over*, the author's latest short story (or novella, if you like) which has not yet been published. It is a story different from most stories in this anthology in terms both of its narrative mode and the 'African flavour' the author infuses into it. The black characters' speech patterns, especially 'MaSelepe's, are based on the North Sotho speech rhythms and peculiarities, as well as on North Sotho idiomatic expressions.

The varied perspectives offered by the stories in this anthology are united by a common focus on the subject of 'pride' and its 'negation'. This topic is developed through focus on issues such as the hurts of humiliation, disappointment, frustration, dissatisfaction, failure and non-fulfilment. Such topical unity is pedagogically useful, because it allows for sharply defined learning activities, as does the stories' largely common geographic focus. It is therefore possible for the teacher and learner to compare and contrast certain stories on the basis of a particular idea.

What emerges from this collection is writers' shared concern with the difficulties of life. The stories demonstrate persuasively that life is sometimes irksome and disappointing, that to live entails a constant struggle against adversity, frustration and belittlement. These stories enhance our understanding of life with subtlety and proficiency.

South Africa is the setting for the disquieting realities depicted in these stories, and South Africans are the people on whom our attention is focused; but each story is concerned with a particular worldwide experience. In each local and private experience we see something universal, and in each universal reality we can find our personal experiences reconstructed.

Because these stories deal with the challenges of life, in each story we find characters who are involved in a struggle to prevail. The creative strategies used by various characters to cope with or rise above unfavourable circumstances constitute a valuable lesson in problem-solving techniques. Even the non-success of some characters teaches us how to avoid failure and situations which may undermine our own sense of 'pride'. Perhaps this, more than anything else, makes these stories so educative.

INTRODUCTION

Section 1: What is a Short Story?

The art of the short story as practised today was solidly established in the nineteenth century by writers such as Edgar Allan Poe. Earlier forms of the short story such as the folk tale, fable, myth, parable, legend, lay and *fabliau* predated the nineteenth-century art form.

The term short story is not is easy to define. The *Macmillan Contemporary Dictionary* (1979) provides, however, a definition that can be profitably used as a starting point. This dictionary defines the short story as a 'fictional prose work with a single theme, full plot, limited number of characters, and shorter in length than a novel'. While this definition does not cover every aspect of the short story as a genre, it does throw up points which, if explained in a little more detail, will allow us to talk about other features of this art form.

1.1 Language

The short story uses 'prose' as a medium; in other words, it employs language in its ordinary or everyday form. This does not, of course, preclude short story writers from giving their stories a poetic character. There are many short stories the world over with distinctive poetic features.

Literary language, whether poetic or prosaic, appeals, in a thoroughgoing fashion, to the reader's senses, emotions, imagination and intellect. Its impact is complete because literary artists rely on a combination of narrative and rhetorical devices such as metaphor, rhythm, tone, symbol, image, point of view, plot, character, conflict, action, setting, atmosphere and so on to appeal to the reader's whole being, and thereby deepen and extend his or her experiences, sympathies and insight. Literary language is used to make us feel what it means to be human, and it achieves this through recreating intense and convincing impressions of the human experience. Through literary language we begin to know ourselves, our society, and the world we live in. The language used by writers anthologized here is no exception.

Because a short story must be short, a careful writer always tries to avoid diffuseness and long, leisurely descriptions. The aim is to economize on the use of words, thus achieving compression. Spare and suggestive writing is the hallmark of good short fiction.

1.2 Fictionality

The short story is also a fictional work, meaning that the characters and situations it deals with are partly or wholly imaginary. Fiction involves an imaginative reconstruction of reality, and such reality may be objective or subjective. The reality of fiction is imaginary, because writers rely on intuitive and imaginative thoughts and feelings for their creative endeavours. However, the characters and incidents they are concerned with can also be a real reconstruction of their past or present experiences. In such a case, then, the fictionality of the story would derive from the fact that it is concerned with characters and situations that are an approximate, rather than an exact, representation of those events and persons. Even though a short story may refer to known people and events, it is the author's imaginative representation of these that makes the work fictional. Fiction approximates life; it does not produce *replicas* of reality. This is so because literary artists create their stories by reordering and reshaping the raw material that is reality. They give a shape, a plan and a sense of organic structure to what we usually experience as *chaotic* and incomplete reality. In a sense, the fictionality of fiction also derives from the impression of organization and completeness in the segment of life it portrays.

There are several reasons why human beings are attracted to the imaginative enactments of fiction. One of the potent reasons is that in fiction we find 'not only the pleasure of recognizing the world we have known and of reliving the past, but also the pleasure of entering worlds we do not know and of experimenting with experiences which we deeply crave but which the limitations of life, the fear of consequences, or the severity of our own principles forbid to us . . . . In fiction we escape limitations and penalties' (Brooks, Purser, and Warren, 1975: 3).

1.3 Theme

It is generally accepted that a short story is concerned with a single major theme that gives it focus and unity. Although it is possible for a story to have more than one main theme, the shortness of the short story also derives from its concern with one main theme. The concept of theme as used here refers to what the writer says about a particular subject or topic. To put it differently, theme is 'the governing idea implicit in the original situation of conflict that becomes, in the end, the focal idea — that is, what we take to be the "meaning" of the whole' (Brooks, Purser, and Warren, 1975: 15). As the central idea of a work, theme says something about people and life in general; it provides existential insight, and is prominent in stories that seek to make a serious comment on the human condition. Although theme is often *suggested in the story*, it can also be stated directly by the author.

All the stories in this anthology are based on the subject of pride, or what can be described as a person's sense of dignity and self-respect. However, this general topic is treated differently by each writer, and is developed through a thematic focus which draws on narrative devices such as characterization, setting, plot, diction, symbolism, point of view, imagery, tone and so on. In Miriam Tlali's *Devil at a Dead End*, for instance, the author seems to suggest that 'a woman whose dignity is at stake fights back cunningly and effectively'. This, then, would be the theme of the story. Theme is therefore a narrative elaboration of a particular subject, and must be teased out of the story. We expect to find in a theme an authorial and dramatic explanation of a given subject.

It is possible for a story to have minor themes in addition to the main theme, but plot often revolves around a single major theme. Subordinate themes, or sub-themes, are dependent on the main theme for their significance and are related to it.

Sub-themes are common in long narrative works such as novellas and novels, and their purpose is to give the writer an opportunity for a detailed treatment of the subject at hand. A fictional work's thematic development can be illustrated thus:

SUBJECT > MAIN THEME(S) > SUB-THEME(S)

1.4 Plot

A single pre-eminent theme in a short story is important, because it not only allows for thematic unity but also ensures that there is a straightforward plot. The plot structure of a short story is often straightforward in the sense that it is uninvolved: its organic development is not as intricate as in novels; it proceeds in what may be described as a fairly 'linear fashion'; it is neither digressive nor padded out. Usually, the plot starts with an incident and then develops through a sequence of events to a climax and resolution of the action. The concept of plot refers to the developmental structure of events in which one incident leads to another. A story has a plot if there is a 'causal connection' or 'link' between events. Many stories, both modern and traditional, follow this pattern in their narrative method.

For example, the following story has a plot because the events have an organic relationship:

> Hundreds of township residents went to the suburb of Houghton yesterday to see a famous film actress tie the knot at a friend's house.

However, the following narrative does not have a plot:

> Hundreds of township residents went to the suburb of Houghton. A famous film actress tied the knot at a friend's house.

In the above example, we have two unrelated events which can, at best, be linked imaginatively only when the reader makes an effort to fill in the gap. There is no textual signal which points to the relation between the two events. In the first example, however, it is clear that the film actress's marriage led to hundreds of township residents going to Houghton. A plotted story, therefore, has causal connection whereas a plotless one doesn't. However, it is important to note that a plotless story is not an inferior form of art; it is simply different. Stories without a plot are often those which dwell on 'inner reality' or the interiority of human consciousness. Plotless stories may also be those which try to suggest that life is without order, coherence, clarity, meaning or plan.

The plot of a short story, even though uncomplicated, is 'full'. In other words, a good short story has a sense of wholeness; it is completely developed. A good story may end on a powerful note of suspense, but will still have a total effect, a sense of integrity, thus giving us the impression of a finished artistic product. We may be left wanting to know more, but the narrative structure coaxes us into accepting the necessity of that particular conclusion.

A plotted story makes use of organic events for its development. The writer arranges these events in a particular order to achieve a particular effect. The portrayal of conflict, whether internal or external, is another strategy writers use to develop their plots.

The final outcome in the plot of a short story often comes swiftly in the last paragraph or sentence after the reader has been kept in suspense throughout. An 'unexpected ending', 'a dramatic unveiling' and 'a surprising twist of plot' are the 'shock tactics' the short story writer uses 'to make the reader think and respond' (Hawthorn, 1985: 23).

1.5 Characterization

One dominant thematic concern and an uninvolved

plot do not allow for numerous characters. This explains why short stories have a limited number of characters and why, consequently, each role-player is a vital and indispensable part in the interrelationship of main events and the story's thematic development. A character's role might be a minor one, but that does not necessarily turn the character into an expendable presence. In fact, such characters are necessary to give the story a sense of fullness.

Literary characters can be known better than real human beings because their inner lives, including their hopes and fears, are closely revealed to us by the author. Situations in which they are placed by the nature of the plot also serve as a test that unveils their personality. In real life we are often not privileged to know individuals as intimately as we do in fiction.

A literary character may be introduced to the reader directly or indirectly. Direct characterization happens when the writer tells the reader openly and straightforwardly the sort of a person the character is. In this case, the person's character traits are made known to the reader directly through the narrative voice. Direct characterization is also made possible when the person in question says something that highlights their personality and behaves in a manner that focuses the reader's attention on their character traits, beliefs and values.

A character is presented indirectly when the author simply shows us how the person behaves and what they think, feel and say, thus allowing us to determine on our own the kind of a person the character is. Sometimes indirect characterization occurs when the writer tells us what other characters in the story say about that character. Whatever method the writer uses, the purpose is always the same: to present believable characters that the reader will be interested in, either because they are pleasing or disagreeable.

A detailed discussion of characterization will be found in section 2 of this introduction.

1.6 Concluding perspectives

Each story in this anthology is dominated by a specific element (character, plot, theme, place, point of view and so on) which gives the narrative a unique make-up and specificity of focus. A story that does not blend several narrative elements is not necessarily mediocre. Its special focus simply means that the author has a different purpose. You will find in this anthology some stories that use a single narrative aspect rather than an integrated treatment of all elements.

Even though it is accepted that a short story must be short, the extent of its shortness is uncertain. Hawthorn (1985: 3) provides what can only be described as a rough guide:

> In practice . . . we usually refer to a prose narrative of some twenty or thirty pages or less as a short story, while works that seem to hover on the awkward boundary between 'short story' and 'novel', having a length of between forty or fifty and a hundred pages, we describe as novelle (singular: novella).

In accordance with this classification, Es'kia Mphahlele's *Crossing Over* in this anthology may be seen as a novella and the rest as stories.

The essence of the short story is constantly elusive. The above definition is certainly neither exhaustive nor final. There are more characteristics of the genre that you will find as you read widely. I have only outlined salient features which you will discover in the short stories anthologized here. As you read more, you will find that there are stories which are exceptions to the norm I have tried to outline. The short story has shown that it is capable of limitless possibilities.

Section 2: Short Story Analysis

Some of the characteristics of the short story just discussed can be found in Njabulo Ndebele's *The Music of the Violin.* (Please read the story before you proceed any further, otherwise this analysis will not make much sense.) This story is presented by a *third-person omniscient narrator*, who observes everything and knows everyone's thoughts and feelings. The greatest strength of this story lies in its characterization, because the author's special focus is on character portrayal and analysis. In the preceding section, brief mention was made of characterization in short fiction. Ndebele's story, on account of its specific focus, now presents us with an opportunity to discuss characterization in detail, including elements of narrative fiction not mentioned before.

The story, set in Soweto, is largely about the emotional and mental distress suffered by Vukani, the *protagonist.* This story is based on the literary notion of *psychological realism*, as it seeks to delineate the intellectual and emotional interiority of the main character. The inner life of the protagonist is troubled by questions of class, culture and identity, which arise from his middle-class background in a largely working-class environment. Vukani's middle-class status derives from his parents' privileged social position. Both mother and father are middle-class professionals, who subscribe to values that are in conflict with those of the ordinary people of Soweto. His parents, especially the mother, impose these values on Vukani in a singularly uncompromising spirit, thus bringing him into conflict with other children whose values and background are working-class.

The Music of the Violin focuses mainly on Vukani and an expensive violin his parents have bought him in order to enhance his musical talent. For both mother and father, the violin is a status symbol, a concrete representation of their deep yearnings for a sophisticated middle-class lifestyle — what Dr Zwane, a family friend, calls 'advancement'. It is interesting to note that Vukani's parents did not buy him a guitar, a musical instrument widely used in black South African townships. To them, a violin symbolizes a higher cultural life unknown to most township residents. They want to be different from, rather than to merge with, the masses. As far as they are concerned, 'otherness', as opposed to 'sameness', is a source of their identity. They take pride in their difference, because they see the dominant proletarian culture around them as inferior.

Vukani's father is a school inspector and the mother a nursing sister. They are professionals whose driving ambition is not only to lead a 'civilized' life, but also to have it rub off on their children. The humble life of the masses is not for them.

The story begins and ends in Vukani's home on a Friday evening. However, the story's unity of place and time does not prevent Ndebele from giving us glimpses of Vukani's experiences outside his home and at different times. He uses the *flashback technique* to give us this extra information — information which is crucial to the development of the story. The use of flashbacks *inverts* the chronological order in which the story is generally told. These flashbacks are important aspects of the story's narrative organization as they provide the reader with revealing answers at crucial moments in the development of the plot. The reader's curiosity as to *why* Vukani behaves the way he does is thus satisfied.

The first flashback takes us to Vukani's school a year previously, and the second to the Friday afternoon of the story. All these flashbacks portray different aspects of Vukani's experiences, which are characterized by a sharp sense of personal alienation and ill-treatment.

At the beginning of the story, we meet a restless Vukani in a state of *conflict*, which is both internal and external. He is in his bedroom, unable to concentrate on his homework because of the noise from the living room. His parents and their visitors are engaged in a conversation that is punctuated with laughter. He is also anxious to avoid the visitors and thereby save himself from 'the usual agony' that would follow. Vukani is in conflict with himself and the people in the living room. The narrator heightens our curiosity deliberately by not explaining what 'the usual agony' is. The stage is now set for the dramatization of Vukani's mental and emotional anguish.

The mystery behind Vukani's anxiety is partly resolved when we learn later that 'the usual agony' is caused by his mother's habit of insisting that he entertains family guests with his violin. Vukani's anxiety builds up as he expects the visitors to be brought to his bedroom at any time. Ndebele uses Vukani's apprehension to generate an atmosphere of tension and uncertainty. We begin to feel that something dramatic is about to happen. This sense of expectation engages us deeply as we read the story. The technique of *suspense* as used here is meant to make the reader speculate about what is going to happen. We become aware that the violin is capable of bringing both 'pain and pleasure' to Vukani. But why pain? Is it not odd for a violin, an instrument we usually associate with musical pleasure, to bring distress to someone?

The Music of the Violin can be described as a *psycho-*

logical drama in that Ndebele relies heavily on Vukani's inner conflict and fear to develop the plot and themes of the story. As Vukani waits in his bedroom, trying 'to brace himself for the coming of the visitors', he is made to look like a defendant in a court of law, anxiously awaiting judgement. It emerges that Vukani is 'an unwilling entertainer', hence his nervousness. He sees the task of entertaining visitors with his violin as 'an agonising nuisance'. But why? It is not clear at this stage why Vukani chafes at the thought of playing the violin, because the narrator provides explanation piecemeal in order to whet the reader's appetite, as it were.

As Vukani waits to see how events will turn out, a rebellious thought comes to his mind: he thinks of refusing to play, of defying his parents. For the first time, the thematically important idea of rebellion is tentatively introduced. Although he was well provided for — he had books, a place for study, plenty of clothing, a transistor radio, a violin, and games — Vukani found home unpleasant. Because he was materially comfortable, thanks to his well-to-do parents, his mother expected him to show his gratitude by being completely dutiful. She equates a demonstration of piety by Vukani with an acceptance of the middle-class values she professes. She was fond of telling him how lucky he was. However, as far as Vukani was concerned, this 'luck' brought only pain and restrictions. Vukani's unhappiness is caused, in the first place, by numerous limitations imposed on him. His room, he reflects, might be as good as any white boy's, but this comfort has turned him into a virtual slave. He then remembers what one of his teachers told them at assembly one morning:

> 'Children, I would rather be a hungry dog that runs freely in the streets than a fat, chained dog burdened

with itself and the weight of the chain. Whenever the white man tells you that he has made you much better off than Africans elsewhere on this continent, tell him he is lying before God!'

Vukani, no doubt, desires freedom and identification with the children of the Soweto proletariat, who are certainly 'hungry' but 'free' — free from the rigours of a 'control culture' represented by his parents. The quest for freedom, for a life without regimentation, is central to Vukani's rejection of his parents' expectations. On this level, the story can be seen as a dramatization of the age-old topic of youthful rebellion and a desire for adventure. He wants to liberate himself from the constraints of a rigid domestic life and join other children roaming the streets. He is a boy in search of peer-group acceptance, of a sense of belonging.

But on another level, the story can be seen as a microcosmic representation of the power relations of apartheid South Africa. Within this interpretive framework, the role played by Vukani's parents can be regarded as symbolizing that of the former paternalistic white establishment, and Vukani's that of the struggling black masses. The white establishment, convinced of its 'civilization' and historic mission — to bring 'prosperity' to South Africa — enjoined blacks to accept their subjugation, because, as the propaganda went, Africans in other parts of the continent were worse off.

In the same vein, Vukani's parents expect him to be thankful and obedient, because, as the mother says to him, 'There is not a single boy in the whole of Soweto . . . who has a room like yours.' Vukani's parents are proud of the apparent success of their civilizing mission, hence they invite guests such as those in the living room to come and see signs of their progress, which are evidenced in particular by Vukani's playing of the violin. The white establishment also entered into this sort of self-congratulation when foreign tourists were invited to South Africa to come and see how white *baaskap* had brought happiness and material advancement to blacks.

Vukani's misery is caused, in the second place, by his *alienation*. His mother likes to 'show off at his expense'. For instance, on Mondays, Wednesdays and Fridays he has to carry his violin to school for after-school musical lessons. The violin sets him apart from other children; he becomes a virtual outcast, is often teased and eventually becomes known as the 'fellow with a strange guitar'. The word 'strange' is an important indicator of the gulf that separates Vukani from the dominant culture of his social environment. He is, in a sense, a foreigner, and his foreignness is typified by the unfamiliar musical instrument he carries with him.

Ndebele seems to suggest that the only solution to Vukani's cultural isolation does not lie in 'difference' but in 'likeness', and that the only viable cultural option for the black elite is incorporation into and participation in the cultural life of the black working class. It is important to note this point, because this story was written when the white state was attempting to drive a wedge between the educated black elite (potential leaders in the struggle against apartheid) and the black masses.

In order to create a strong fund of sympathy for Vukani, the narrator takes us, through an important flashback, to an incident a year before when Vukani's violin was stolen at school. We begin to see him as a helpless victim. As he says to his friend Doksi, 'The whole class seems to have ganged up on me.' This flashback also makes us aware that Vukani is treated as a pariah not only because of the violin but also because he is the inspector's son. His middle-class background has earned him adversaries in a largely working-class environment. While searching for the violin, a girl called Topsana makes cruel fun of him:

> 'Hey you, Vukani,' called Topsana, 'I want to soothe your heart. I've long been waiting for this moment. Come and kiss me.' The smaller girls giggled. . . . 'I mean it,' said Topsana. 'I know who took your violin. It's safe. You'll find it at home. I made them promise to take it there. There now, I want my kiss. I want to kiss the inspector's son.'

Class rivalry among blacks is a crucial theme in this story. Vukani's mother, for example, is determined to make sure that her family remains distinctly middle class and superior to the township 'animals' and 'savages' and determined to ensure that her children are not won over by these inferiors. For instance, when she found the stolen violin on the doorstep of their house the following morning, she went into uncontrollable rage as she interpreted that as an act of spiteful ingratitude on the part of Vukani. Her attempts to transmit 'civilized' values to him, she reckoned, were being spurned. By contrast, Vukani's father is shown as a reasonable, if not somewhat ineffectual, parent. As a school inspector, he sees his task as that of 'uplift[ing] the black nation'. However, his role in the whole process of 'enlightenment' is not characterized by the irrationality of Vukani's mother; he is the voice of reason in the family, and his yearning for a comfortable lifestyle is tempered with a sense of good judgement. Ndebele constantly shows him as the *antithesis* of Vukani's mother.

For example, he tries, in the manner of a gentleman, to calm down his wife after she has found the violin on the doorstep:

'What's happening Dorcas?' Vukani saw his father entering the bedroom. 'Can you believe this? I found this violin on the doorstep outside as I was leaving for work. Can you believe this?'

'Vukani,' said his father. 'What on earth could have made you do such a thing?'

'I didn't put it there, Baba,' Vukani replied.

'Nonsense,' shouted his mother, 'You don't have to lie. Ungrateful boy, you have the nerve to tell your parents a lie.'

'Wait a minute, dear, maybe we should hear what he has to say.' Vukani had nothing to say. The deep feeling of having been wronged could only find expression in tears. He heard the violin land next to him and he recoiled from its coldness. He also heard his mother leave, saying that he was crying because of his sins. She never knew what had happened . . .

Although a likeable character, the father's moderating influence is not always effective, because he is not sufficiently assertive. It would not be far-fetched to see in the father a representation of South Africa's English-speaking liberals and Afrikaner *verligtes*, historically rational, gentle and receptive, but eventually ineffective in the face of *verkramptes' kragdadigheid* and stubbornness, symbolized in the story by Vukani's mother.

In another important flashback, Ndebele takes us a few hours back to an incident on the Friday afternoon that illustrates Vukani's perpetual humiliation. It is yet another strategy used by Ndebele to create sympathy for Vukani.

A gang of boys had stopped him on his way home just to harass him. Again the violin was the cause of his misery. This gang had always referred to him as 'music man', and on this Friday afternoon their persecution had been particularly vicious:

> A hand grabbed Vukani's collar behind and jerked him to a halt. The leader of the gang came round and faced him. He held Vukani by the knot of his tie . . .
>
> 'Do you have a sister?' Bhuka [the gang leader] snapped. Vukani had trouble breathing now. Bhuka realised this and loosened the grip. Vukani thought of Teboho at home. If she came here she would fight for him. 'I asked you a question. Do you have a sister?' Vukani nodded. 'Hey man, talk! Is your voice precious? His master's voice!'
>
> 'Yes,' answered Vukani in a whisper.
>
> 'I want to fuck her. Do you hear? I want to eat her up thoroughly. Do you hear? Tell her that.' Bhuka then paused and jerked Vukani to and fro so that Vukani's head bobbed. He then stopped and glowered at Vukani. 'And what song will you play when I am on top of her?' There was a festive laugh from the crowd. Bhuka looked round in acknowledgement. 'Tell me now, can you play *Thoko Ujola Nobani?*' It was a current hit.
>
> Vukani felt tears in his eyes. He blinked many times to keep them in. Why couldn't they just leave him alone. That day would be final, he would simply tell his parents that he did not want to play the violin again. If they still insisted, he would run away from home.

The element of conflict is at the core of this story. Here Ndebele uses the flashback technique to bring a historical conflict into the present, thus providing the reader with sufficient reasons for Vukani's disquiet at the prospect of playing the violin for the visitors. In fact, all the past conflicts that Vukani has experienced are reconstructed through the flashback.

The vulgarity of Bhuka's language may disturb readers with fine sensibilities, but then we have to bear in mind that this story is written in the realist tradition. Ndebele allows individuals to speak in a manner that highlights their character and morality. For example, Bhuka's coarse language is in keeping with his character: he is a hooligan and a bully; he lacks self-respect and his rudeness towards others says something about his view of human relations.

The above flashback is the last in the story. The flashbacks have played their role: we are now privy to Vukani's dislike of the violin and the reasons behind his uneasiness about the visitors. As he waits apprehensively for the visitors to be brought to his bedroom, one cannot but share his suffering. '*Then the door opened. "Here he is!" said Vukani's mother as she led the visitors in.*' The quarry has been found and the torment must begin.

Again, Ndebele takes his time to prepare us for the showdown involving parents and son. He gives us details of the psychological trauma the violin has caused in Vukani, as well as the reasons for his inability to say no to his parents, and thereby bring his suffering to an end. He cannot act in his own interests because he has no resolve, and his lack of determination is through his fear.

But he is emboldened by his sister's courage when she stands up to her mother, who berates her for breaking her 'precious' and 'expensive' dish from Hong Kong: '*He decided then that he would not let his sister down.*' Brother and sister are about to band together in an attempt to restore their self-worth. The fact that Vukani's revolt is inspired by his sister Teboho is worth noting. According to the mother,

'Since Teboho went to that university in the north,

> she has come back with some very strange ideas . . . . Yesterday she said I was a slave of the things I bought; that the white man had planned it that way. To give us a little of everything so that we can so prize the little we have that we completely forget about the most important things in life, like our freedom. I won't have that nonsense in my house.'

What does this mean? It seems that Ndebele sees this university and education in general as a source of new political ideas that can liberate the oppressed. Importantly, appears to suggest that the black elite — Vukani and his sister are members of this group on account of their social background — are morally and socially obliged to take on the mantle of leadership in the black community, and that in this role they have to challenge those blacks whose values and actions make them collaborators in the maintenance of white supremacy. Seen from this perspective, this story becomes an artistic product of its own time, responding, as it does, to the political difficulties that faced the black community.

With compelling skill and feeling, Ndebele has prepared the ground for a dramatic and unforgettable rebellion. After some hesitation and reflection, Vukani eventually asserts his will in a climax of great power:

> 'Ma, I don't want to play the violin any more . . . Today those boys stopped me again . . . I do not want to play . . . I do not want to play . . . not any more . . .'

The violin, it must be noted, is shown in the story as a *symbol* of an oppressive culture and social class. Vukani has now rejected this culture and class, and is about to enter and participate in the dominant proletarian culture of his social environment. Naturally, Vukani finds his rebellion liberating: '*He felt free. There was a vast expanse of open space inside him. He was free. He could fly into the sky.*' His mother, as might be expected, is enraged and responds violently but Teboho rushes into the bedroom to side with her brother. Intensely disappointed by the disapproval of the woman visitor and of Vukani's father, the mother can only resort to 'the wail of the bereaved'; her pride has been undermined.

The Music of the Violin, like other stories in this anthology, is typically South African, and yet universal. It is a story that succeeds in combining the historical and the trans-historical. Only the peculiar history of South Africa could have led to the sort of experience portrayed here; yet the story has a universal significance, because it is also a dramatization of *archetypal experiences*: social climbing, the tyranny of those who have power, youthful desire for freedom, class conflict, human pretentiousness and alienation. The universality of the story allows the author to focus our attention on the human condition.

Vukani, a Zulu word which means 'wake up', has significant resonance. It seems that through this character Ndebele was calling for some kind of awakening and assertiveness. As this story was written during the apartheid era, it is possible that Ndebele was appealing for social and political consciousness among fellow blacks, for the black elite's solidarity with the masses — something that seems to be implied by Vukani's revolt against the elitism of his parents. However, the story's historical significance does not limit its attraction to readers who are interested in South Africa's past. Even today socio-political awareness is still a vital necessity, and the story's archetypal experiences make its appeal timeless.

On a broader level, Vukani's awakening and rebellion can be seen as an awareness of one's rights and the need for revolt if such rights are denied. He becomes a *hero* at the end of the story, an admirable character who represents a high ideal. He is likely to become a better leader, because he has achieved new *awareness* and a sense of identity with the poor and the oppressed.

The foregoing analysis is certainly not complete. There are so many things that can be said about a fictional work, especially if it is loaded with meaning to the fullest possible extent. I have not, for instance, analysed the language of the story although there is much that can be said about it from a linguistic/stylistic perspective. Every critical endeavour involves a choice as prompted by the critic's interpretive framework and priorities. It is important to note this, because criticism, in the final analysis, is a process rather than a finished product.

WORKS CITED

1. Brooks, Cleanth, John Thibaut Purser, and Robert Penn Warren. *An Approach to Literature.* 5th edn. Englewood Cliffs, New Jersey: Prentice-Hall, 1975.
2. Halsey, William D. *Macmillan Contemporary Dictionary.* New York: Macmillan, 1979.
3. Hawthorn, Jeremy. *Studying the Novel: An Introduction.* London: Edward Arnold, 1985.

I thank my colleague Professor Adrian Roscoe for reading and commenting on a first draft of this introduction.

Marcus Ramogale
Department of English
University of the North, South Africa
January 1996

H.C. Bosman

UNTO DUST

I have noticed that when a young man or woman dies, people get the feeling that there is something beautiful and touching in the event, and that it is different from the death of an old person. In the thought, say, of a girl of twenty sinking into an untimely grave, there is a sweet wistfulness that makes people talk all kinds of romantic words. She died, they say, young, she that was so full of life and so fair. She was a flower that withered before it bloomed, they say, and it all seems so fitting and beautiful that there is a good deal of resentment, at the funeral, over the crude questions that a couple of men in plain clothes from the landdrost's office are asking about cattle-dip.

But when you have grown old, nobody is very much interested in the manner of your dying. Nobody except you yourself, that is. And I think that your past life has got a lot to do with the way you feel when you get near the end of your days. I remember how, when he was lying on his death-bed, Andries Wessels kept on telling us that it was because of the blameless path he had trodden from his earliest years that he could compose himself in peace to lay down his burdens. And I certainly never saw a man breathe his last more tranquilly, seeing that right up to the end he kept on murmuring to us how happy he was, with heavenly hosts and invisible choirs of angels all around him.

Just before he died, he told us that the angels had even become visible. They were medium-sized angels, he said, and they had cloven hoofs and carried forks. It was obvious that Andries Wessels's ideas were getting a bit confused by then, but all the same I never saw a man die in a more hallowed sort of calm.

Once, during the malaria season in the Eastern Transvaal, it seemed to me, when I was in a high fever and like to die, that the whole world was a big burial-ground. I thought it was the earth itself that was a graveyard, and not just those little fenced-in bits of land dotted with tombstones, in the shade of a Western Province oak tree or by the side of a Transvaal koppie. This was a nightmare that worried me a great deal, and so I was very glad, when I recovered from the fever, to think that we Boers had properly marked-out places on our farms for white people to be laid to rest in, in a civilized Christian way, instead of having to be buried just anyhow, along with a dead wild-cat, maybe, or a Bushman with a claypot, and things.

When I mentioned this to my friend, Stoffel Oosthuizen, who was in the Low Country with me at the time, he agreed with me wholeheartedly. There were people who talked in a high-flown way of death as the great leveller, he said, and those high-flown people also declared that everyone was made kin by death. He would still like to see those things proved, Stoffel Oosthuizen said. After all, that was one of the reasons why the Boers trekked away into the Transvaal and the Free State, he said, because the British Government wanted to give the vote to any Cape Coloured person walking about with a *kroes* head and big cracks in his feet.

The first time he heard that sort of talk about death coming to all of us alike, and making us all equal, Stoffel Oosthuizen's suspicions were aroused. It sounded like something out of a speech made by one of those liberal Cape politicians, he explained.

I found something very comforting in Stoffel Oosthuizen's words.

Then, to illustrate his contention, Stoffel Oosthuizen told me a story of an incident that took place in a bygone Transvaal Kafir War. I don't know whether he told the story incorrectly, or whether it was just that kind of story, but, by the time he had finished, all my uncertainties had, I discovered, come back to me.

'You can go and look at Hans Welman's tombstone any time you are at Nietverdiend,' Stoffel Oosthuizen said. 'The slab of red sandstone is weathered by now, of course, seeing how long ago it all happened. But the inscription is still legible. I was with Hans Welman on that morning when he fell. Our commando had been ambushed by the kafirs and was retreating. I could do nothing for Hans Welman. Once, when I looked round, I saw a tall kafir bending over him and plunging an assegai into him. Shortly afterwards I saw the kafir stripping the clothes off Hans Welman. A yellow kafir dog was yelping excitedly around his black master. Although I was in grave danger myself, with several dozen kafirs making straight for me on foot through the bush, the fury I felt at the sight of what that tall kafir was doing made me hazard a last shot. Reining in my horse, and taking what aim I could under the circumstances, I pressed the trigger. My luck was in. I saw the kafir fall forward beside the naked body of Hans Welman. Then I set spurs to my horse and galloped off at full speed, with the foremost of my pursuers already almost upon me. The last I saw was that yellow dog bounding up to his master – whom I had wounded mortally, as we were to discover later.

'As you know, that kafir war dragged on for a long time. There were few pitched battles. Mainly, what took place were bush skirmishes, like the one in which Hans Welman lost his life.

'After about six months, quiet of a sort was restored to the Marico and Zoutpansberg districts. Then the day came when I went out, in company of a handful of other burghers, to fetch in the remains of Hans Welman, at his widow's request, for burial in the little cemetery plot on the farm. We took a coffin with us on a Cape-cart.

'We located the scene of the skirmish without difficulty. Indeed, Hans Welman had been killed not very far from his own farm, which had been temporarily abandoned, together with the other farms in that part, during the time that the trouble with the kafirs had lasted. We drove up to the spot where I remembered having seen Hans Welman lying dead on the ground, with the tall kafir next to him. From a distance I again saw that yellow dog. He slipped away into the bush at our approach. I could not help feeling that there was something rather stirring about that beast's fidelity, even though it was bestowed on a dead kafir.

'We were now confronted with a queer situation. We found that what was left of Hans Welman and the kafir consisted of little more than pieces of sun-dried flesh and the dismembered fragments of bleached skeletons. The sun and wild animals and birds of prey had done their work. There was a heap of human bones, with here and there leathery strips of blackened flesh. But we could not tell which was the white man and which the kafir. To make it still more confusing, a lot of bones were missing altogether, having no doubt been dragged away by wild animals into their lairs in the bush. Another thing was that Hans Welman and that kafir had been just about the same size.'

Stoffel Oosthuizen paused in his narrative, and I let my imagination dwell for a moment on that situation. And I realized just how those Boers must have felt about it: about the thought of bringing the remains of a Transvaal burgher home to his widow for Christian burial, and perhaps having a lot of kafir bones mixed up with the burgher – lying with him in the same tomb on which the mauve petals from the oleander overhead would fall.

'I remember one of our party saying that that was the worst of these kafir wars,' Stoffel Oosthuizen continued. 'If it had been a war against the English, and part of a dead Englishman had got lifted into that coffin by mistake, it wouldn't have mattered so much,' he said.

There seemed to me in this story to be something as strange as the African veld. Stoffel Oosthuizen said that the little party of Boers spent almost a whole afternoon with the remains in order to try to get the white man sorted out from the kafir. By the evening they had laid all they could find of what seemed like Hans Welman's bones in the coffin in the Cape-cart.

The rest of the bones and flesh they buried on the spot.

Stoffel Oosthuizen added that, no matter what the difference in the colour of their skin had been, it was impossible to say that the kafir's bones were less white than Hans Welman's. Nor was it possible to say that the kafir's sun-dried flesh was any blacker than the white man's. Alive, you couldn't go wrong in distinguishing between a white man and a kafir. Dead, you had great difficulty in telling them apart.

'Naturally, we burghers felt very bitter about this whole affair,' Stoffel Oosthuizen said, 'and our resentment was something that we couldn't explain, quite. Afterwards, several other men who were there that day told me that they had the same feelings of suppressed anger that I did. They wanted somebody – just once – to make a remark such as "in death they were not divided". Then you would have seen an outburst all right. Nobody did say anything like that, however. We all knew better. Two days later a funeral service was conducted in the little cemetery on the Welman farm, and shortly afterwards the sandstone memorial was erected that you can still see there.'

That was the story Stoffel Oosthuizen told me after I had recovered from the fever. It was a story that, as I have said, had in it features as strange as the African veld. But it brought me no peace in my broodings after that attack of malaria. Especially when Stoffel Oosthuizen spoke of how he had occasion, one clear night when the stars shone, to pass that quiet graveyard on the Welman farm. Something leapt up from the mound beside the sandstone slab. It gave him quite a turn, Stoffel Oosthuizen said, for the third time – and in that way – to come across that yellow kafir dog.

Sarah Gertrude Millin

A SACK FOR NINEPENCE

The tall native, with his dirty shirt and trousers, the colour of mud, with his greenish-brown coat and dusty peppercorn hair and bare feet, stood in the dock, and his eyes were concentrated on the interpreter. The interpreter was translating to him the judge's concluding remarks to the jury:

'. . . On the other hand, gentlemen, you must bear in mind, as the learned counsel for the defence has pointed out, that when a native says he will kill a man, he is not necessarily threatening to take his life. He may only mean that he will hurt him. The expression, "You shall not see the sun tomorrow" is another such exclamation of rage which may have no real significance. Moreover, it must be remembered that the principal testimony against the prisoner is that of his wife, Masangape, who has lost her child, and who has been badly treated by him. The matter of the stone has not been satisfactorily explained, yet there is no evidence that the prisoner placed it where it was found, nor did anyone see the burning of the hut. The child is dead. The man who wore the sack is dead. All the inhabitants of the hut are dead. Only Masangape, the wife, is here to tell the story of that day and night. It is for you to say whether you believe Masangape, and whether in the light of the other evidence I have outlined to you, you think the prisoner committed this crime. If you find the evidence insufficient to establish his guilt beyond reasonable doubt, it is your duty to find him not guilty. Consider your verdict . . .'

Pepetwayo listened to the interpreter, but he could discover no meaning in the judge's words. Thc jurymen scrambled to their feet. The judge gathered together his red robes and stood up, and, as he did so, the people in court — mostly natives — rose. The policeman touched the prisoner's arm. The prisoner gave a start, looked round with rolling eyes and, on the policeman's word, began hurriedly to descend the steps that led from the dock to the cells below.

He was still thinking about the sack.

This was the story of the sack:

Pepetwayo had married his wife when she was a widow with a year-old child. And it was now seven years since their marriage, and this child she had borne by another man was still the only child in their hut. Pepetwayo spoke to her about it often, and sometimes he beat her. He consulted a witch-doctor and he fought men who made jokes, but the days passed and the days passed and forever he had to father only this child of the dead man.

He grew to hate the child with a terrible deep hatred. He could not bear to see the small white teeth crunching the bread for which he had to break his back hauling up stones on the Transvaal diamond diggings. In summer Gule ran naked, but this winter he had been bought a thick cotton singlet, and Pepetwayo could not rest his eyes on it without wanting to tear it from the boy's back. He could not keep his voice from scolding him or his hands from striking him. He said to Masangape in their speech: 'Send Gule away, or there will be great trouble.'

She decided finally to bestow Gule on some friends in a neighbouring hut. It was, like all the other huts, a circular construction of rags and reeds and mud, a dozen feet in diameter, with no opening for entrance or exit but a flap of sacking. It stood, surrounded by a reed fence, on the side of a low, stony hill, a little apart from the rest of the location where Masangape lived with her husband. In the whole of that location there was no tree or flower or blade of grass. There was no well for water. Little girls, with tin cans on their heads, walked three miles to fetch the muddy water of the Vaal River. Only on the top of the hill there grew, near the half-hearted and abandoned beginnings of a stone wall, a few prickly pears, and, when the sun went down in a flare of scarlet scribbled with fire, these bold and fleshy weeds leaned against the sky in black relief, and the huts themselves clung together like the hives of gigantic wasps.

In this hut there were already five people maintained on the sixteen shillings a week carned by the head of the household. But no native ever questions the right of a fellow-tribesman to share with him, and Gule was accepted without bargain or comment.

Yet only for a few days was there peace in Pepetwayo's home. It happened that he returned from his work on the diggings and Masangape was not there. Where she was he knew, of course. But he particularly resented her absence this evening because he was happy, because he wanted her to exult with him over a bargain. He had bought a grain-sack from the shop for ninepence when everyone knew that the price of one so large as this was always a shilling. But he had said to the store-keeper: 'Look, Baas, how poor I am, and how the weather is cold. I want this sack to wear on my body to keep the wind out. But it is Monday today and I have just this ninepence, and why shall such a great person as the Baas wait till next Saturday for only a little threepence? Let the Baas give me the sack for ninepence.'

And, actually, the Baas had done it, and Pepetwayo loved the sack as if it were a trophy in a game he had won.

Now he wanted his wife to open the sides for him and cut a hole for his head so that he might wear it against the cold. He could work better with his hands than she could — he had in his day sewn together the skins of jackals with sinew to make those great rugs which are called karosses — but it simply was his desire that she should do this thing for him.

And the hut was empty. There was no fat-soaked mealie-meal cooking in the tripod pot. His belly was fainting against his backbone, for he had eaten nothing all day except, at twelve o'clock, a piece of bread. There was no one to share his triumph about the sack.

He flung it down in a corner of the hut, and rushed over to the neighbours who housed Gule.

There his wife sat chattering with other women. There his wife's child ran about playing with other children. The air was leaping with gaiety. The terrific smell of a sheep's head and trotters cooking in a tripod pot attacked his nostrils . . .

He thought of his quiet hut, of his unused pot, of the absence of small, rotund, black bodies and rushing noises and high laughter in his yard, of his bargain of a sack lying rumpled, unhailed, in a corner, and he ran up to his wife and jerked her up by the shoulder and shouted awful words at her and dragged her home.

He beat her when they got home, and would not eat, and would not let her make in the hut the smoky fire of dung and sticks with which they kept themselves warm in the winter nights. And throughout the black hours, wearing still the clothes they used by day, they lay side by side on the goatskins which separated them from the naked earth, covered with two cotton blankets, bitter, hostile, and yet drawn together by the cold.

In the morning Pepetwayo went to work as usual, a white scurf of frost in his face and hands. And when he was gone, his wife packed her belongings into the sack she found lying in the corner and left him, to go and live in the hut that sheltered also her child.

Pepetwayo was hungry and tired and cold all day long. And for this he blamed his wife and her child. If his wife had not neglected him the night before to go to see her child, he would have had something in his belly, he thought, he would have slept in the night, he would have been able to wear the sack today against the whipping wind. He could not forget the animation in the other people's yard.

In the evening he walked towards the location, picking up here and there as he went along a stick for the fire. But again, as he reached home, no smoke rose to greet him, and he saw soon enough that Masangape was gone, and her belongings. He stood in the hut looking at he knew not what, and suddenly he remembered his sack. Where was his sack? Had she had the effrontery to take his sack, to steal his sack for which only the day before he had paid ninepence . . . not a shilling, as was usual, but — a bargain, a diplomatic achievement — ninepence?

Once more he ran along to the other hut. This time

there were no visitors in the yard, only the inhabitants of the hut were present, and his wife was sitting, silent, in their midst. She was frightened. She could not live with her husband any more, and she did not know what he would now do to her.

But he entered in among them shouting the word 'sack'.

'Give me my sack. What have you done with my sack?'

He pulled his wife up by the stuff of her dress between her shoulders.

'You —'

His eyes fell on the child.

'He shall not see the sun tomorrow!' he cried. 'There will not be cause for you to leave me again. Where is my sack?'

His wife looked at him dumbly.

He let her go, for his eyes had seen something. There was a man barely visible in the smoke-filled hut and he was wearing a baggy garment over his shoulders. Pepetwayo sprang at the man, and they struggled towards the yard. He could see now, in the last light of the day, that the man was the brother of Gule's protector, and that here was his very sack.

He attempted to pull it from the man as they fought. 'You shall not,' he panted, '— none of you — see the sun tomorrow.'

The sack was torn. His own clothes were torn. People flung themselves forward and separated them. He threatened to kill his wife if she did not come back with him. She walked beside him, weeping.

And, as on the night before they lay down together on the ground in the small, dark hut.

But this time, in the middle of the night, Pepetwayo got up, and began fumbling about the hut. His wife lay still, listening to his movements. Then she felt that — something — was happening. Terror filled her. 'Pepetwayo! What are you doing? ' 'Nothing,' he said, in a voice unexpectedly peaceable.

She heard the rattle of matches as in the dark he put his hand on the box. Now he went outside. She sat up.

'Pepetwayo! Where are you going? Pepetwayo!' He came back to the hut. 'Lie still. I will be here again in a minute.' She began to moan.

'Are you mad?' he said. 'Be quiet. I am not going to leave you for long. Wait for me. Don't make this noise. If I do not find you here when I come in I will kill you.' She drew the blankets over her head, and lay waiting and shivering. He was gone for minutes — for an hour. When he returned he put his arms round her.

'I am happy again. Let us sleep,' he said.

In the morning the hut that contained Gule and the man who had worn Pepetwayo's sack and four other people was found burnt down, and everyone in it was dead. A stone was lying against the flap that was the only opening to the hut, and the inhabitants had thus been fastened in while the old sacks and reeds of which the hut was made burnt round them and over them. Masangape was led, screaming, to the police-station to tell her story. Pepetwayo was arrested. 'I know nothing,' he said. The police did not question him, and when, towards the end of the six months that intervened before his trial, his young counsel came to talk with him he maintained firmly: 'I know nothing.' At the trial he was not put in the box. And when he gathered dimly that the defending advocate was explaining to the jury how ridiculous it was that a man should kill six people for the sake of an empty sack, he nodded his head slightly. Yes, that was wise talk. 'I need not inform you, gentlemen,' the advocate continued, 'how often native huts are burnt down, or how often sleeping natives are suffocated because the fire made for warmth has not been removed . . .'

The judge addressed the jury. Pepetwayo was led back to his cell. The jury went away to deliberate.

They returned presently. The prisoner was once more prodded up the steps to the dock. The judge, who had retired, resumed his seat on the bench. The people in court duly stood up and sat down.

The registrar addressed the foreman of the jury.

'Have you considered your verdict?'

'We have.'

'Are you all agreed?'

'We are.'

'What is your verdict?'

'Not guilty.' The judge addressed Pepetwayo. He put the facts as he saw them before the jury, though it was reasonably clear to him that Pepetwayo had committed the crime. However, they had apparently considered the evidence insufficient.

He sat up and looked at Pepetwayo from under his heavy brow. 'The jury have found you not guilty. You may go.'

'You may go,' the interpreter translated.

The policeman tapped his shoulder.

'You may go.' Pepetwayo looked from one to the other. What had happened? Was he free? He could not believe it.

'Hurry up,' said the policeman.

The native did not move.

The policeman pushed him. The man began to scramble down as if an hypnotic influence were directing him.

Outside the court other natives surrounded Pepetwayo, giving him tobacco to chew, and cigarettes.

He was free. He was a hero. The justice of the white man was a miracle.

He blew out a mouthful of smoke, and in a voice hushed by six months of waiting in gaol, he began to tell his worshipful audience about this sack, worth a shilling, which he had bought for ninepence, and which had been given by his wife to the brother of the man who had sheltered Gule.

Can Themba
THE SUIT

Five-thirty in the morning, and the candlewick bedspread frowned as the man under it stirred. He did not like to wake his wife lying by his side – as yet – so he crawled up and out by careful peristalsis. But before he tiptoed out of his room with shoes and socks under his arm, he leaned over and peered at the sleeping serenity of his wife: to him a daily matutinal miracle.

He grinned and yawned simultaneously, offering his wordless Te Deum to whatever gods for the goodness of life; for the pure beauty of his wife; for the strength surging through his willing body; for the even, unperturbed rhythms of his passage through days and months and years – it must be – to heaven.

Then he slipped soundlessly into the kitchen. He flipped aside the curtain of the kitchen window, and saw outside a thin drizzle, the type that can soak one to the skin, and that could go on for days and days. He wondered, head aslant, why the rain in Sophiatown always came in the morning when workers had to creep out of their burrows; and then at how blistering heatwaves came during the day when messengers had to run errands all over; and then at how the rain came back when workers knocked off and had to scurry home.

He smiled at the odd caprice of the heavens, and tossed his head at the naughty incongruity, as if, 'Ai, but the gods!'

From behind the kitchen door, he removed an old rain cape, peeling off in places, and swung it over his head. He dashed for the lavatory, nearly slipping in a pool of muddy water, but he reached the door. Aw, blast, someone had made it before him. Well, that is the toll of staying in a yard where twenty . . . thirty other people have to share the same lean-to. He was dancing and burning in that climactic moment when trouser-fly will not come wide soon enough. He stepped round the lavatory and watched the streamlets of rainwater quickly wash away the jet of tension that spouted from him. That infinite after-relief. Then he dashed back to his kitchen. He grabbed the old baby-bathtub hanging on a nail under the slight shelter of the gutterless roof-edge. He opened a large wooden box and quickly filled the bathtub with coal. Then he inched his way back to the kitchen door and inside.

He was huh-huh-huhing one of those fugitive tunes that cannot be hidden, but often just occur and linger naggingly in the head. The fire he was making soon licked up cheerfully, in mood with his contentment.

He had a trick for these morning chores. While the fire in the old stove warmed up, the water kettle humming on it, he gathered and laid ready the things he would need for the day: briefcase and the files that go with it; the book that he was reading currently; the letters of his lawyer boss which he usually posted before he reached the office; his wife's and his own dry-cleaning slips for the Sixty-Minutes; his lunch tin solicitously prepared the night before by his attentive wife; and, today, the battered rain cape. By the time the kettle on the stove sang (before it actually boiled), he poured water from it into a washbasin, refilled and replaced it on the stove. Then he washed himself carefully: across the eyes, under, in and out the armpits, down the torso and in between the legs. This ritual was thorough, though no white man a-complaining of the smell of wogs knows anything about it. Then he dressed himself fastidiously. By this time he was ready to prepare breakfast.

Breakfast! How he enjoyed taking in a tray of warm breakfast to his wife, cuddled in bed. To appear there in his supremest immaculacy, tray in hand when his wife comes out of ether to behold him. These things we blacks want to do for our own . . . not fawningly for the whites for whom we bloody-well got to do it. He wasn't one of those who believed in putting his wife in her place even if she was a good wife. Not he.

Matilda, too, appreciated her husband's kindness, and only put her foot down when he offered to wash up also.

'Off with you,' she scolded him on his way.

At the bus-stop he was a little sorry to see that jovial old Maphikela was in a queue for a bus ahead of him. He would miss Maphikela's raucous laughter and uninhibited, bawdy conversations in fortissimo. Maphikela hailed him nevertheless. He thought he noticed hesitation in the old man, and a slight clouding of his countenance, but the old man shouted back at him, saying that he would wait for him at the terminus in town.

Philemon considered this morning trip to town

with garrulous old Maphikela as his daily bulletin. All the township news was generously reported by loud-mouthed heralds, and spiritedly discussed by the bus at large. Of course, 'news' included views on bosses (scurrilous), the Government (rude), Ghana and Russia (idolatrous), America and the West (sympathetically ridiculing), and boxing (bloodthirsty). But it was always stimulating and surprisingly comprehensive for so short a trip. And there was no law of libel.

Maphikela was standing under one of those token bus-stop shelters that never keep out rain nor wind nor sun-heat. Philemon easily located him by his noisy ribbing of some office boys in their khaki-green uniforms. They walked together into town, but from Maphikela's suddenly subdued manner, Philemon gathered that there was something serious coming up. Maybe a loan.

Eventually, Maphikela came out with it.

'Son,' he said sadly, 'if I could've avoided this, believe you me I would, but my wife is nagging the spice out of my life for not talking to you about it.'

It just did not become blustering old Maphikela to sound so grave and Philemon took compassion upon him.

'Go ahead, dad,' he said generously. 'You know you can talk to me about anything.'

The old man gave a pathetic smile. 'We-e-ell, it's not really any of our business . . . er . . . but my wife felt . . . you see. Damn it all! I wish these women would not snoop around so much.' Then he rushed it. 'Anyway, it seems there's a young man who's going to visit your wife every morning . . . ah . . . for these last bloomin' three months. And that wife of mine swears by her heathen gods you don't know a thing about it.'

It was not quite like the explosion of a devastating bomb. It was more like the critical breakdown in an infinitely delicate piece of mechanism. From outside, the machine just seemed to have gone dead. But deep in its innermost recesses, menacing electrical flashes were leaping from coil to coil, and hot, viscous, molten metal was creeping up on the fuel tanks . . .

Philemon heard gears grinding and screaming in his head . . .

'Dad,' he said hoarsely, 'I . . . I have to go back home.'

He turned round and did not hear old Maphikela's anxious, 'Steady, son. Steady, son.'

The bus ride home was a torture of numb dread and suffocating despair. Though the bus was now emptier Philemon suffered crushing claustrophobia. There were immense washerwomen whose immense bundles of soiled laundry seemed to baulk and menace him. From those bundles crept miasmata of sweaty intimacies that sent nauseous waves up and down from his viscera. Then the wild swaying of the bus as it negotiated Mayfair Circle hurtled him sickeningly from side to side. Some of the younger women shrieked delightedly to the driver, '*Fuduga!* . . . Stir the pot!' as he swung his steering-wheel this way and that. Normally, the crazy tilting of the bus gave him a prickling exhilaration. But now . . .

He felt like getting out of there, screaming, elbowing everything out of his way. He wished this insane trip were over, and then again, he recoiled at the thought of getting home. He made a tremendous resolve to gather in all the torn, tingling threads of his nerves contorting in the raw. By a merciless act of will, he kept them in subjugation as he stepped out of the bus back in the Victoria Road terminus,

Sophiatown.

The calm he achieved was tense . . . but he could think now . . . he could take a decision . . .

With almost boyishly innocent urgency, he rushed through his kitchen into his bedroom. In the lightning flash that the eye can whip, he saw it all . . . the man beside his wife . . . the chestnut arm around her neck . . . the ruffled candlewick bedspread . . . the suit across the chair. But he affected not to see.

He opened the wardrobe door, and as he dug into it, he cheerfully spoke to his wife: 'Fancy, Tilly, I forgot to take my pass. I had already reached town, and was going to walk up to the office. If it hadn't been for wonderful old Mr Maphikela.'

A swooshing noise of violent retreat and the clap of his bedroom window stopped him. He came from behind the wardrobe door and looked out from the open window. A man clad only in vest and underpants was running down the street. Slowly, he turned round and contemplated . . . the suit.

Philemon lifted it gingerly under his arm and looked at the stark horror in Matilda's eyes. She was now sitting up in bed. Her mouth twitched, but her throat raised no words.

'Ha,' he said, 'I see we have a visitor,' indicating the blue suit. 'We really must show some of our hospitality. But first, I must phone my boss that I can't come to work today . . . mmmm-er, my wife's not well. Be back in a moment, then we can make arrangements.' He took the suit along.

When he returned he found Matilda weeping on the bed. He dropped the suit beside her, pulled up the chair, turned it round so that its back came in front of him, sat down, brought down his chin onto his folded arms before him, and waited for her.

After a while the convulsions of her shoulders ceased. She saw a smug man with an odd smile and meaningless inscrutability in his eyes. He spoke to her with very little noticeable emotion; if anything, with a flutter of humour.

'We have a visitor, Tilly.' His mouth curved ever so slightly. 'I'd like him to be treated with the greatest of consideration. He will eat every meal with us and share all we have. Since we have no spare room, he'd better sleep in here. But the point is, Tilly, that you will meticulously look after him. If he vanishes or anything else happens to him . . . ' A shaft of evil shot from his eye . . . 'Matilda, I'll kill you.'

He rose from the chair and looked with incongruous supplication at her. He told her to put the fellow in the wardrobe for the time being. As she passed him to get the suit, he turned to go. She ducked frantically, and he stopped.

'You don't seem to understand me, Matilda. There's to be no violence in this house if you and I can help it. So, just look after that suit.' He went out.

He went out to the Sophiatown Post Office, which is placed on the exact line between Sophiatown and the white man's surly Westdene. He posted his boss's letters, and walked to the beerhall at the tail end of Western Native Township. He had never been inside it before, but somehow the thunderous din laved his bruised spirit. He stayed there all day.

He returned home for supper . . . and surprise. His dingy little home had been transformed, and the air of stern masculinity it had hitherto contained had been wiped away, to be replaced by anxious feminine touches here and there. There were even gay, colourful curtains swirling in the kitchen window. The old-fashioned coal stove gleamed in its blackness. A clean, chequered oil cloth on the table. Supper ready.

Then she appeared in the doorway of the bedroom. Heavens! Here was the woman he had married; the young, fresh, cocoa-coloured maid who had sent rushes of emotion shuddering through him. And the dress she wore brought out all the girlishness in her, hidden so long beneath German print. But no hint of coquettishness, although she stood in the doorway and slid her arm up the jamb, and shyly slanted her head to the other shoulder. She smiled weakly.

What makes a woman like this experiment with adultery, he wondered.

Philemon closed his eyes and gripped the seat of his chair on both sides as some overwhelming, undisciplined force sought to catapult him towards her. For a moment some essence glowed fiercely within him, then sank back into itself and died . . .

He sighed and smiled sadly back at her. 'I'm hungry, Tilly.'

The spell snapped, and she was galvanized into action. She prepared his supper with dexterous hands that trembled a little only when they hesitated in mid-air. She took her seat opposite him, regarded him curiously, clasped her hands waiting for his prayer, but in her heart she murmured some other, much more urgent prayer of her own.

'Matilda!' he barked. 'Our visitor!' The sheer savagery with which he cracked at her jerked her up, but only when she saw the brute cruelty in his face did she run out of the room, toppling the chair behind her.

She returned with the suit on a hanger, and stood there quivering like a feather. She looked at him with helpless dismay. The demoniacal rage in his face was evaporating, but his heavy breathing still rocked his thorax above the table, to and fro.

'Put a chair, there.' He indicated with a languid gesture of his arm. She moved like a ghost as she drew a chair to the table.

'Now seat our friend at the table . . . no, no, not like that. Put him in front of the chair, and place him on the seat so that he becomes indeed the third person.'

Philemon went on relentlessly: 'Dish up for him. Generously. I imagine he hasn't had a morsel all day, the poor devil.'

Now, as consciousness and thought seeped back into her, her movements revolved so that always she faced this man who had changed so spectacularly. She started when he rose to open the window and let in some air.

She served the suit. The act was so ridiculous that she carried it out with a bitter sense of humiliation. He came back to sit down and plunge into his meal. No grace was said for the first time in this house. With his mouth full, he indicated by a toss of his head that she should sit down in her place. She did so. Glancing at her plate, the thought occurred to her that someone, after a long famine, was served a sumptuous supper, but as the food reached her mouth it turned to sawdust. Where had she heard it?

Matilda could not eat. She suddenly broke into tears.

Philemon took no notice of her weeping. After supper, he casually gathered the dishes and started washing up. He flung a dry cloth at her without saying a word. She rose and went to stand by his side drying up. But for their wordlessness, they seemed a very devoted couple.

After washing up, he took the suit and turned to

her. 'That's how I want it every meal, every day.' Then he walked into the bedroom.

So it was. After that first breakdown, Matilda began to feel that her punishment was not too severe, considering the heinousness of the crime. She tried to put a joke into it, but by slow, unconscious degrees, the strain nibbled at her. Philemon did not harass her much more, so long as the ritual with the confounded suit was conscientiously followed.

Only once, he got one of his malevolent brainwaves. He got it into his head that 'our visitor' needed an outing. Accordingly the suit was taken to the dry-cleaners during the week, and, come Sunday, they had to take it out for a walk. Both Philemon and Matilda dressed for the occasion. Matilda had to carry the suit on its hanger over her back and the three of them strolled leisurely along Ray Street. They passed the church crowd in front of the famous Anglican Mission of Christ the King. Though the worshippers saw nothing unusual in them, Matilda felt, searing through her, red-hot needles of embarrassment, and every needle-point was a public eye piercing into her degradation.

But Philemon walked casually on. He led her down Ray Street and turned into Main Road. He stopped often to look into shop windows or to greet a friend passing by. They went up Toby Street, turned into Edward Road, and back home. To Philemon the outing was free of incident, but to Matilda it was one long, excruciating incident.

At home, he grabbed a book on abnormal psychology, flung himself into a chair and calmly said to her, 'Give the old chap a rest, will you, Tilly?'

In the bedroom, Matilda said to herself that things could not go on like this. She thought of how she could bring the matter to a head with Philemon; have it out once and for all. But the memory of his face that first day she had forgotten to entertain the suit, stayed her. She thought of running away, but where to? Home? What could she tell her old-fashioned mother had happened between Philemon and her? All right, run away clean then. She thought of many young married girls who were divorcees now, who had won their freedom.

What had happened to Staff Nurse Kakile? The woman drank heavily now, and when she got drunk, the boys of Sophiatown passed her around and called her the Cesspot.

Matilda shuddered.

An idea struck her. There were still decent, married women around Sophiatown. She remembered how after the private schools had been forced to close with the advent of Bantu Education, Father Harringay of the Anglican Mission had organized cultural clubs. One, she seemed to remember, was for married women. If only she could lose herself in some cultural activity, find absolution for her conscience in some doing good; that would blur her blasted home life, would restore her self-respect. After all, Philemon had not broadcast her disgrace abroad . . . nobody knew; not one of Sophiatown's slander-mongers suspected how vulnerable she was. She must go and see Mrs Montjane about joining a cultural club. She must ask Philemon now if she might . . . she must ask him nicely.

She got up and walked into the other room where Philemon was reading quietly. She dreaded disturbing him, did not know how to begin talking to him . . . they had talked so little for so long. She went and stood in front of him, looking silently upon his deep concentration. Presently, he looked up with a frown on his face.

Then she dared, 'Phil, I'd like to join one of those cultural clubs for married women. Would you mind?'

He wrinkled his nose and rubbed it between thumb and index finger as he considered the request. But he had caught the note of anxiety in her voice and thought he knew what it meant.

'Mmm,' he said, nodding. 'I think that's a good idea. You can't be moping around here all day. Yes, you may, Tilly.' Then he returned to his book.

The cultural club idea was wonderful. She found women like herself with time (if not with tragedy) on their hands, engaged in wholesome refreshing activities. The atmosphere was cheerful and cathartic. They learned things and they did things. They organized fêtes, bazaars, youth activities, sport, music, self-help and community projects. She got involved in committees, meetings, debates, conferences. It was for her a whole new venture into humancraft, and her personality blossomed. Philemon gave her all the rein she wanted.

Now, abiding by that silly ritual at home seemed a little thing . . . a very little thing . . .

Then one day she decided to organize a little party for her friends and their husbands. Philemon was very decent about it. He said it was all right. He even gave her extra money for it. Of course, she knew nothing of the strain he himself suffered from his mode of castigation.

There was a week of the most hectic preparation. Philemon stepped out of its cluttering way as best he could. So many things seemed to be taking place simultaneously. New dresses were made. Cakes were baked; three different orders of meat prepared; beef for the uninvited chancers; mutton for the normal guests; turkey and chicken for the inner pith of the club's core. To Philemon, it looked as if Matilda planned to feed the multitude on the Mount with no aid of miracles.

On the Sunday of the party, Philemon saw Matilda's guests. He was surprised by the handsome grace with which she received them. There was a long table with enticing foods and flowers and serviettes. Matilda placed all her guests round the table, and the party was ready to begin in the mock-formal township fashion. Outside a steady rumble of conversation went on where the human odds and ends of every Sophiatown party had their 'share'.

Matilda caught the curious look on Philemon's face. He tried to disguise his edict when he said, 'Er . . . the guest of honour.'

But Matilda took a chance. She begged, 'Just this once, Phil.'

He became livid. 'Matilda!' he shouted. 'Get our visitor!' Then with incisive sarcasm, 'Or are you ashamed of him?'

She went ash-grey; but there was nothing for it but to fetch her albatross. She came back and squeezed a chair into some corner, and placed the suit on it. Then she slowly placed a plate of food before it. For a while the guests were dumbfounded. Then curiosity flooded in. They talked at the same time. 'What's happening?' Some just giggled in a silly way. Philemon carelessly swung his head towards Matilda. 'You better ask my wife. She knows the fellow best.'

All interest beamed upon poor Matilda. For a moment she could not speak, all enveloped in misery. Then she said, unconvincingly, 'It's just a game that my husband and I play at mealtime.' They roared with laughter. Philemon let her get away with it.

The party went on, and every time Philemon's glare sent Matilda scurrying to serve the suit each course; the guests were no-end amused by the persistent mock-seriousness with which this husband and wife played out their little game. Only, to Matilda, it was no joke; it was a hot poker down her throat. After the party, Philemon went off with one of the guests who had promised to show him a joint 'that sells genuine stuff, boy, genuine stuff.'

Reeling drunk, late that sabbath, he crashed through his kitchen door, onwards to his bedroom. Then he saw her.

They have a way of saying in the argot of Sophiatown, 'Cook out of the head!' signifying that someone was impacted with such violent shock that whatever whiffs of alcohol still wandered through his head were instantaneously evaporated and the man stood sober before stark reality.

There she lay, curled as if just before she died she begged for a little love, implored some implacable lover to cuddle her a little . . . just this once . . . just this once more.

In screwish anguish, Philemon cried, 'Tilly!'

Alan Paton
HA'PENNY

Of the six hundred boys at the reformatory, about one hundred were from ten to fourteen years of age. My Department had from time to time expressed the intention of taking them away, and of establishing a special institution for them, more like an industrial school than a reformatory. This would have been a good thing, for their offences were very trivial, and they would have been better by themselves. Had such a school been established I should have liked to be Principal of it myself, for it would have been an easier job; small boys turn instinctively towards affection, and one controls them by it, naturally and easily.

Some of them, if I came near them, either on parade or in school or at football, would observe me watchfully, not directly or fully, but obliquely and secretly; sometimes I would surprise them at it, and make some small sign of recognition, which would satisfy them so that they would cease to observe me, and would give their full attention to the event of the moment. But I knew that my authority was thus confirmed and strengthened.

The secret relations with them were a source of

continuous pleasure to me. Had they been my own children I would no doubt have given a greater expression to it. But often I would move through the silent and orderly parade, and stand by one of them. He would look straight in front of him with a little frown of concentration that expressed both childish awareness of and manly indifference to my nearness. Sometimes I would tweak his ear, and he would give me a brief smile of acknowledgement, or frown with still greater concentration. It was natural, I suppose, to confine these outward expressions to the very smallest, but they were taken as symbolic, and some older boys would observe them and take themselves to be included. It was a relief, when the reformatory was passing through times of turbulence and trouble, and when there was danger of estrangement between authority and boys, to make these simple and natural gestures, which were reassurances to both me and them that nothing important had changed.

On Sunday afternoons when I was on duty I would take my car to the reformatory and watch the free boys being signed out at the gate. This simple operation was also watched by many boys not free, who would tell each other, 'in so many weeks I'll be signed out myself.' Among the watchers were always some small boys, and these I would take by turns in the car. We would go out to the Potchefstroom Road with its ceaseless stream of traffic, and to the Baragwanath crossroads, and come back by the Van Wyksrus road to the reformatory. I would talk to them about their families, their parents, their sisters and brothers, and I would pretend to know nothing of Durban, Port Elizabeth, Potchefstroom and Clocolan, and ask them if these places were bigger than Johannesburg.

One of the small boys was Ha'penny, and he was about twelve years old. He came from Bloemfontein and was the biggest talker of them all. His mother worked in a white person's house, and he had two brothers and two sisters. His brothers were Richard and Dickie, and his sisters Anna and Mina.

'Richard and Dickie?' I asked.

'Yes, meneer.'

'In English,' I said, 'Richard and Dickie are the same name.'

When we returned to the reformatory, I sent for Ha'penny's papers; there it was plainly set down; Ha'penny was a waif, with no relatives at all. He had been taken in from one home to another, but he was naughty and uncontrollable, and eventually had taken to pilfering at the market.

I then sent for the Letter Book, and found that Ha'penny wrote regularly, or rather that others wrote for him till he could write himself, to Mrs Betty Maarman, of 48 Vlak Street, Bloemfontein. But Mrs Maarman had never once replied to him. When questioned, he had said, perhaps she is sick. I sat down and wrote at once to the Social Welfare Officer at Bloemfontein, asking him to investigate.

The next time I had Ha'penny out in the car I questioned him again about his family. And he told me the same as before, his mother, Richard and Dickie, Anna and Mina. But he softened the 'D' of Dickie, so that it sounded now like Tickie.

'I thought you said Dickie,' I said.

'I said Tickie,' he said.

He watched me with concealed apprehension, and I came to the conclusion that this waif of Bloemfontein was a clever boy, who had told me a story that was all imagination, and had changed one single letter of it to make it safe from any question. And I thought I understood it all too, that he was ashamed of being without a family and had invented them all, so that no one might discover that he was fatherless and motherless and that no one in the world cared whether he was alive or dead. This gave me a strong feeling for him, and I went out of my way to manifest towards him that fatherly care that the State, though not in those words, had enjoined upon me by giving me this job.

Then the letter came from the Social Welfare Officer in Bloemfontein, saying that Mrs Betty Maarman of 48 Vlak Street was a real person, and that she had four children, Richard and Dickie, Anna and Mina, but that Ha'penny was no child of hers, and she knew him only as a derelict of the streets. She had never answered his letters, because he wrote to her as 'Mother', and she was no mother of his, nor did she wish to play any such role. She was a decent woman, a faithful member of the church, and she had no thought of corrupting her family by letting them have anything to do with such a child.

But Ha'penny seemed to me anything but the usual delinquent; his desire to have a family was so strong, and his reformatory record was so blameless, and his anxiety to please and obey so great, that I began to feel a great duty towards him. Therefore I asked him about his 'mother'.

He could not speak enough of her, nor with too high praise. She was loving, honest, and strict. Her home was clean. She had affection for all her children. It was clear that the homeless child, even as he had attached himself to me, would have attached himself to her; he had observed her even as he had observed me, but did not know the secret of how to open her heart, so that she would take him in, and save him from the lonely life that he led.

'Why did you steal when you had such a mother?' I asked.

He could not answer that; not all his brains nor his courage could find an answer to such a question, for he knew that with such a mother he would not have stolen at all.

'The boy's name is Dickie,' I said, 'not Tickie.'

And then he knew the deception was revealed. Another boy might have said, 'I told you it was Dickie,' but he was too intelligent for that; he knew that if I had established that the boy's name was Dickie, I must have established other things too. I was shocked by the immediate and visible effect of my action. His whole brave assurance died within him and he stood there exposed, not as a liar, but as a homeless child who had surrounded himself with mother, brothers, and sisters, who did not exist. I had shattered the very foundations of his pride and his sense of human significance.

He fell sick at once, and the doctor said it was tuberculosis. I wrote at once to Mrs Maarman, telling her the whole story, of how this small boy had observed her, and had decided that she was the person he desired for his mother. But she wrote back saying that she could take no responsibility for him. For one thing, Ha'penny was a Mosuto, and she was a coloured woman; for another, she had never had a child in trouble, and how could she take such a boy?

Tuberculosis is a strange thing; sometimes it manifests itself suddenly in the most unlikely host, and swiftly sweeps to the end. Ha'penny withdrew himself from the world, from all Principals and mothers, and the doctor said there was little hope. In desperation I sent money for Mrs Maarman to come.

She was a decent, homely woman, and seeing that the situation was serious, she, without fuss or embarrassment, adopted Ha'penny for her own. The whole reformatory accepted her as his mother. She sat the whole day with him, and talked to him of Richard and Dickie, Anna and Mina, and how they were all waiting for him to come home. She poured out her affection on him, and had no fear of his sickness, nor did she allow it to prevent her from satisfying his hunger to be owned. She talked to him of what they would do when he came back, and how he would go to the school, and what they would buy for Guy Fawkes night.

He in his turn gave his whole attention to her, and when I visited him he was grateful, but I had passed out of his world. I felt judged in that I had sensed only the existence and not the measure of his desire. I wished I had done something sooner, more wise, more prodigal.

We buried him on the reformatory farm, and Mrs Maarman said to me, 'When you put up the cross, put he was my son.'

'I'm ashamed,' she said, 'that I wouldn't take him.'

'The sickness,' I said, 'the sickness would have come.'

'No,' she said, shaking her head with certainty. 'It wouldn't have come. And if it had come at home, it would have been different.'

So she left for Bloemfontein, after her strange visit to a reformatory. And I was left too, with the resolve to be more prodigal in the task that the State, though not in so many words, had enjoined on me.

Dan Jacobson
BEGGAR MY NEIGHBOUR

Michael saw them for the first time when he was coming home from school one day. One moment the street had been empty, glittering in the light from the sun behind his back, with no traffic on the roadway and apparently no pedestrians on the broad sandy pavement; the next moment these two were before him, their faces raised to his. They seemed to emerge directly in front of him, as if the light and shade of the glaring street had suddenly condensed itself into two little piccanins with large eyes set in their round, black faces.

'*Stukkie brood?*' the elder, a boy, said in a plaintive voice. A piece of bread. At Michael's school the slang term for any African child was just that: *stukkie brood.* That was what African children were always begging for.

'*Stukkie brood?*' the little girl said. She was wearing a soiled white dress that was so short it barely covered her loins; there seemed to be nothing at all beneath the dress. She wore no socks, no shoes, no cardigan, no cap or hat. She must have been about ten years old. The boy, who was dressed in a torn khaki shirt and a pair of grey shorts much too large for him, was about Michael's age, about twelve, though he was a little smaller than the white boy. Like the girl, he was barefoot. Their limbs were painfully thin; their wrists and ankles stood out in knobs, and the skin over these protruding bones was rougher than elsewhere. The dirt on their skin showed up as a faint greyness against the black.

'I've got no bread,' the white boy said. He had halted in surprise at the suddenness of their appearance before him. They must have been hiding behind one of the trees that were planted at intervals along the pavement. 'I don't bring bread from school.'

They did not move. Michael shifted his school case from one hand to the other and took a pace forward. Silently, the African children stood aside. As he passed them, Michael was conscious of the movement of their eyes; when he turned to look back he saw that they were standing still to watch him go. The boy was holding one of the girl's hands in his.

It was this that made the white child pause. He was touched by their dependence on one another, and disturbed by it too, as he had been by the way they had suddenly come before him and by their watchfulness and silence after they had uttered their customary, begging request. Michael saw again how ragged and dirty they were, and thought of how hungry they must be. Surely he could give them a piece of bread. He was only three blocks from home.

He said, 'I haven't any bread here. But if you come home with me, I'll see that you get some bread. Do you understand?'

They made no reply; but they obviously understood what he had said. The three children moved down the pavement. Only Michael's shod feet crunched on the sand; the footfalls of the others were silent. They walked a little behind Michael, and to one side of him. Once he asked them if they went to school, and the boy shook his head; when he asked them if they were brother and sister, the boy nodded.

When they reached Michael's house, he went inside and told Dora, the cook-girl, that there were two piccanins in the lane outside, and that he wanted her to cut some bread and jam for them. Dora grumbled that she was not supposed to look after every little beggar in town, and Michael answered her angrily, 'We've got lots of bread. Why shouldn't we give them some?' He was particularly indignant because he felt that Dora, being of the same race as the two outside, should have been even readier than he was to help them. When Dora was about to take the bread out to the back gate, where the children waited, he stopped her. 'It's all right, Dora,' he said in a tone of reproof, 'I'll take it,' and he went out into the sunlight, carrying the plate in his hand.

'Stukkie brood,' he called out to them. 'Here's your *stukkie brood.'*

The children stretched their hands out eagerly, and Michael let them take the inch-thick slices from the plate. He was pleased to see that Dora had put a scraping of apricot jam on the bread. Each of them held the bread in both hands, as if afraid of dropping it. The girl's mouth worked a little, but she kept her eyes fixed on the white boy.

'What do you say?' Michael asked.

They replied in high, clear voices, 'Thank you, baas.'

'That's better. Now you can eat.' He wanted to see them eat it; he wanted to share their pleasure in satisfying their strained appetites. But without saying a word to him, they began to back away, side by side.

They took a few paces, and then they turned and ran along the lane towards the main road they had walked down earlier. The little girl's dress fluttered behind her, white against her black body. At the corner they halted, looked back once, and then ran on, out of sight.

A few days later, at the same time and in the same place, Michael saw them again, on his way home from school. They were standing in the middle of the pavement, and he saw them from a long way off. They were obviously waiting for him to come. Michael was the first to speak, as he approached them.

'What? Another piece of bread?' he called out from a few yards away.

'Yes, baas,' they answered together. They turned immediately to join him as he walked by. Yet they kept a respectful pace or two behind.

'How did you know I was coming?'

'We know the baas is coming from school.'

'And how do you know that I'm going to give you bread?'

There was no reply; not even a smile from the boy, in response to Michael's. They seemed to him, as he glanced casually at them, identical in appearance to a hundred, a thousand, other piccanins, from the peppercorns on top of their heads to their wide, calloused, sand-grey feet.

When they reached the house, Michael told Dora, 'Those *stukkie broods* are waiting outside again. Give them something, and they can go.'

Dora grumbled once again, but did as she was told. Michael did not go out with the bread himself; he was in a hurry to get back to work on a model car he was making, and was satisfied to see, out of his bedroom window, Dora coming from the back gate a few minutes later with an empty plate in her hand. Soon he had forgotten all about the two children. He did not go out of the house until a couple of hours had passed; by then it was dusk, and he took a torch with him to help him find a piece of wire for his model in the darkness of the lumber-shed. Handling the torch gave Michael a feeling of power and importance, and he stepped into the lane with it, intending to shine it about like a policeman on his beat. Immediately he opened the gate, he saw the two little children standing in the half-light, just a few paces away from him.

'What are you doing here?' Michael exclaimed in surprise.

The boy answered, holding his hand up, as if warning Michael to be silent. 'We were waiting to say thank you to the baas.'

'What!' Michael took a step towards them both, and they stood their ground, only shrinking together slightly.

For all the glare and glitter there was in the streets of Lyndhurst by day, it was winter, midwinter; and once the sun had set, the air turned bitterly cold as swiftly as the light disappeared. The cold at night wrung deep notes from the contracting iron roofs of the houses, and froze the fish-ponds in all the gardens of the white suburbs. Already Michael could feel its sharp touch on the tips of his ears and fingers. And the two African children stood there barefoot, in a flimsy dress and torn shirt, waiting to thank him for the bread he had sent out to them.

'You mustn't wait,' Michael said. In the half-darkness he saw the white dress on the girl more clearly than the boy's clothing; and he remembered the nakedness and puniness of her black thighs. He stretched his hand out, with the torch in it. 'Take it,' he said. The torch was in his hand, and there was nothing else that he could give to them. 'It's nice,' he said. 'It's a torch. Look.' He switched it on and saw in its beam of light a pair of startled eyes, darting desperately from side to side. 'You see how nice it is,' Michael said, turning the beam upwards, where it lost itself against the light that lingered in the sky. 'If you don't want it, you can sell it. Go on, take it.'

A hand came up and took the torch from him. Then the two children ran off, in the same direction they had taken on the first afternoon. When they reached the corner all the street lights came on, as if at a single touch, and the children stopped and stared at them, before running again. Michael saw the torch glinting in the boy's hand, and only then did it occur to him that despite their zeal to thank him for the bread they hadn't thanked him for the torch. The size of the gift must have surprised them into silence, Michael decided; and the thought of his own generosity helped to console him for the regret he couldn't help feeling when he saw the torch being carried away from him.

Michael was a lonely child. He had neither brothers nor sisters; both his parents worked during the day, and he had made few friends at school. But he was not unhappy in his loneliness. He was used to it, in the first place; and then, because he was lonely, he was all the better able to indulge himself in his own fantasies. He played for hours, by himself, games of his own invention – games of war, of exploration, of seafaring, of scientific invention, of crime, of espionage, of living in a house beneath or above his real one. It was not long before the two African children, who were now accosting him regularly, appeared in some of his games, for their weakness, poverty, and dependence gave Michael ample scope to display in fantasy his kindness, generosity, courage and decisiveness. Sometimes in his games Michael saved the boy's life, and was thanked for it in broken English. Sometimes he saved the girl's, and then she humbly begged his pardon for having caused him so much trouble. Sometimes he was just too late to save the life of either, though he tried his best, and then there were affecting scenes of farewell.

But in real life, Michael did not play with the children at all: they were too dirty, too ragged, too strange, too persistent. Their persistence eventually drove Dora to tell Michael's mother about them; and his mother did her duty by telling Michael that on no account should he play with the children, nor should he give them anything of value.

'Play with them!' Michael laughed at the idea. And apart from bread and the torch he had given them nothing but a few old toys, a singlet or two, a pair of old canvas shoes. No one could begrudge them those gifts. Michael's mother certainly didn't. What she was anxious to do was simply to prevent her son playing with the piccanins, fearing that he would pick up germs, bad language, and 'Kaffir ways' generally from them. Hearing both from Michael and Dora that he did not play with them, and that he had never even asked them into the backyard, let alone the house, she was satisfied.

They came to Michael about once a week, meeting him as he walked back from school, or simply waiting for him outside the back gate. The spring winds had already blown the cold weather away, almost overnight, and still the children came. Their words of thanks never varied, whatever Michael gave them; but they had revealed, in response to his questions, that the boy's name was Frans and the girl's name was Annie, that they lived in Green Point Location, and that their mother and father were both dead. During all this time Michael had not touched them, except for the fleeting contact of their hands when he passed a gift to them. Yet sometimes Michael wished that they were more demonstrative in their expressions of gratitude to him; he thought that they could, for instance, seize his hand and embrace it; or go down on their knees and weep, just once. As it was, he had to content himself with fantasies of how they spoke of him among their friends, when they returned to the tumbled squalor of Green Point Location; of how incredulous their friends must be to hear their stories about the kind white *kleinbaas* who gave them food and toys and clothing.

One day Michael came out to them carrying a possession he particularly prized – an elaborate pen and pencil set which had been given to him for a recent birthday. He had no intention of giving the outfit to the African children, and he did not think that he would be showing off with it in front of them. He merely wanted to share his pleasure in it with someone who had not already seen it. But as he noticed the way the children were looking at the open box, Michael knew the mistake he had made. 'This isn't for you,' he said abruptly. The children blinked soundlessly, staring from the box to Michael and back to the box again. 'You can just look at it,' Michael said. He held the box tightly in his hand stretching it forward, the pen and the propelling pencils shining inside the velvet-lined case. The two heads of the children came together over the box; they stared deeply into it.

At last the boy lifted his head. 'It's beautiful,' he breathed out. As he spoke, his hand slowly came up towards the box.

'No,' Michael said, and snatched the box away.

'Baas?'

'No.' Michael retreated a little from the beseeching eyes and uplifted hand.

'Please, baas, for me?'

And his sister said, 'For me also, baas.'

'No, you can't have this.' Michael attempted to laugh, as if at the absurdity of the idea. He was annoyed with himself for having shown them the box, and at the same time shocked at them for having asked for it. It was the first time they had asked for anything but bread.

'Please, baas. It's nice.' The boy's voice trailed away on the last word, in longing; then his sister repeated the word, like an echo, her own voice trailing away too. 'Ni-ce.'

'No! I won't give it to you! I won't give you anything if you ask for this. Do you hear?'

Their eyes dropped, their hands came together, they lowered their heads. Being sure now that they would not again ask for the box, Michael relented. He said, 'I'm going in now, and I'll tell Dora to bring you some bread.'

But Dora came to him in his room a few minutes later. 'The little Kaffirs are gone.' She was holding the plate of bread in her hand. Dora hated the two children, and Michael thought there was some kind of triumph in her voice and manner as she made the announcement.

He went outside to see if she was telling the truth.

The lane was empty. He went to the street, and looked up and down its length, but there was no sign of them there either. They were gone. He had driven them away. Michael expected to feel guilty; but to his own intense surprise he felt nothing of the kind. He was relieved that they were gone, and that was all.

When they reappeared a few days later, Michael felt scorn towards them for coming back after what had happened on the last occasion. He felt they were in his power. 'So you've come back?' he greeted them. 'You like your *stukkies brood,* hey? You're hungry, so today you'll wait, you won't run away.'

'Yes, baas,' they said, in their low voices.

Michael brought the bread out to them; when they reached for it he jokingly pulled the plate back and laughed at their surprise. Then only did he give them the bread.

'Thank you, baas.'

'Thank you, baas.'

They ate the bread in Michael's presence; watching them, he felt a little more kindly disposed towards them. 'All right, you can come another day, and there'll be some more bread for you.'

'Thank you, baas.'

'Thank you, baas.'

They came back sooner than Michael had expected them to. He gave them their bread and told them to go. They went off, but again did not wait for the usual five or six days to pass, before approaching him once more. Only two days had passed, yet here they were with their eternal request – '*Stukkie brood,* baas?'

Michael said, 'Why do you get hungry so quickly now?' But he gave them their bread.

When they appeared in his games and fantasies, Michael no longer rescued them, healed them, casually presented them with kingdoms and motor-cars. Now he ordered them about, sent them away on disastrous missions, picked them out to be shot for cowardice in the face of the enemy. And because something similar to these fantasies was easier to enact in the real world than his earlier fantasies, Michael soon was ordering them about unreasonably in fact. He deliberately left them waiting; he sent them away and told them to come back on days when he knew he would be in town; he told them there was no bread in the house. When he did give them anything, it was bread only now; never old toys or articles of clothing.

So, as the weeks passed, Michael's scorn gave way to impatience and irritation, irritation to anger. What angered him most was that the two piccanins seemed too stupid to realize what he now felt about them, and instead of coming less frequently, continued to appear more often than ever before. Soon they were coming almost every day, though Michael shouted at them and teased them, left them waiting for hours, and made them do tricks and sing songs for their bread. They did everything he told them to do; but they ignored his instruction as to which days they should come. Invariably, they would be waiting for him in the shade of one of the trees that grew alongside the main road from school, or standing at the gate behind the house with sand scuffed up about their bare toes. They were as silent as before; but more persistent, inexorably persistent. Michael took to walking home by different routes, but they were not to be so easily discouraged. They simply waited at the back gate, and whether he went into the house by the front or the back gate he could not avoid seeing their upright, unmoving figures.

Finally, he told them to go and never come back at all. Often he had been tempted to do this, but some shame or pride had always prevented him from doing it; he had always weakened previously, and named a date, a week or two weeks ahead, when they could come again. But now he shouted at them, 'It's finished! No more bread – nothing! Go on, *voetsak!* If you come back I'll tell the garden-boy to chase you away.'

From then on they came every day. They no longer waited right at the back gate, but squatted in the sand across the lane. Michael was aware of their eyes following him when he went by, but they did not approach him. They did not even get up from the ground when he passed. A few times he shouted at them to go, and stamped his foot, but he shrank from hitting them. He did not want to touch them. Once he sent out Jan, the garden-boy, to drive them away; but Jan, who had hitherto always shared Dora's views on the children, came back muttering angrily and incomprehensibly to himself; when Michael peeped into the lane he saw that they were still there. Michael tried to ignore them, to pretend he did not see them. He hated them now; even more, he began to dread them.

But he did not know how much he hated and feared the two children until he fell ill with a cold, and lay feverish in bed for a few days. During those days the two children were constantly in his dreams, or in his half-dreams, for even as he dreamed he knew he was turning in his bed; he was conscious of the sun shining outside by day, and at night of the passage-light that had been left on inside the house. In these dreams he struck and struck again at the children with weapons he found in his hands; he fled in fear from them down lanes so thick with sand his feet could barely move through it; he committed lewd, cruel acts upon the bare-thighed girl, and her brother shrieked to tell the empty street what he was doing. Michael struck out at him with a piece of heavy cast-iron guttering. Its edge dug sharply into his hands as the blow fell, and when he lifted the weapon he saw the horror he had made of the side of the boy's head, and how the one remaining eyeball still stared unwinkingly at him.

Michael thought he was awake, and suddenly calm. The fever seemed to have left him. It was as though he had slept deeply, for days, after that last dream of violence; yet his impression was that he had woken directly from it. The bedclothes felt heavy on him and he threw them off. The house was quite silent. He got out of bed and went to look at the clock in the kitchen: it was early afternoon. Dora and Jan were resting in their rooms across the yard, as they always did after lunch. Outside, the light of the sun was unremitting, a single golden glare. He walked back to his bedroom; there, he put on his dressing-gown and slippers, feeling the coolness inside his slippers on his bare feet. He went through the kitchen again and on to the stoep, and then across the yard. The sun seemed to seize the back of his neck as firmly as a hand grasping, and its light was so bright he was aware of it only as a darkness beyond the little stretch of ground he looked down upon. He opened the back gate. Inevitably, as he had known they would be, the two were waiting.

He did not want to go beyond the gate in his pyjamas and dressing-gown, so, shielding his eyes from the glare with one hand, he beckoned them to him with the other. Together, in silence, they rose and crossed the lane. It seemed to take them a long time to come to him, but at last they stood in front of him, with their hands interlinked. Michael stared into their dark faces, and they stared into his.

'What are you waiting for?' he asked.

'For you.' First the boy answered; then the girl repeated, 'For you.'

Michael looked from the one to the other, and he remembered what he had been doing to them in his dreams. Their eyes were fathomlessly black to look into. Staring forward, Michael understood what he should have understood long before: that they came to him not in hope or appeal or even in reproach, but in hatred. What he felt towards them, they felt towards him; what he had done to them in his dreams, they did to him in theirs.

The sun, their staring eyes, his own fear came together in a sound that seemed to hang in the air of the lane – a cry, the sound of someone weeping. Then Michael knew that he was the one who was crying. He felt the heat of the tears in his eyes, their moisture running down his cheeks. With the same fixity of decision that had been his in his dreams of violence and torture, Michael knew what he must do. He beckoned them forward, closer. They came. He stretched out his hands, he felt under his fingers the springy hair he had looked at so often before from the distance between himself and them; he felt the smooth skin of their faces; their frail, rounded shoulders, their hands. Their hands were in his, and he led them inside the gate.

He led them into the house, through the kitchen, down the passage, into his room, where they had never been before. They looked about at the pictures on the walls, the toys on top of the low cupboard, the twisted white sheets and tumbled blankets on the bed. They stood on both sides of him, and for the first time since he had met them, their lips parted into slow, grave smiles. Michael knew that what he had to give them was not toys or clothes or bread, but something more difficult. Yet it was not difficult at all, for there was nothing else he could give them. He took the girl's face in his hands and pressed his lips to hers. He was aware of the darkness of her skin, and of the smell of it, and of the faint movement of her lips, a single pulse that beat momentarily against his own. Then it was gone. He kissed the boy, too, and let them go. They came together, and grasped each other by the hand, staring at him.

'What do you want now?' he asked.

A last anxiety flickered in Michael and left him, as the boy slowly shook his head. He began to step back pulling his sister with him. When he was through the door he turned his back on Michael and they walked away down the passage. Michael watched them go. At the door of the kitchen, on their way out of the house, they paused, turned once more, and lifted their hands, the girl copying the boy, in a silent, tentative gesture of farewell.

Michael did not follow them. He heard the back gate swing open and then bang when it closed. He went wearily back to his bed, and as he fell upon it, his relief and gratitude that the bed should be there to receive him, changed suddenly into grief at the knowledge that he was already lying upon it – that he had never left it.

His cold grew worse, turned into bronchitis, kept him in bed for several weeks. But his dreams were no longer of violence; they were calm, spacious, empty of people. As empty as the lane was, when he was at last allowed out of the house, and made his way there immediately, to see if the children were waiting for him.

He never saw them again, though he looked for them in the streets and lanes of the town. He saw a hundred, a thousand, like them, but not the two he hoped to find.

Bessie Head

THE WIND AND A BOY

Like all the village boys, Friedman had a long wind blowing for him, but perhaps the enchanted wind that blew for him, filled the whole world with magic.

Until they became ordinary, dull grown men, who drank beer and made babies, the little village boys were a special set all on their own. They were kings whom no one ruled. They wandered where they willed from dawn to dusk and only condescended to come home at dusk because they were afraid of the horrible things in the dark that might pounce on them. Unlike the little girls who adored household chores and drawing water, it was only now and then that the boys showed themselves as useful attachments to any household. When the first hard rains of summer fell, small dark shapes, quite naked except for their loin-cloths, sped out of the village into the bush. They knew that the first downpour had drowned all the wild rabbits, moles and porcupines in their burrows in the earth. As they crouched down near the entrances to the burrows, they would see a small drowned nose of an animal peeping out; they knew it had struggled to emerge from its burrow, flooded by the sudden rush of storm water, and as they pulled out the animal, they would say, pityingly: 'Birds have more sense than rabbits, moles and porcupines. They build their homes in trees.' But it was hunting made easy, for no matter how hard a boy and his dog ran, a wild rabbit ran ten times faster; a porcupine hurled his poisonous quills into the body; and a mole stayed where he thought it was safe – deep under the ground. So it was with inordinate pride that the boys carried home armfuls of dead animals for their families to feast on for many days. Apart from that, the boys lived very much as they pleased, with the wind and their own games.

Now and then, the activities of a single family could captivate the imagination and heart of all the people of their surroundings; for years and years, the combination of the boy, Friedman, and his grandmother, Sejosenye, made the people of Ga-Sefete-Molemo ward, smile, laugh, then cry.

They smiled at his first two phases. Friedman came home as a small bundle from the hospital, a bundle his grandmother nursed carefully near her bosom and crooned to day and night with extravagant care and tenderness.

'She is like that,' people remarked, 'because he may be the last child she will ever nurse. Sejosenye is old now and will die one of these days; the child is a gift to keep her heart warm.'

Indeed, all Sejosenye's children were grown, married and had left home. Of all her children, only her last-born daughter was unmarried and Friedman was the result of some casual mating she had indulged in, in a town a hundred miles away where she had a job as a typist. She wanted to return to her job almost immediately, so she handed the child over to her mother and that was that; she could afford to forget him as he had a real mother now. During all the time that Sejosenye haunted the hospital awaiting her bundle, a friendly foreign doctor named Friedman took a fancy to her maternal, grandmotherly ways. He made a habit of walking out of his path to talk to her. She never forgot it and on receiving her bundle she called the baby, Friedman.

They smiled at his second phase, a small dark shadow who toddled silently and gravely beside a very tall grandmother; wherever the grandmother went, there went Friedman. Most women found this phase of the restless, troublesome toddler tedious; they dumped the toddler onto one of their younger girls and were off to weddings and visits on their own.

'Why can't you leave your handbag at home sometimes, granny?' they said.

'Oh, he's no trouble,' Sejosenye would reply.

They began to laugh at his third phase. Almost overnight he turned into a tall, spindly-legged, graceful gazelle with large, grave eyes. There was an odd, musical lilt to his speech and when he teased, or was up to mischief, he moved his head on his long thin neck from side to side like a cobra. It was he who became the king of kings of all the boys in his area; he could turn his hand to anything and made the best wire cars with their wheels of shoe polish tins. All his movements were neat, compact, decisive, and for his age he was a boy who knew his own mind. They laughed at his knowingness and certainty on all things, for he was like the grandmother who had had a flaming youth all her own too. Sejosenye had scandalized the whole village in her days of good morals by leaving her own village ward to live with a married man in Ga-Sefete-Molemo ward. She had won him from his wife and married him and then lived down the scandal in the way only natural queens can. Even in old age, she was still impressive. She sailed through the village, head in the air, with a quiet, almost expressionless face. She had developed large buttocks as time went by and they announced their presence firmly in rhythm with her walk.

Another of Sejosenye's certainties was that she was a woman who could plough, but it was like a special gift. Each season, in drought or hail or sun, she removed herself to her lands. She not only ploughed but nursed and brooded over her crops. She was there all the time till the corn ripened and the birds had to be chased off the land, till harvesting and threshing were done; so that even in drought years with their scanty rain, she came home with some crops. She was the envy of all the women of the surroundings.

'Sejosenye always eats fine things in her house,' they said. 'She ploughs and then sits down for many months and enjoys the fruits of her labour.'

The women also envied her beautiful grandson. There was something special there, so that even when Friedman moved into his bad phase, they forgave him crimes other boys received a sound thrashing for. The small boys were terrible thieves who harassed people by stealing their food and money. It was all a part of the games they played but one which people did not like. Of them all, Friedman was the worst thief, so that his name was mentioned more and more in any thieving that had been uncovered.

'But Friedman showed us how to open the window with a knife and string,' the sobbing, lashed boys would protest.

'Friedman isn't as bad as you,' the parents would reply, irrationally. They were hypnotised by a beautiful creature. The boy Friedman, who had become a real nuisance by then, also walked around as though he were special. He couldn't possibly be a thief and he added an aloof, offended, disdainful expression to his pretty face. He wasn't just an ordinary sort of boy in Ga-Sefete-Molemo ward. He was . . .

It happened, quite accidentally, that his grandmother told him all those stories about the hunters, warriors, and emissaries of old. She was normally a quite absentminded woman, given to dreaming by herself, but she liked to sing the boy a little song now and then as they sat by the outdoor fire. A lot of them were church songs and rather sad; they more or less passed as her bed-time prayer at night – she was one of the old church-goers. Now and then she added a quaint little song to her repertoire and as the night-time, firelight flames flicked between them, she never failed to note that this particular song was always well-received by the boy. A little light would awaken in his eyes and he would bend forward and listen attentively.

'Welcome, Robinson Crusoe, welcome,' she would sing, in clear, sweet tones. 'How could you stay, so long away, Robinson, how could you do so?'

When she was very young, Sejosenye had attended the mission school of the village for about a year; made a slight acquaintance with the ABC and one, two, three, four, five, and the little song about Robinson Crusoe. But girls didn't need an education in those days when ploughing and marriage made up their whole world. Yet Robinson Crusoe lived on as a gay and out-of-context memory of her school-days. One evening the boy leaned forward and asked: 'Is that a special praise-poem song for Robinson Crusoe, grandmother?'

'Oh yes,' she replied, smiling.

'It appears that the people liked Robinson Crusoe much,' the boy observed. 'Did he do great things for them?'

'Oh yes,' she said, smiling.

'What great things did he do?' the boy asked, pointedly.

'They say he was a hunter who went by Gweta side and killed an elephant all by himself,' she said, making up a story on the spot. 'Oh! In those days, no man could kill an elephant by himself. All the regiments had to join together and each man had to thrust his sword into the side of the elephant before it died. Well, Robinson Crusoe was gone many days and people wondered about him: "Perhaps he has been eaten by a lion," they said. "Robinson likes to be a solitary person and do foolish things. We won't ever go out into the bush by ourselves because we know it is dangerous." Well, one day, Robinson suddenly appeared in their midst and people could see that he had a great thing on his mind. They all gathered around him. He said: "I have killed an elephant for all the people." The people were surprised: "Robinson!" they said. "It is impossible! How did you do it? The very thought of an elephant approaching the village makes us shiver!" And Robinson said: "Ah, people, I saw a terrible sight! I was standing at the feet of the elephant. I was just a small ant. I could not see the world any more. Elephant was above me until his very head touched the sky and his ears spread out like great wings. He was angry but I only looked into one eye which was turning round and round in anger. What to do now? I thought it better to put that eye out. I raised my spear and threw it at the angry eye. People! It went right inside. Elephant said not a word and he fell to one side. Come, I will show you what I have done." Then the women cried in joy: "Loo-loo-loo!" They ran to fetch their containers as some wanted the meat of the elephant; some wanted the fat. The men made their knives sharp. They would make shoes and many things from the skin and bones. There was something for all the people in the great work Robinson Crusoe did.'

All this while, as he listened to the story, the boy's eyes had glowed softly. At the end of it, he drew in a long breath.

'Grandmother,' he whispered, adroitly stepping into the role of Robinson Crusoe, the great hunter. 'One day, I'm going to be like that. I'm going to be a hunter like Robinson Crusoe and bring meat to all the people.' He paused for breath and then added tensely: 'And what other great thing did Robinson Crusoe do?'

'Tsaa!' she said, clicking her tongue in exhaustion. 'Am I then going away that I must tell *all* the stories at once?'

Although his image of Robinson Crusoe, the great hunter, was never to grow beyond his everyday boyish activities of pushing wire cars, hunting in the fields for wild rabbits, climbing trees to pull down old birds' nests and yelling out in alarm to find that a small snake now occupied the abandoned abode, or racing against the wind with the spoils of his latest theft, the stories awakened a great tenderness in him. If Robinson Crusoe was not churning up the dust in deadly hand-to-hand combat with an enemy, he was crossing swollen rivers and wild jungles as the great messenger and ambassador of the chief – all his activities were touchingly in aid of or in defence of the people. One day Friedman expressed this awakened compassion for life in a strange way. After a particularly violent storm, people found their huts invaded by many small mice and they were hard-pressed to rid themselves of these pests. Sejosenye ordered Friedman to kill the mice.

'But grandmother,' he protested. 'They have come to us for shelter. They lost all their homes in the storm. It's better that I put them in a box and carry them out into the fields again once the rains are over.'

She had laughed in surprise at this and spread the story around among her women friends, who smiled tenderly then said to their own offspring: 'Friedman isn't as bad as you.'

Life and its responsibilities began to weigh down heavily on Friedman as he approached his fourteenth year. Less time was spent in boyish activities. He grew more and more devoted to his grandmother and concerned to assist her in every way. He wanted a bicycle so that he might run up and down to the shops for her, deliver messages, or do any other chore she might have in mind. His mother, who worked in a town far away, sent him the money to purchase the bicycle. The gift brought the story of his life abruptly to a close.

Towards the beginning of the rainy season, he accompanied his grandmother to her lands which were some twenty miles outside the village. They sowed seed together after the hired tractor had turned up the land but the boy's main chore was to keep the household pot filled with meat. Sometimes they ate birds Friedman had trapped, sometimes they ate fried tortoise-meat or wild rabbit; but there was always something as the bush abounded with animal life. Sejosenye only had to take a bag of mealie meal, packets of sugar, tea, and powdered milk as provisions for their stay at the lands; meat was never a problem. Mid-way through the ploughing season, she began to run out of sugar, tea, and milk.

'Friedman,' she said that evening, 'I shall wake you early tomorrow morning. You will have to take the bicycle into the village and purchase some more sugar, tea, and milk.'

He was up at dawn with the birds, a solitary figure cycling on a pathway through the empty bush. By nine, he had reached the village and first made his way to Ga-Sefete-Molemo ward and the yard of a friend of his grandmother, who gave him a cup of tea and a plate of porridge. Then he put one foot on the bicycle and turned to smile at the woman with his beautiful gazelle eyes. His smile was to linger vividly before her for many days as a short while later, hard pounding feet came running into her yard to report that Friedman was dead.

He pushed the bicycle through the winding, sandy pathway of the village ward, reached the high embankment of the main road, pedalled vigorously up it and out of the corner of his eye saw a small green truck speeding towards him. In the devil-may-care fashion of all the small boys, he cycled right into its path, turned his head and smiled appealingly at the driver. The truck caught him on the front bumper, squashed the bicycle and dragged the boy along at a crazy speed for another hundred yards, dropped him and careered on another twenty yards before coming to a halt. The boy's pretty face was a smear all along the road and he only had a torso left.

People of Ga-Sefete-Molemo ward never forgot the last coherent words Sejosenye spoke to the police. A number of them climbed into the police truck and accompanied it to her lands. They saw her walk slowly and enquiringly towards the truck, they heard the matter-of-fact voice of the policeman announce the death, then they heard Sejosenye say piteously: 'Can't you return those words back?'

She turned away from them, either to collect her wits or the few possessions she had brought with her. Her feet and buttocks quivered anxiously as she stumbled towards her hut. Then her feet tripped her up and she fell to the ground like a log.

The people of Ga-Sefete-Molemo ward buried the boy Friedman but none of them would go near the hospital where Sejosenye lay. The stories brought to them by way of the nurses were too terrible for words. They said the old woman sang and laughed and talked to herself all the time. So they merely asked each other: 'Have you been to see Mma-Sejosenye?' 'I'm afraid I cannot. It would kill my heart.' Two weeks later, they buried her.

As was village habit, the incident was discussed thoroughly from all sides till it was understood. In this timeless, sleepy village, the goats stood and suckled their young ones on the main road or lay down and took their afternoon naps there. The motorists either stopped for them or gave way. But it appeared that the driver of the truck had neither brakes nor a driving licence. He belonged to the new, rich civil-servant class whose salaries had become fantastically high since independence. They had to have cars in keeping with their new status; they had to have any car, as long as it was a car; they were in such a hurry about everything that they couldn't be bothered to take driving lessons. And thus progress, development, and a pre-occupation with status and living-standards first announced themselves to the village. It looked like being an ugly story with many decapitated bodies on the main road.

Nat Nakasa

MR NAKASA GOES TO HARLEM

Harlem, like all New York, is the most indescribable place I have ever seen. It humbles the visitor by its size alone. After weeks of being there, I was still trying to understand and describe it to myself.

Before coming here, I had read stories by Langston Hughes and powerful essays by James Baldwin. They often made Harlem sound like one of the townships in Johannesburg. When Baldwin spoke of the ghetto, I likened Harlem to Sophiatown.

I had visions of private homes turned into shebeens – illegal drinking clubs. Here I would find the drinking fraternity and be welcomed like a long-missed cousin. But Harlem drinks in night clubs and bars, like the white fold. In Harlem I missed the sense of danger which characterized our drinking sessions, many of which were so rudely interrupted by the Johannesburg police.

Harlem has a facade of respectability, the kind I associate with white suburbia. Many people here chew cigars, while others read newspapers on the back seats of licensed taxis. I am more accustomed to the overloaded pirate taxis which used to find their way into Johannesburg through devious routes. None of these were driven by whites.

Harlem even has its banks in the community, despite all the talk about how rough it is. Now, nobody ever risked opening a bank in Sophiatown or Edenvale. Those were outfits of the sedate, more secure white world.

The townships in Johannesburg were neatly separated from the white area, in accordance with the official policy of apartheid. Some were fenced in like game reserves, which is what we called them. Harlem is not like that. My friends had difficulty in showing me where it began. Besides, I hear there are whites living there as well, which would not be tolerated where I come from.

Yet, at the same time, Harlem is quite different from white or integrated New York – that is, those few parts of both places that I saw. I felt more at home in Harlem than I could ever be in the plush hotels downtown. A lot of Harlem's battles and preoccupations are no different from mine. The people here are still fighting for a place in the sun, just like me.

I saw filth and squalor and saw people climb from plush cars into disgusting hovels – their homes. For, even though Harlem had its cigars, I did not see poodles and fox terriers in the place. I did not see housewives take dogs for afternoon walks, a practice I know only as having something to do with white affluence.

When I asked if the community had its poodle-raising set, I was told a story about the last riot. Apparently, someone swiped yards of sausage from a shop during the riot lootings, only to be besieged by Harlem's dogs as he went down the sidewalk. The dogs, it is said, forced the man to the ground and made off with much of his loot. I can well imagine the same thing happening in Edenvale, Johannesburg.

Finally, the white folks downtown seem to be somewhat apprehensive about going uptown. Taxi-men kept turning me down on many occasions when I wanted a ride to my hotel in Harlem. Some would slow down on seeing my raised hand then sweep past me without stopping. One cab driver left me in the rain after stopping. When I mentioned Harlem, he said: 'I thought you were going downtown. I would take you if you were going the right way.' Negroes told me this was something I would have to expect a good deal of the time.

Some whites drive through Harlem, but take care not to stop any place. It is worse for Southern motorists. A friend from Alabama, a white journalist, had to use a false registration plate on his car in order to drive through Harlem. In this respect, as in many others, Harlem is reminiscent of Johannesburg. The few whites who do go to our townships do so at their peril. Our drunken brawls and weekend brutalities, as well as anti-white feelings, have long put God's fear into them.

So much for invidious comparisons. The most I can do is put down my reactions to Harlem, just how it felt to be there . . .

I lived at the Hotel Theresa, apparently the Negro Waldorf of yesteryear. This is the tall, ageing building where 7th Avenue meets 125th Street. From my room, I could see Harlem Square, where the local soapbox men hold forth in the summer.

The Theresa was built in 1895, strictly for whites. As Harlem went black, however, it was taken over by Negro celebrities. Joe Louis, Ella Fitzgerald and other personages have lived there. More recently, its guests included Fidel Castro and Cassius Clay. The world champion gave instructions that all walls and furniture in his suite be painted pink.

But there were no celebrities in the Theresa when I checked in. Even Malcolm X, who had an office there, spent most of his time elsewhere. I never saw him there, although I tried many times.

The Theresa has survived three riots and, last summer, a group of young men moved into the place carrying rifles. The police were called in, but they could make no arrests as the rifles turned out to be unloaded.

The police were among the most fascinating people to speak with in Harlem. They are a lonely crowd, and people stare coldly at them with accusing eyes. I never saw anybody talk with them. One of them, white, smiled like a schoolboy when I introduced myself as a stranger from South Africa.

'You're a long ways from home,' he said.

Across the street, advertising a book, stood a weatherbeaten placard. It proclaimed in bold lettering: THE GODDAM WHITE MAN. This made me uneasy, but the policeman seemed to take no notice of it.

Nervously, I lit a cigarette and offered the policeman one. 'Can't take it,' he said. 'Not allowed to smoke in uniform.' I should have known better, I thought. But then I don't have much experience of chatting with policemen on the sidewalks.

'This is a bad neighbourhood,' he warned, almost confidentially, 'you must be careful.'

'But why? The people seem to be nice and harmless to me.'

'Yes, you're looking at the church people. This is Sunday and the bad ones aren't up yet,' he said.

'What places do you think I should go and see?' I asked.

'The museum downtown. Been there yet?'

'No. But I went to the Solomon Guggenheim.'

'Right. That's a good one. What about the Empire State Building?'

'Yes, I went there, but I got scared before we reached the top . . . Tell me, were you here during the last riot?'

'What do they call it?'

'Disturbance.'

In this officer's view, the junkies and the hoodlums of Harlem were responsible for the disturbance. The good folks had nothing to do with the whole business. It was true that many people were badly housed, but that was their own fault. They did not look after their apartments properly.

'Who owns the apartments?' I asked.

The officer explained that most of the people in Harlem did not own the apartments. But then they lived in them, sublet them and overcrowded the place. He himself did not live there and his parents did not like him working in the neighbourhood.

I could have talked to the policeman much longer. But I soon noticed that our chat was slowly stirring the crowd in Harlem Square. Passers-by stared fiercely, directly at us, apparently suspecting impending trouble. Another policeman joined us, and I thought it was curious that the Harlem police were almost always in pairs. Meanwhile, teen-age boys snuggled close to us, obviously to listen in without asking what was going on. Harlem has obviously not forgotten the shooting of Jimmy Powell by a policeman, shortly before the last riot.

I got the feeling in Harlem that people are not

always amused by outsiders coming to write about the community. Like Jews, they seem to resent the situation being turned into party conversation or tourist-story material.

Also, like white Americans, Negroes do not like outsiders lashing out at the United States, especially as foreigners almost always get their facts and local nuances mixed up. This is nothing peculiar to the United States. I have seen Africans get irritated in Johannesburg when white and black foreigners begin to assail South Africa and get their facts mixed up.

Harlem loves America dearly, bitterly. Its people will stop at nothing to change America and make it a better home for themselves. But they do not want to see the country hurt or disparaged unduly. Not by outsiders, anyway. Harlemites are like the South African refugees who are desperate for a change back home, but remain irrevocably in love with the country.

My relationship with Harlem is largely what Joe Louis meant to me when he rocked the myth of white supremacy in the ring. To this day, Africans in South Africa would fork out their last cents to see the Brown Bomber, even without his gloves. I think, in turn, when Africans arrive at the United Nations, Negroes identify with them and see a new dawn in their own lives.

The same Harlemites, however, do not like too much interference with the details of their situation. 'I really think it is presumptuous for people to come here for a short while and go writing about Harlem,' a young, talented novelist said to me. Another person, a Negro woman, put it more frankly. 'You know,' she said, 'you really have no right to write about Harlem. You don't know anything about it.'

A bearded Negro actor – I'll call him Vos – took a slightly different attitude. He welcomed me into his studio with the warm greetings of Negro-African brotherhood. Vos answered my questions diligently until I told him I was writing for the *New York Times*.

'Give me that notebook,' he said, suddenly, firmly. 'I don't want to have anything to do with white papers.' For a moment I felt like a spy in Harlem. I tore off the pages which contained the actor's comments and gave them to him. I also told him I failed to see the logic of his thinking. But the matter did not end there.

I was to meet more nationalists. Vos and the others invited me and a friend to a party, adding bitterly, 'But please don't bring any white folks with you.' Vos had recently fought with a Nigerian student who brought a white date to one of Harlem's parties.

I got the impression that Vos belonged to a new world in Harlem, the world beyond Malcom X, if such is possible. For Malcolm now stands for brotherhood to those who offer friendship, and enmity to those who threaten the black man's cause. He has conceded, time and again, publicly, that not all whites are the same. But Vos and his fellow nationalists want no truck with whites, however good they may be.

Time moves fast, even for the Malcolms, although most whites I met regarded Malcolm as the worst in Negro extremism. If anything, my own guess is that Malcolm, like Martin Luther King, may yet be charged with 'cooling it' too soon with the white folks. I can see the younger nationalists sneering at him for his appearances at Harvard and in the pages of the *Saturday Evening Post* which carried his biography.

This aspect of Harlem's many faces left me a little frightened. I am, by nature, somewhat easy to scare. But this was something else, something quite apart from my unbrave makeup. It was a brand of blackmanship such as I had not met anywhere else before.

Harlem has this element of resilient, unapologising blackmanship and not all of it is negative. I saw this at the Schomburg Library in Harlem where, for the first time in my life, I saw a collection of writings by distinguished black men. Here, again for the first time, I saw busts of black men.

This came as a thrill to me. For, where I come from, all great men are whites. The heroes in our schoolbooks and films and all the statues in our capitals are those of white men. The only black statue I ever saw was that of the great Zulu king, uShaka. Even that lies out of the way, far from the cities, and we were taught to despise the statue as a relic from our savage past.

Like any other place Harlem has its great contradictions. I met Negroes who sat at my feet and listened for hours to the clicks in my Zulu language. Some asked me to teach them the language. I also met Negroes who wished to have little or nothing to do with me. I think that this was partly because of a sense of embarrassment which many Negroes still feel in being associated with Africans.

There was the churchman I met in the cafeteria at the basement of his church. I told him I was a journalist from South Africa and that I wished to talk with anybody who had some time. There were many people in the cafeteria, all engaged in the chit-chats which make Sunday a great social occasion in Harlem.

The churchman led me to an empty table and gave

me coffee. I thought he would sit with me and talk, but he went to join the rest of the chatting crowd. He later returned to ask how I was enjoying my coffee. I said, lamely, that I was doing fine and would like to have a chat with anyone. Now the man offered me some food, but I told him I did not want to eat. At this stage, he went to the kitchen and fetched half of a roasted chicken and six or eight buns. I was to take that away with me, he said. 'That's the best I can do for you, my friend,' he said.

Thus, minus my chat, I left the place clutching a parcel of roasted chicken in one hand, plus half a dozen buns in the other. My next interviews that night were to be conducted with the splendid smell of chicken under my arm.

Rightly or unfairly, I drew certain inferences from this incident. There can be no doubt that there are many Negroes in Harlem who look down on Africans in the same way that many Johannesburg Africans foolishly despise other Africans, or the English condescend, insufferably, to Americans.

It's no use saying the churchman misunderstood me. If anything, Negroes are forever telling me how clearly I speak English. Besides, there are several similar incidents I know of. Not so long ago, an African girl was proposed to by a Negro boy. Yet, shortly before the two met for the first time, the young man had told his uncle that he might not know what to do with the girl when she appeared. 'Is she going to come with those spears and African drums, Uncle?' he had asked. I myself have been asked by Negroes if we still eat people where I come from.

Now, for this sort of thing, I am inclined to blame the white world more than anyone else. For years now, white cartoonists have been churning out stereotypes of Africans putting white hunters into black pots and boiling them. I have never lunched on anybody's ribs, and it's no use pointing at the Congo. The cartoons I speak of were done scores of years before the Congo erupted. I wonder how London or Rome or New York would feel if Africans began producing caricatures, based on true stories, of whites lynching black men or cutting their hands off as was done by the Belgians.

But there is another side to the story of Negro-African relations. A lot of people complained, for instance, that many Africans who came to New York remained downtown where the 'white girls show them a good time.' It was said that few Africans ever came among the people in Harlem.

A man recalled that some of the African politicians used to live in Africa House in Harlem when they were students. The same man charged that these Africans now spent most of their time with whites, having acquired a new status as diplomats. He said that, until recently, Africans employed white secretaries and white clerks in their embassies and no Negroes.

When Sekou Touré came to Harlem, he apparently brought a white girl to interpret from French for him. This was evidently unsatisfactory for Harlem and a Negro interpreter was hurriedly produced to replace the white one.

Yet, whatever the current feelings may be between Africans and Negroes, it would be a mistake to underestimate the sentiments of kinship between the two.

Even *Ebony,* while peddling wigs and skin-bleaching creams, is currently running a series on 'Africa's Golden Past'. The magazine feeds Harlem constantly on stories of progress and success by Africans.

Perhaps the people I met came to life most when

they spoke of the ways in which they continuously survived and beat the odds against them. There was the young, college-trained businessman who told of the difficulties he had trying to get a job. 'They just wouldn't hire me,' he said, 'so I borrowed money and opened my own business. I figured the best thing to do was to hire them, and send them to places where my black skin would not be welcomed.'

A woman traced this attitude to a Jewish source. 'If the Jews go into a shop and get discriminated against,' she quipped, 'they buy the joint.' This seemed an attractive philosophy to me, although, heaven knows, there are too many who never reach college or know where to borrow cash to open shop.

Lewis Michaux, a bookstore owner at Harlem Square, made it the hard way. A former labourer, he 'took' and sold three pigs from his boss's farm before going into the book business. Now he is one of the pillars of Harlem.

A small man, Mr Michaux has been a nationalist of the Marcus Garvey breed for decades now. His bookstore is filled with books and magazines by and about black men all over the world. 'The House of Common Sense and the Home of Proper Propaganda' his store is called.

This is where Dr W E B Du Bois, the late Negro scholar, first met his wife, Shirley Graham. In the back room, Mr Michaux keeps something like a hall of fame. The walls of this room are covered with big and small portraits of former American Presidents.

Mr Michaux believes that Jesus was a black man. 'They lynched Jesus,' he said, 'and they don't lynch white folks!'

Old Michaux had made this claim to many groups of students from white universities, some of whom come to the shop to hear him talk. He is now writing a biography of a former American President who, Mr Michaux is satisfied, had a Negro mother.

On the Negroes in Harlem, Mr Michaux said: 'The so-called Negro has been woke up for years now, but he never got up yet. It's not enough to open your eyes and stay in bed. You got to get up and go to work as well.'

I suppose few people would go to Harlem and take no interest in the churches there. For some of the people of Harlem, the church is the very core of their lives, something which has to do with their day-to-day survival. I remember clearly the power of the organ and the singing inside those storefront churches. At times it was tragic and yet beautiful. At no time was it comical.

I saw a girl take a position behind the mike while the rest of the congregation clapped to her song, and somebody pumped the organ. At first there was a suggestion of suffering and self-pity in her voice. Then this transformed into pain, agony, which almost drove me out of the place. The handclapping took on a faster pace and more people said, 'Amen, praise the Lord, Sister!' Then, as if in a trance, the girl let out some gibberish and moaned and twisted her body and contorted her face until I thought she would smash her head on the floor. Finally, the congregation switched to a new, cheerful tune and the girl began to swing and sing the gospel blues like Mahalia Jackson.

I understood this because I used to preach in the street myself. In those few moments, the girl told the long story of misery, pain and an unbending will to survive. I visited other churches, Daddy Grace's for instance, and found people going through the same experience. Beautiful, ebony-black women rose in turn to the mike and unleashed gospel blues, sometimes with a jazzy beat, transforming the service into a great jazz festival.

The odd men out in Harlem are the businessmen, the white shopkeepers. I saw them straining to be polite and friendly to unresponsive black customers. Some of them were aware of the disadvantages at which Harlem is placed inside those decaying tenements, with all the dope-peddling and the numbers business. They even conceded that something ought to be done, perhaps by the Negroes themselves. Yet they seemed so removed from Harlem that I wondered if they had any intimate understanding of its problems.

The most sympathetic businessman said to me: 'But for the grace of God, I could also have been born black.' He told me about a number of Negro organisations which he supported financially and in many other ways. I had no way of explaining effectively to him that what he had just said might annoy a lot of black men. For I doubt that there are many black men who enjoy being pitied in this way.

One of the things which Le Roi Jones says in his play *The Slave* is about just this. The central character in the play, a Negro, says to his ex-wife, a white woman: ' . . . you were certain, my God, so certain . . . emotionally and intellectually, that you were right until the only idea you had about me was to pity me . . . '

This does not mean, however, that all Harlem is suspicious or resentful of all whites. There are white people who have good names in certain quarters of Harlem. One of them was President Kennedy. A number of people had a good word for him. 'He was one of the few Presidents that ever came to Harlem,' one man said, 'and he really cared about civil rights.'

Yet even Kennedy had his critics. I remember the large Harlem housewife who said: 'I never trusted him. I don't like nothin' Irish. That dirty Irishman stole the idea of the Peace Corps from us. We was going to do it ourselves.' This lady, I gathered later, was an ardent Republican.

I asked a seasoned newspaperman in Harlem to name six top Negro leaders in the order of their importance according to his judgement. He listed Martin Luther King, Roy Wilkins, Whitney Young, James Farmer, Dorothy Height and A Philip Randolph.

Of Malcolm X he said: 'I know Malcolm. He's a friend of mine. Malcolm X is a necessary evil. As long as our society is as twisted as it is, there will always be a place for the Malcolm Xs'. If you want to get rid of Malcolm X, begin by getting rid of the imperfections in our society.'

I did not meet any of the six leaders listed above, but I developed a deep respect for their work from what I heard people say. Harlem functions on a vast, complex scale, comprising innumerable fronts, some of which appear to be in desperate competition with each other. Harlem has its branch of the NAACP, Mobilisation for Youth, Har-you-Act and other groups. Somewhere, somehow, all these organisations as well as many others, find a common focal point where most of their pressure converges, all in the business of finding a place in the sun for black America. This is the only way I could explain finding a drawing of Du Bois, Martin Luther King and Ralph Bunche in Malcolm X's head office.

Richard Rive

THE VISITS

It was on the evening The Student had gone out that The Woman had first arrived. It wasn't actually a visit, but that was the nearest he could come to it. He remembered it very clearly. First the phone call for The Student, some girl or other (the ringing sounded brazen and adolescent), then the front-door banging. The Student revving his engine and the tortured whine as the Honda gathered speed up the driveway.

He was distinctly annoyed. He went to the front-door, opened it, peered out from long habit, then closed the door gently as if to make up to it for The Student's treatment. He returned to his study and sat down at the cluttered desk. Should he read or mark books? He was busy fighting his way through *A Century of South African Verse in English.* What a bore. What a boring bore. Should he mark the Standard Ten compos instead? Mark books?

There was a quietness which settled over the flat. It was like that whenever The Student went out and he took the phone off the cradle. The silence surging softly . . . but first the storm before the calm. The phone, then the revving of that damn engine, then peace. Mark books. Standard Ten compos. Remember, dearest children, the word *can* denotes ability, whereas *may* denotes possibility. Ability and possibility. Can ability. May possibility. Can-ability, may-possibility. He repeated it mentally until a rhythm formed. May-possibility sounded clumsy, so he changed it to canability, mayability. But that was wrong. Sacrificing meaning for rhythm. Maybe he could use it on his seniors. His students. The Student?

He got up, uncomfortable at the triviality of his ideas. Must be getting old. Mr Chips. Old at forty-five. Young at forty-five. He walked to the kitchen to make some tea and turned on the tap for hot water. The gurgle echoed through the flat. How vacant the place sounded without The Student. How empty when he wasn't there. How empty when he was there. A different kind of emptiness.

Impossible to speak to him any longer. He was too . . . too physical. Throwing his weight and looks around. Girls, the telephone and the Honda. Looks and muscle. A student of rags and tatters. He switched on the stove reflectively, and put on the water. May-ability, canability. Canability, mayability.

It was then that he heard the knocking at the door. Not loudly but it could be heard throughout the flat. Who could it be? He was curious but didn't answer the door at once. He fussed loudly in the kitchen to show that he was in (he knew he could be heard at the entrance), until the knocking was repeated. He coughed and said, 'Coming.'

When he opened the door he was surprised and disappointed to see the African woman standing there.

'Yes?' he asked somewhat annoyed.

She said nothing, just stood there, her eyes downcast. He took in her appearance. She was extremely unattractive, seemed all of a heap from her doughy bosom to her thick ankles hanging over her shoes.

'Yes?' he repeated, showing his impatience.

She looked at him for the first time and he noticed a mixture of shyness and aggression. He felt like shutting the door on her, but was incapable of such behaviour. He braced himself and became the teacher. (For God's sake boy, open your mouth when you recite. Can denotes ability. May possibility.)

Then she said in a half-whisper, 'I want food.' And as an afterthought, 'Please.'

It was the way she said it that made him look at her more closely. Although she whispered, her tone was not servile or pleading. She spoke almost as if the asking for food was hers by right. Not quite a demand, more a taking for granted. He wanted her to go, but there was something about her he didn't quite understand. He couldn't see her eyes very clearly but sensed they were laughing and mocking him. When he tried to see she cast them down.

'Food?' he repeated, and knew he sounded foolish. She maintained her silence, not looking him in the face.

'Wait here, I'll see.' He realized that this was a sign of defeat. But why should he be defeated? There was no contest, or was there? What he knew was that he had to get away from her. He wished The Student was there. He could deal physically with the situation. But this was so different. He went back to the kitchen and stood for some time staring at the water boiling over on the stove and hissing on the plate. Then he opened the provisions cupboard and started filling an empty carrier bag. Sugar, rice, a tin of mushrooms. There was some apricot jam left over, a bottle of pickles, stuffed olives. What the hell could she do with stuffed olives? He opened the fridge and removed cheese, butter and two pints of milk. Then he opened the bread bin. He stared at the bulging carrier on the kitchen table.

He seemed afraid to face her and hoped she would be gone by the time he returned to the door. He decided to have a cup of tea while playing for time. Should he invite her in? He smiled and decided against the tea. Then resolutely he took the paper carrier. Give her the food and tell her to get the hell away.

When he handed over the provisions she made a slight, old-fashioned bow. It seemed comical because he estimated she could not be more than forty. Still, one could never tell with these people. Or could one?

'Thank you,' she said in the same whisper. Then she was gone. He returned to the kitchen and felt relieved, and for no reason at all, he felt completely exhausted.

The second time The Woman came it was almost like her first visit. Had she visited him? One did not visit and ask for food. The Student was out again (flexing his muscles at some giddy fresher in a coffee bar). He had been in his study for some time reading the book on South African verse. It wasn't quite as boring as he had thought at first.

Roy Campbell. *Upon a dark and gloomy night.* Yes it was a dark and gloomy night. Outside it was dark with squalls of north-wester. *Upon a gloomy night with nobody in sight, I went abroad when all my house was hushed.* To waste the poetry of that great Spanish mystic St John of the Cross upon the snot-nosed brats in his matriculation class. (For goodness sake, try to feel what the poet is trying to get at.

Feel the *brio.)* They lived for Hondas and girls and pop. Telephones and screaming singers. The Animals. The Insecticides.

He settled down for more Roy Campbell. *In safety, in disguise, in darkness up the secret stair I crept . . .* he recognized the knock at once when it came and was afraid to answer.

She stood halfway in the shadow of the entrance but he had no difficulty recognizing the dumpy figure, the heavy legs and the downcast eyes. This time he was determined that she should speak first. She had the empty carrier bag with her. He didn't want to break the silence. Somehow he seemed afraid of his own voice. She held out the bag without saying anything.

'What is it this time?' he said in his schoolmaster voice. Then he regretted his tone and felt his attitude was wrong, far too aggressive. There was certainly no cause for aggression.

'More food?' he asked, hoping he sounded friendly.

'Yes, please,' she said at last.

He went into the kitchen and half-filled the bag with all the left-overs he could find. By the time he returned he felt more at ease, more in control of himself, and was determined to speak.

'Tell me,' he said without handing over the bag, 'what is your name? Who are you?'

She mumbled something which sounded like Edith. The surname was inaudible. He didn't bother to ask her to repeat it.

'Now look here, Edith or whoever you are.' He spoke faster than usual, his voice a trifle raspy. 'Now look here. You're a grown woman. You should be working instead of begging like this. Take the carrier but don't come back here again. Do you understand?'

She nodded slightly and took the food with the same old-fashioned bow. Then, like the first time, she was gone.

He went back to his study and slumped down in the chair. He took up his book but had no further interest in Roy Campbell. Edith something or other. For God's sake why must she come to him? What had he done to her? What had he done for her? He felt guilty but there was nothing he could think of to feel guilty about. He had given her food. He had done his duty. What was his duty and why should he do it? Again the nagging feeling of guilt. Well, he had to tell her not to come again. Couldn't keep giving food away. Not a charitable institution. He wished The Student would come home earlier so that they could talk. No, not about The Woman necessarily. Only just talk.

He sat in the dark until well after eleven o'clock when he heard The Student's Honda whining up the driveway. Then he went to bed.

Even after her third visit he said nothing to The Student about it. They seldom spoke and communicated only when it was necessary. (The Student was in sometimes now because examinations were pressing.) The night of her third visit, however, The Student was out, and he was alone in the flat, although himself on the verge of going out. He was going out more frequently now. He sometimes visited two members of his staff with whom he was quite intimate, and his one married sister. Most times he sat in the Public Library reading until closing time. He even went to cinemas although he detested them. What he seemed afraid of was being alone in the flat. The loneliness got him down. Or was it the aloneness. He used to enjoy it before. The silence, his books, his pipe. A cup of tea and a small brandy with water before turning in for the night. He couldn't stand the sameness any longer. And the loneliness. One tired of too much routine.

He had put on his overcoat and prepared himself mentally for the brisk walk to the library. The dark shadows of the trees lining the avenue, the smell of rain. He was about to pick up his books when the knock came. He looked around for possible escape routes but there was only the bathroom window and he realized how absurd it was for him to climb through that.

She stood in the doorway holding the same empty carrier.

'But I told you not to come back!' He tried to control himself. 'I told you not to come again.'

She maintained her silence, her eyes, as usual, downcast. He clenched the library books till he could feel the edges cutting into his palm.

'Do you understand me?'

She nodded slightly.

'I told you to stay away! Do you understand? Stay away!' She stood dumbly, not looking at him.

'If you come again I'll be forced to call the police. Police!' he repeated.

She started slightly and cast a quick glance at him. He felt it was hostile.

'Police!' he repeated. 'Police!'

There was a pause that lasted longer than it should have done.

'Hell,' he said, dropping the books on the table. 'Hell, what do I do now?' He decided to try to be reasonable and sat down wearily. 'Where you from?'

She kept her eyes down, not replying.

'Look,' he said frustratedly, 'I'll give you food for

the last time. For the last time. You understand? You must never come again. If you do come I'll call the police. Then you'll go to jail! Understand?'

She stared at him, her eyes no longer downcast.

'Jail! Police! Jail!'

Then he noticed, almost with a start, that she was crying. Two tears rolled down her cheeks but her face remained immobile. The tears did not seem part of her. He felt the sense of guilt again, felt like assuring her that he would not call the police. That he was only pretending. But she must not come again.

He went into the kitchen, and when he returned she took the carrier with the same quaint bow. He watched her walking down the driveway. Then he saw another dark figure joining her. They seemed to speak for a short time, but it was too far for him to hear what they were saying. She pointed at him still standing in the open doorway. The other figure (he could not make out the sex) also turned. He heard their loud laughter. He shut the door and felt sick to the stomach.

She came again the following week after that, and every week after that. Now he merely went to the door, took her empty carrier and then filled it. No words passed between them, only the ritual. The quaint bow and she was gone. He bought extra groceries which he set aside for her. She did not always come on the same evening, but she never came more than once a week. She seemed to time it so that The Student was out and he was in.

Although he watched her when she left, he never saw her companion again. He started suffering from lack of sleep, was short tempered with his pupils at school and was seriously thinking of giving The Student notice and then himself moving from the flat. There was no one to whom he could speak seriously about the visits.

He told The Student about it one evening but he turned it into a joke and they both laughed. He seemed to welcome and dread her visits at the same time. He wanted to find out more about her, follow her and see where she lived. Was she married? Did she have children? Why did she have to beg? Was it only to him she came? But somehow he was afraid, afraid he might find out. He could ask her in, give her some tea and then ask questions. He was afraid of her answers.

Then one week she did not appear. Her groceries remained in the closet. The following week she did not come either. He kept her groceries in case. After she had not appeared for a month he decided to use the provisions he had bought for her. With a strange sense of fear he opened the bags and was relieved when nothing happened. He felt as if an enormous burden had dropped from his shoulders and wanted to speak to someone about it. Anyone. The Student was in his room trying in vain to study. He made some coffee and took it to The Student, standing in the doorway, attempting to keep the conversation alive.

'By the way,' The Student said, not annoyed at being disturbed, 'your girl friend turned up last week but you were out.'

'I was out?' he said, bewildered. He was eager to know more.

'I answered the door and there she was. What an ugly bitch.'

'Yes?' He hoped he didn't sound over-anxious.

'I told her to get away, clear off, hamba!' He waved his arms to indicate the action. 'She wouldn't.'

'What did you do?' His lips were trembling.

'What you should have done the first time.'

'What I should have done?'

'Yes. I took her by her black neck and frog-marched her down the driveway. Then threw her out.'

He felt a tightening across his chest. His fists balled and he felt like hitting The Student. He was shivering all over.

'She won't come again,' The Student assured him.

'You shouldn't have done that.' He tried to control his voice.

'Why the hell not?' The Student looked at him puzzled.

'You shouldn't have done that,' he repeated lamely.

'Are you sick or something?' The Student asked.

'I'm all right. Only have to get back to my books. Marking to be done.'

The Student looked at him in a strange way. Then the phone rang.

He went into his study and slumped down at the desk. He felt like crying but couldn't. He heard The Student banging the front door then the revving of the Honda engine. Long after the whine had faded away he sat at his desk just staring in the dark.

Doris Lessing

NO WITCHCRAFT FOR SALE

The Farquars had been childless for years when little Teddy was born; and they were touched by the pleasure of their servants, who brought presents of fowls and eggs and flowers to the homestead when they came to rejoice over the baby, exclaiming with delight over his downy golden head and his blue eyes. They congratulated Mrs Farquar as if she had achieved a very great thing, and she felt that she had – her smile for the lingering, admiring natives was warm and grateful.

Later, when Teddy had his first haircut, Gideon the cook picked up the soft gold tufts from the ground, and held them reverently in his hand. Then he smiled at the little boy and said: 'Little Yellow Head.' That became the native name for the child. Gideon and Teddy were great friends from the first. When Gideon had finished his work, he would lift Teddy on his shoulders to the shade of a big tree, and play with him there, forming curious little toys from twigs and leaves and grass, or shaping animals from wetted soil. When Teddy learned to walk it was often Gideon who crouched before him, clucking encouragement, finally catching him when he fell, tossing him up in the air till they both became breathless with laughter. Mrs Farquar was fond of the old cook because of his love for her child.

There was no second baby; and one day Gideon said: 'Ah missus, missus, the Lord above sent this one; Little Yellow Head is the most good thing we have in our house.' Because of that 'we' Mrs Farquar felt a warm impulse towards her cook; and at the end of the month she raised his wages. He had been with her now for several years; he was one of the few natives who had his wife and children in the compound and never wanted to go home to his kraal, which was some hundreds of miles away. Sometimes a small piccanin, who had been born the same time as Teddy, could be seen peering from the edge of the bush, staring in awe at the little white boy with his miraculous fair hair and northern blue eyes. The two little children would gaze at each other with a wide, interested gaze, and once Teddy put out his hand curiously to touch the black child's cheeks and hair.

Gideon, who was watching, shook his head wonderingly, and said: 'Ah, missus, these are both children, and one will grow up to be a Baas, and one will be a servant,' and Mrs Farquar smiled and said sadly, 'Yes, Gideon, I was thinking the same.' She sighed. 'It is God's will,' said Gideon, who was a mission boy. The Farquars were very religious people; and this shared feeling about God bound servant and masters even closer together.

Teddy was about six years old when he was given a scooter, and discovered the intoxications of speed. All day he would fly around the homestead, in and out of flowerbeds, scattering squawking chickens and irritated dogs, finishing with a wide dizzying arc into the kitchen door. There he would cry: 'Gideon, look at me!' And Gideon would laugh and say: 'Very clever, Little Yellow Head.' Gideon's youngest son, who was now a herdboy, came especially up from the compound to see the scooter. He was afraid to come near it, but Teddy showed off in front of him. 'Piccanin,' shouted Teddy, 'get out of my way!' And he raced in circles around the black child until he was frightened, and fled back to the bush.

'Why did you frighten him?' asked Gideon, gravely reproachful.

Teddy said defiantly: 'He's only a black boy,' and laughed. Then, when Gideon turned away from him without speaking, his face fell. Very soon he slipped into the house and found an orange and brought it to Gideon, saying: 'This is for you.' He could not bring himself to say he was sorry; but he could not bear to lose Gideon's affection either. Gideon took the orange unwillingly and sighed. 'Soon you will be going away to school, Little Yellow Head,' he said wonderingly, 'and then you will be grown up.' He shook his head gently and said, 'And that's how our lives go.' He seemed to be putting a distance between himself and Teddy, not because of resentment, but in the way a person accepts something inevitable. The baby had lain in his arms and smiled up into his face: the tiny boy had swung from his shoulders, had played with him by the hour. Now Gideon would not let his flesh touch the flesh of the white child. He was kind, but there was a grave formality in his voice that made Teddy pout and sulk away. Also, it made him into a man: with Gideon he was polite, and carried himself formally, and if he came into the kitchen to ask for something, it was in the way a white man uses towards a servant, expecting to be obeyed.

But on the day that Teddy came staggering into the kitchen with his fists to his eyes, shrieking with pain, Gideon dropped the pot full of hot soup that he was holding, rushed to the child, and forced aside his fingers. 'A snake!' he exclaimed. Teddy had been on his scooter, and had come to a rest with his foot on the side of a big tub of plants. A tree-snake, hanging by its tail from the roof, had spat full into his eyes. Mrs Farquar came running when she heard the commotion. 'He'll go blind,' she sobbed, holding Teddy close against her. 'Gideon, he'll go blind!' Already the eyes, with perhaps half an hour's sight left in them, were swollen up to the size of fists: Teddy's small white face was distorted by great purple oozing protuberances. Gideon said: 'Wait a minute, missus, I'll get some medicine.' He ran off into the bush.

Mrs Farquar lifted the child into the house and bathed his eyes with permanganate. She had scarcely heard Gideon's words; but when she saw that her remedies had no effect at all, and remembered how she had seen natives with no sight in their eyes, because of the spitting of a snake, she began to look for the return of her cook, remembering what she had heard of the efficacy of native herbs. She stood by the window, holding the terrified, sobbing little boy in her arms, and peered helplessly into the bush. It was not more than a few minutes before she saw Gideon come bounding back, and in his hand he held a plant.

'Do not be afraid, missus,' said Gideon, 'this will cure Little Yellow Head's eyes.' He stripped the leaves from the plant, leaving a small white fleshy root. Without even washing it, he put the root in his mouth, chewed it vigorously, and then held the spittle there while he took the child forcibly from Mrs Farquar. He gripped Teddy down between his knees, and pressed the balls of his thumbs into the swollen eyes, so that the child screamed and Mrs Farquar cried out in protest: 'Gideon, Gideon!' But Gideon took no notice. He knelt over the writhing child, pushing back the puffy lids till chinks of eye-ball showed, and then he spat hard, again and again, into first one eye and then the other. He finally lifted Teddy gently into his mother's arms, and said: 'His eyes will get better.' But Mrs Farquar was weeping with terror, and she could hardly thank him: it was impossible to believe that Teddy could keep his sight. In a couple of hours the swellings were gone; the eyes were inflamed and tender but Teddy could see. Mr and Mrs Farquar went to Gideon in the kitchen and thanked him over and over again. They felt help-less because of their gratitude: it seemed they could do nothing to express it. They gave Gideon presents for his wife and children, and a big increase in wages, but these things could not pay for Teddy's now completely cured eyes. Mrs Farquar said: 'Gideon, God chose you as an instrument for His goodness,' and Gideon said: 'Yes, missus, God is very good.'

Now, when such a thing happens on a farm, it cannot be long before everyone hears of it. Mr and Mrs Farquar told their neighbours and the story was discussed from one end of the district to the other. The bush is full of secrets. No one can live in Africa, or at least on the veld, without learning very soon that there is an ancient wisdom of leaf and soil and season – and, too, perhaps most important of all, of the darker tracts of the human mind – which is the black man's heritage. Up and down the district people were telling anecdotes, reminding each other of things that had happened to them.

'But I saw it myself, I tell you. It was a puff-adder bite. The kaffir's arm was swollen to the elbow, like a great shiny black bladder. He was groggy after half a minute. He was dying. Then suddenly a kaffir walked out of the bush with his hands full of green stuff. He smeared something on the place, and next day my boy was back at work, and all you could see was two small punctures in the skin.'

This was the kind of tale they told. And, as always, with a certain amount of exasperation, because while all of them knew that in the bush of Africa are waiting valuable drugs locked in bark, in simple-looking leaves, in roots, it was impossible to ever get the truth about them from the natives themselves.

The story eventually reached town; and perhaps it was at a sundowner party, or some such function, that a doctor, who happened to be there, challenged it. 'Nonsense,' he said. 'These things get exaggerated in the telling. We are always checking up on this kind of story, and we draw a blank every time.'

Anyway, one morning there arrived a strange car at the homestead, and out stepped one of the workers from the laboratory in town, with cases full of test-tubes and chemicals.

Mr and Mrs Farquar were flustered and pleased and flattered. They asked the scientist to lunch, and they told the story all over again, for the hundredth time. Little Teddy was there too, his blue eyes sparkling with health, to prove the truth of it. The scientist explained how humanity might benefit if this new drug could be offered for sale; and the Farquars were even more pleased: they were kind, simple people, who liked to think of something good coming about because of them. But when the scientist began talking of the money that might result, their manner showed discomfort. Their feelings over the miracle (that was how they thought of it) were so strong and deep and religious, that it was distasteful to them to think of money. The scientist, seeing their faces, went back to his first point which was the advancement of humanity. He was perhaps a trifle perfunctory: it was not the first time he had come salting the tail of a fabulous bush-secret.

Eventually, when the meal was over, the Farquars called Gideon into their living-room and explained to him that this baas, here, was a Big Doctor from the Big City, and he had come all that way to see Gideon. At this Gideon seemed afraid; he did not understand; and Mrs Farquar explained quickly that it was because of the wonderful thing he had done with Teddy's eyes that the Big Baas had come.

Gideon looked from Mrs Farquar to Mr Farquar, and then at the little boy, who was showing great importance because of the occasion. At last he said grudgingly: 'The Big Baas wants to know what medicine I used?' He spoke incredulously, as if he could not believe his old friends could so betray him. Mr Farquar began explaining how a useful medicine could be made out of the root, and how it could be put on sale, and how thousands of people, black and white, up and down the continent of Africa, could be saved by the medicine when that spitting snake filled their eyes with poison. Gideon listened, his eyes bent on the ground, the skin of his forehead puckering in discomfort. When Mr Farquar had finished he did not reply. The scientist, who all this time had been leaning back in a big chair, sipping his coffee and smiling with sceptical good-humour, chipped in and explained all over again, in different words, about the making of drugs and the progress of science. Also, he offered Gideon a present.

There was silence after this further explanation, and then Gideon remarked indifferently that he could not remember the root. His face was sullen and hostile, even when he looked at the Farquars, whom he usually treated like old friends. They were beginning to feel annoyed; and this feeling annulled the guilt that had been sprung into life by Gideon's accusing manner. They were beginning to feel that he was unreasonable. But it was at that moment that they all realized he would never give in. The magical drug would remain where it was, unknown and useless except for the tiny scattering of Africans who had the knowledge, natives who might be digging a ditch for the municipality in a ragged shirt and a pair of patched shorts, but who were still born to healing, hereditary healers, being the nephews or sons of the old witchdoctors whose ugly masks and bits of bone and all the uncouth properties of magic were the outward signs of real power and wisdom.

The Farquars might tread on that plant fifty times a day as they passed from house to garden, from cow kraal to mealie field, but they would never know it.

But they went on persuading and arguing, with all the force of their exasperation; and Gideon continued to say that he could not remember, or that there was no such root, or that it was the wrong season of the year, or that it wasn't the root itself, but the spit from his mouth that had cured Teddy's eyes. He said all these things one after another, and seemed not to care they were contradictory. He was rude and stubborn. The Farquars could hardly recognize their gentle, loveable old servant in this ignorant, perversely obstinate African, standing there in front of them with lowered eyes, his hands twitching his cook's apron, repeating over and over whichever one of the stupid refusals that first entered his head.

And suddenly he appeared to give in. He lifted his head, gave a long, blank angry look at the circle of whites, who seemed to him like a circle of yelping dogs pressing around him, and said: 'I will show you the root.'

They walked single file away from the homestead down a kaffir path. It was a blazing December afternoon, with the sky full of hot rain-clouds. Everything was hot: the sun was like a bronze tray whirling overhead, there was a heat shimmer over the fields, the soil was scorching underfoot, the dusty wind blew gritty and thick and warm in their faces. It was a terrible day, fit only for reclining on a verandah with iced drinks, which is where they would normally have been at that hour.

From time to time, remembering that on the day of the snake it had taken ten minutes to find the root, someone asked: 'Is it much further, Gideon?' And Gideon would answer over his shoulder, with angry politeness: 'I'm looking for the root, baas.' And indeed, he would frequently bend sideways and trail his hand among the grasses with a gesture that was insulting in its perfunctoriness. He walked them through the bush along unknown paths for two hours, in that melting destroying heat, so that the sweat trickled coldly down them and their heads ached. They were all quite silent: the Farquars because they were angry, the scientist because he was being proved right again; there was no such plant. His was a tactful silence.

At last, six miles from the house, Gideon suddenly decided they had had enough; or perhaps his anger evaporated at that moment. He picked up, without an attempt at looking anything but casual, a handful of blue flowers from the grass, flowers that had been growing plentifully all down the paths they had come.

He handed them to the scientist without looking at him, and marched off by himself on the way home, leaving them to follow him if they chose.

When they got back to the house, the scientist went to the kitchen to thank Gideon: he was being very polite, even though there was an amused look in his eyes. Gideon was not there. Throwing the flowers casually into the back of his car, the eminent visitor departed on his way back to his laboratory.

Gideon was back in his kitchen in time to prepare dinner, but he was sulking. He spoke to Mrs Farquar like an unwilling servant. It was days before they liked each other again.

The Farquars made enquiries about the root from their labourers. Sometimes they were answered with distrustful stares. Sometimes the natives said: 'We do not know. We have never heard of the root.' One, the cattle boy, who had been with them a long time, and had grown to trust them a little said: 'Ask your boy in the kitchen. Now, there's a doctor for you. He's the son of a famous medicine man who used to be in these parts, and there's nothing he cannot cure.' Then he added politely: 'Of course, he's not as good as the whiteman's doctor, we know that, but he's good for us.'

After some time, when the soreness had gone from between the Farquars and Gideon, they began to joke: 'When are you going to show us the snake-root, Gideon?' And he would laugh and shake his head, saying, a little uncomfortably: 'But I did show you, missus, have you forgotten?'

Much later, Teddy, as a schoolboy, would come into the kitchen and say: 'You old rascal, Gideon! Do you remember that time you tricked us all by making us walk miles all over the veld for nothing? It was so far my father had to carry me!'

And Gideon would double up with polite laughter. After much laughing, he would suddenly straighten himself up, wipe his old eyes, and look sadly at Teddy, who was grinning mischievously at him across the kitchen: 'Ah, Little Yellow Head, how you have grown! Soon you will be grown up with a farm of your own . . . '

Nadine Gordimer
SIX FEET OF THE COUNTRY

My wife and I are not real farmers – not even Lerice, really. We bought our place, ten miles out of Johannesburg on one of the main roads, to change something in ourselves, I suppose; you seem to rattle about so much within a marriage like ours. You long to hear nothing but a deep satisfying silence when you sound a marriage. The farm hasn't managed that for us, of course, but it has done other things, unexpected, illogical. Lerice, who I thought would retire there in Chekhovian sadness for a month or two, and then leave the place to the servants while she tried yet again to get a part she wanted and become the actress she would like to be, has sunk into the business of running the farm with all the serious intensity with which she once imbued the shadows in a playwright's mind. I should have given it up long ago if it had not been for her. Her hands, once small and plain and well kept – she was not the sort of actress who wears red paint and diamond rings – are hard as a dog's pads.

I, of course, am there only in the evenings and at weekends. I am a partner in a luxury-travel agency, which is flourishing – needs to be, as I tell Lerice, in order to carry the farm. Still, though I know we can't afford it, and though the sweetish smell of the fowls Lerice breeds sickens me, so that I avoid going past their runs, the farm is beautiful in a way I had almost forgotten – especially on a Sunday morning when I get up and go out into the paddock and see not the palm trees and fishpond and imitation-stone bird bath of the suburbs but white ducks on the dam, the lucerne field brilliant as window dresser's grass, and the little stocky, mean-eyed bull, lustful but bored, having his face tenderly licked by one of his ladies. Lerice comes out with her hair uncombed, in her hand a stick dripping with cattle dip. She will stand and look dreamily for a moment, the way she would pretend to look sometimes in those plays. 'They'll mate tomorrow,' she will say. 'This is their second day. Look how she loves him, my little Napoleon.' So that when people come out to see us on Sunday afternoon, I am likely to hear myself saying as I pour out the drinks, 'When I drive back home from the city every day, past those rows of suburban houses, I wonder how the devil we ever did stand it . . . Would you care to look around?' And there I am, taking some pretty girl and her young husband stumbling down to our riverbank, the girl catching her stockings on the mealie-stooks and stepping over cow turds humming with jewelgreen flies while she says, '. . . the tensions of the damned city. And you're near enough to get into town to a show, too! I think it's wonderful. Why, you've got it both ways!'

And for a moment I accept the triumph as if I *had* managed it – the impossibility that I've been trying for all my life – just as if the truth was that you could get it 'both ways', instead of finding yourself with not even one way or the other but a third, one you had not provided for at all.

But even in our saner moments, when I find Lerice's earthy enthusiasms just as irritating as I once found her histrionical ones, and she finds what she calls my 'jealousy' of her capacity for enthusiasms as big a proof of my inadequacy for her as a mate as ever it was, we do believe that we have at least honestly escaped those tensions peculiar to the city about which our visitors speak. When Johannesburg people speak of 'tension', they don't mean hurrying people in crowded streets, the struggle for money, or the general competitive character of city life. They mean the guns under the white men's pillows and the burglar bars on the white men's windows. They mean those strange moments on city pavements when a black man won't stand aside for a white man.

Out in the country, even ten miles out, life is better than that. In the country, there is a lingering remnant of the pretransitional stage; our relationship with the blacks is almost feudal. Wrong, I suppose, obsolete, but more comfortable all around. We have no burglar bars, no gun. Lerice's farm boys have their wives and their piccanins living with them on the land. They brew their sour beer without the fear of police raids. In fact, we've always rather prided ourselves that the poor devils have nothing much to fear, being with us; Lerice even keeps an eye on their children, with all the competence of a woman who has never had a child of her own, and she certainly doctors them all – children and adults – like babies whenever they happen to be sick.

It was because of this that we were not particularly startled one night last winter when the boy Albert came knocking at our window long after we had gone to bed. I wasn't in our bed but sleeping in the little dressing-room-*cum*-linen-room next door, because Lerice had annoyed me and I didn't want to find myself softening towards her simply because of the sweet smell of the talcum powder on her flesh after her bath. She came and woke me up. 'Albert says one of the boys is very sick,' she said. 'I think you'd better go down and see. He wouldn't get us up at this hour for nothing.'

'What time is it?'

'What does it matter?' Lerice is maddeningly logical.

I got up awkwardly as she watched me – how is it I always feel a fool when I have deserted her bed? After all, I know from the way she never looks at me when she talks to me at breakfast the next day that she is hurt and humiliated at my not wanting her – and I went out, clumsy with sleep.

'Which of the boys is it?' I asked Albert as we followed the dance of my torch.

'He's too sick. Very sick, *Baas,*' he said.

'But who? Franz?' I remembered Franz had had a bad cough for the past week.

Albert did not answer; he had given me the path, and was walking along beside me in the tall dead grass. When the light of the torch caught his face, I saw that he looked acutely embarrassed. 'What's this all about?' I said.

He lowered his head under the glance of the light. 'It's not me, *Baas.* I don't know. Petrus he send me.'

Irritated, I hurried him along to the huts. And there, on Petrus's iron bedstead, with its brick stilts, was a young man, dead. On his forehead there was still a light, cold sweat; his body was warm. The boys stood around as they do in the kitchen when it is discovered that someone has broken a dish – unco-operative, silent. Somebody's wife hung about in the shadows, her hands wrung together under her apron.

I had not seen a dead man since the war. This was very different. I felt like the others – extraneous, useless. 'What was the matter?' I asked.

The woman patted at her chest and shook her head to indicate the painful impossibility of breathing.

He must have died of pneumonia.

I turned to Petrus. 'Who was this boy? What was he doing here?' The light of a candle on the floor showed that Petrus was weeping. He followed me out the door.

When we were outside, in the dark, I waited for him to speak. But he didn't. 'Now, come on, Petrus, you must tell me who this boy was. Was he a friend of yours?'

'He's my brother, *Baas*. He came from Rhodesia to look for work.'

The story startled Lerice and me a little. The young boy had walked down from Rhodesia to look for work in Johannesburg, had caught a chill from sleeping out along the way, and had lain ill in his brother Petrus's hut since his arrival three days before. Our boys had been frightened to ask us for help for him because we had never been intended ever to know of his presence. Rhodesian natives are barred from entering the Union unless they have a permit; the young man was an illegal immigrant. No doubt our boys had managed the whole thing successfully several times before; a number of relatives must have walked the seven or eight hundred miles from poverty to the paradise of zoot suits, police raids, and black slum townships that is their *Egoli,* City of Gold – the Bantu name for Johannesburg. It was merely a matter of getting such a man to lie low on our farm until a job could be found with someone who would be glad to take the risk of prosecution for employing an illegal immigrant in exchange for the services of someone as yet untainted by the city.

Well, this was one who would never get up again.

'You would think they would have felt they could tell *us,*' said Lerice next morning. 'Once the man was ill. You would have thought at least –' When she is getting intense over something, she has a way of standing in the middle of a room as people do when they are shortly to leave on a journey, looking searchingly about her at the most familiar objects as if she had never seen them before. I had noticed that in Petrus's presence in the kitchen, earlier, she had had the air of being almost offended with him, almost hurt.

In any case, I really haven't the time or inclination any more to go into everything in our life that I know Lerice, from those alarmed and pressing eyes of hers, would like us to go into. She is the kind of woman who doesn't mind if she looks plain, or odd; I don't suppose she would even care if she knew how strange she looks when her whole face is out of proportion with urgent uncertainty. I said, 'Now I'm the one who'll have to do all the dirty work, I suppose.'

She was still staring at me, trying me out with those eyes – wasting her time, if she only knew.

'I'll have to notify the health authorities,' I said calmly. 'They can't just cart him off and bury him. After all, we don't really know what he died of.'

She simply stood there, as if she had given up – simply ceased to see me at all.

I don't know when I've been so irritated. 'It might have been something contagious,' I said. 'God knows.' There was no answer.

I am not enamoured of holding conversations with myself. I went out to shout to one of the boys to open the garage and get the car ready for my morning drive to town.

As I had expected, it turned out to be quite a business. I had to notify the police as well as the health authorities, and answer a lot of tedious questions: How was it I was ignorant of the boy's presence? If I did not supervise my native quarters, how did I know that that sort of thing didn't go on all the time? Et cetera, et cetera. And when I flared up and told them that so long as my natives did their work, I didn't think it my right or concern to poke my nose into their private lives, I got from the coarse, dull-witted police sergeant one of those looks that come not from any thinking process going on in the brain but from that faculty common to all who are possessed by the master-race theory – a look of insanely inane certainty. He grinned at me with a mixture of scorn and delight at my stupidity.

Then I had to explain to Petrus why the health authorities had to take away the body for a post-mortem – and, in fact, what a post-mortem was. When I telephoned the health department some days later to find out the result, I was told that the cause of death was, as we had thought, pneumonia, and that the body had been suitably disposed of. I went out to where Petrus was mixing a mash for the fowls and told him that it was all right, there would be no trouble; his brother had died from that pain in his chest. Petrus put down the paraffin tin and said, 'When can we go to fetch him, *Baas?*'

'To fetch him?'

'Will the *Baas* please ask them when we must come?'

I went back inside and called Lerice, all over the house. She came down the stairs from the spare bedrooms, and I said, '*Now* what am I going to do? When I told Petrus, he just asked calmly when they could go and fetch the body. They think they're going to bury him themselves.'

'Well, go back and tell him,' said Lerice. 'You must tell him. Why didn't you tell him then?'

When I found Petrus again, he looked up politely. 'Look, Petrus,' I said. 'You can't go to fetch your brother. They've done it already – they've *buried* him, you understand?'

'Where?' he said slowly, dully, as if he thought that perhaps he was getting this wrong.

'You see, he was a stranger. They knew he wasn't from here, and they didn't know he had some of his people here so they thought they must bury him.' It was difficult to make a pauper's grave sound like a privilege.

'Please, *Baas,* the *Baas* must ask them.' But he did not mean that he wanted to know the burial place. He simply ignored the incomprehensible machinery I told him had set to work on his dead brother; he wanted the brother back.

'But, Petrus,' I said, 'how can I? Your brother is buried already. I can't ask them now.'

'Oh, *Baas!*' he said. He stood with his bran-smeared hands uncurled at his sides, one corner of his mouth twitching.

'Good God, Petrus, they won't listen to me! They can't, anyway. I'm sorry, but I can't do it. You understand?'

He just kept on looking at me, out of his knowledge that white men have everything, can do anything; if they don't, it is because they won't.

And then, at dinner, Lerice started. 'You could at least phone,' she said.

'Christ, what d'you think I am? Am I supposed to bring the dead back to life?'

But I could not exaggerate my way out of this ridiculous responsibility that had been thrust on me. 'Phone them up,' she went on. 'And at least you'll be able to tell him you've done it and they've explained that it's impossible.'

She disappeared somewhere into the kitchen quarters after coffee. A little later she came back to tell me, 'The old father's coming down from Rhodesia to be at the funeral. He's got a permit and he's already on his way.'

Unfortunately, it was not impossible to get the body back. The authorities said that it was somewhat irregular, but that since the hygiene conditions had been fulfilled, they could not refuse permission for exhumation. I found out that, with the undertaker's charges, it would cost twenty pounds. Ah, I thought, that settles it. On five pounds a month, Petrus won't have twenty pounds – and just as well, since it couldn't do the dead any good. Certainly I should not offer it to him myself. Twenty pounds – or anything else within reason, for that matter – I would have spent without grudging it on doctors or medicines that might have helped the boy when he was alive. Once he was dead, I had no intention of encouraging Petrus to throw away, on a gesture, more than he spent to clothe his whole family in a year.

When I told him, in the kitchen that night, he said,

'Twenty pounds?'

I said, 'Yes, that's right, twenty pounds.'

For a moment, I had the feeling, from the look on his face, that he was calculating. But when he spoke again I thought I must have imagined it. 'We must pay twenty pounds!' he said in the faraway voice in which a person speaks of something so unattainable that it does not bear thinking about.

'All right, Petrus,' I said, and went back to the living-room.

The next morning before I went to town, Petrus asked to see me. 'Please, *Baas,*' he said, awkwardly handing me a bundle of notes. They're so seldom on the giving rather than the receiving side, poor devils, that they don't really know how to hand money to a white man. There it was, the twenty pounds, in ones and halves, some creased and folded until they were soft as dirty rags, others smooth and fairly new – Franz's money, I suppose, and Albert's, and Dora the cook's, and Jacob the gardener's, and God knows who else's besides, from all the farms and small-holdings round about. I took it in irritation more than in astonishment, really – irritation at the waste, the uselessness of this sacrifice by people so poor. Just like the poor everywhere, I thought, who stint themselves the decencies of life in order to insure themselves the decencies of death. So incomprehensible to people like Lerice and me, who regard life as something to be spent extravagantly and, if we think about death at all, regard it as the final bankruptcy.

The servants don't work on Saturday afternoon anyway, so it was a good day for the funeral. Petrus and his father had borrowed our donkey cart to fetch the coffin from the city, where, Petrus told Lerice on their return, everything was 'nice' – the coffin waiting for them, already sealed up to save them from what must have been a rather unpleasant sight after two weeks' interment. (It had taken all that time for the authorities and the undertaker to make the final arrangements for moving the body.) All morning, the coffin lay in Petrus's hut, awaiting the trip to the little old burial ground, just outside the eastern boundary of our farm, that was a relic of the days when this was a real farming district rather than a fashionable rural estate. It was pure chance that I happened to be down there near the fence when the procession came past; once again Lerice had forgotten her promise to me and had made the house uninhabitable on a Saturday afternoon. I had come home and been infuriated to find her in a pair of filthy old slacks and with her hair uncombed since the night before, having all the varnish scraped off the living-room floor, if you please. So I had taken my No. 8 iron and gone off to practise my approach shots. In my annoyance, I had forgotten about the funeral, and was reminded only when I saw the procession coming up the path along the outside of the fence towards me; from where I was standing, you can see the graves quite clearly, and that day the sun glinted on bits of broken pottery, a lopsided homemade cross, and jam jars brown with rain water and dead flowers.

I felt a little awkward, and did not know whether to go on hitting my golf ball or stop at least until the whole gathering was decently past. The donkey cart creaks and screeches with every revolution of the wheels, and it came along in a slow, halting fashion somehow peculiarly suited to the two donkeys who drew it, their little potbellies rubbed and rough, their heads sunk between the shafts, and their ears flattened back with an air submissive and downcast; peculiarly suited, too, to the group of men and women who came along slowly behind. The patient ass. Watching, I thought, you can see now why the creature became a Biblical symbol. Then the procession drew level with me and stopped, so I had to put down my club. The coffin was taken down off the cart – it was a shiny, yellow-varnished wood, like cheap furniture – and the donkeys twitched their ears against the flies. Petrus, Franz, Albert, and the old father from Rhodesia hoisted it on their shoulders and the procession moved on, on foot. It was really a very awkward moment. I stood there rather foolishly at the fence, quite still, and slowly they filed past, not looking up, the four men bent beneath the shiny wooden box, and the straggling troop of mourners. All of them were servants or neighbours' servants whom I knew as casual, easygoing gossipers about our lands or kitchen. I heard the old man's breathing.

I had just bent to pick up my club again when there was a sort of jar in the flowing solemnity of their processional mood; I felt it at once, like a wave of heat along the air, or one of those sudden currents of cold catching at your legs in a placid stream. The old man's voice was muttering something; the people had stopped, confused, and they bumped into one another, some pressing to go on, others hissing them to be still. I could see that they were embarrassed, but they could not ignore the voice; it was much the way that the mumblings of a prophet, though not clear at first, arrest the mind. The corner of the coffin the old man carried was sagging at an angle; he seemed to be trying to get out from under the weight of it. Now Petrus expostulated with him.

The little boy who had been left to watch the donkeys dropped the reins and ran to see. I don't know why – unless it was for the same reason people crowd around someone who has fainted in a cinema – but I parted the wires of the fence and went through, after him.

Petrus lifted his eyes to me – to anybody – with distress and horror. The old man from Rhodesia had let go of the coffin entirely, and the three others, unable to support it on their own, had laid it on the ground, in the pathway. Already there was a film of dust lightly wavering up its shiny sides. I did not understand what the old man was saying; I hesitated to interfere. But now the whole seething group turned on my silence. The old man himself came over to me, with his hands outspread and shaking, and spoke directly to me, saying something that I could tell from the tone, without understanding the words, was shocking and extraordinary.

'What is it, Petrus? What's wrong?' I appealed.

Petrus threw up his hands, bowed his head in a series of hysterical shakes, then thrust his face up at me suddenly. 'He says, "My son was not so heavy". '

Silence. I could hear the old man breathing; he kept his mouth a little open, as old people do.

'My son was young and thin,' he said at last, in English.

Again silence. Then babble broke out. The old man thundered against everybody; his teeth were yellowed and few, and he had one of those fine, grizzled, sweeping moustaches that one doesn't often see nowadays, which must have been grown in emulation of early Empire builders. It seemed to frame all his utterances with a special validity, perhaps merely because it was the symbol of the traditional wisdom of age – an idea so fearfully rooted that it carries still something awesome beyond reason. He shocked them; they thought he was mad, but they had to listen to him. With his own hands he began to prise the lid off the coffin and three of the men came forward to help him. Then he sat down on the ground; very old, very weak, and unable to speak, he merely lifted a trembling hand towards what was there. He abdicated, he handed it over to them, he was no good any more.

They crowded round to look (and so did I), and now they forgot the nature of this surprise and the occasion of grief to which it belonged, and for a few minutes were carried up in the astonishment of the surprise itself. They gasped and flared noisily with excitement. I even noticed the little boy who had held the donkeys jumping up and down, almost weeping with rage because the backs of the grown-ups crowded him out of his view.

In the coffin was someone no one had ever seen before: a heavily built, rather light-skinned native with a neatly stitched scar on his forehead – perhaps from a blow in a brawl that had also dealt him some other, slower-working injury which had killed him.

I wrangled with the authorities for a week over the body. I had the feeling that they were shocked, in a laconic fashion, by their own mistake, but that in the confusion of their anonymous dead they were helpless to put it right. They said to me, 'We are trying to find out,' and 'We are still making inquiries.' It was as if at any moment they might conduct me into their mortuary and say, 'There! Lift up the sheets; look for him – your poultry boy's brother. There are so many black faces – surely one will do?'

And every evening when I got home, Petrus was waiting in the kitchen. 'Well, they're trying. They're still looking. The *Baas* is seeing to it for you, Petrus,' I would tell him. 'God, half the time I should be in the office I'm driving around the back end of the town chasing after this affair,' I added aside, to Lerice, one night.

She and Petrus both kept their eyes turned on me as I spoke, and, oddly, for those moments they looked exactly alike, though it sounds impossible: my wife, with her high, white forehead and her attenuated Englishwoman's body, and the poultry boy, with his horny bare feet below khaki trousers tied at the knee with string and the peculiar rankness of his nervous sweat coming from his skin.

'What makes you so indignant, so determined about this now?' said Lerice suddenly.

I stared at her. 'It's a matter of principle. Why should they get away with a swindle? It's time these officials had a jolt from someone who'll bother to take the trouble.'

She said, 'Oh.' And as Petrus slowly opened the kitchen door to leave, sensing that the talk had gone beyond him, she turned away, too.

I continued to pass on assurances to Petrus every evening, but although what I said was the same and the voice in which I said it was the same, every evening it sounded weaker. At last, it became clear that we would never get Petrus's brother back, because nobody really knew where he was. Somewhere in a graveyard as uniform as a housing scheme, somewhere under a number that didn't belong to him, or in the medical school, perhaps, laboriously reduced to layers of muscle and strings of nerve?

Goodness knows. He had no identity in this world anyway.

It was only then, and in a voice of shame, that Petrus asked me to try and get the money back.

'From the way he asks, you'd think he was robbing his dead brother,' I said to Lerice later. But as I've said, Lerice had got so intense about this business that she couldn't even appreciate a little ironic smile.

I tried to get the money; Lerice tried. We both telephoned and wrote and argued, but nothing came of it. It appeared that the main expense had been the undertaker, and after all he had done his job. So the whole thing was a complete waste, even more of a waste for the poor devils than I had thought it would be.

The old man from Rhodesia was about Lerice's father's size, so she gave him one of her father's old suits, and he went back home rather better off, for the winter, than he had come.

Ahmed Essop

THE HAJJI

When the telephone rang several times one evening and his wife did not attend to it as she usually did, Hajji Hassen, seated on a settee in the lounge, cross-legged and sipping tea, shouted: 'Salima, are you deaf?' And when he received no response from his wife and the jarring bell went on ringing, he shouted again: 'Salima, what's happened to you?'

The telephone stopped ringing. Hajji Hassen frowned in a contemplative manner, wondering where his wife was now. Since his return from Mecca after the pilgrimage, he had discovered novel inadequacies in her, or perhaps saw the old ones in a more revealing light. One of her salient inadequacies was never to be around when he wanted her. She was either across the road confabulating with her sister, or gossiping with the neighbours, or away on a shopping spree. And now, when the telephone had gone on assaulting his ears, she was not in the house. He took another sip of the strongly spiced tea to stifle the irritation within him.

When he heard the kitchen door open he knew that Salima had entered. The telephone burst out again in a metallic shrill and the Hajji shouted for his wife. She hurried to the phone.

'Hullo . . . Yes . . . Hassen . . . Speak to him? . . . Who speaking? . . . Caterine? . . . Who Caterine? . . . Au-right . . . I call him.'

She put the receiver down gingerly and informed her husband in Gujarati that a woman named 'Caterine' wanted to speak to him. The name evoked no immediate association in his memory. He descended from the settee and, squeezing his feet into a pair of crimson sandals, went to the telephone.

'Hullo . . . Who? . . . Catherine? . . . No, I don't know you . . . Yes . . . Yes . . . Oh . . . now I remember . . . Yes . . . '

He listened intently to the voice, urgent, supplicating. Then he gave his answer: 'I am afraid I can't help him. Let the Christians bury him. His last wish means nothing to me . . . Madam, it's impossible . . . No . . . Let him die . . . Brother? Pig! Pig! Bastard!' He banged the receiver onto the telephone in explosive annoyance.

'O Allah!' Salima exclaimed. 'What words! What is this all about?'

He did not answer but returned to the settee, and she quietly went to the bedroom.

Salima went to bed and it was almost midnight when her husband came into the room. His earlier vexation had now given place to gloom. He told her of his brother Karim who lay dying in Hillbrow. Karim had cut himself off from his family and friends ten years ago; he had crossed the colour line (his fair complexion and grey eyes serving as passports) and gone to cohabit with a white woman. And now that he was on the verge of death he wished to return to the world he had forsaken and to be buried under

Muslim funeral rites and in a Muslim cemetery.

Hajji Hassen had, of course, rejected the plea, and for good reason. When his brother had crossed the colour line, he had severed his family ties. The Hajji at that time had felt excoriating humiliation. By going over to the white Herrenvolk, his brother had trampled on something that was vitally part of him, his dignity and self-respect. But the rejection of his brother's plea involved a straining of the heartstrings and the Hajji did not feel happy. He had recently sought God's pardon for his sins in Mecca, and now this business of his brother's final earthly wish and his own intransigence was in some way staining his spirit.

The next day Hassen rose at five to go to the mosque. When he stepped out of his house in Newtown the street lights were beginning to pale and clusters of houses to assume definition. The atmosphere was fresh and heavy, and he took a few deep breaths. The first trams were beginning to pass through Bree Street and were clanging along like decrepit yet burning spectres towards the Johannesburg City Hall. Here and there a figure moved along hurriedly. The Hindu fruit and vegetable hawkers were starting up their old trucks in the yards, preparing to go out for the day to sell to suburban housewives.

When he reached the mosque the Somali muezzin in the ivory-domed minaret began to intone the call for prayers. After prayers, he remained behind to read the Koran in the company of two other men. When he had done the sun was shining brilliantly in the courtyard onto the flowers and the fountain with its goldfish.

Outside the house he saw a car. Salima opened the

door and whispered, 'Caterine'. For a moment he felt irritated, but realising that he might as well face her he stepped boldly into the lounge.

Catherine was a small woman with firm fleshy legs. She was seated cross-legged on the settee, smoking a cigarette. Her face was almost boyish, a look that partly originated in her auburn hair which was cut very short, and partly in the smallness of her head. Her eye-brows, firmly pencilled, accentuated the grey-green glitter of her eyes. She was dressed in a dark grey costume.

He nodded his head at her to signify that he knew who she was. Over the telephone he had spoken with aggressive authority. Now, in the presence of the woman herself, he felt a weakening of his masculine fibre.

'You must, Mr Hassen, come to see your brother.'

'I am afraid I am unable to help,' he said in a tentative tone. He felt uncomfortable; there was something so positive and intrepid about her appearance.

'He wants to see you. It's his final wish.'

'I have not seen him for ten years.'

'Time can't wipe out the fact that he's your brother.'

'He is a white. We live in different worlds.'

'But you must see him.'

There was a moment of strained silence.

'Please understand that he's not to blame for having broken with you. I am to blame. I got him to break with you. Really you must blame me, not Karim.'

Hassen found himself unable to say anything. The thought that she could in some way have been responsible for his brother's rejection of him had never occurred to him. He looked at his feet in awkward silence. He could only state in a lazily recalcitrant tone: 'It is not easy for me to see him.'

'Please come Mr Hassen, for my sake, please. I'll never be able to bear it if Karim dies unhappily. Can't you find it in your heart to forgive him, and to forgive me?'

He could not look at her. A sob escaped from her, and he heard her opening her handbag for a handkerchief.

'He's dying. He wants to see you for the last time.'

Hassen softened. He was overcome by the argument that she had been responsible for taking Karim away. He could hardly look on her responsibility as being in any way culpable. She was a woman.

'If you remember the days of your youth, the time you spent together with Karim before I came to separate him from you, it will be easier for you to pardon him.'

Hassen was silent.

'Please understand that I am not a racialist. You know the conditions in this country.'

He thought for a moment and then said: 'I will go with you.'

He excused himself and went to his room to change. After a while they set off for Hillbrow in her car.

He sat beside her. The closeness of her presence, the perfume she exuded stirred currents of feeling within him. He glanced at her several times, watched the deft movements of her hands and legs as she controlled the car. Her powdered profile, the outline taut with a resolute quality, aroused his imagination. There was something so businesslike in her attitude and bearing, so involved in reality (at the back of his mind there was Salima, flaccid, cowlike and inadequate) that he could hardly refrain from expressing his admiration.

'You must understand that I'm only going to see my brother because you have come to me. For no one else would I have changed my mind.'

'Yes, I understand. I'm very grateful.'

'My friends and relatives are going to accuse me of softness, of weakness.'

'Don't think of them now. You have decided to be kind to me.'

The realism and the commonsense of the woman's words! He was overwhelmed by her.

The car stopped at the entrance of a building in Hillbrow. They took the lift. On the second floor three white youths entered and were surprised at seeing Hassen. There was a separate lift for non-whites. They squeezed themselves into a corner, one actually turning his head away with a grunt of disgust. The lift reached the fifth floor too soon for Hassen to give a thought to the attitude of the three white boys. Catherine led him to apartment 65.

He stepped into the lounge. Everything seemed to be carefully arranged. There was her personal touch about the furniture, the ornaments, the paintings. She went to the bedroom, then returned and asked him in.

Karim lay in bed, pale, emaciated, his eyes closed. For a moment Hassen failed to recognize him: ten years divided them. Catherine placed a chair next to the bed for him. He looked at his brother and again saw, through ravages of illness, the familiar features. She sat on the bed and rubbed Karim's hands to wake him. After a while he began to show signs of consciousness. She called him tenderly by his name.

When he opened his eyes he did not recognize the man beside him, but by degrees, after she had repeated Hassen's name several times, he seemed to understand. He stretched out a hand and Hassen took it, moist and repellent. Nausea swept over him, but he could not withdraw his hand as his brother clutched it firmly.

'Brother Hassen, please take me away from here.'

Hassen's agreement brought a smile to his lips.

Catherine suggested that she drive Hassen back to Newtown where he could make preparations to transfer Karim to his home.

'No, you stay here. I will take a taxi.' And he left the apartment.

In the corridor he pressed the button for the lift. He watched the indicator numbers succeeding each other rapidly, then stop at five. The doors opened – and there they were again, the three white youths. He hesitated. The boys looked at him tauntingly. Then suddenly they burst into deliberately brutish laughter.

'Come into the parlour,' one of them said.

'Come into the Indian parlour,' another said in a cloyingly mocking voice.

Hassen looked at them, annoyed, hurt. Then something snapped within him and he stood there, transfixed. They laughed at him in a raucous chorus as the lift doors shut.

He remained immobile, his dignity clawed. Was there anything so vile in him that the youths found it necessary to maul that recess of self-respect within him? 'They are whites,' he said to himself in bitter justification of their attitude.

He would take the stairs and walk down the five floors. As he descended he thought of Karim. Because of him he had come there and because of him he had been insulted. The enormity of the insult bridged the gap of ten years when Karim had spurned him, and diminished his being. Now he was diminished again.

He was hardly aware that he had gone down five floors when he reached ground level. He stood still, expecting to see the three youths again. But the foyer was empty and he could see the reassuring activity of street life through the glass panels. He quickly walked out as though he would regain in the hubbub of the street something of his assaulted dignity.

He walked on, structures of concrete and glass on either side of him, and it did not even occur to him to take a taxi. It was in Hillbrow that Karim had lived with the white woman and forgotten the existence of his brother; and now that he was dying he had sent for him. For ten years Karim had lived without him. O Karim! The thought of the youth he had loved so much during the days they had been together at the Islamic Institute, a religious seminary though it was governed like a penitentiary, brought the tears to his eyes and he stopped against a shop window and wept. A few pedestrians looked at him. When the shopkeeper came outside to see the weeping man, Hassen, ashamed of himself, wiped his eyes and walked on.

He regretted his pliability in the presence of the white woman. She had come unexpectedly and had disarmed him with her presence and subtle talk. A painful lump rose in his throat as he set his heart against forgiving Karim. If his brother had had no personal dignity in sheltering behind his white skin, trying to be what he was not, he was not going to allow his own moral worth to be depreciated in any way.

When he reached central Johannesburg he went to the station and took the train. In the coach with the blacks he felt at ease and regained his self-possession. He was among familiar faces, among people who respected him. He felt as though he had been spirited away by a perfumed, well-made, wax doll, but had managed with a prodigious effort to shake her off.

When he reached home Salima asked him what had been decided and he answered curtly, 'Nothing'. But feeling elated after his escape from Hillbrow he added condescendingly, 'Karim left of his own accord. We should have nothing to do with him.'

Salima was puzzled, but she went on preparing supper.

Catherine received no word from Hassen and she phoned him. She was stunned when he said: 'I'm sorry but I am unable to offer any help.'

'But . . . '

'I regret it. I made a mistake. Please make some other arrangements. Goodbye.'

With an effort of will he banished Karim from his mind. Finding his composure again he enjoyed his evening meal, read the paper and then retired to bed. Next morning he went to mosque as usual, but when he returned home he found Catherine there again. Angry that she should have come, he blurted out: 'Listen to me, Catherine. I can't forgive him. For ten years he didn't care about me, whether I was alive or dead. Karim means nothing to me now.'

'Why have you changed your mind? Do you find it so difficult to forgive him?'

'Don't talk to me of forgiveness. What forgiveness, when he threw me aside and chose to go with you? Let his white friends see to him, let Hillbrow see to him.'

'Please, please, Mr Hassen, I beg you . . . '

'No, don't come here with your begging. Please go

away.'

He opened the door and went out. Catherine burst into tears. Salima comforted her as best she could.

'Don't cry Caterine. All men hard. Dey don't understand.'

'What shall I do now?' Catherine said in a defeated tone. She was an alien in the world of the non-whites. 'Is there no one who can help me?'

'Yes, Mr Mia help you,' replied Salima.

In her eagerness to find some help, she hastily moved to the door. Salima followed her and from the porch of her home directed her to Mr Mia's. He lived in a flat on the first floor of an old building. She knocked and waited in trepidation.

Mr Mia opened the door, smiled affably and asked her in.

'Come inside, lady; sit down . . . Fatima,' he called to his daughter, 'bring some tea.'

Mr Mia was a man in his fifties, his bronze complexion partly covered by a neatly trimmed beard. He was a well-known figure in the Indian community. Catherine told him of Karim and her abortive appeal to his brother. Mr Mia asked one or two questions, pondered for a while and then said: 'Don't worry, my good woman. I'll speak to Hassen. I'll never allow a Muslim brother to be abandoned.'

Catherine began to weep.

'Here, drink some tea and you'll feel better.' He poured tea. Before Catherine left he promised that he would phone her that evening and told her to get in touch with him immediately should Karim's condition deteriorate.

Mr Mia, in the company of the priest of the Newtown mosque, went to Hassen's house that evening. They found several relatives of Hassen's seated in the lounge (Salima had spread the word of Karim's illness). But Hassen refused to listen to their pleas that Karim should be brought to Newtown.

'Listen to me Hajji,' Mr Mia said. 'Your brother can't be allowed to die among the Christians.'

'For ten years he has been among them.'

'That means nothing. He's still a Muslim.'

The priest now gave his opinion. Although Karim had left the community, he was still a Muslim. He had never rejected the religion and espoused Christianity, and in the absence of any evidence to the contrary it had to be accepted that he was a Muslim brother.

'But for ten years he has lived in sin in Hillbrow.'

'If he has lived in sin that is not for us to judge.'

'Hajji, what sort of a man are you? Have you no feeling for your brother?' Mr Mia asked.

'Don't talk to me about feeling. What feeling had he for me when he went to live among the whites, when he turned his back on me?'

'Hajji, can't you forgive him? You were recently in Mecca.'

This hurt Hassen and he winced. Salima came to his rescue with refreshments for the guests.

The ritual of tea-drinking established a mood of conviviality and Karim was forgotten for a while. After tea they again tried to press Hassen into forgiving his brother, but he remained adamant. He could not face Catherine without looking ridiculous. Besides he felt integrated now; he would resist anything that negated him.

Mr Mia and the priest departed. They decided to raise the matter with the congregation in the mosque. But they failed to move Hassen. Actually his resistance grew in inverse ratio as more people came to learn of the dying Karim and Hassen's refusal to forgive him. By giving in he would be displaying mental dithering of the worst kind, as though he were a man without an inner fibre, decision and firmness of will.

Mr Mia next summoned a meeting of various religious dignitaries and received their mandate to transfer Karim to Newtown without his brother's consent. Karim's relatives would be asked to care for him, but if they refused Mr Mia would take charge.

The relatives, not wanting to offend Hassen and also feeling that Karim was not their responsibility, refused.

Mr Mia phoned Catherine and informed her of what had been decided. She agreed that it was best for Karim to be amongst his people during his last days. So Karim was brought to Newtown in an ambulance hired from a private nursing home and housed in a little room in a quiet yard behind the mosque.

The arrival of Karim placed Hassen in a difficult situation and he bitterly regretted his decision not to accept him into his own home. He first heard of his brother's arrival during the morning prayers when the priest offered a special prayer for the recovery of the sick man. Hassen found himself in the curious position of being forced to pray for his brother. After prayers several people went to see the sick man, others went up to Mr Mia to offer help. Hassen felt out of place and as soon as the opportunity presented itself he slipped out of the mosque.

In a mood of intense bitterness, scorn for himself, hatred of those who had decided to become his brother's keepers, infinite hatred for Karim, Hassen went home. Salima sensed her husband's mood and did not say a word to him.

In his room he debated with himself. In what way should he conduct himself so that his dignity remained intact? How was he to face the congregation, the people in the streets, his neighbours? Everyone would soon know of Karim and smile at him half sadly, half ironically, for having placed himself in such a ridiculous position. Should he now forgive the dying man and transfer him to his home? People would laugh at him, snigger at his cowardice, and Mr Mia perhaps even deny him the privilege: Karim was now *his* responsibility. And what would Catherine think of him? Should he go away somewhere (on the pretext of a holiday) to Cape Town, to Durban? But no, there was the stigma of being called a renegade. And besides, Karim might take months to die, he might not die at all.

'O Karim, why did you have to do this to me?' he said, moving towards the window and drumming at the pane nervously. It galled him that a weak, dying man could bring such pain to him. An adversary could be faced, one could either vanquish him or be vanquished, with one's dignity unravished, but with Karim what could he do?

He paced his room. He looked at his watch; the time for afternoon prayers was approaching. Should he expose himself to the congregation? 'O Karim! Karim!' he cried, holding on to the burglar-proof bar of his bedroom window. Was it for this that he had made the pilgrimage – to cleanse his soul in order to return into the penumbra of sin? If only Karim would die he would be relieved of his agony. But what if he lingered on? What if he recovered? Were not prayers being said for him? He went to the door and shouted in a raucous voice: 'Salima!'

But Salima was not in the house. He shouted again

and again, and his voice echoed hollowly in the rooms. He rushed into the lounge, into the kitchen, he flung the door open and looked into the yard.

He drew the curtains and lay on his bed in the dark. Then he heard the patter of feet in the house. He jumped up and shouted for his wife. She came hurriedly.

'Salima, Salima, go to Karim, he is in a room in the mosque yard. See how he is, see if he is getting better. Quickly!'

Salima went out. But instead of going to the mosque, she entered her neighbour's house. She had already spent several hours sitting beside Karim. Mr Mia had been there as well as Catherine – who had wept.

After a while she returned from her neighbour. When she opened the door her husband ran to her. 'How is he? Is he very ill? Tell me quickly!'

'He is very ill. Why don't you go and see him?'

Suddenly, involuntarily, Hassen struck his wife in the face.

'Tell me, is he dead? Is he dead?' he screamed.

Salima cowered in fear. She had never seen her husband in this raging temper. What had taken possession of the man? She retired quickly to the kitchen. Hassen locked himself in the bedroom.

During the evening he heard voices. Salima came to tell him that several people, led by Mr Mia, wanted to speak to him urgently. His first impulse was to tell them to leave immediately; he was not prepared to meet them. But he had been wrestling with himself for so many hours that he welcomed a moment when he could be in the company of others. He stepped boldly into the lounge.

'Hajji Hassen,' Mr Mia began, 'please listen to us. Your brother has not long to live. The doctor has seen him. He may not outlive the night.'

'I can do nothing about that,' Hassen replied, in an audacious matter-of-fact tone that surprised him and shocked the group of people.

'That is in Allah's hand,' said the merchant Gardee. 'In our hands lie forgiveness and love. Come with us now and see him for the last time.'

'I cannot see him.'

'And what will it cost you?' asked the priest who wore a long black cloak that fell about his sandalled feet.

'It will cost me my dignity and my manhood.'

'My dear Hajji, what dignity and what manhood? What can you lose by speaking a few kind words to him on his death-bed? He was only a young man when he left.'

'I will do anything, but going to Karim is impossible.'

'But Allah is pleased by forgiveness,' said the merchant.

'I am sorry, but in my case the circumstances are different. I am indifferent to him and therefore there is no necessity for me to forgive him.'

'Hajji,' said Mr Mia, 'you are only indulging in glib talk and you know it. Karim is your responsibility, whatever his crime.'

'Gentlemen, please leave me alone.'

And they left. Hassen locked himself in his bedroom and began to pace the narrow space between bed, cupboard and wall. Suddenly, uncontrollably, a surge of grief for his dying brother welled up within him.

'Brother! Brother!' he cried, kneeling on the carpet

beside his bed and smothering his face in the quilt. His memory unfolded a time when Karim had been ill at the Islamic Institute and he had cared for him and nursed him back to health. How much he had loved the handsome youth!

At about four in the morning he heard an urgent rapping. He left his room to open the front door.

'Brother Karim dead,' said Mustapha, the Somali muezzin of the mosque, and he cupped his hands and said a prayer in Arabic. He wore a black cloak and a white skull-cap. When he had done he turned and walked away.

Hassen closed the door and went out into the street. For a moment his release into the street gave him a feeling of sinister jubilation, and he laughed hysterically as he turned the corner and stood next to Jamal's fruitshop. Then he walked on. He wanted to get away as far as he could from Mr Mia and the priest who would be calling upon him to prepare for the funeral. That was no business of his. They had brought Karim to Newtown and they should see to him.

He went up Lovers' Walk and at the entrance of Orient House he saw the night-watchman sitting beside a brazier. He hastened up to him, warmed his hands by the fire, but he did this more as a gesture of fraternization as it was not cold, and he said a few words facetiously. Then he walked on.

His morbid joy was ephemeral, for the problem of facing the congregation at the mosque began to trouble him. What opinion would they have of him when he returned? Would they not say: he hated his brother so much that he forsook his prayers, but now that his brother is no longer alive he returns. What a man! What a Muslim.

When he reached Vinod's Photographic Studio he pressed his forehead against the neon-lit glass showcase and began to weep.

A car passed by filling the air with nauseous gas. He wiped his eyes, and looked for a moment at the photographs in the showcase; the relaxed happy, anonymous faces stared at him, faces whose momentary expressions were trapped in film. Then he walked on. He passed a few shops and then reached Broadway Cinema where he stopped to look at the lurid posters. There were heroes, lusty, intrepid, blasting it out with guns; women in various stages of undress; horrid monsters from another planet plundering a city; Dracula.

Then he was among the quiet houses and an avenue of trees rustled softly. He stopped under a tree and leaned against the trunk. He envied the slumbering people in the houses around him, their freedom from the emotions that jarred him. He would not return home until the funeral of his brother was over.

When he reached the Main Reef Road the east was brightening up. The lights along the road seemed to be part of the general haze. The buildings on either side of him were beginning to thin and on his left he saw the ghostly mountains of mine sand. Dawn broke over the city and when he looked back he saw the silhouettes of tall buildings bruising the sky. Cars and trucks were now rushing past him.

He walked for several miles and then branched off onto a gravel road and continued for a mile. When he reached a clump of blue-gum trees he sat down on a rock in the shade of the trees. From where he sat he could see a constant stream of traffic flowing along the highway. He had a stick in his hand which he had picked up along the road, and with it he prodded a crevice in the rock. The action, subtly, touched a chord in his memory and he was sitting on a rock with Karim beside him. The rock was near a river that flowed a mile away from the Islamic Institute. It was a Sunday. He had a stick in his hand and he prodded a crevice and the weather-worn rock flaked off and Karim was gathering the flakes.

'Karim! Karim!' he cried, prostrating himself on the rock, pushing his fingers into the hard roughness, unable to bear the death of that beautiful youth.

He jumped off the rock and began to run. He would return to Karim. A fervent longing to embrace his brother came over him, to touch that dear form before the soil claimed him. He ran until he was tired, then walked at a rapid pace. His whole existence precipitated itself into one motive, one desire, to embrace his brother in a final act of love.

His heart beating wildly, his hair dishevelled, he reached the highway and walked on as fast as he could. He longed to ask for a lift from a passing motorist but could not find the courage to look back and signal. Cars flashed past him, trucks roared in pain.

When he reached the outskirts of Johannesburg it was nearing ten o'clock. He hurried along, now and then breaking into a run. Once he tripped over a cable and fell. He tore his trousers in the fall and found his hands were bleeding. But he was hardly conscious of himself, wrapped up in his one purpose.

He reached Lovers' Walk, where cars growled around him angrily; he passed Broadway Cinema, rushed towards Orient House, turned the corner at Jamal's fruitshop. And stopped.

The green hearse, with the crescent moon and stars emblem, passed by; then several cars with mourners followed, bearded men, men with white skull-caps on their heads, looking rigidly ahead, like a procession of puppets, indifferent to his fate. No one saw him.

Mbulelo Mzamane

MY OTHER COUSIN, SITHA

Just how I happened to fall for the paraffin one, week in and week out, still puzzles me. I never approved of Sitha's weekly disappearance. I loathed Slakes, the fellow who always hijacked her. I simply couldn't understand why she preferred him to her other boyfriend, Martin, who didn't land her in the same trouble. But come Friday and I became an accessory, as it were, after the fact.

When my father was transferred to Johannesburg, my mother remained with relatives in Brakpan, in order to be near the Far East Rand Non-European Hospital where she worked. She only came home when she was day-off. My father worked in the vast parish of Moroka, which has since been divided into four parishes. The main church in Senaoana, where he also had his office, was a good distance from home. When he was not in his office, he was doing parish visits, on a bicycle. Most of the time, therefore, we were left to our own devices. Being the eldest among us, my cousin Sitha then became the mistress of the house. We enjoyed so much freedom that I seldom went to school. On the few occasions when I did, it was because I had a rock group which practised daily, after lessons.

On Fridays, when Sitha returned from school, she made fire and placed the pots on the stove. Then she instructed my sisters, who remained playing outside, to watch over the pots – which meant we often ate charcoal-flavoured food for supper. She vanished into the bathroom to wash, as though she hadn't washed in the morning before going to school, and emerged with shiny legs and a face masked in Butone. Because I have such a passion for music, I duly resented being dragged from under my pile of records to accompany her to the shops.

'Sabelo, get the paraffin container ready, we're going to the shops,' she'd say.

We bought our groceries from Khanyile's General Dealers. Tat' uKhanyile, the proprietor, was our church warden. We were more than just important customers, we behaved like virtual shareholders. We helped Bhut' Plum, who ran the shop, supervise the lady who baked fatcakes at the back of the store; we checked to see if the customers had collected in sufficient numbers in the shop and, if they had, served them, ourselves, shovelling malted toffees and sharps into our pockets as we did so. When we were sent to buy anything, we behaved as at a self-service supermarket and then paid or kept the money, as our fancy dictated. Sitha considered herself above the racket and so let us steal whatever we'd been sent to buy, while she retained the money.

On Fridays, when we went to buy paraffin, I left Sitha on the verandah of the shop, overlooking the Moroka West taxi rank, sauntered in, bided my time, filled up the tin with paraffin and then came out. Invariably, I'd find Slakes already with her.

Slakes belonged to a group which appropriately called itself The Black Swine. They wore black and white fung kong shoes, rustler suits and black skull-caps with elongated tailpieces, rather like the devil's tail. They ruled with an iron hand over White City, which had the only high school, serving more than ten townships. That put all of us who attended the school, from Naledi to Mofolo, at the mercy of the Black Swine. For the girls, salvation lay in falling in love. Just how much free will counted in Sitha's case, and how much she was swayed by intimidation, just to what extent she became Slakes's willing victim, I can't tell. There were many girls in her position. My own girlfriend, Puni, from whom I'd had to part, used to argue that she had no alternative. I couldn't believe that when I caught her putting her hand, voluntarily, round Kali's shoulders – he wasn't wielding any knife blade that I could see. She told me that it was all flattery, that she had to make the affair look authentic, for the safety of us both. I thought differently. I rather thought my safety lay in breaking with her, if I didn't want my jaws socked. However, since the boys had virtually nothing to offer the Black Swine, not even some token resistance, our fate was more or less sealed. We paid sixpence, every Monday, as protection fee. As the Black Swine had no system of accounting, one had to pay this fee as often as it was demanded, which was on every school day and sometimes twice a day. Occasionally, Slakes rescued me, but most of the time his shifty eyes just passed me over.

'Take it home,' Sitha would say. 'I won't be long.'

I'd take the paraffin home.

She'd disappear until Sunday evening when she came back to get her gym-dress pressed, in readiness for school. I couldn't understand why she took so much trouble over her gyms, since she wasn't a regular at school. I was only prevented from reporting the matter to my father by the fact that I wasn't such a model of attendance either.

My father is very long-suffering. But when he gets angry, you thank your ancestors you aren't on the receiving end. He never fails to point out that even our Lord wasn't averse to using the whip, and applies the maxim himself with apostolic zeal. In Sitha's case, he first tried every possible method to reform her. He pleaded with her and sometimes adopted a very menacing tone; he begged her to show some consideration for his public image; he appealed to her not to jeopardise her own future; he reasoned with her, threatened her, but all to no avail.

One Friday afternoon he returned home much earlier than usual. We'd already left for the shops. He changed into his great overcoat, although the evening temperature in December was very high, and followed us. I bumped into him, on my way back home, at the corner near the Nazarene church.

'Where's she?' he asked.

'Tata?' I still have the habit of pretending deafness and incomprehension when I'm at a loss for an answer. I expected my father to repeat his question, instead of which he fixed me with an unnerving stare. I hated to betray Sitha. 'I left her talking to some friends.'

'Where?'

'Outside Khanyile's.'

'What friends?'

'Some gentlemen . . . '

He didn't wait for my reply. I knocked into a small boy, pushing a tyre, as I craned my neck to catch my father's disappearing figure. He vanished into a thick crowd around the taxi rank. I knew then that Sitha had had it.

He mingled with the crowd but kept a close watch on the couple, who were holding hands on the stoep outside the shop. In due course, Sitha and Slakes took a taxi. My father also got into an empty one and ordered the driver to trail the one in which Sitha and Slakes were travelling.

I can only fill in the rest from my father's report: at the crossroads in White City the taxi in front stopped, and the one behind drove on a few blocks before stopping. With his coat collar raised to the level of his ears, my father followed them to a house in White City. Since he only wanted to find out where they were going, he turned at the gate of the house they'd entered and went for the police.

They were in bed when he returned in the black maria, accompanied by about ten policemen from the Moroka police station. They had little trouble in persuading Slakes to open the door. In fact, he had hoped to satisfy their enquiries at the door, and opened it with only a blanket around his body. The police squadron barged in, my father at the tail end.

What followed was, strictly speaking, illegal – but the police realized just how necessary it was for my father to let off steam a bit, and so they let it continue for a while. From under his greatcoat he produced a sjambok. One of my father's few boasts is the expert way in which he used to fight with sticks as a boy, looking after cattle in the Transkei. I once witnessed his expertise in Brakpan the day he thrashed Don, who was regarded by all who knew him as the boss of the township. Don was an indiscriminate bully who thrived on the cautious nature of township folk. He could close a function, be it a stokvel or a church bazaar, merely by telling everybody to leave the premises. But my father had never heard of Don before their encounter at a party to celebrate the christening of a daughter of one of my father's parishioners. Don descended on the gathering like a Philistine and demanded liquor. When he was told that there was none, he ordered the host to close the party. My father was so furious that he slipped into one of the bedrooms, unobserved, and returned with a stick. He gave Don a beating which remained the talk of the township long after we'd left Brakpan. The thrashing Slakes received that evening left him with welts the size of hose-pipes. No doubt worse damage would have been done if, at a certain stage, the police had not thought it fit to intervene. When he decided to turn to Sitha, the police again threw themselves between them.

Sitha and Slakes were marched into the black maria in their birthday suits, with only their blankets around them. Dad carried her clothes in a bundle, under his armpit. They drove them to the police station, where the police went through the motions of taking statements. After more intimidation, they were released and told they'd hear from the police as soon as a day had been fixed for their trial. There was to be no trial but the whole show was calculated to act as a repellent, which it did. Slakes was released and told to make himself scarce. The police drove Sitha and my father home.

Thanks to the township telegraphic system, the following morning the story was all over the place. For days afterwards, Slakes elicited giggles wherever he appeared. His swaggering walk had lost a bit of its former bounce, I noticed.

We became a complete family again, from Friday to Friday. Even my mother eventually transferred from the Far East to Baragwanath Hospital.

At this time, the happiest man alive was undoubtedly Martin.

Martin had matriculated at Lovedale Institution. He worked as a dispatch clerk at some factory in Doornfontein. He wanted to become a lawyer and was studying for a diploma, by correspondence, through the University of South Africa. He also taught Sunday School, sang in the church choir and was generally every parent's idea of a decent young man. Naturally, he was as suited to his environment as is a specialist surgeon who suddenly finds he has to exchange positions with a village butcher.

On Saturday afternoons we attended church choir practices: my mother, Sitha and I. We even formed a double quartet with some close family friends and met on alternate Sundays, when my mother was afternoon-off. Martin, who had not the slightest respect for pitch, tune or time, was in it from the beginning. He never missed a practice. His enthusiasm made up for his tone-deafness and assured him a permanent place in the choir. Just how the grown-ups tolerated him, I couldn't understand. We'd never have considered him, even during a crisis or for comic effects, in my pop group.

My family is sharply divided into two: those who can sing and those who can't. The latter group is invariably more critical than the former. Their ears are paradoxically more faultless, and their taste more cultivated. They try to hide their inability to correct any false notes they hear by producing equally off-key guffaws. They were always present at our practices because Martin's singing gave them no end of amusement. They were untiring in their efforts to provide us with new songs, especially those with very complicated transitions. My only good memory of these practices lies in the consolatory fact that we never actually performed in public.

These choral occasions also served as amorous encounters between Martin and Sitha. To be able to check your girlfriend, as they say, at her home, before her parents, is no mean achievement. That sort of thing does not occur commonly outside our white suburbs. It is not customary, but where it occurs it is the measure of the boyfriend's acceptability.

Many a squabble between families has arisen over the issue of children in love. My younger brother, Soso, once created strained relations between my family and the Qwathis, who had several daughters, because every time he went to check, he rained such stones over their roof to summon his girl out that one evening, unable to bear it any longer, Tat' uQwathi came out in person and chased him right to the doorstep of our house. I was once punched in the face by an outraged parent who found me and his daughter locked in a tight embrace, in his sitting room. It's always best to grab your girl and disappear with her, into the bushes. You dare not risk even taking her out for a walk in a township teeming with Black Swine.

In a way, I envied Martin, who actually had supper with us every Sunday. Not that I really care much for that kind of affair. It may have class but it lacks adventure. Besides, the other family always imagines it has a permanent claim on you, a thing which makes it very difficult to break the silver cup. Still it is something to boast about when you are actually admitted to her home.

After Sunday practices, Sitha and Martin would go out for a walk. They usually went to watch soccer or to the library which was converted to a hall over weekends for ballroom dancing. They seldom strayed far from home. He always brought her back dead on time for supper.

One Sunday afternoon they invited me to accompany them to Baragwanath, to visit a sick aunt of Martin's. At Moroka West we waited in vain for a taxi and eventually decided to try Moroka Central. Near Elkah Stadium we bumped into a gang of Black Swine. It was all so unexpected there was no turning back. They simply emerged from nowhere, Slakes among them.

Fortunately they let Martin and me pass, unmolested, but Slakes stayed Sitha behind.

Martin had bought some fruit for his aunt which he and Sitha had been carrying in a paper-bag between them. The paper-bag remained with Sitha.

We walked up a steep hill to the taxi rank in silence, occasionally glancing back to see if Sitha was following.

At the taxi rank I met a schoolmate, Mafa, and we began to chat about all sorts of irrelevant matters. Half an hour later, Mafa decided to proceed on his way to the football ground, to watch a soccer derby between the local rivals, Moroka Swallows and Desert Rats. I wanted to accompany Mafa to the match but Martin pleaded with me to remain with him.

An hour passed, still no Sitha!

'It's almost past visiting time,' Martin said. 'We could at least drop the fruit at the hospital. Will you go and see if she'll give us the paper-bag?'

One of Boswell's famous acts was popping his head

in and out of a live lion's mouth. But the circus king fell victim to his own pranks. He was eaten alive by one of his own lions. I've a very well-developed survival instinct. I'm as mad as my neighbour, no worse, and equally sensitive to danger. Martin's suggestion fell on deaf ears.

We stood at the rank watching and never for a moment letting them out of sight.

Slakes decided to sit on the grass near the road. After a while Sitha followed his example.

Excited voices rose from the nearby soccer pitch. Slakes and Sitha eventually stood up and, hand in hand, decided to walk in the direction from which we'd come. That did it.

'I'm going to the ground,' I said.

'Let's get the fruit,' Martin said.

I looked him up and down and wondered where he was born.

'It's well past the visiting hour,' I said.

'Please, Sabelo, my *swaar,* what shall we say when we get home?'

'I'm not going home, at least not just yet. We can go home after the match. She'll be home by then.'

I walked resolutely across the street. Martin followed me.

The match was in the second half. My side was trailing Desert Rats by an odd goal. It was a very stiff match. Gloom enveloped the Swallows camp, until Rhee got the ball near the centre line. He dribbled past two opponents and passed the ball to Aarah who heeled it to Differ. Differ unleashed a cannonball from outside the eighteens which left the opposing goalkeeper as flat-footed as a duck. From then on it was us all the way. In the closing stages of the game Carlton intercepted a loose ball and dished it to the evergreen Differ, who was standing unmarked inside the opponents' eighteens. Baboon, Desert Rats' running back, charged in and brought Differ down with a tackle that would have been discouraged even in rugby. The referee unhesitatingly awarded a penalty. Desert Rats disputed his decison. Chaos broke loose. Supporters of both teams swarmed onto the field. Martin forgot himself and rushed on with the rest, muttering something about 'infringement' and 'constitution'. The referee blew his whistle to signal the end of the match. The last we saw of him, he was running for dear life in the direction of Moroka police station with three youths, brandishing glittering blades, in hot pursuit.

The players went to change into their clothes at one corner of the field. We clustered round them, indulging in a post-mortem of the match, as liberal with advice as only spectators can be.

Martin was explaining the league's constitution to someone who seemed to pay very little attention to him.

Soon everybody began to trickle away. Martin and I were among the last to leave.

It was almost dark when we got back home, now trooping as solemnly as tragedians.

'What shall we say?' Martin asked, when we reached the gate.

'Say we left her dancing at the library and went to the football ground.'

'But we can't say that. We should have gone straight to the police and not procrastinated. Suppose something happens to her? This chap could be hauled in for forcible abduction and possible seduction.'

Damn the fellow with his long words and his law!

'Better say we left her at the library, if we're asked,

that is.'

Someone opened the door and terminated our argument.

'Thought I recognized your voices. Come in. Supper's almost ready. Mom was beginning to worry about your whereabouts.' Sitha held the door for us and shut it after us.

When we had mixed fruit for dessert, I didn't ask where the fruit had come from. I ate with an appetite which astonished my mother.

'You should take him out more often,' she told Martin.

I didn't choke at the remarks which followed either.

'Oh! Don't think we're ungrateful,' she continued. 'Thanks a lot for the fruit.'

Mtutuzeli Matshoba

TO KILL A MAN'S PRIDE

Every man is born with a certain amount of pride in his humanity. But I have come to believe that pride is only a mortal thing, and that there are many ways to destroy it. One sure way is to take a man and place him in a Soweto hostel.

At the mention of the word 'hostel' those who have never been near the Soweto version, or live in places where all people are treated as people, if there is any such place in the world, will immediately think of an establishment along Salvation Army lines. They would be infinitely far from the truth. A nearer comparison would be a Nazi concentration camp. North of our location lies our own Auschwitz. From its long grey structures the chimneys jut out of asbestos roofs into the sky; row upon monotonous row of low-built rough brick is packed into a triangular patch north of Mzimhlope and the adjacent Killarney, south east of Meadowlands. These three locations are separated from the hostel by one street on two sides; the third side faces the golden mine dunes across a rocky veld depression with an almost dry stream meandering in the middle from a small dam, which is more like a swamp, in Florida.

The hostel is, by conservative estimate, the home of some twenty thousand migrant labourers from all parts of Southern Africa, some of whom begin the trek as far away as Malawi and Zambia. Since the Kliptown floods at the beginning of 'seventy-seven, the families whose shanties were swept away in the deluge have been 'located' in a section of the hostel complex near Meadowlands. (This section was evacuated in 'seventy-six after certain tragic events about which I shall find the opportunity one day to tell you.) There they waited, a family to a five by three metre cubicle, until the WRAB could figure out what to do with them. Opposite Killarney a space just big enough for two soccer fields side by side was left vacant when the hostel was built. That is all the whole complex can boast by way of recreation facilities. There was also a bottle store, a beer lounge for fifty people all seated around rusty metal tables, and a *mai-mai* (sorghum beer) beerhall, an open square with benches along the walls and under a sort of continuous verandah. Along a street off the Soweto highway were prospering shops where the hostel inmates used to buy food. Today, the ruins of these buildings are ghastly monuments of the day of fire in June 'seventy-six.

It was there, in room 413, that my friend Somdali stayed. We had met at work. I had just been hired and was still keeping to myself, working at the tedious paper guillotine impatiently, with repeated glances at the clock high up on the wall. Lunch-time was forty-five minutes away and it seemed to me that Detail Die-cut Limited worked to a different time scale. The minutes were crawling, and Pieters had just come to instruct me about something I knew, for the thousandth time. Perhaps he underestimated my intelligence; but more likely he was 'breaking me in', measuring my tolerance. The die-cutting machines were whining incessantly and above their noise the maddening sound of Springbok Radio screeched out of a small home-made soundbox hanging from the whitewashed concrete roof which was supported by colossal, whitewashed cylindrical pillars. The walls too were whitewashed. The thirty or so factory 'girls' were working noisily at their tables behind me, chattering and giggling as if trying to outdo the machines and the radio.

Tea-break, my first there, had been an ordeal of eyes studying me from behind large mugs and the tins that were used as teacups. Fortunately, the 'girls' had their own tea-room, otherwise it would have been worse. There were sixteen 'boys', including myself, round the long unvarnished table. I was sitting at the far side, a pungent toilet door behind me – not the type that you sit on, but a hole in the floor for squatting over. I could never bring myself to use it during all the eight months I spent working there. The tea was the only thing the firm could offer. You bought your own bread and anything that you could afford to go with it. Since I hadn't known that, and hadn't had a cent in my pocket when I was taken on in the morning, I was not eating. After being tipped by a neighbour who worked next door to Detail that one 'boy' had severed his fingers with the guillotine and there might be a 'space', I had borrowed a twenty cent piece for the train ticket and rushed there. So now I sat at the end of the table, not knowing what to do with my hands and feeling like a specimen for human study and contemplation while the others were hurriedly eating their first meal of the day. The 'girls' were chatting at the tops of their voices in the other room. One of the 'boys' suggested that John had cut his fingers on purpose to get workers' insurance money. They talked about it until the buzzer sounded after fifteeen minutes.

At lunch I had nowhere to go. I decided to familiarise myself with the neighbourhood. It was one of those rusty industrial outskirts of town where one sees no one but grease-stained overall-clad mechanics and handy-men. Nothing but trucks and vans off-loading semi-processed goods. Our firm was at the southern end of Mooi street, under a maze of highways, with Heidelberg road forming a T with Mooi street, and running into mine dunes. I followed Mooi street in the direction of Carlton Centre. I had an hour, a hungry hour to kill. Not that my empty stomach worried me; well, it worried me only because it was an uncomfortable sensation which could not be totally ignored. Someone was walking beside me. His tall shadow had fallen in line with mine. Both of us had our hands in our pockets. I moved aside to give him way to pass but he did not.

'Hawu, sawubona mfowethu.' He extended his massive hand to greet. It was one of the 'boys' from the firm; tall, receding forehead, smooth dark skin and one eye. In the one eye and the wide grin I could read recognition, although I had never seen the man myself. His Elmer skipper that was no longer its original white but brownish, and the flimsy dark trousers that came to just above his naked ankles, were worn without any thought of physical decoration, but only to cover the body. I gave him my hand.

'Seems you don't recognise me, but I know you. I have seen you at Mzimhlope.' He was telling the truth.

I felt slightly embarrassed at not knowing a man

who knew me. It's always like that. Anyway he did not know me by name either. 'I can't even recognise you. Let alone place you,' I answered, also showing my teeth.

'My name is Somdali. I also stay at Mzimhlope,' he said by way of introduction.

'Mzimhlope? Which side?' I was asking with due regard for his feelings, not wishing to make him feel awkward. I had already placed him in 'Auschwitz' from his appearance and the way he spoke with a deep Zulu accent. People born and bred in Soweto speak every language in a characteristic way.

'The northern side of the station,' and seeing that he had finally to divulge the guarded domicile, he amassed enough courage to tell me, 'in the hostel.'

'Oh, I see. My name is Mtutu. I stay in . . . in the location.'

'Yes. I have seen you there, when I'm going to and from the station.' They hold a servitude, a right of way in the location and are hardly worth a second glance from the location residents, except maybe the dark night's children who never fail to collect the dues on Fridays and month-ends, or the fallen women who provide the hostelers with female company for sale.

I did not have anything to say. We went a few paces before he continued. 'You were lucky to arrive first. One guy cut his fingers with the guillotine yesterday. That thing needs to be operated with care, it's dangerous. You've filled that guy's space.' I did not comment. 'They're going to teach you the machines too.' I let him go on. 'But you won't be paid before you're registered. They first take a person on trial.'

That was interesting. 'How long is the trial?'

'Two, three weeks – Pieters decides. But ag, it's only a way to get free labour out of the people they employ before they register them. Pieters is the owner of the firm. He takes the good-looking girls away in his VW station wagon 'to clean his house' before he registers them. You should see him among the girls – acts like a bull that has been kept alone for months, when it is released among a herd of cows. Some of the girls are married. When their husbands want to talk to them on the phone, or come looking for them at lunch or after work, he refers to them as 'boyfriends'. Otherwise he has a little sense of humour when he has not got out on the wrong side of his bed in the morning. His assistant is aloof and has an affair with one of the two Indian girls in the office.'

'How much is the starting pay?'

'Twenty-five rand a week. Thirty for those who have been with the firm over three years. The women, I don't know.'

He told me a little more about himself, that he had come from Mondlo near Vryheid in Natal to work in Johannesburg with a forged pass eight years before, that he had been with Detail for two years and (he must have guessed I was curious to know) that he had lost his eye in a stick-fight competition when he was a teenager, an unfortunate accident for which no-one could be blamed. 'Your mouth is dry. You must be hungry.'

'I'm used to it, mfo. Don't worry,' I said politely.

'Say it again, mfowethu. We are all used to it at one time or another of our lives. But I have fifty cents here. Let's go buy some magewu.'

That was how I struck up a friendship with the man from the hostel. At the end of the first week he lent me money to buy a weekly ticket, gave me cigarettes every day without being asked; we ate and talked together during lunch and entrained together at Mzimhlope and Faraday Stations.

Tell me – who could deny such a man friendship? I could see that people we met who knew me always wondered what I was up to with a 'country boy', but I knew better. However I never invited him home – what could I invite him for? To remind him that he also had a family he was denied? And it was not until after I had been registered that he invited me to the hostel 'just to see where I live'.

Registration for work is such an interesting example of a way of killing a man's pride that I cannot pass it by without mention. It was on Monday, after two weeks of unrewarded labour and perseverance, that Pieters gave me a letter which said I had been employed as a general labourer at his firm. I was to take the letter to the notorious 80 Albert Street. Monday is usually the busiest day there because everybody wakes up on this day determined to find a job. They end up dejected, crowding the labour office for 'piece' jobs.

That Monday I woke up elated, whistling all the way as I cleaned the coal stove, made fire to warm the house for those who were still asleep, and took my toothbrush and washing rags to the tap outside the toilet. The cold water was revivifying as I splashed it over my upper body. I greeted 'Star', also washing at the tap diagonally opposite my home. Then I took the washing basin, half-filled it with water and went into the lavatory to wash the rest of me. When I had finished washing and dressing I bade them goodbye at home and set out, swept into the torrent of workers rushing to the station. Somdali had reached the station first and we waited for our trains with the hundreds already on the platform. The guys from the location prefer to wait for trains on the station bridge. Many of them looked like children who did not want to go to school. I did not sympathize with them. The little time my brothers have to themselves, Saturday and Sunday, some of them spend worshipping Bacchus.

The train schedule was geared to the morning rush hour. From four in the morning the trains had rumbled in with precarious frequency. If you stay near the road to the hostel you are woken up by the shuffle of a myriad footfalls long before the first train. I have seen these people on my way home when the nocturnal bug has bitten me. All I can say is that an endless flow of resolute men, hastening in the inky, misty morning down Mohale street to the station, is an awesome apparition.

I had arrived ten minutes early at the station. The 'ninety-five' to George Goch passed Mzimhlope while I was there. This train brought the free morning stuntman show. The daredevils ran along the roof of the train, a few centimetres from the naked cable carrying thousands of electric volts, and ducked under every pylon. One mistimed step, a slip – and reflex action would send his hand clasping for support. No comment from any of us at the station. The train shows have been going on since time immemorial and have lost their magic.

My train to Faraday arrived, bursting along the seams with its load. The spaces between the adjacent coaches were filled with people. So the only way I could get on the train was by wedging myself among those hanging on perilously by hooking their fingers into the narrow runnels along the tops of the coaches, their feet on the door ledges. A slight wandering of the mind, a sudden swaying of the train as it switched lines, bringing the weight of the others on top of us, a lost grip – and another labour unit would be abruptly terminated. We hung on for dear life until Faraday.

In Pieters's office. Four automatic telephones, two scarlet and two orange coloured, two fancy ashtrays, a gilded ball-pen stand complete with gilded pen and chain, two flat plastic trays, the one on the left marked IN and the other one OUT, all displayed on the bland face of a large highly-polished desk. Under my feet a thick carpet that made me feel like a piece of dirt. On the soft opal green wall on my left a big framed 'Desiderata' and above me a ceiling of heavenly splendour. Behind the desk, wearing a short cream-white safari suit, leaning back in a regal flexible armchair, his hairy legs (the pale skin of which curiously made me think of a frog's ventral side) balanced on the edge of the desk in the manner of a sheriff in an old-fashioned western, blue-eyed, slightly bald, jackal-faced overlord.

'You've got your pass?'

'Yes, mister Pieters.' That one did not want to be called baas.

'Let me see it. I hope it's the right one. You got a permit to work in Johannesburg?'

'I was born here, mister Pieters.' My hands were respectfully behind me.

'It doesn't follow.' He removed his legs from the edge of the table and opened a drawer. Out of it he took a small bundle of typed papers. He signed one of them and handed it to me. 'Go to the pass office. Don't spend two days there. Otherwise you come back and I've taken somebody else in your place.'

He squinted his eyes at me and wagged his tongue,

trying to amuse me the way he would try to make a baby smile. That really amused me, his trying to amuse me the way he would a baby. I thought he had a baby's mind.

'Esibayeni'. Two storey red-brick building occupying a whole block. Address: 80 Albert street, or simply 'Pass Office'. Across the street, half the block (the remaining half a parking space and 'home' of the homeless methylated spirit drinkers of the city) taken up by another red-brick structure. Not offices this time, but 'Esibayeni' (at the kraal) itself. No question why it has been called that. The whole black population of Johannesburg above pass age knows that place.

Like I said, it was full on a Monday, full of wretched men with defeated eyes sitting along the gutters on both sides of Albert Street, others grouped where the sun's rays leaked through the skyscrapers, and the rest milling about. When a car driven by a white man went up the street pandemonium broke loose as men, I mean dirty slovenly *men,* trotted behind it and fought to give their passes first. If the white person had not come for that purpose they cursed him until he went out of sight. Occasionally a truck or van would come to pick up labourers for a piece job. The clerk would shout out the number of men that were wanted for such and such a job, say forty, and double the number would be all over the truck before you could say 'stop'. None of them would want to miss the cut, which caused quite some problems for the employer. A shrewd businessman would take all and simply divide the money he had laid out among the whole group, as it was left to him to decide how much to pay for a piece job. Everybody was satisfied in the end – the temporary employer having his work done in half the time he had bargained for, and each of the labourers with enough for a ticket back to the pass-office the following day, and maybe ten cents worth of dish-water and bread from the oily restaurants in the neighbourhood, for three days. Those who were smart and familiar with the ways of the pass-office handed their passes in with twenty and/or fifty-cent pieces between the pages. This gave them first preference, and they could choose the better jobs.

The queue to 'Esibayeni' was moving slowly. It snaked about thirty metres around the corner of Polly street. It had taken me more than an hour to reach the door. Inside the ten-foot wall was an asphalt rectangle, longitudinal benches along the opposite wall in the shade of narrow tin ledges, filled with bored-looking men, toilets on the lower side of the rectangle, facing wide bustling doors. It would take me another three hours to reach the clerks. If I finished there just before lunch-time, it would mean that I would not be through with my registration by four in the afternoon when the pass office closed. Fortunately I had twenty cents and I knew that the blackjacks who worked there were nothing but starving leeches. One took me up the queue to four people who stood before a snarling white boy. Those whose places ahead of me in the queue had been usurped wasted their breath grumbling.

The man in front of me could not understand what was being bawled at him in Afrikaans. The clerk gave up explaining, not prepared to use any other language than his own. I felt that at his age, about twenty, he should be at RAU learning to speak other languages. That way he wouldn't burst a vein trying to explain everything in one tongue just because it was his. He was either bone-headed or downright lazy or else impatient to 'rule the Bantus'.

He took a rubber stamp and banged it furiously on one of the pages of the man's pass, and threw the book into the man's face. 'Go to the other building, stupid!'

The man said, 'Thanks,' and elbowed his way to the door.

'Next! Wat soek jy?' he asked in a bellicose voice when my turn to be snarled at came. He had freckles all over his face, and a weak jaw.

I gave him the letter of employment and explained in Afrikaans that I wanted E and F cards. My use of his language eased some of the tension out of him. He asked for my pass in a slightly calmer manner. I gave it to him and he paged through. 'Good, you have permission to work in Johannesburg right enough.' He took two cards from a pile in front of him and laboriously wrote my pass numbers on them. Again I thought that he should still be at school, learning to write properly. He stamped the cards and told me to go to room six in the other block. There were about twelve other clerks growling at people from behind a continuous U-shaped desk, and the space in front of the desk was overcrowded with people who made it difficult to get to the door.

Another blackjack barred the entrance to the building across the street. 'Where do you think you're going?'

'Awu! What's wrong with you? I'm going to room six to be registered. You're wasting my time,' I answered in an equally unfriendly way. His eyes were bloodshot, as big as a cow's and as stupid, his breath was fouled with 'mai-mai', and his attitude was a long way from helpful.

He spat into his right hand, rubbed his palms together and grabbed a stick that was leaning against the wall near him. 'Go in,' he challenged, indicating with a tilt of his head, and dilating his gaping nostrils.

His behaviour perplexed me, more than angering or dismaying me. It might be that he was drunk; or was I supposed to produce something first, and was he so uncouth as not to tell me why he would not allow me to go in? Whatever the reason, I regretted that I could not kick some of the 'mai-mai' out of the sagging belly, and proceeded on my way. I turned to see if there was anyone else witnessing the unnecessary aggression.

'No, mfo. You've got to wait for others who are also going to room six,' explained a man with half his teeth missing, wearing a tattered overcoat and nothing to cover his large, parched feet. And, before I could say thanks: 'Say, mnumzane, have you got a cigarette on you? Y'know, I haven't had a single smoke since yesterday.'

I gave him the one shrivelled Lexington I had in my shirt-pocket. He indicated that he had no matches either. I searched myself and gave the box to him. His hands shook violently when he lit and shielded the flame. 'Ei! Babalaaz has me.'

'Ya, neh,' I said, for the sake of saying something. The man turned and walked away as if his feet were sore. I leaned against the wall and waited. When there were a good many of us waiting the gatekeeper grunted that we should follow him inside to another bustling 'kraal'. That was where the black clerks shouted out the jobs at fifty cents a piece or more, depending on whether they were permanent or temporary. The men in there were fighting like mad to reach the row of windows where they hand in their passes. We followed the blackjack up a sloping cement way rising to a green double door.

There was nowhere it wasn't full at the pass-office. Here too it was full of the same miserable figures that were buzzing all over the place, but this time they stood in a series of queues at a long counter like the one across the street, only this one was L-shaped and the white clerks behind the brass grille wore ties. I decided that they were of a better class than the others, although there was no doubt that they also had the same rotten manners and arrogance. The blackjack left us with another one who told us which queues to join. Our cards were taken and handed to a lady filing clerk who went to look for our records.

I was right! The clerks were, at bottom, all the same. When I reached the counter I pushed my pass under the grille. The man who took it had close-cropped hair and a thin sharp face. He went through my pass checking it against a photostat record with my name scrawled on top in a handwriting that I did not know.

'Where have you been from January until now, September?' he said in a cold voice, looking at me from behind the grille like a god about to admonish a sinner.

I have heard some funny tales, from many tellers, when it comes to answering that question. See if you recognise this one:

CLERK:	Heer, man. Waar was jy al die tyd, jong? (Lord, man. Where have you been all the time, jong?)
MAN:	I . . . I was mad, baas.
CLERK:	Mad!? You think I'm your uncle, kaffer?

KAFFER: No baas, I was mad.
CLERK: Jy . . . jy dink . . . (and the white man's mouth drops open with no words coming out.)
KAFFER: (Coming to the rescue of the baas with an explanation) At home they tell me that I was mad all along, baas. 'Strue.
CLERK: Where are the doctor's papers? You must have been to hospital if you were mad! (With annoyance.)
KAFFER: I was treated by a witchdoctor, baas. Now I am better and have found a job.

Such answers serve them right. If it is their aim to harass the poor people with impossible questions, then they should expect equivalent answers. I did not, however, say something out of the way. I told the truth. 'Looking for work.'

'Looking for work, who?'

'Baas.'

'That's right. And what have you been living on all along?' he asked, like a god.

'Scrounging, and looking for work.' Perhaps he did not know that among us blacks a man is never thrown to the dogs.

'Stealing, huh? You should have been caught before you found this job. Do you know that you have contravened section two, nine, for nine months? Do you know that you would have gone to jail for two years if you had been caught, tsotsi? These policemen are not doing their job anymore,' he said, turning his attention to the stamps and papers in front of him.

I had wanted to tell him that if I had had a chance

to steal, I would not have hesitated to do so, but I stopped myself. It was the wise thing to act timid in the circumstances. He gave me the pass after stamping it. The blackjack told me which corridor to follow. I found men sitting on benches alongside one wall and stood at the end of the queue. The man in front of me shifted and I sat on the edge. This time the queue was reasonably fast. We moved forward on the seats of our pants. If you wanted to prevent them shining you had to stand up and sit, stand up and sit. You could not follow the line standing. The patrolling blackjack made you sit in an embarrassing way. Halfway to the door we were approaching, the man next to me removed his upper clothes. All the others nearer to the door had their clothes bundled under their armpits. I did the same.

We were all vaccinated in the first room and moved on to the next one where we were X-rayed by some impatient black technicians. The snaking line of black bodies reminded me of prisoners being searched. That was what 80 Albert Street was all about.

The last part of the medical examination was the most disgraceful. I don't know whether it was designed to save expense or on some other ground of expediency, but on me it had the effect of dishonour. After being X-rayed we could put on our shirts and cross the corridor to the doctor's cubicle. Outside were people of both sexes waiting to settle their own affairs. You passed them before entering the cubicle, inside which sat a fat white man in a white dust-coat with a face like an owl, behind a simple desk. The man who had gone in ahead of me was zipping up his fly. I unzipped mine and stood facing the owl behind the desk, holding my trousers with both hands. He tilted his fat face to the right and left twice or thrice.

'Ja. Your pass.'

I hitched my trousers up while he harried me to give him the pass before I could zip my trousers. I straightened myself at leisure, in spite of his 'Gou, gou, gou!' My pride had been hurt enough by exposing myself to him, with the man behind me preparing to do so and the one in front of me having done the same, a row of men of different ages parading themselves before a bored owl. When I finished dressing I gave him the pass. He put a little maroon stamp somewhere in amongst the last pages. It must have meant that I was fit to work.

The medical examination was over and the women on the benches outside pretended they did not know. The young white ladies clicking their heels up and down the passages showed you they knew. You held yourself together as best as you could until you vanished from their sight, and you never told anybody else about it.

'Maar, my friend. Why don't you come with me to the hostel one day? Just to see where I stay, and meet some of the guys who come from Natal with me. Are you afraid?' Somdali asked as we went through the barriers at Faraday station.

It was the third week after I had been to the pass office. I was even beginning to get used to the twenty-five rand and few cents in a brown envelope that the Indian lady bookkeepers in the office had given me, and which made me feel very ashamed each time I received it. I felt like a dupe when I had to go to the office to sign for chicken feed after working honestly for a whole week and taking Pieters's scorn without any complaint. He seemed to think that we, the workers, depended on him for a living – and to forget that he, in turn, depended on our labour for his easy life. Maybe this was because he knew that the greater demand was for jobs, for work, not for labour. Everybody was at his mercy. Somdali had been right about the bull-like behaviour of our boss. He behaved like a sheikh in a harem. None of the women liked it, but they had to hide their disapproval as long as they wanted to remain working. We only gritted our teeth and let him continue.

I could not refuse Somdali's invitation. It was not an invitation to a cocktail party but it was an invitation right enough. Such are the invitations of the simple. Apart from the fact that he was my friend, in the evenings I usually had nothing to do at home but listen to the hysterical screams of my sisters' babies, while being asked to shift this way and that in the doll's house. And the hostel was no longer dangerous: 'seventy-six had come and gone. Before Somdali invited me there, the hostel was to me a place I knew of and didn't know about. I knew it must be hell to live there – family men without families, married men without wives. That was how I had seen it, and that was where my concern ended. But when it comes to the misery of life one has to partake to really understand. The deepest pangs of the man caught up in squalor are never really felt from a safe distance. Most people shrink from experiencing what it feels like to be down, licking the base of the drain. Somdali's invitation was my chance to get to the core of hostel life.

In order for you to understand why I had never cared about the hostel, I think a brief description of how I viewed the hostel from afar will be necessary. At first the security of the hostel was tight, with watchmen at every gate, preventing outsiders from entering the premises. Perhaps someone still had a little conscience, and wished to try and hide the shameful place. As time went on this security slackened until there was free traffic between the location and the hostel, although only men went there – it would have been sheer madness for a woman to go into that encampment of deprived men. Even then it was mainly the location drunks who went in after the poisonous brew of yeast, brown bread, brown sugar and water – mbamba, skokiaan and other variations of the same thing which they consumed there out of sight of the people of the location. We only went there to sell something – a watch maybe, the hostelers being ever prepared to 'snatch a bargain' – or to use the showers and quickly return to the location.

The few inmates with a venturesome spirit or having relatives 'outside', most of whom had been discovered there in the Golden City by the tracing of lineage, went out to mix with the location people. Black people seem to believe that they are all related to each other in this way. This way you can never be lost, wherever you go, because everybody with the same surname or clan-name as you is regarded as a relative and is obliged to you. Others formed bands who invaded the location at night solely to rape and kill, so that there was someone lying dead somewhere in the small location once in every week. This gave the hostel people a formidableness that made it difficult to befriend them or to sympathise with their terrible lot.

The bulk of the inmates chose to stay 'inside' at weekends, filling in the emptiness of their lives with alcohol and traditional song that brought them nostalgia for the places of their birth, the barren hopelessness of which had driven them to gather scraps in the human jungles of Johannesburg. Murder was also rife inside. Dehumanized people lose their concern for life: 'We live like hogs, wild dogs or any other neglected animals. The pets of abeLungu live better than we,' Somdali would say to me on a day when he was in a really depressed mood. Normally he never complained.

'Okay Somdali, I'll go with you today. It's still early,' I said and saw that he was pleased.

At the station a man named Joe, who was already quite familiar with Somdali from dice games in the hostel, joined us. Somdali and Joe were friends, only that was rather costly to the former. What kept them going was that Somdali provided beers. Innocent Somdali was not aware of the exploitation and derived great satisfaction from living with amajita, as he would say. There was no need to wise him up. I could not help laughing inside when I heard Joe promising to get Somdali a woman and to lead the latter to a 'spot'. The expeditions always ended up with both of them drunk and Somdali claiming that he had been pickpocketed at the 'spot', but not sore about it, perhaps considering it as part of the sacrifice of learning to live Soweto-style. The three of us went up Mohale street with the wave of countless people, turned down Carr street and fifty metres later crossed the new Soweto highway where it started skirting Mzimhlope.

We entered the first 'street' to our left. It was the first time that I had been to the hostel to visit someone (I had gone there on impersonal matters) and naturally my senses were sharp. The first thing that told you you were in a different place was the smell hanging in the air, the stench of rotting rubbish, urine, dirty water and neglected toilets, an unhygienic mucky atmosphere that almost made you puke. If you've ever been near a pigsty, then you have the right idea. Not that I rate the location much better, but at least the location smells of life, not neglect. As we went deeper into the hostel I was disgusted to think that it was humans who let other humans live like that, in the lowest state of dereliction: and yet their sweat fuelled the economy of the country to keep it going. The so-called last bastion against roving Marxism; a bastion of men scraping small sooty enamel pots to cook the tomatoes, onions and mealie meal they had in plastic carriers. A bastion of men wasting away on skokiaan, a bastion of men washing overalls in the water-troughs; a bastion of men walking in the open in their underpants. Don't count me in, and count Somdali out too.

The first dormitory was fifty short paces long. Three doors. A gap. Another pile of brownish, greyish bricks and undulating asbestos on top, this time the toilets. Six basins in a row in an enclosure with no door and the wall going only halfway up so that a passerby could see a person sitting inside. Adjacent to this: high narrow troughs, apparently to wash dishes in. Behind this: low, deep cement troughs for washing clothes in. The longitudinal half of this place an empty room with eight showers. A man was vigorously rubbing soap on his naked glistening body under one of them. The long dormitories alternated with the toilets. A man obeying the call of nature in the middle of the night had to walk outside for not less than fifteen paces – well, like in the location. The wise thing to do was to be armed when going to the toilet.

There had been an attempt to make the place

homely, maybe when it was still new. Peach trees lined our way on both sides and through the gaps between the buildings I saw that there were garden patches with wilting plants, mostly maize and potatoes. The grass behind and between the buildings grew waist high. The stench was unbearable.

At length, after jumping and stepping around the puddles, we came to where Somdali stayed. He pushed the metal door inwards without knocking. The noise it made put our teeth on edge. He went in ahead and as we followed, my foot sank into stagnant water just in front of the door. There was a buzz of agitated insects.

When you go into a place where people are living, you expect to find something, at least, which indicates that this is so. But in the hostel you are utterly disheartened. The door opened into a medium-sized room. The floor was bare, dust-laden cement. Near the wall facing the door, which had two squares cut into it for windows that had never been cleaned since the hostel was built, were two tables made of cement slabs on metal stilts coming out of the floor. The benches on opposite sides of the tables were also made of cement slabs resting on sewerage pipes. Two old men in denim overalls sat at one table talking in a dull murmur and apparently drinking from a plastic container between them. They did not even raise their eyes to see who was coming in. Against the side walls were long steel cabinets from which the green paint had peeled long ago and which rust now covered almost completely. They extended from the front wall half the length of the side walls to two openings on the left and right. The walls were not plastered and the asbestos roof rested on rafters that were coated with thick layers of soot and spider-webs.

The soot might have come from a brazier during winter.

We followed Somdali to the opening on the right, into a closet for four people sleeping in the corners. The first opening led to another, into a closet exactly the same as the one we had passed, except that it was the last and had only one opening to it. Eight men on either side of the central room, which meant sixteen men to one door and, there being three doors in the long dormitories, forty-eight men to one unit fifty paces long. There is absolutely no privacy there. You sleep in your corner of the closet, on the door-like lid of a brick kist in which you are supposed to keep your possessions, a metre from the man next to you and the men below you.

The last closet was full of men huddled around a small one-plate stove hardly a foot high from which a thin battered chimney pipe rose to a small hole in the roof. The sun was setting and it was cold in the 'house', although the middle of summer was not long gone. Worn, dirty shreds and blankets were heaped on the wooden lids and from the smutty rafters hung all sorts of dust-covered rags, jackets, overcoats, jerseys and whatever you may care to name. There was even a bicycle suspended with a wire, and two electric guitars. A smell of rotting food, sweat and the coal-smoke from the miniature stove stifled the air. Suddenly the naked bulb blinked alive and shed a light that made the room eerie, casting darkness in the corners.

'This is my bed, majita, make yourselves at home,' Somdali said and took off his jacket which he added to the clothes hanging near his 'bed'. We sat on the kist, Joe settling down beside me without showing any sign of surprise at the unspeakable living conditions. As I said, he was used to personal visits to the hostel. As for me, I was shocked.

After hanging his coat Somdali turned to greet the others. When we had come in they had just glanced at us and resumed their conversation. The African way of entering the company of others is for the newcomer to announce himself by greeting first. It is the 'umthakathi' (wizard) who arrives unseen. 'Sonibonani ekhaya (Good evening at home).'

'Awu, Somdali! You are back from esiLungwini. Athin'ama Bhunu? (What do the Boers say?)' They greeted him enthusiastically, as if they were noticing Somdali for the first time.

'What can they say, but continue to give us the scorpion's bite? Er, madoda, I have brought you a friend of mine that I work with . . . ' and he introduced me, starting with my first name and inserting the possessive preposition 'ka' before my surname. 'Well, this skelm Joe you know.'

One man held my hand and introduced himself. The others followed suit. I counted eight of them. Somdali came to sit next to me. 'You seem not to be at ease, my friend. Relax. You must be shocked by this stable when you see it for the first time. You'll get used to it, mfowethu.'

'Let's hope I will. But I doubt it,' I replied.

'This is our reward for working for the whites. They don't care how you live, as long as you turn up for work the following day,' said Somdali bitterly.

'They don't know. Otherwise they'd be ashamed of themselves,' I answered, thinking that no normal human being could consciously tolerate other people living that way.

'You think so?' Somdali seemed to disagree. 'What do you say of the very idea of building such a place, of removing men from their families after taking their livestock and what little land they had, and burying them in filth? Is that not meant to kill a man's pride in himself?'

I understood what Somdali meant. Before I could make that known in so many words he went on, with gall in his voice, 'If you take a man, a married man, from his wife it's tantamount to castrating him. A bullock is castrated to make it strong for labour purposes.'

'Yes, Somdali is right, ndodana (son).' It was old Khuzwayo, the grey-head sexagenarian Somdali had told me was like a father to them in their labour camp dens. 'Come nearer boy, I want to see you when I talk to you. Fana, sit yourself somewhere.' Fana stood up from the tin of paint he was sitting on. I replaced him beside the old man. The little stove was beginning to glow on the sides, a solitary pot filling its whole face and boiling furiously. The heat-wave was too much for me, so I shifted a little backward. The old man also positioned himself to look directly into my face. His Bushman-like features were attractive.

'Ya, ndodana ka . . . ? (Yes, son of?)' I answered him by finishing his greeting with my name. I did this twice before he heard me well. 'You defend abeLungu by saying they do not know? Now, my boy, tell me this: is this – the way we live, all of us blacks – our rightful legacy from the ancestors, or from Tixo who made heaven and earth?' He paused, looking at me. 'Or is it an apportionment that our conquerors think fit for us?'

'It is the latter, baba,' I replied without certainty, as I did not know what old Khuzwayo was getting around to. Everybody was listening. Doubtless they were all sensitive about the question of their status in the social stratification. They knew that a man could not sink lower down than they were, and the only way they could let off steam was by damning the system that degraded them. To them every white man stood for the forces that held them down with their faces in the muck of the hostel. In other words, their hopelessness bred a volcanic racism.

'That is right, my boy. You are following my words well. You see, they have laid claim to everything that you can turn your eyes to see. If everything had gone according to their desires they would have owned even us black people, to till the soil for them until the end of the world. But one human being cannot be owned by another. And since they are unable to own us, all they lack is a way to justify genocide. You can remove a man from the face of a piece of paper, scratch his name out and pretend that he does not exist, but you cannot remove him physically from the face of the earth without murdering him. For he is born here and so he dies here, fighting perhaps for the one square metre he owns in the world. For man was created by Nkulunkulu so that he might avail himself of that which umhlaba (earth) was made to give. Man was not created to divide for others that which is bad and to keep that which is good for himself. We all die in the end and leave everything as we found it when we were born.'

'Ya. The old man is right, mfowethu. No man is ordained to determine the fate of another. If he has, by some vile means, usurped the other's right to self-determination, then peace is disturbed. When peace is disturbed it is always a sign that someone who is dissatisfied is trying to get his rightful share from the world.' So said the man who had introduced himself as Bongani. I had tried to vindicate their oppressors and they assailed me from all directions.

I attempted to manoeuvre out of the spot I was in by explaining exactly what I had meant. 'What I intended to say was that the majority of whites do not know how you live because the whole rotten situation is camouflaged. The harsh enforcement of the inhumane laws that result in such conditions produces a calm of sorts, and this deceives them into thinking that everybody is satisfied except a few anarchists and agitators who must be weeded out. I think that the people are very apt when they refer to the police as "the camouflage" these days, because they camouflage black vexations with brute violence – and whenever there is a marked "calm" the whites are made to believe that all is peaceful. Whatever the cause of strife was, it has been settled and things are under control. The means by which this has been brought about are made light of, or deliberately and unscrupulously suppressed. A counterfeit peace is produced for them. They don't know what is going on "in their own backyard". That's what I meant.'

They seemed satisfied with my clarification, for no one attacked me after that.

Old Khuzwayo had taken to me. He slapped my shoulder amicably. 'You know, my son, you know. For a moment I thought that you were lost. Your explanation takes my mind back to the end of the Second World War. When the time came to ask the German nation why they had allowed people to be decimated in front of their eyes, they shamefully claimed that they had not known what was taking place until it was too late to do anything about it but stand up in defence of the sovereignty of their country. It did not help them any because everybody was against them. Their country was divided among their enemies because they allowed some fanatics to control their destiny. Blind obedience and gullibility are suicidal.'

I stayed longer than I had intended with Somdali and his mates. Bongani, who had been cooking – boiling an assortment of old vegetables into a thick soup – cut our topic short by announcing supper. Each man dived to where he kept his spoon and, at the drop of an eyelid, I was alone in front of the small stove. Even Khuzwayo had been surprisingly swift for his age. Joe came from the shadows to sit on the old man's plastic milk crate.

I saw why they had been so fast in their reactions to Bongani's call. They all ate together from the steaming pot. Three loaves of bread were placed on a sheet of paper that was spread on the dusty floor. They broke pieces from the loaves and scooped from the pot with their spoons. You could see that they were racing, each wanting to down more soup and pieces of bread than the next man. I don't wish to insult those brothers of ours, but have you ever seen the deadly excitement of a predator after making a killing? They even fought over space.

'Damn it, Fana, don't push!' snarled one of them.

'Give me space. How do you think I'll reach the pot?' retorted Fana with a full mouth.

'You're cheeky, you Fana. One day I'll beat it out of you,' the other one threatened.

Old Khuzwayo ruled for peace. 'Awu, don't fight over food like puppies, boys. You're spoiling everybody's meal. And while you're busy fighting, the food is getting finished.'

Supper over, Somdali sent Fana to buy him 'mai-mai' from the opposite dormitory. Bongani went to wash the pot and the spoons in the sink outside. Another one took a broom to sweep where they had been eating. 'No, boy. You'll sweep tomorrow morning. The dust will take time to settle down,' said Somdali, preventing him. He collected only the crumbs they had made. There was a certain organisation in the way they lived. The young ones did the chores.

When Bongani returned he removed the guitars from their perches and gave one to Fana. They connected the guitars to an amplifier with a PM 10 and strummed for some seconds. Then, with extraordinary dexterity, they played a moving 'mbaqanga' (a fast African beat that is still a favourite with country people). The sound of an electric guitar in that gloomy lair, with the men sitting around the small stove and listening sorrowfully to the melodious twangs, the overhanging dust-covered rags, the bicycle, the shadows cast by the dim, stained light bulb, mesmerised me in a way which I fail to find words to describe. Somdali was drinking his beer in slow sips. He passed the can to the next man, who took a few draughts and also passed it on. If you did not want to drink you gave the can to the man beside you. The music paused while Bongani and Fana drank. They started another song immediately after that.

'What's the time, Somdali?' I asked, thinking that at home they would be wondering why I had not returned from work. I was three hours late already.

'I don't know, my friend. You want to go now? Madoda, any of you got a watch?' None had, so one of the younger men had to go and ask the time in the opposite house, and bring another can of beer.

'Yes, ndoda, I should be running away before my people decide to go looking for me at the police-stations.' It was after nine. I bade everybody good-night and stood to go. Joe did the same. Somdali took us out. 'So you've seen where I stay, my friend. Hope you come by yourself when you've got time. So long.'

'Sweet, Somdali. See you tomorrow morning,' I said, and we parted.

As we came out of the gaping fence onto the highway, I remarked about our visit to Joe.

'You know, Joe, I've never spent such a long time in the hostel. Jesus, man, these people live like animals. To travel the whole distance from where they come from to stay like this!'

'Ya. It's bad, sonny. Think of the many other such places in Soweto alone. How many are there? Let's see – it's this one, Dube, Nhlazane, Merafe, Nancefield,' counted Joe.

'And Diepkloof. All about the same size. Hundreds of thousands of disgruntled men, leaving hundreds of thousands of starving families in the so-called homelands. That's not counting us location people, because we're not much better off than the hostel residents except in that we are allowed a temporary sojourn with our families.'

'Not counting the rest of South Africa either. It's not only Johannesburg. All over the country there are people who have uprooted from normal family life to slave in the cities. Take Somdali's bitterness and multiply it about twenty million times and see if you don't arrive at a very sad and volcanic state of affairs,' said Joe, and I silently agreed with him.

At home I thought about the hostel before I dozed off. The more I recalled all the details of my visit the more I felt depressed. My last thought was that the world was still too far from perfection and that those who hoped for world peace at this point in time were building castles in the air.

It would not be the last time I visited Somdali. Something about the dirt and the desolation of the hostel attracted me strongly towards the place. Instead of going there for vice, like many of the location people, I went there out of sympathy with my friends and maybe that is why I felt so strongly about the way they lived. What's more, sharing the emptiness of the life of Somdali and his comrades filled, for me, the listless evenings on street corners, outside the shops and at the station. Every day we gave vent to our feelings and it was amazing how therapeutic the exercise was for me. It gave me the satisfaction of knowing much more about life than those who prefer the escapism of artificiality.

As I continued going there, I discovered that song was the only solace of those lonely people. At least two days a week they sang traditional choral music. After supper they would assemble in the adjoining closet and start singing with the conscientiousness of a stage group rehearsing for a fête. Hearing this, Mbobo and others would come from the opposite house and join in the singing. Some of the songs were performed with graceful dances, so elegantly carried out that I wondered where they could all have learnt the same paces. When they sang, it was from the core of their souls, their eyes glazed with memories of where they had first sung those lyrics; and interruptions were not tolerated. Sometimes I was so moved by their music that I yearned to join them, and because I did not know the songs I sailed away in my mind for paradises that I conjured up, where people sang their troubles away. After an evening of invigorating talk and untainted African traditional song I went away feeling as if I had found treasure in a graveyard. Those men might be buried there in the labour camps, but they are still people and, because they live in the throes of debasement, human adaptability has given them a most simple and practical approach to life, and none of the illusions of people who live comfortable lives or strive only for that throughout their time on earth, never achieving it but ending up drowning their frustrations in the pleasures of the flesh, half-immersed in intoxicants and half out of their minds half the time, until their humanity rots inside them. I would rather depend on a poor man for help, because a rich man, never having known hunger himself, will let you go away with an empty stomach.

The weekends were most exciting. They made me think of words I heard from a friend (I don't know where he picked them up). He would look at some of the people we worked with, who came from the rural areas and say, 'You can take the man out of the country, but you can never take the country out of the man.' On Friday the dreariness was stirred by a din that reached a crescendo on Sunday afternoon.

A typical weekend went like this: after looking in at home on Friday, I would go up to the hostel in the company of Joe or some of the guys who went there to augment their scanty paypackets with Soweto's favourite game of chance, shooting craps (dice). Somdali was a loyal worshipper of Bacchus. I would find him sitting like a lord in the shadows of his kist with two or three bottles of beer between his legs, the rest of a whole crate inside the multi-purpose 'bed'. When I came in he would greet me like a long-lost friend, as if we had not been together only an hour or so before.

'Aah, son of my mother! You came just in time. Borrow a mug from one of our brothers here and let us drink to our ancestors. Bongani, give him something to drink with.'

'Here, Somdali. You're drinking the sweat of your brow? Is this what you have been working for, the whole week?' I would reply jokingly, and accept the mug that Bongani handed to me.

'Of course – what do you think? It's Friday today; everybody drinks white man's beer and feels rich. Come on, use your mouth for what it should be used now, not for preaching.'

When Joe was with me, he did not wait to be invited, but took a container and gulped down as much as he could before Somdali protested that he was drinking as if it was his last day on earth.

Meanwhile, the game would be warming up in the main room. 'Five I do, five I do . . . Eê, pop! Eê, six three!' we would hear them singing out with great gusto. On that evening the stove would burn itself to ashes with no one tending it. Fridays they did not dine together. Everyone ate an almost substantial meal in one of the city 'chesanyamas' and returned to the hostel replete. Old Khuzwayo never returned at weekends because of the boisterousness, which was too much for his aged nerves. He slept in the sky slums on the roof of the Golden City. When we felt that the game was hot enough, we went in for the gambit. Sometimes we won and at other times we lost, but mostly we lost. The foolish lost their whole pay envelopes there and it was such a pity to watch them begging to be advanced more money, only to lose that as well. Depending on the amount of money involved, it was possible for the game to last the whole night. The winners never hung around the game long, but went off to drink their crumpled scoops in one of the countless haunts of vice. When you are poor there is no form of entertainment that you can afford to drown your misfortunes in besides over-indulgence of one kind or another.

At Msomi's you got everything: cigarettes, dagga, any concoction you wanted, and the profligate women whose sole source of income was peddling themselves to the famished hostel men. The latter were only too eager to part with a little hard-earned cash for the company of anything in skirts, no matter what she was like. Msomi's traffic in vice was booming and there was no fear of interference from the police, any sign of whom in the hostel invoked among the inhabitants a primordial bloodlust. Stoning and hacking to death of 'sellout intruders', as they referred to them, occurred from time to time.

When it got late I went home or somewhere else in the location. The difference was striking. In the location the presence of womenfolk and children contributed a certain amount of warmth and a reason for living; a man's delight is a loving woman and growing children.

Saturday morning was always a drab spectacle. Many woke up with a whole day to themselves. Before the beerhall was destroyed, everybody swarmed there to sink what had remained of their Friday earnings in beer. There was nothing else they could do. When the bar went up in flames the Msomis saw a chance to go into business supplying their hostel mates with debauchery. However, even before that, as soon as the sun surfaced in the east on Saturdays, everybody came out of their lairs to soak up the mild morning beams. They made me think of a plague-stricken concentration camp although I had never seen one. That is why when I learnt of Auschwitz, the Nazi camp in Poland, I simply dubbed the hostel 'our Auschwitz'. Grim-looking men sat or stood against the wall drinking from tins at every house. Some did their washing at the troughs and others clustered together playing dice. Door-to-door merchants had their colourful goods draped over their shoulders and arms with the rest of their stocks in bulging paper bags. The clothing they sold ranged from men's underwear to overcoats, and even female garments which were bought and locked away until such time as the buyer took them home to present to his family. The street vendors would be preparing their makeshift shops to start selling everything from sheep entrails to chicken pieces that hummed with green flies, while the rib-cages of mongrels kept themselves at a safe salivating distance. As the day got older, the tempo would increase to a fast drunken frenzy until the night came to cover it all up.

Then, on Sunday, a sleeping social consciousness, underlined by a strong traditional inclination, showed itself. The men drank together according to their places of origin. Don't mistake this for a reflection of tribalism. It was only their recollection of how they used to spend their Sundays in the different country areas they came from – not necessarily Sundays, but those days that were traditionally set aside for social gatherings where the young and nimble entertained their elders with dances to the sound of tom-toms and songs which were sung by the great-grandfathers and handed down from father to son.

Sunday morning was no different from a Saturday except that you could see that something important was being prepared for. The few converts wore their 'Zionist' uniforms of blue on snow-white and clutched their staffs and bibles to join other worshippers in the locations. Groups of dancers wearing distinctive garb left the hostel singing, whistling, waving their dancing sticks and pausing at every busy street corner to treat the location people to some dancing and singing. The disappointing part was that many location people regarded it as backwardness. 'You'll never see whites doing such things where they stay,' they would say. Why should the whites do them? Mos they're not black like I am. And who told you that your whites are the measuring standard of right and wrong? I wanted to ask the critics but chose not to because I knew their minds had been stolen from them in order to 'civilize' them. Other groups came from other hostels to ours in the same fashion, their sorrows forgotten for a while.

At two in the afternoon, after preparing themselves, the groups went out to the 'market-place' (an open space near where the beerhall used to be and where most of the vendors sold their assortments of goods). The first sound of the tom-tom and the flutes of the Pedis brought people to watch from all corners of the hostel.

The baPedi formed a line and swayed gracefully from side to side, blowing their flutes in typical fashion while others played the drums of diminishing size, the biggest of them made out of paraffin drums and the smallest the size of a gallon of paint.

A most exciting entertainment was provided by the foot-stomping Zulus. They dressed in traditional attire and danced to the sound of a single drum with amazing rhythm. They sat or knelt in formations of four, five or six, according to the size of the competing groups, clapping hands in unison with the drum and singing or humming in high spirits. They kept themselves going with long draughts from a big black clay vessel which was refilled from large plastic containers. The competitors took the 'stage' like waves, those in front vigorously stomping the ground with their tyre sandals until you thought you could feel it vibrating. Their feet rose above their heads and came down thunderously. Endurance and physical fitness is basic to the African 'ballet', and a weakling does not waste his time going on the stage. As I say, the dance was performed with superb rhythm. If you missed a step you were penalized by having to leave the stage to await your partners, and your group lost points for that.

The drum, the clapping hands, the songs, shouts of 'Usuthu!' and the rising and falling legs went on and on, the muscular and wiry black bodies glistening with sweat until sunset, when the sun would lie on Meadowlands like a glowing half-circle, and the smoke from the chimneys would blanket the slumbering Soweto.

Njabulo Ndebele

THE MUSIC OF THE VIOLIN

Vukani was doing homework in his bedroom when voices in the living room slowly filtered into his mind. He lifted his head to look up, as if to focus his ears. No. He could not recognise the voices. Now and again the hum of conversation was punctuated with laughter. Then he grew apprehensive, the continuing conversation suddenly filling him with dread. He tried to concentrate on his work: 'Answer the following questions: How did the coming of the whites lead to the establishment of prosperity and peace among the various Bantu tribes? . . . ' But the peace had gone from his mind. The questions had become a meaningless task. Instinctively, he turned round to look at his music stand at the foot of his bed. Yesterday he had practised some Mozart. Then he saw the violin leaning against the wall next to the stand. Would they come to interrupt him? He felt certain they would. He stood up, thinking of a way of escape.

There was another peal of laughter from the living room, and Vukani wondered again who the visitors were. As he opened the door slowly, he was met by another thunderous roar. Escape would be impossible.

He had to go through the living room and would certainly be called by his mother to be introduced to the visitors, and then the usual agony would follow. A delicate clink of cups and saucers told Vukani that the visitors had been served with tea. Another roar. His father and the male visitor were laughing. He knew now that the visitors were a man and a woman, but he did not recognise their voices. Growing curious, he opened the door by another inch or so, and saw the woman visitor, who sat close to where the passage to the bedrooms began. Vukani's mother, still in her white nursing uniform, sat close to the woman visitor in another heavily cushioned chair. They were separated by a coffee table.

'I couldn't make it at all to the meeting last Saturday,' said Vukani's mother.

'Which meeting?' asked the woman.

The men laughed again.

'Don't you laugh so loudly,' Vukani's mother shouted.

'You see,' Vukani's father was saying, 'I had caught the fellow by surprise, the way I like to catch them.'

'That's the only way to ensure that the work gets done,' said the other man.

'Indeed,' agreed Vukani's father.

'So?' asked the other man.

'So I said: "Show me the students' garden plots." I saw a twitch of anguish across his face. But he was a clever fellow, you see. He quickly recovered and said: "Of course Sir, of course, come along." So we went. There was a wilderness around the school. These bush schools: I wouldn't have been surprised if a python had stopped us in our tracks. So, after about two hundred yards of walking, and all the wilderness around us, I began to wonder. So I said to this teacher:

"Mr Mabaso," – that was the fellow's name – "these plots, they are quite far, aren't they?" "We're just about there, Sir," he said.'

'Man alive!' exclaimed the other man. 'This story is getting hot. Let me sip one more time.' There was silence while the man sipped his tea. Vukani's mother also lifted her cup to her lips. The women were now listening too.

'So,' continued Vukani's father, 'we walked another two hundred yards and I turned to look at the man. "We're just about there, Sir." '

Everybody laughed. 'You see, the fellow was now sweating like a horse.'

'So?' asked the woman visitor, laughing some more. She was wiping her eyes with a tissue.

'Then this fellow, Mabaso, shows me a hill about a mile away and says: "We're going there, to that hill, Sir, the plots are behind it. You see, Sir, I figured that since the wind normally hits the hill on the side we are looking at now, I should have the plots on the leeward side to protect the plants." What bosh!'

There was more laughter and the male visitor said, in the middle of it: 'Beatrice, give me some Kleenex, please.' His wife stood up and disappeared from Vukani's view. She returned. Vukani heard the blowing of a nose. It must have been the man.

'Please don't laugh, fellow Africans,' said Vukani's father. 'The man is a genius. What's this poem by the English poet? The man blushes unseen in the wilderness. He knew I would not go any further. So I really have no proof that there were no garden plots.'

'Of course there weren't any,' asserted Vukani's mother.

'Of course there weren't,' everybody agreed.

'You school inspectors,' said the male visitor, 'have

real problems with these bush schools.'

'You haven't heard anything yet,' agreed Vukani's father. 'We just can't get it into these teachers' heads that we have to uplift the black nation. And we cannot do that through cheating and laziness. We will not develop self-reliance that way. That fellow was just not teaching the students gardening, and that is dead against government policy.' Vukani shut the door. In spite of himself, he had been amused by the story. He went back to the desk and tried to continue with the homework. He could not. What about going out through the window? No. That would be taking things too far. He wondered where Teboho, his sister was. Probably in her bedroom.

Teboho and their mother were getting involved in too many heated exchanges these days. Their mother tended to make too many demands on them. Vukani wished he could go and talk to Teboho. They had grown very close. Then he suddenly became frantic again and went to the door. He had to escape. When he opened the door, slightly again, it was the woman named Beatrice who was talking.

'You just don't know what you missed, you,' she was saying. The men laughed again.

'Please, you men!' appealed Vukani's mother. But they laughed once again.

'Do you want us to leave you and go to the bedroom?' threatened Vukani's mother. 'And you know if we go in there we won't come out.'

'Peace! Peace!' shouted Vukani's father. 'Peace, women of Africa!'

Then he lowered his voice as he continued to talk to the other man.

'What have I missed?' asked Vukani's mother, eagerly.

'Well, you just don't know what you've missed,' said Mrs Beatrice, pulling the bait away from the fish.

'Please don't tease me.'

'I want to do just that,' said Mrs Beatrice, clapping once and sitting forward in her chair, her legs thrust underneath. She kept on pulling her tight-fitting skirt down over her big knees. But after each effort, the skirt slipped back, revealing the knees again.

'You women are on again about the Housewives' League,' interrupted Vukani's father.

'Day in and day out,' supported the other man.

'Of course yes!' said Mrs Beatrice with emphatic pride.

'Forget about these men,' pleaded Vukani's mother, 'and give me a pinch of the story.'

'Mother-of-Teboho, you really missed,' Mrs Beatrice started. 'A white woman came all the way from Emmarentia, a high-class exclusive suburb, to address the meeting on Jewish recipes. Came all the way to Soweto for that. It was wonderful.'

'Was it not Mrs Kaplinsky?'

'As if you knew!'

'Eh, please, give me! Give me!' shouted Vukani's mother with great excitement, clapping her hands repeatedly. 'I'm fetching my pen, I'm fetching my pen. Give me those recipes.' But she did not leave to go and fetch her pen.

'I'm selling them, dearie. Business first, friendship after.' They laughed.

'*Ei*! Women and food!' exclaimed the other man.

'What! We cook for you,' retorted his wife.

'Exactly,' concurred Vukani's mother. 'More tea?'

'No thanks, dearie.'

'Hey you men, more tea?' But the men were already back to their conversation. Vukani's father answered while laughing, suddenly coming into Vukani's view as he brought his empty cup to the coffee table that separated the women.

'No thanks,' he was saying, 'No thanks . . . he he he hehehehe . . . that was a good one . . . no thanks . . . what a good one.' Then he took out a handkerchief from the pocket of his trousers, wiped his eyes, wiped his whole face, and then wiped his lips. 'A jolly good evening, tonight.' Then he went back to his chair, disappearing from Vukani's view.

'Thanks for the tea,' said the other man, blowing his nose.

'Teboho!' called Vukani's mother. 'Please come and clear up here!'

Teboho appeared carrying a tray. She had on denim jeans and a loose blouse.

'That was a nice cup of tea, Teboho,' said the other man. Teboho smiled shyly. 'When are you going back to varsity?'

'We have six more weeks,' replied Teboho.

'You are lucky to have children who are educating themselves, dearie,' said Mrs Beatrice.

'Oh, well,' said Vukani's mother shrugging her shoulders, as Teboho disappeared into the kitchen. There was silence.

'Sometimes these South African Jews sicken me,' said the other man reflectively.

'Why?' the two women asked.

'Well, they're hypocrites! I mean look, they say they were killed left and right by the Germans, but here they are helping the Boers to sit on us.'

'How can you say such a thing?' asked his wife. 'People like Mrs Kaplinsky are very good friends of ours. Some of her best friends are Africans.'

'Because she gives you recipes?'

'Food, my dear husband, belongs to mankind, not just to one race.'

'Yes, exactly,' agreed Vukani's mother, 'like art, literature and things. Completely universal.'

'Well . . . ' said the man, but he did not pursue the matter further.

'In fact this reminds me,' said Vukani's mother with sudden enthusiasm, her eyes glittering, 'instead of sitting here talking politics, we should be listening to some music. Have you heard my son play? He plays the violin. A most wonderful instrument!'

'Yes,' said Vukani's father, 'you know . . . '

Vukani swiftly shut the door, shutting out the living room conversation with an abruptness that brought him sharply to himself as he moved to the centre of the room. He began to feel very lonely and noticed that he was trembling. It was coming now. He looked at the history homework on the desk, then looked at the reading lamp with its circular light which seemed to be baking the open pages of the books on the desk with its intensity, while the books looked as if they were waiting for that delicate moment when they would burst into flame. Then he thought of Doksi his friend. He wondered where he was and what he was doing at that moment. Friday evening? Probably watching his father cutting the late evening customers' hair and trimming it carefully while he murmured a song as always. Doksi had said to Vukani one day that when he was a grown-up, he would like to be a barber like his father. And Doksi did love hair. Vukani remembered his favourite game: a weekly ritual of hair burning. Every Saturday afternoon Doksi would make a fire out in the yard and when it was burning steadily, toss knots of hair into it. The hair would catch fire with a crackling brilliance that always sent him into raptures of delight. He never seemed to mind the smell of the burning hair. One Saturday after his bonfire Doksi had said, while making the sign of the cross over the smoking fire: 'When God had finished burning hair he thought that it was good.' Vukani had playfully accused him of sacrilege. But Doksi, suddenly looking serious, had said, 'Dead things catch fire.' Now Vukani was suddenly fascinated by a desire to see the books on the desk aflame. Perhaps he should lower the lamp, bringing it closer to the books. It was a silly idea but he lowered the lamp all the same. But the papers shone defiantly with a sheen. It was futile. Then he saw his violin again, and felt the sensation of fear deep in his breast.

He looked at the violin with dread, as something that could bring both pain and pleasure at once. It was like the red dress which Miss Yende, their class teacher in Standard Four, occasionally wore. She had once said to the class: 'When I wear this red dress, children, know that I shall not stomach any nonsense that day. Know that I shall expect sharp minds: I shall expect quick responses to my questions, and I shall expect absolute seriousness. And I shall use the stick with the vengeance of the God of the Old Testament.' That dress! It was a deep, rich velvety red that gave the impression that the dress had a flowery fragrance. Yet, because it also signalled the possibility of pain, it had a dreadful repulsiveness.

Vukani tried to brace himself for the coming of the visitors. It was always like that. Every visitor was brought to his room, where he was required to be doing his school work or practising on the violin.

Then he had to entertain these visitors with violin music. It was always an agonising nuisance to be an unwilling entertainer. What would happen if he should refuse to play that night? He knew what his mother would say. It was the same thing all the time. His eyes swept round the room. He was well provided for. There was the beautiful desk on which he did his work; bookshelves full of books, including a set of the *Encyclopaedia Britannica*; a reading lamp on the desk; two comfortable easy chairs; a wardrobe full of clothes; his own portable transistor radio; a violin and a music stand; a chest full of games: Monopoly, chess and many others. His mother never tired of telling him how lucky he was. 'There is not a single boy in the whole of Soweto, not even here in Dube, who has a room like yours. This room is as good as any white boy's. Isn't it exactly like Ronnie Simpson's? You yourself, you ungrateful boy, saw that room when we visited the Simpsons in Parktown North. Kaffir children! That's what. Always ungrateful!'

What did all this really mean to him when it brought so much pain? Vukani remembered what teacher Maseko had said at assembly one morning: 'Children, I would rather be a hungry dog that runs freely in the streets, than a fat, chained dog burdened with itself and the weight of the chain. Whenever the white man tells you that he has made you much better off than Africans elsewhere on this continent, tell him he is lying before God!' There were cheers that morning at assembly, and the children had sung the morning's hymn with a feeling of energetic release:

I will make you fishers of men
Fishers of men
Fishers of men
I will make you fishers of men
If you follow me.

Three weeks later, teacher Maseko was fired. The

Principal had made the announcement at morning assembly. He spoke in Afrikaans, always. Concluding the announcement, he said: 'Children, a wandering dog, that upsets garbage bins and ejects its dung all over the place, is a very dangerous animal. It is a carrier of disease and pestilence, and when you see it, pelt it with stones. What should you do to it?'

'Pelt it with stones!' was the sombre response of the assembled children that morning. Vukani had wondered whether teacher Maseko was that dog. But how could anybody pelt teacher Maseko with stones?

Vukani heard another roar of laughter from the living room. But why did his mother have to show off at his expense like this? That Friday, as on all Mondays, Wednesdays and Fridays, he had carried his violin to school. The other children at school never got used to it. It was a constant source of wonder and ridicule. 'Here's a fellow with a strange guitar!' some would say. Others would ask him to play the current township hits. It was so every day. Then one day his violin disappeared from class while he went out to the boys' toilet. He was met with stony faces when after school he pleaded for its return. Everybody simply went home and there was no sign of the violin. What would he say to his music teacher in town? What would he say to his mother? When he went out of the classroom, he found Doksi waiting for him. They always went home together, except on the days when Vukani had to go to town for his music lessons after school. 'Doksi,' he said, 'I can't find my violin. Somebody took it.'

'These boys of shit!' Doksi cursed sympathetically. He had not waited for details. He knew his friend's problem. 'Do you suspect anybody?'

'I can't say,' replied Vukani. 'The whole class

seems to have ganged up on me. There are some things that always bring them together.' 'Even Gwendoline?' asked Doksi, with a mischievous smirk on his face. Gwendoline was the frail, brilliant, beautiful girl who vied with Vukani for first position in class. Vukani had always told Doksi that he would like to marry that girl one day. And Doksi would always say: 'With you it's talk, talk all the time. Why don't you just go to this girl and tell her you love her? Just look at how she looks at you. She's suffering, man!'

'Look,' said Vukani, 'this is no time for jokes. My violin is lost.'

'The trouble with you, Vukani, is that you are too soft. I would never stand this nonsense. I'd just face the whole class and say, "Whoever took my violin is a coward. Why doesn't he come out and fight?" I'm sure it was taken by one of those big boys whom everybody fears. Big bodies without minds. They ought to be working in town. Just at school to avoid paying tax. But me, they know me. They know what my brothers would do. My whole family would come here looking for the bastards.' Most of the children had gone now. Only those whose turn it was to clean the classrooms remained.

'Let's go and tell the Principal,' suggested Vukani. The Principal was one of those Vukani had entertained one day in his bedroom. He was a friend of his father's. 'But maybe we shouldn't,' said Vukani, changing his mind.

'Let's go and find out from the girls sweeping your classroom,' suggested Doksi. They went back. The girls were singing loudly and the room was full of dust. 'Leave it to me,' said Doksi. There were four girls in there. Gwendoline and Manana were as old as

Doksi and Vukani. The other two girls, Topsana and Sarah were older. Much older.

'Hey, you girls!' shouted Doksi, squaring his shoulders and looking like a cowboy about to draw. 'Where is the bloody violin?' The bigger girls simply laughed.

'And who are you, toughie?' asked Sarah, pushing a desk out of the way for Topsana to sweep.

'Hey you, Vukani,' called Topsana, 'I want to soothe your heart. I've long been waiting for this moment. Come and kiss me.' The smaller girls giggled, and Vukani regretted that they had come back. 'I mean it,' said Topsana. 'I know who took your violin. It's safe. You'll find it at home. I made them promise to take it there. There now, I want my kiss. I want to kiss the inspector's son.'

Doksi turned to the younger girls, 'Hey you, what is the joke? What's there to laugh at?'

'Hha!' protested Manana, sweeping rather purposefully. 'We have a right to laugh.'

'I can show you a thing or two,' Doksi said. 'Punch you up or something.'

'Doksi,' appealed Vukani, 'please let's go.' Doksi clearly felt the need for retreat, but it had to be done with dignity. He addressed all the girls with a sweep of his hand, 'You are all useless. One of these days I'll get you. Come on, Vukani, let's go.'

The walk home for Vukani had been a long one. Better not to tell the parents. If Topsana had been telling the truth, then he should wait. Nobody asked him about the violin. But he would never forget the morning following that day when his mother stormed into his bedroom, black with anger. She had simply come in and pulled the blankets off him. She glared at him, holding the violin in one of her hands. Vukani had felt so exposed – as if his mother was about to hit him with the violin. It was very early in the morning. His mother was already dressed up in her uniform, ready to go to work. If she was on day duty, she had to leave very early for the hospital.

'Vukani!' she was shouting. 'What desecration is this? What ultimate act of ungratefulness is this? Is this to spite me? Is this an insult? Tell me before I finish you off!'

'What's happening, Dorcas?' Vukani saw his father entering the bedroom. 'Can you believe this? I found this violin on the doorstep outside as I was leaving for work. Can you believe this?'

'Vukani,' said his father. 'What on earth could have made you do such a thing?'

'I didn't put it there, *Baba,*' Vukani replied.

'Nonsense,' shouted his mother, 'you have the nerve to tell your parents a lie.'

'Wait a minute, dear, maybe we should hear what he has to say.' Vukani had nothing to say. The deep feeling of having been wronged could only find expression in tears. He heard the violin land next to him and he recoiled from its coldness. He also heard his mother leave, saying that he was crying because of his sins. She never knew what had happened.

But that had been a year ago. Today he had been humiliated again in public, and there were people in that living room who wanted to humiliate him again. Right inside his home. It was all because of this violin. The homework had made him forget the latest ordeal for a while. The homework was like a jigsaw puzzle; you simply looked for pieces which fitted. All the answers were there in the chapter. You just moved your finger up and down the page until you spotted the correct answer. There was no thinking involved. But now it was all gone. It was not South African History, the story of the coming of the white man he was looking at, he was now faced with the reality of the violin.

There was that gang of boys who always stood under the shop verandah at Maponya's shopping complex. They shouted, 'Hey, music man!' whenever he went past their 'headquarters' on his way home to Dube. That very Friday they had done more than shout at him from a distance. They had stopped him and humiliated him before all those workers who were returning from work in town.

'Hey, music man,' the one who seemed to be their leader had called. Vukani, as a rule, never answered them. He just walked on as if he had not heard anything. But that afternoon, as he was coming up from Phefeni station, and was turning round the corner to go down towards the AME church, it was as if the gang had been waiting for him.

'Hey, music man!' This time it was a chorus. Out of the corner of his eye, Vukani saw two boys detach themselves from the gang. He dare not turn to look. He had to act unconcerned. He tried to quicken his steps as imperceptibly as possible.

'Music man! Don't you know your name?' They were behind him now. Crossing the street had been no problem for them. They simply walked into the street and cars came to a screeching halt. They were the kings of the township. They just parted the traffic as Moses must have parted the waves of the sea. Vukani wanted to run but he was not going to give himself away. If he ran and they caught up with him, they could do a lot of harm to him. He had had that feeling of wanting to take advantage of something weaker than himself when he found a stray dog trying to topple a garbage bin. If the dog had stood its ground and growled, he would have been afraid. But the dog had taken to its heels, tail tucked between legs, and Vukani had been filled with the urge to run after the dog, catch it, and beat it to death. A fleeing impala must excite the worst destructive urge in a lion. Vukani had once seen a film in which a lion charged at a frightened impala. There had been a confidence in the purposeful strides of the lion, as if it felt this was just a game that would surely end with the bringing down of the prey.

A hand grabbed Vukani's collar behind and jerked him violently to a halt. The leader of the gang came round and faced him. He held Vukani by the knot of his tie. He was short but heavily built. He had puffed up cheeks with scars on them. His bloodshot eyes suggested the violence in him. He must have been four or five years older than Vukani.

'Spy!' the leader cursed, glaring at Vukani. 'So you are special! So we had to cross the street and risk death in order to talk to you. You don't know your name, music man? Every day we greet you nice and you don't answer. Because you think you are being greeted by shit. By scum, hey? Why, spy? Are we shit?'

'Ja! Just answer that,' said the fellow behind, 'are we shit?' Vukani tried to free his neck.

'Shit!' screamed the leader, 'we just wanted to talk to you nice-nice. That's all. We just wanted to dance to your music a little. Dance to your guitar a little. But no. You don't even look at us. Do we smell, music man? Do we smell?' There was a crowd of workers now who were watching the spectacle quietly.

'Shake him up, Bhuka!' was the chorus from the rest of the gang about thirty yards away at the shop.

'What are you rogues doing to this poor boy?' asked an old lady who had a bundle of washing on her head.

'Shut up!' said Bhuka. 'Go and do your white man's washing, he'll want it tomorrow.' Some of the crowd laughed at this.

'Dogs of the street! Don't talk like that to your mother. Whose child are you?'

'I'm your child,' said Bhuka with a certain flourish. This time more of the crowd laughed.

'He's the child of his mother!' said the boy behind Vukani. None laughed at that one. He was in the shadow of his leader.

'You are laughing,' said the woman, bravely addressing the crowds. 'You are laughing at this boy being harassed and you are laughing at me being insulted by these street urchins. I could be your mother and this could be your son. *Sies!* You rogues, just let decent people be.' The woman then left, taking Vukani's hopes with her. But she unsettled Bhuka slightly. He had to move his prey to safer ground. Too many lesser animals could be a disturbance. He tightened his grip around Vukani's tie, pulling him across the street towards the 'headquarters'. Vukani looked at the fist below his chin, and saw that it had a little sixth finger. There were two shining copper bangles round the wrist. Part of the crowd left but another part wanted to see the game to its end. They followed the trio to the shop. The gang had then completely encircled Vukani.

'Do you have a sister?' Bhuka snapped. Vukani had trouble breathing now. Bhuka realised this and loosened the grip. Vukani thought of Teboho at home. If she came here she would fight for him. 'I asked you a question. Do you have a sister?' Vukani nodded. 'Hey man, talk!'

'Is your voice precious? His master's voice!'

'Yes,' answered Vukani in a whisper.

'I want to fuck her. Do you hear? I want to eat her up thoroughly. Do you hear? Tell her that.' Bhuka then paused and jerked Vukani to and fro so that Vukani's head bobbed. He then stopped and glowered at Vukani. 'And what song will you play when I am on top of her?' There was a festive laugh from the crowd. Bhuka looked round in acknowledgement. 'Tell me now, can you play *Thoko Ujola Nobani?'* It was a current hit.

Vukani felt tears in his eyes. He blinked many times to keep them in. Why couldn't they just leave him alone. That day would be final, he would simply tell his parents that he did not want to play the violin again. If they still insisted, he would run away from home. 'Please, leave me alone,' he heard himself say.

'I asked you. Can you play *Thoko Ujola Nobani?'*

Vukani shook his head.

'Why, music man?'

'I'd have to see it written first. I can't just play it like that.'

'Next time you pass here you must know that song. And come with your sister!' Then he gave Vukani a shove in the chest, and Vukani reeled backwards and fell on his back. But he still held onto the violin. 'Next time we greet you nice-nice, you must greet nice-nice.' Vukani got up timidly and hurried away, glancing backwards occasionally. Somehow he felt relieved. It could have been worse. The stories he had heard about the violence of this gang were simply unbelievable. He felt deep inside him the laughter that followed him as he slunk away. Just after passing the AME church, he saw the rubbish heap that people had created at the corner and wished he was brave enough to throw the violin there.

'My son,' his mother had said one day when Vukani had complained about the harassment he suffered as a result of the violin, 'you should never yield to ignorance.'

'But maybe you should buy me a piano,' Vukani had said. 'I can't carry that in the street.'

'If Yehudi Menuhin had listened to fools, he wouldn't be the greatest living violinist. A violin you have, and a violin you shall play.'

That's how it had ended. But his agony had continued three times a week.

Then the door opened. 'Here he is!' said Vukani's mother as she led the visitors in. His father took the rear. Vukani blankly looked at the homework: Question Three: Who introduced the European type of education among the Bantu . . . ? But Vukani felt only the solid presence of four people behind him.

'Vuka,' said his mother, 'I did not hear you practise today.' It was not clear from her voice whether she was finding fault with her son or was just trying to say something by way of introduction. Vukani turned round and smiled sheepishly. They all looked at him as if they expected him to defend himself, their eyes occasionally going to the table as if to see what he was doing.

'Are you doing your homework, son?' asked the male visitor.

'*E*!'

'Good, hard-working boy!' he said, patting him on the shoulder. And Vukani felt in that hand the heaviness of condescension.

'He's a very serious-minded boy,' added his mother with obvious pride.

'You are very happy, dearie, to have a child who loves school,' commented Mrs Beatrice.

'And here is my Mozart's violin,' said Vukani's father, pointing at the violin against the wall. He took the case, opened it and took out the violin.

'Vuka!'

'Ma!'

'These visitors are the mother and father of Lauretta. Do you know her?'

'No, I don't think I do,' said Vukani, shaking his head.

'But you are at the same school together. Surely you know Lauretta, the daughter of Doctor Zwane? Stand up to greet them.'

Vukani then remembered the girl, who was well known at school for her brilliance. She was two classes ahead of Vukani. But Vukani wondered if she could beat Gwendoline. Vukani greeted the visitors and went back to his seat.

'Vuka, you will play the visitors something, won't you? What will you play us?' asked his mother. Vukani looked at the violin in his father's hands. He was explaining to Dr Zwane the various kinds of violins.

'This type,' he was saying, 'is very rare. You do not find it easily these days. Not at all.'

'It must have been very expensive,' observed Dr Zwane appreciatively, 'one can judge from its looks.'

'Five hundred and fifty rands down,' butted in Vukani's mother, 'made to specifications. You just tell them how you want it and they just make it. This is special.'

'One has to pay to produce a Mozart,' said Vukani's father with finality.

'We had Lauretta start on ballet recently,' said Mrs Zwane, as if suggesting that they were also doing their duty. 'I'm happy to note that she seems to be doing well. All these things have to be taught at school. You school inspectors have a duty to ensure that it happens.'

'Indeed,' agreed Vukani's father. 'But do you think the Boers would agree? Never. Remember they say Western Civilisation is spoiling us. So we have to cultivate the indigenous way of life.' The conversation was stopped by Vukani's mother.

'Okay now.' She clapped her hands. 'What will you play us?'

Vukani's father brought the violin to him. He took it with his visibly shaking hands. He saw the red, glowering eyes of Bhuka that afternoon. He heard the laughter of people in the streets. He remembered being violently shaken awake by his angry mother one morning. He remembered one of his dreams which came very frequently. He was naked in the streets and people were laughing. He did not know how he had come to be naked. It always occurred that way. He would be naked in the streets and people would be laughing. Suddenly he would reach home and his mother would scold him for bringing shame to the family. But the dream would always end with him leaving home and flying out into the sky with his hands as wings.

Vukani found that he had instinctively put the violin on his left shoulder. And when he became aware, he felt its irksome weight on him. What did people want of him? He did not want to play. He did not want to play. And for the second time that day, he felt the tears coming to his eyes and again he blinked repeatedly to keep them from flowing. This was the time.

'Mama!'

'Yes, son.' But Vukani did not go on.

His mother continued: 'Why don't you play some selections from Brahms? You know some extracts from his only violin concerto? Perhaps Mozart? Yes Mozart. I know that sometimes one is in the mood for a particular composer. What about Liszt? Where are your music books? There is something on the music stand: what is it? Ahh! it's the glorious beautiful Dvorak. Tum tee tum!' She shook her head, conducting an imaginary orchestra. 'Come up and play some of this Dvorak.'

Vukani wanted to shout, but his throat was completely dry. He wanted to sink into the ground. He tried to swallow. It was only dryness he swallowed and it hurt against the throat. Standing up would be agonising. His strength and resistance were all gathered up in his sitting position. All that strength would be dissipated if he stood up. And he would feel exposed, lonely and vulnerable. The visitors and his parents soon noticed that there was something amiss.

'What is it, Vuka?' asked his mother. 'Is there something wrong?'

'Nothing wrong, ma.' He had missed his opportunity. Why did he fear? Why did he not act decisively for his own good? Then he felt anger building up in him, but he was not sure whether he was angry with himself or with his parents — together with the visitors whose presence was now forcing him to come to terms with his hitherto unexpressed determination to stop doing what brought him suffering. At that moment there was a dull explosion from the kitchen, of something massive suddenly disintegrating into pieces. There was silence for a while. Then Vukani's mother muttered: 'The bloody street girl has done it again.' And she stormed out of the bedroom. Her voice could be heard clearly in the kitchen: '*Awu*, Lord of the heavens! My . . . my expensive . . . my precious . . . my expensive . . . this girl has done it again. Teboho, has the devil got into you again? Do you have to break something every day?' Vukani's mother was now shrieking with anger. 'Do you know what? Maybe you don't. I gave Mrs Willard three hundred rands to bring me this set from Hong Kong when she went there on holiday. And I have told you countless times that you should be extra careful when you handle those dishes. Such care doesn't cost much. How many households in the whole of Johannesburg, white and black, can boast of owning such a set – a genuine set? But you, you refuse to appreciate that. Don't just stand there . . . '

'Mama, can you please just stop that,' said Teboho in a voice that sounded urgently restrained.

'Is that how you are talking to me?'

Then Teboho's voice seemed to lose all restraint: 'You don't want to listen to anybody, you just come in shouting.' The voice was loud and defiant.

'Is that how they teach you to talk to your parents at the university?'

'Mama, that is not the point.'

'Are you arguing with me?'

'The point is that you have been showing more interest in your dishes and your furniture than in your children.'

'What?'

'I'm not going to say anything more.'

'Slut! That's what you are! What decent girl would talk like that to her mother?'

'Mama, will you stop.' There was the sound of a

slap. Another explosion. Lighter this time – perhaps a glass.

'I'm leaving this house,' screamed Teboho. Then the door to her room banged shut, rattling some cutlery. Vukani's father was about to leave for the kitchen when he met his wife at the door. She grinned at the visitors.

'I'm sorry for that unfortunate diversion. Children can be destructive. Since Teboho went to that university in the north, she has come back with some very strange ideas. Opposes everything. Defiant. Yesterday she said I was a slave of the things I bought; that the white man had planned it that way. To give us a little of everything so that we can so prize the little we have that we completely forget about the most important things in life, like our freedom. I won't have that nonsense in my house. Fancy, doing all that rubbish when the visitors are here. I've had enough. I felt I had to remind that girl that I was her parent. I wonder what all this showing-off is for?'

'One can never know with children, dearie,' observed Mrs Zwane.

'Indeed!' said her husband.

'Well, Vuka,' said Vukani's father, 'can you heal our broken spirits?'

'Yes,' agreed his mother. 'We have been waiting for too long.'

Vukani thought of his sister. He wanted to go to her. They were very lonely. Their parents disapproved of some of their friends. Even Doksi. His mother had said he should have friends of his own station in life. What would a barber's son bring him? This had brought Vukani and Teboho very close. He decided then that he would not let his sister down. But could he? He thought of smashing the violin against the wall and then rushing out of the house. But where would he go? Who did he know nearby? The relatives he knew lived very far away. He did not know them all that well anyhow. He remembered how envious he would be whenever he heard other children saying they were going to spend their holidays with their relatives. Perhaps with a grandmother or an uncle. He remembered that he had once asked his mother when they were ever going to visit his uncle. His mother had not answered him. But then there was that conversation between his parents.

'By the way,' asked Vukani's mother, 'when did you say your sister would be coming?'

'Next month.' There was a brief silence and then his father continued, 'Why do you ask? I have been telling you practically every day.'

'I was just asking for interest's sake.'

'Well,' said the father, putting down the *Daily Mail* and picking up the *Star*, 'I just feel there is more to the question than casual interest.'

'You think so?'

'Yes, I think so.' There was silence.

'Relatives,' the mother came out, 'can be a real nuisance. Once you have opened the door, they come trooping in like ants. We cannot afford it these days. Not with the cost of living. These are different times. Whites saw this problem a long time ago. That is why they have very little time for relatives. The nuclear family! That's what matters. I believe in it. I've always maintained that. If relatives want to visit, they must help with the groceries. There I'm clear, my dear. Very clear.'

Vukani's father had said something about 'whites are whites; blacks are blacks' but Vukani's aunt never came. Nobody ever said anything about her. Doksi liked to say: 'It's nice to have many relatives. Then when you are in trouble at home, you can always hide with one of them. And your father will go from relative to relative looking for you. When he finds you, he will be all smiles trying to please the relatives.'

'Vukani!' called his mother. 'We are still waiting, will you start playing now.'

Vukani stood up slowly and walked round to the music stand. Then he faced his mother and something yielded in him.

'Ma, I don't want to play the violin any more.' There was a stunned silence. Vukani's mother looked at her husband, a puzzled expression on her face. But she quickly recovered.

'What?' she shouted.

'I don't want to play the violin any more.' Vukani was surprised at his steadiness.

'This is enough!' screamed his mother. 'Right now . . . right now. You are going to play that violin right now.'

'Now you just play that instrument. What's going on in this house?'

His father's voice put some fear into him.

'Wait, dearie,' pleaded Mrs Zwane. 'Maybe the boy is not well.'

'Beatrice,' answered Vukani's mother, 'it's nothing like that. We are not going to be humiliated by such a little flea. Play, cheeky brute!'

'Today those boys stopped me again.' Vukani attempted to justify his stand.

'Who?' shrieked his mother, 'those dogs of the street? Those low things?'

'What's bothering him?' asked Dr Zwane. Vukani's mother explained briefly. Then turning towards her husband she said, 'As I told you the other day, he keeps complaining that people laugh at him because he plays the violin.'

'Jealousy,' shouted Mrs Zwane. 'Plain jealousy. Jealousy number one. Nothing else. Township people do not want to see other Africans advance.'

'Dear,' answered Vukani's mother, 'you are showing them a respect they do not deserve. If you say they are jealous, you make them people with feelings. No. They do not have that. They are not people; they are animals. Absolutely raw. They have no respect for what is better than they. Not these. They just trample over everything. Hey, you, play that instrument and stop telling us about savages.'

Vukani trembled. He felt his head going round now. He did not know what to do to escape from this ordeal. The tears came back, but this time he did not stop them. He felt them going down his cheeks and he gave in to the fury in him: 'I do not want to play . . . I do not want to play . . . not any more . . . ' Then he choked and could not speak further. But what he had already said had carried everything he felt deep inside him. He felt free. There was a vast expanse of open space deep inside him. He was free. He could fly into the sky. Then he heard Dr Zwane say: 'How difficult it is to bring up a child properly in Soweto! To give them culture. Black people just turn away from advancement.'

Those words seemed to build a fire in Vukani's mother. They had sounded like a reflection on her. She let go at Vukani with the back of her hand. Vukani reeled back and fell on the bed letting the violin drop to the floor. It made no noise on the carpet. Vukani's mother lifted him from the bed and was about to strike him again when Teboho rushed into the bedroom and pulled her mother away from her brother.

'Ma! What are you doing? What are you doing?' she was screaming.

'Are you fighting me?' shrieked her mother. 'You laid a hand on your mother. Am I bewitched?'

'You never think of anybody else, just yourself.'

'Teboho,' called her father. 'Don't say that to your mother.'

'Please, dearie, please,' appealed Mrs Zwane, 'there is no need for all this. How can you do this to your children?'

'*Sies*! What disgraceful children! I am a nursing sister, your father is an inspector of schools. What are you going to be, listening to savages? You cannot please everybody. Either you please the street, in which case you are going to be a heap of rubbish, something to be swept away, or you please your home which is going to give you something to be proud of for the rest of your useless life!'

'Dorcas! That's enough now!' She looked at her husband with disbelief, a wave of shock crossing her face. Then she turned towards the door and went to her bedroom, banging the door violently. There was bitter sobbing in the main bedroom. Then it turned into the wail of the bereaved.

Miriam Tlali

DEVIL AT A DEAD END*

She arrived at Ficksburg Station at 2.30 p.m. It would be a good half-hour before the Durban train to Bethlehem arrived. The thought made her smile. She was early. Her mother would have congratulated her for the achievement. She remembered, with the smile still on her face, how she would always say to them, 'My children, learn to be in time always. The passenger should wait for the train, and not expect the train to wait for her.'

She descended the stairs facing the open window of the booking office. Through the round opening at eye-level, she could hear that the booking clerk was engaged in conversation with someone, a female.

She carefully placed a R10 banknote on the small, concave, coinerroded wooden base, letting it protrude into the other side through the semi-circular opening over the plank. She waited, wondering about the contact and remembering what the taxi driver had said: 'You don't know this Boer clerk here. He can be very

* This story was banned in South Africa in 1979 before publication. The censorship board claimed at the time that because the story had been seen by two people (the postman and himself) it was as good as having been published.

furious when you ask for a second-class ticket without having made a booking beforehand. Anyway, try. Speak to him in "SeBuru" and not English. They are more tolerant when you address them in their own language.'

'Ja?' the clerk said, banging impatiently on the base and startling her.

'Can I . . . Kan ek 'n tweede-klas kaartjie kry na Johannesburgtoe, asseblief?'

'Het jy bespreking gemaak?' 'Nee, ek . . . ' 'Wel, nee. Natuurlik kan jy nie!' he snapped.

And without much ado, he grabbed the money and deposited (or shall I say he flung) a ticket and change in banknotes with some silver and bronze coins on the base. The girl tried to plead, saying she was from very far away, in the outlying areas of Leribe district in Lesotho. The clerk gazed at her, his fierce-looking, cat-like, bespectacled grey eyes looking like an abyss, with the pupils dilating and contracting. She flinched and dropped her eyes. In that instant, the furious clerk grunted, with a hard bang drew the wooden shutter over the window-pane. The girl bent down slowly. A black railway policeman who was standing a few metres away scurried nearer, and together, they picked up some of the coins which had landed on the concrete floor. He asked, 'Did you want a second-class ticket, my sister?'

'Yes '

'They usually insist that you make a booking two weeks before the intended date of departure.'

'How does one make a booking when you come from so far away? I would have to spend two days along the way. You know where Nqechane is.'

'I know,' said the policeman, nodding. 'And when you make a booking by phone, they ignore you. Some even try sending telegrams; but these are never noted.

Anyway, don't worry. When you get to Bethlehem, ask the ticket examiner to convert your ticket to second class. The new Line trains via Balfour are usually never fully booked. Then at least you won't have to stand the whole night right up to Johannesburg.'

The siren of the oncoming steam locomotive became audible and minutes later the train pulled into the platform. The kind policeman helped the girl into the packed third-class coach and one of the passengers on the train extended his arms to receive the girl's bags. She thanked both men for their courtesy.

There seemed to be no sitting space available, and there was no point in attempting to move any further than where she was. She leaned against a window and arranged her three bags on the floor along the side of the passage wall. One bag she clamped between her feet and the other two she nestled against her jutting slim ankles. She could at least feel her bags all the time, she thought gratefully, as she clung to her handbag.

The train moved on slowly, stopping at the many sidings and stations and winding its way laboriously over the steep slopes. She closed her eyes and listened, wishing that she were at least lying down. That distance she had walked on foot! She thought of the booking clerk at Ficksburg and his eyes.

'It will be raining by the time we get to Bethlehem, can you see that, my sister?'

Only then was she aware of the presence of the kind man who had received her on to the train. She opened her eyes and noticed that the clouds were gathering fast and she nodded in response to the question. She could not make out whether the young man was coloured or Indian or African; she finally decided to dismiss the matter and not let her mind dwell on it. She looked through the open window into the peaceful receding landscape outside. Her searching eyes quickly spotted the mountain peak of Nqechane and she thought of the tranquillity of the past three weeks she had spent at the beautiful village bearing the name of the peak. Everything was just as she remembered it when she was still a child.

She closed her eyes and thoughts drifted on, rocked by the swaying rhythmic movements of the train . . . She thought of the horrible eyes of the booking clerk at Ficksburg.

She recollected that she had not been in contact with a single white person for the duration of her holiday. She had had perfect peace. No; she corrected herself — with the exception of 'Me Sistere, the Mother Superior at the nearby Nqechane Anglican Mission, and 'Ntate Fatere, the Priest-in-Charge. But those were different, she argued with herself. They even extended a friendly arm to greet you. That is why she had forgotten about them. But of course there was her first contact with those white people at the border post of Ficksburg* — how on earth could she forget that? She could not remember that contact because she had the Open Sesame — the *brown* Travel Document of the Republic and not the *green* Lesotho Local Passport. It was precisely because of those first contacts that she had at last decided to change from green to brown. The nauseating numerous questions they used to ask when you wanted to come to any part of this Republic, especially Johannesburg. As if crossing a mere river meant the same thing as going from heaven to hell or vice versa. What did it matter what you crossed to get where anyway? They would ask you:

* Border between Lesotho and South Africa. Crossing into South Africa is always confrontational and often traumatic for Blacks.

Why do you want to go to Johannesburg? To what address? How long are you going to be there?
Who is the person you are visiting there?
How much money have you got in your purse — will you be able to pay for a return ticket?

And more often than not, you would be refused permission. Your *green* document would be flung at you and you would have to turn right back with your carefully prepared chicken provision and dumplings in your tin trunk and all. They wouldn't even consider the sacrifices you made to get to that post at all. Like how many days and nights you travelled on foot; or whether there are any buses where you come from; or if there are buses, whether you were able to pay the fare or not. Whether your reasons for visiting the Republic were valid or not depended mainly on whether the 'nonnie' had prepared a good breakfast for the particular 'baas' at the post at the time or not. Of late, even when you claimed that there was a death of a close relation of yours at that address in the Republic they would turn you back. *Death*, not illness, Death what is worse than Death? And even if you actually produced a telegram to prove your claim they were not ashamed to ask you whether you were going to *eat* that corpse. 'What are you going to do with the dead person?' they ask you. She remembered how when she got tired of all those stinking questions, she had taken the advice of her friend: leave the green thing in the bag and cross the river — walk or swim over it or across it, that's all.

But that too presented problems: the inevitable arrangements with the 'professional' river escorts, the ones who knew, or professed to know, when, where, and how to cross the Caledon in order to avoid contact with the whites at the border post with your green book. Armed sentries are known to carry on continuous patrols along the banks of the river. And these do not hesitate to open fire. These are some of the reasons which make those escorts indispensable. In addition, the escorts would have to come to some agreement with the inspectors at the customs barriers. These would have to pass your luggage without asking too many questions. Some prior negotiations with people near the river on the other side to accommodate you where you could sit and dry your clothes while you waited to be reunited with your luggage. Some accidents were known to happen and this could incur heavy losses of valuables especially if the escorts were not adequately compensated. The whole process became more and more expensive.

She thought of the last straw, when she decided to bury her green book forever and vowed to go to any lengths to acquire a brown one. She recalled bitterly that it was all because of that abominable barbed wire fence. Who ever thought that those white officials on this side would ever think of going to the extent of actually erecting a barbed wire fence right along the meandering Caledon River? Honestly! Just to bring about that contact. She had first to be carried across the full river, and then over a nearly seven-foot-high barbed wire fence by yelling, giggling, curious youths who obviously found it amusing and gratifying — the experience of coddling ordinarily inaccessible parts of anatomy of a partially clad woman! She had her brown travel documents in her handbag now, and all that ordeal was over, thank God.

She thought of those eyes of the white booking clerk.

Just after 6 p.m., the train steamed steadily into Platform One at Bethlehem. A strong wind blew from the Drakensberg Mountains in the east and swept the raindrops into the faces of the alighting passengers, now rushing towards the smelly non-White waiting-rooms just outside the station, about twenty metres from the railway line.

'I will take these, my sister,' said the voice of the kind young man, relieving her of two of her bags.

'Thanks,' she said.

They joined the seemingly endless moving stream of passengers to the waiting-rooms.

At exactly 7 p.m. the black announcer came round swinging a large loudspeaker and shouting into its mouthpiece, 'Ba eang Gauteng ba ee ho Platform Three! Ba eang Gauteng ba ee ho Platform Three! . . '

Still accompanied by the willing strange young man, the girl followed the long procession over the narrow bridge.

On Platform Three, there were two guards standing and chatting near the wooden benches. The girl said to the young man, 'I want to ask the guard to convert my ticket from third- to second-class, but I'm reluctant. I travelled on foot and by bus the whole day and I'm tired. I wouldn't be able to stand the whole night right to Johannesburg.'

'Where are you from, my sister?'

'Nqechane, in the Leribe District.'

'Oh. I don't even know where that is; I'm from Bloemfontein. Do go. I'll accompany you into the compartment and return to the third-class coaches.'

'And where are *you* going to?'

'Also Johannesburg.'

Reluctantly, and with a feeling of apprehension, the girl moved towards the two guards, who looked at her questioningly as she approached. She suddenly became conscious of her high platform shoes. She moved slowly. She would have to avoid the risk of tripping, she thought. She was thankful that her wide-bottomed balooba denim pair of slacks concealed her knees which were by now impulsively knocking against each other. Her step, which was normally graceful and confident, was faltering . . . She thought of the white booking clerk at Ficksburg. Not knowing who of the two white men to refer her request to, she held her ticket before them and asked, 'Kan ek hierdie kaartjie verander tot tweede-klas asseblief?'

And without appearing to pay much attention, the man on her right-hand side said, signalling to the near-by coach with the 'Non-Whites — Reserved' sign on it, 'Gaan in die "C" Kompartement.'

With great relief and a smile on her face, she obeyed. She had been fortunate . . . She thought of the furious eyes of the clerk at the booking office in Ficksburg. On her way, she passed the 'B' compartment and noticed that there was only one black lady in it. She smiled and nodded expectantly when the girl greeted her. The girl hesitated. She stopped and asked her, 'Are you with other passengers in here, Mother?'

'No, my child, I'm alone in here. Haven't seen any others arriving.'

He did say 'C' she thought, puzzled.

She passed on to the next compartment. It was also unoccupied. She put her bags on the cushioned green bunk. She looked around. It was clean and comfortable — a welcome change from the third-class coaches she had been standing in from Ficksburg. Only the stale familiar odour of the inevitable Dettol that, she had come to know, one would have to learn to live with. It was permanent, and it seemed to have been built into the very heavily wood-panelled walls of the compartments. Like the inlaid, meaningless landscape photographs of the sunny South Africa which seemed to strive to create beauty in surroundings where most of the time only ugliness and cruelty prevailed.

She decided to speak to the elderly lady next-door. After exchanging the usual formalities, she remarked, 'I wonder why the guard said I must go into "C" when you are alone here. The usual procedure is to let females share the same compartment, and the male passengers also their own, isn't it?'

'I wondered why you passed into "C", but then I thought you had more ladies accompanying you, my child.'

'No, I'm alone.'

They both smiled. She folded her arms over her bosom and sighed, still smiling, and remarked, twisting the ends of her lips and raising her eyebrows, 'Perhaps he wants to pay you a visit.'

'A visit?' the girl asked, surprised . . . She thought of the booking clerk at Ficksburg, and realised that she would have the image of those grey cruel eyes on her for a long time. She said, 'I don't think he'd do that.'

'Why, my child?'

The girl shrugged her shoulders vigorously, and answered, 'I don't know. But somehow they don't seem to know that we are human beings like them.'

'You're still very young, aren't you?' and she peeped through the window, pointing. 'You see that train in that platform on the other side? It's full of soldiers. All those white soldiers there, can you see them?'

'Yes. All carrying guns and filing into the train with kitbags. What about them?'

'Yes. They're soldiers. I don't know who they are fighting or why. One teacher told me that they are fighting black people somewhere in the north. They have a big camp just outside Bethlehem. That's where they learn how to shoot and all about fighting. When you pass there, you'll always see them drilling, playing all sorts of games. No black woman moves in that area without men to protect her. They chase them into the dongas and grab them by force. Would they do that if they didn't think we're humans?'

The girl shook her head. 'I'd like to go into the cloakroom or toilet there and do some washing up before I sit and eat something. Shall I leave my bags in your compartment? Surely he can't expect me to sit alone there. What happens if I should want to visit the small house, take everything with me? The same thing applies with you too. People want to sit together and speak. It can be very lonely. I'd rather be in here with you.'

The train left Bethlehem. The ticket examiner came and issued the new second-class ticket without appearing to notice anything amiss or out of order. He did not seem to mind the two women being together. They both ordered bedding. He was very formal and to the point; he then left.

'I'll wait until you come back, then it will be my turn and you can stay with the luggage.'

The girl left, taking her handbag and adding into it a few of the items she would need. She returned about twelve minutes later, feeling refreshed and no longer so tired. 'It's your turn now, Mother,' she said to the smiling lady.

'Hm . . . You smell sweet, and look like a fresh peach!'

'Thanks.' The girl blushed.

She was just reaching up to ease her sling bag into the baggage rack above, when the guard stood at the door. He looked at the girl noticing the bare portion of her ebony torso and the pronounced umbilical groove, reducing her slim waistline even more. Trying to look at him and noticing his fixed stare, she withdraw her arms almost instinctively and readjusted the hem of her short blouse. She pulled it down to cover her bare waist and felt uncomfortable when he shifted his eyes from her body to meet hers.

'Where's your companion?' he asked, smiling and frowning. 'Who?'

'Your escort or husband. The man who was with you when you entered the coach.'

'Oh. He . . .'

The man did not wait to hear what the girl said because just then, the elderly woman appeared at the end of the narrow passage and he moved away, tapping at the next door, smiling and giving her way to pass. She went into the compartment and shut the door behind her, whispering and smiling. 'What did I tell you? Didn't I tell you that he'd pay you a visit?'

'He asked me where the man who was carrying my bags had gone to. He said something about "husband" and when I tried to explain, he saw *you* coming and just left.'

'Oh, jealous!'

They both laughed.

'He knows I'm getting off at Villiers; but don't worry, it will be dawn already. I suppose he'll get tired of waiting.'

Not long after they had shared their provisions, and they had exhausted their long 'introductions' in the usual African way, the coloured attendant came to prepare their beds from the 'non-white' bedding kits. They went to bed and switched off the lights. The swaying train and the steady drizzle outside lulled them into a peaceful sleep as it traversed the unending beautiful maize fields.

During the early hours of the morning, the guard

knocked at the door to warn the elderly lady that the train was nearing Villiers, and disappeared. She felt reluctant to wake up the girl to bid her goodbye; thinking that she might find it difficult to sleep again after her departure. She decided to wake her up, anyway, as she felt just that it would be cruel for her to walk out. She bade the girl farewell and assured her that there was the coloured attendant in the nearby compartment and that she thought she had heard other passengers move into the other compartments. She explained, 'I know most third-class people usually come to the coach where the guard is only to get their tickets and then go back to third. But perhaps some of them were second-class passengers.' She bent down and whispered into the girl's ear, 'I don't think he'll ignore their presence. Besides — the law! Just make sure you lock the door from inside, my child.'

The train glided out of the platform. It was a smooth quiet motion and she remembered that the coaches were now being drawn by an electric engine. She lay quietly, listening . . . She thought of the ticket examiner's strange behaviour, and she remembered those eyes of the booking clerk at Ficksburg station.

From afar, came the low rumble of thunder. She moved out of her bed and walked to the other window, rolled up the blind and opened it. She looked out. The wide expanse of farm-lands lay completely deserted, enveloped in pitch-black darkness. The lights piercing through the train windows struck the falling raindrops and formed rays of oblique streaks of glittering lines, descending heavily against the side of the coaches. The rain was pouring in torrents. There was no sign of life in the coach in which she was. Where was the coloured attendant anyway, fast asleep, she wondered. Was Johannesburg still far to go? She could not sleep.

The train stopped. It was a big station — 'Balfour North', the sign read. When the train was about to leave, the guard emerged from a room on the platform and stood next to the train facing expectantly towards the fore end. He noticed the girl withdraw her head into the compartment, and draw the blinds.

He blew his whistle and shouted, 'Balfour North!' and the train pulled out of the platform.

The door yielded easily when the guard prised the lever with his key. She turned, startled, and aware that she was scantily dressed in her flimsy nightie. She tried to move towards her bed and he intercepted her saying, 'It's dark. You needn't be afraid. I've just come to chat with you that's all, please. I'm lonely in my cubicle, please. Please,' he begged, speaking calmly.

She asked, 'Chat about what?'

He smiled, asking, 'Where did you say your husband went to?'

'He's not my husband. He was a stranger. He helped me carry my luggage over the steps in Bethlehem.'

'What is he of yours?'

'What do you mean?'

'Call I turn on the very dim light, please? I like to see your beautiful face; can l?' the man said, reaching for the switch. The dim light came on. He smiled into the girl's face, and she draw away.

'I mean; is he your "nyatsi" or what?' he said, twisting his eyebrows and smiling mischievously.

She sat on the cushioned bunk and watched him remove his cap and put it on the steel peg above the door. It struck her that the man's manner and tone of speech, which had been formal and austere in the presence of the middle-aged lady, had now changed to familiarity. His behaviour had altered like a reversible cloak; like a garment you either decided to keep on or strip off, just like that. She was not sure she liked the metamorphosis, but she became more curious . . . She thought of the Ficksburg station booking clerk's eyes.

She remembered that she once heard a person saying that most whites first learnt swear words in the vocabulary of the African languages. She asked, 'What did you say he was of mine?'

'Your "nyatsi",' he repeated, emphasising the word.

'We travelled together from Ficksburg. He helped me with my baggage; and I was late. The train nearly left me. I was lucky to meet a sympathetic person.'

'Why were you late? Flirting, I suppose.'

'No. I was pleading with the booking clerk to sell me a second-class ticket and he was refusing.'

'And so your companion came to *console* you?' and he mentioned the word 'troos' (console) already moving towards her. He asked. 'How about letting *me* do that, then? I'd like to comfort you. I'd enjoy it very much,' he said, coming near her as the girl receded, petrified. 'Don't be afraid, please. Come; just stand up. Come, man; don't be so lazy. Just stand up and let's have some fun. Just a little love making,' the guard implored, touching her slim shoulders tenderly and stroking them. 'Come. It won't hurt, please. Come on, hold me tight, tight!' he demanded, taking the girl's hands and crossing them behind him. The girl slackened her grip, but he stopped her. 'Don't do that, please. All right, just clasp me tightly against you and I'll be satisfied.'

He held her face in both his hands and pressed it against his warm impetuous body, raising her chin. The girl closed her eyes. 'Don't close your eyes, please. They're so beautiful. Look at me. Look into my eyes, please.'

The girl kept her eyes closed. She was thinking of the haunting, furious eyes of the booking clerk at

Ficksburg. He switched off the light. 'Come now. Stand up. We shall soon be in Johannesburg. Please. You're hard, man — unyielding. Why?' he asked. He looked at his wrist watch in the dark. The green arms and the circle of dots were vivid and luminous. 'Just wait for me; I'm coming. There's a station nearby.'

The girl sat trembling and feeling guilty. She reprimanded herself, I should be screaming for help or something. She sat waiting. She was surprised at herself. She had been like a bewildered beholder, powerless. She had abandoned herself into the arms of a strange white man who did not even know her name. An expert who obviously knew what he was doing. She was taken aback at what seemed to be a response by a part of herself over which she had no control. She felt like a being apart, looking on. She waited, dismayed.

She listened. It was quiet outside. The storm had subsided. There was no downpour here. The torrent seemed to have been cut with a knife.

She heard the now-familiar voice of the ticket examiner. He yelled, 'Union!'

The train glided slowly out of the platform.

The next moment, the guard darted stealthily up the two steps in a single stride. He sneaked quietly into the dimly lit compartment. Without uttering a word, and with one powerful wrench, he gathered the tender body of the woman in his arms and her face came to rest against his. He breathed the words tenderly into her ear, 'Come on now, please!'

She slowly wrapped her shaky reluctant arms around the warm neck of the guard. They stood there and kissed. She could feel his strong muscles move as he gently stroked her back. He moved his exploring hands down her midrif and below. His knees seemed to sag and he knelt on the edge of the cushioned bunk. As his left hand caressed the girl's firm nipple, his right hand felt for the switch and lowered it. The darkness surrounded them completely, isolating them from the rest of the world. She thought of the fiery, bottomless eyes of the booking clerk at Ficksburg station.

Almost in a whisper, his warm breath pouring like steam over her naked body, he pleaded. 'Kom,' he said, 'kom nou, toe, kom. Dis net die twee van ons; toemaar. Dis net ons twee; kom.' In the darkness, and with his eyes closed tightly, his warm quavering, salivating tongue groped towards the girl's navel, and spotting it, sank into its hollow warmness.

'Oh God help me. Let *something* happen . . .' The girl's conscience, her soul, stood aloof, untouched, admonishing. Her heart was pounding fast, but only with a feeling of guilt. 'What if my parents, my husband . . . What if. . ? Oh no, no, no!'

Still kneeling and salivating like Pavlov's dog, the man continued to plead anxiously, 'Kom nou, kom . . . ag tog . . . asseblief, kom . . . '

She draw a deep breath, lifting her face and looking up into the darkness; waiting for something, some miracle.

In times of threat, some invisible omnipotent power seems always to be waiting to come to the aid of the helpless, the weak, the defenceless. It was not through a cannon that David vanquished Goliath.

The girl remembered . . . Somewhere in the Christian scriptures, they say, a maiden had hidden a potion in her bosom, and she did not want to be searched. The words entered her mind and she uttered them mechanically: 'Ntate se nkame hobane ke silafetse . . . ' Her lips mumbled the entreaty, softy and uncertainly . . . 'Father, do not touch me because I am unclean . . .'

Then repeating loudly, drawing back and pushing the kneeling man, she gasped, 'Se nkame hobane ke silafetse . . . ke metse *mokoala*!' (Do not touch me because I am afflicted with a venereal sickness.)

'Mokoala!' . . . One of those detestable, ominous words. The impact of that word was quick, merciless, shocking and immediately disarming. Like when in a dark alley you suddenly grope into a dead end. She stood still listening to the sound of receding breath. She reached below the bunk above and lowered the dim switch. She watched the recoiling devilish figure and drew a sigh of relief.

Gcina Mhlophe

THE TOILET

Sometimes I wanted to give up and be a good girl who listened to her elders. Maybe I should have done something like teaching or nursing as my mother wished. People thought these professions were respectable, but I knew I wanted to do something different, though I was not sure what. I thought a lot about acting. . . My mother said that it had been a waste of good money educating me because I did not know what to do with the knowledge I had acquired. I'd come to Johannesburg for the December holidays after writing my matric exams, and then stayed on, hoping to find something to do.

My elder sister worked in Orange Grove as a domestic worker, and I stayed with her in her back room. I didn't know anybody in Jo'burg except my sister's friends whom we went to church with. The Methodist church up Fourteenth Avenue was about the only outing we had together. I was very bored and lonely.

On weekdays I was locked in my sister's room so that the Madam wouldn't see me. She was at home most of the time: painting her nails, having tea with her friends, or lying in the sun by the swimming pool. The swimming pool was very close to the room, which is why I had to keep very quiet. My sister felt bad about locking me in there, but she had no alternative. I couldn't even play the radio, so she brought me books, old magazines, and newspapers from the white people. I just read every single thing I came across: *Fair Lady*, *Woman's Weekly*, anything. But then my sister thought I was reading too much.

'What kind of wife will you make if you can't even make baby clothes, or knit yourself a jersey? I suppose you will marry an educated man like yourself, who won't mind going to bed with a book and an empty stomach.'

We would play cards at night when she knocked off, and listen to the radio, singing along softly with the songs we liked.

Then I got this temporary job in a clothing factory in town. I looked forward to meeting new people, and liked the idea of being out of that room for a change. The factory made clothes for ladies' boutiques. The whole place was full of machines of all kinds. Some people were sewing, others were ironing with big heavy irons that pressed with a lot of steam. I had to cut all the loose threads that hang after a dress or a jacket is finished. As soon as a number of dresses in a certain style were finished, they would be sent to me and I had to count them, write the number down, and then start with the cutting of the threads. I was fascinated to discover that one person made only sleeves, another the collars, and so on until the last lady put all the pieces together, sewed on buttons, or whatever was necessary to finish.

Most people at the factory spoke Sotho, but they were nice to me — they tried to speak to me in Zulu or Xhosa, and they gave me all kinds of advice on things I didn't know. There was this girl, Gwendolene — she thought I was very stupid — she called me a 'bari' because I always sat inside the changing room with something to read when it was time to eat my lunch, instead of going outside to meet guys. She told me it was cheaper to get myself a 'lunch boy' — somebody to buy me lunch. She told me it was wise not to sleep with him, because then I could dump him anytime I wanted to. I was very nervous about such things. I thought it was better to be a 'bari' than to be stabbed by a city boy for his money.

The factory knocked off at four-thirty, and then I went to a park near where my sister worked. I waited there till half past six, when I could sneak into the house again without the white people seeing me. I had to leave the house before half past five in the mornings as well. That meant I had to find something to do with the time I had before I could catch the seven-thirty bus to work — about two hours. I would go to a public toilet in the park. For some reason it was never locked, so I would go in and sit on the toilet seat to read some magazine or other until the right time to catch the bus.

The first time I went into this toilet, I was on my way to the bus stop. Usually I went straight to the bus stop outside the OK Bazaars where it was well lit, and I could see. I would wait there, reading, or just looking at the growing number of cars and buses on their way to town. On this day it was raining quite hard, so I thought I would shelter in the toilet until the rain had passed. I knocked first to see if there was anyone inside. As there was no reply, I pushed the door open and went in. It smelled a little — a dryish kind of smell, as if the toilet was not used all that often, but it was quite clean compared to many 'Non-European' toilets I knew. The floor was painted red and the walls were cream white. It did not look like it had been painted for a few years. I stood looking around, with the rain coming very hard on the zinc roof. The noise was comforting — to know I had escaped the wet — only a few of the heavy drops had got me. The plastic bag in which I carried my book and purse and neatly folded pink handkerchief was a little damp, but that was because I had used it to cover my head when I ran to the toilet. I pulled my dress down a little so that it would not get creased when I sat down. The closed lid of the toilet was going to be my seat for many mornings after that.

I was really lucky to have found that toilet because the winter was very cold. Not that it was any warmer in there, but once I'd closed the door it used to be a little less windy. Also the toilet was very small — the walls were wonderfully close to me — it felt like it was made to fit me alone. I enjoyed that kind of privacy. I did a lot of thinking while I sat on that toilet seat. I did a lot of daydreaming too — many times imagining myself in some big hall doing a really popular play with other young actors. At school, we took set books like *Buzani KuBawo* or *A Man for All Seasons* and made school plays which we toured to the other schools on weekends. I loved it very much. When I was even younger I had done little sketches taken from the Bible and on big days like Good Friday, we acted and sang happily.

I would sit there dreaming . . .

I was getting bored with the books I was reading — the love stories all sounded the same, and besides that I just lost interest. I started asking myself why I had not written anything since I left school. At least at school I had written some poems, or stories for the school magazine, school competitions and other magazines like *Bona* and *Inkqubela*. Our English teacher was always so encouraging; I remembered the day I showed him my first poem — I was so excited I couldn't concentrate in class for the whole day. I didn't know anything about publishing then, and I didn't ask myself if my stories were good enough. I just enjoyed writing things down when I had the time. So one Friday, after I'd started being that toilet's best customer, I bought myself a notebook in which I was hoping to write something. I didn't use it for quite a while, until one evening.

My sister had taken her usual Thursday afternoon off, and she had delayed somewhere. I came back from work, then waited in the park for the right time to go back into the yard. The white people always had their supper at six-thirty and that was the time I used to steal my way in without disturbing them or being seen. My comings and goings had to be secret because they still didn't know I stayed there.

Then I realised that she hadn't come back, and I was scared to go out again, in case something went wrong this time. I decided to sit down in front of my sister's room, where I thought I wouldn't be noticed. I was reading a copy of *Drum Magazine* and hoping that she would come back soon — before the dogs sniffed me out. For the first time I realised how stupid it was of me not to have cut myself a spare key long ago. I kept on hearing noises that sounded like the gate opening. A few times I was sure I had heard her footsteps on the concrete steps leading to the servant's quarters, but it turned out to be something or someone else.

I was trying hard to concentrate on my reading again, when I heard the two dogs playing, chasing each other nearer and nearer to where I was sitting. And then, there they were in front of me, looking as surprised as I was. For a brief moment we stared at each other, then they started to bark at me. I was sure they would tear me to pieces if I moved just one finger, so I sat very still, trying not to look at them, while my heart pounded and my mouth went dry as paper.

They barked even louder when the dogs from next door joined in, glared at me through the openings in the hedge. Then the Madam's high-pitched voice rang out above the dogs' barking.

'Ireeeeeeeene!' That's my sister's English name, which we never use. I couldn't move or answer the call — the dogs were standing right in front of me, their teeth so threateningly long. When there was no reply, she came to see what was going on.

'Oh, it's you? Hello.' She was smiling at me, chewing that gum which never left her mouth, instead of calling the dogs away from me. They had stopped barking, but they hadn't moved — they were still growling at me, waiting for her to tell them what to do.

'Please Madam, the dogs will bite me,' I pleaded, not moving my eyes from them.

'No, they won't bite you.' Then she spoke to them nicely, 'Get away now — go on,' and they went off. She was like a doll, her hair almost orange in colour, all curls round her made-up face. Her eyelashes fluttered like a doll's. Her thin lips were bright red like her long nails, and she wore very high-heeled shoes. She was still smiling; I wondered if it didn't hurt after a while. When her friends came for a swim, I could always hear her forever laughing at something or other.

She scared me — I couldn't understand how she could smile like that but not want me to stay in her house.

'When did you come in? We didn't see you.'

'I've been here for some time now — my sister isn't here. I'm waiting to talk to her.'

'Oh — she's not here?' She was laughing, for no reason that I could see. 'I can give her a message — you go on home — I'll tell her that you want to see her.'

Once I was outside the gate, I didn't know what to do

or where to go. I walked slowly, kicking my heels. The street lights were so very bright! Like big eyes staring at me. I wondered what the people who saw me thought I was doing, walking around at that time of the night. But then I didn't really care, because there wasn't much I could do about the situation right then. I was just thinking how things had to go wrong on that day particularly, because my sister and I were not on such good terms. Early that morning, when the alarm had gone for me to wake up, I did not jump to turn it off, so my sister got really angry with me. She had gone on about me always leaving it to ring for too long, as if it was set for her, and not for me. And when I went out to wash, I had left the door open a second too long, and that was enough to earn me another scolding.

Every morning I had to wake up straight away, roll my bedding and put it all under the bed where my sister was sleeping. I was not supposed to put on the light although it was still dark. I'd light a candle, and tiptoe my way out with a soap dish and a toothbrush. My clothes were on a hanger on a nail at the back of the door. I'd take the hanger and close the door as quietly as I could. Everything had to be ready set the night before. A washing basin full of cold water was also ready outside the door, put there because the sound of running water and the loud screech the taps made in the morning could wake the white people and they would wonder what my sister was doing up so early. I'd do my everything and be off the premises by five-thirty with my shoes in my bag — I only put them on once I was safely out of the gate. And that gate made such a noise too. Many time I wished I could jump over it and save myself all that sickening careful-careful business!

Thinking about all these things took my mind away from the biting cold of the night and my wet nose, until

I saw my sister walking towards me.

'Mholo, what are you doing outside in the street?' she greeted me. I quickly briefed her on what had happened.

'Oh Yehovah! You can be so dumb sometimes! What were you doing inside in the first place? You know you should have waited for me so we could walk in together. Then I could say you were visiting or something. Now, you tell me, what am I supposed to say to them if they see you come in again? Hayi!'

She walked angrily towards the gate, with me hesitantly following her. When she opened the gate, she turned to me with an impatient whisper.

'And now why don't you come in, stupid?'

I mumbled my apologies, and followed her in. By some miracle no one seemed to have noticed us, and we quickly munched a snack of cold chicken and boiled potatoes and drank our tea, hardly on speaking terms. I just wanted to howl like a dog. I wished somebody would come and be my friend, and tell me that I was not useless, and that my sister did not hate me, and tell me that one day I would have a nice place to live . . . anything. It would have been really great to have someone my own age to talk to.

But also I knew that my sister was worried for me, she was scared of her employers. If they were to find out that I lived with her, they would fire her, and then we would both be walking up and down the streets. My eleven rand wages wasn't going to help us at all. I don't know how long I lay like that, unable to fall asleep, just wishing and wishing with tears running into my ears.

The next morning I woke up long before the alarm went off, but I just lay there feeling tired and depressed. If there was a way out, I would not have gone to work, but there was this other strong feeling or longing inside me. It was some kind of pain that pushed me to do everything at double speed and run to my toilet. I call it my toilet because that is exactly how I felt about it. It was very rare that I ever saw anybody else go in there in the mornings. It was like they all knew I was using it, and they had to lay off or something. When I went there, I didn't really expect to find it occupied.

I felt my spirits really lifting as I put on my shoes outside the gate. I made sure that my notebook was in my bag. In my haste I even forgot my lunchbox, but it didn't matter. I was walking faster and my feet were feeling lighter all the time. Then I noticed that the door had been painted, and that a new window pane had replaced the old broken one. I smiled to myself as I reached the door. Before long I was sitting on that toilet seat, writing a poem.

Many mornings saw me sitting there writing. Sometimes it did not need to be a poem; I wrote anything that came into my head — in the same way I would have done if I'd had a friend to talk to. I remember some days when I felt like I was hiding something from my sister. She did not know about my toilet in the park, and she was not in the least interested in my notebook.

Then one morning I wanted to write a story about what had happened at work the day before; the supervisor screaming at me for not calling her when I'd seen the people who stole two dresses at lunch time. I had found it really funny. I had to write about it and I just hoped there were enough pages left in my notebook. It all came back to me, and I was smiling when I reached for the door, but it wouldn't open — it was locked!

I think for the first time I accepted that the toilet was not mine after all. . . Slowly I walked over to a bench nearby, watched the early spring sun come up, and wrote my story anyway.

Maude Motanyane
TWO MINUTES

Tosh and I were an odd pair; she was tall and thin, and I was short and plump. People called us the big and small twins, or B & S for short. In very many ways we were different, and yet there was something strong that bound us together. We stood out like sore thumbs from the rest of the girls, who were adventurous and full of pranks. They were wild, while Tosh and I tried to lead a life as pure as possible.

It is twenty years since I last saw Tosh, and I feel guilty that I have not been back to see her. I am sure she is plagued by the same guilt. We made a vow many years ago, and we promised to keep it whatever happened. We crossed each other's hearts and spat on the ground as we promised. "'Strue's God, my friend, if I ever do it I will come back and tell you." There was only one 'it' that little girls in a convent school could promise not to get themselves involved in. According to Sister Marietta, the matron of the convent, boys came second after witches and ghosts as the deadliest poison for little girls. It could take less than two minutes for a boy to ruin a girl's entire life, she said.

The Little Flower Girls' Hostel formed part of a huge

mission station founded by Catholic missionaries at the turn of the century. Most of them were of European origin, but over the years the mission, set in the village of Asazi in Natal, had become a fully fledged community, producing its own breed of African nuns and priests from the surrounding villages.

Sister Marietta was a mouse-like creature of German origin. Armed with a bible and a strict Catholic upbringing, she was determined to save the whole African continent from death and destruction. Her biggest challenge while at The Little Flower was to keep the girls away from the evil clutches of men. Old Marie, as the girls referred to her, made it her business to slot in her anti-male propaganda whenever she could. Her best performances were a day or two before we broke up for the school holidays. She seemed to think that a good dose of lecturing would protect us from the menacing world outside.

She marvelled at the story of a boy who once cast a spell on a girl by simply looking at her. The girl, she said, had trusted her own worldly strength instead of asking for protection from the Virgin Mary. The boy had looked at the girl, the story went, and, without him saying a word, the girl had felt weak. So weak was she that, of her own accord, without the boy even propositioning her, she asked him to 'please kiss me and carry me to the bush'.

'I need not tell you what happened in the bush,' the nun would conclude.

As a rule, anyone who was caught eyeing the boys, whether in church, in class, or in the street, was punished severely. Ten bad marks in Sister Marietta's black book was the highest number one could get at a go, and they indicated the seriousness of the crime. As a result, trying to avoid boys and not being seen with them in a lonely place became our biggest challenge at The Little Flower.

'They will take you and use you, leaving you an empty shell,' Sister Marietta would say, indicating with her hand how a girl would be tossed away as something useless. So ominous was the prospect of being thrown away as a useless shell that Tosh and I would spend long nights discussing ways and means to avoid being subjected to that kind of treatment. Although we did not admire Sister Marietta personally, the idea of being sinless and celibate appealed to us a great deal. Often our night sessions would end with us saying the rosary together, asking for forgiveness for sins we had never committed.

Anastasia, Tasi to her friends, was the most popular girl at The Little Flower. While the rest of the girls loved and admired her, Tosh and I despised her. She dressed in the best fashion clothes, and had all the answers to life's problems. A dark person by nature, Tasi relied on skin-lightening cream to make her skin look lighter. So light was her face at one stage that her ebony hands looked borrowed next to it. Somehow her ears never got lighter, no matter how much cream she used on them. They stuck out like little appendages above her oval face. Tosh and I laughed about her ears behind her back. We did not dare do so in her presence. Tasi's tongue was much too scathing.

'I wonder how Old Marie can be so knowledgeable about matters of the flesh when she has never been involved in them,' Tasi would say mockingly. 'She must be displacing her own fears and using us to fight her own inward physical desire. Celibacy . . . what nonsense. Old Marie must be jealous of our freedom. After all, we never sent her to tie herself to a life devoid of male pleasure.'

Tasi had quite a following, and her bed, which was at the corner of the hundred-bed dormitory, became the girls' rendezvous. This was where all subjects ranging from politics to sex were discussed. Tasi owned a small transistor radio, and often her gang would convene at her bed to listen to the 'Hit Parade'. This had to happen behind Sister Marietta's back because to her, love and rock 'n roll constituted mortal sins. Often the music-listening session would end in a row, with the participants arguing about the lyrics of a song, or which song had been number one on the 'Hit Parade' the previous week.

It was at the rendezous that the anti-missionary politics were discussed. As far as Tasi was concerned, the missionaries, and that included Sister Marietta, had left Europe because of frustration, hunger and poverty. 'Under the guise of Christianity, they came to save us. Save us from what? When they themselves are guilty of racism and bigotry?' Tasi would ask, pointing at the stone building in which the black nuns were housed.

The Little Flower was not immune from the country's racial laws, which decreed that blacks and whites live separately. The white missionaries were clearly a privileged class. They lived in a glass building at the top of the hill, while their black counterparts were housed in a stone and brick building at the bottom of the hill. lt looked more like a cave than a hut and, because of the density of the trees around it, it was cold and dark in winter.

Politics was a sacred subject at The Little Flower, and Tasi was the only one who openly challenged the racism of the convent. 'If they were like Jesus, they would be defying the laws of the country,' Tasi would say angrily. When Tasi questioned the school principal at assembly one day, we feared that she would be expelled from school. She was not. Instead she was fobbed off with an 'it was not the policy of the church to involved in politics' statement, and asked never to bring the subject up again. That did not deter Tasi. She continued to question and attack what she termed inexcusable behaviour from the people of God.

It was at the rendezvous that a perfect plan for smuggling letters was hatched. As a rule, letters sent in and out of the convent were read and censored by Sister Marietta. Incoming parcels were opened too, and every little gift considered to be too fancy for life in a convent school was kept, and not given to the owner until we broke up for the school holidays.

Love story books were banned from the library, and any pages with kissing couples, or people holding hands, were either cut out or blocked with paper. The same applied to movies. Scenes which were remotely sexual were edited out of the movie. We were allowed to watch *The Sound of Music* in my matric class. The movie was so butchered that when I saw it again a couple of years later, it looked completely new.

The smuggling of letters to and from the boys' side took place during morning mass. As the heads bowed down in silent prayer after holy communion, letters would be thrown across the aisle dividing the boys' from the girls' pews. The little pieces of paper, which for some reason were called schemes, would fly like missiles right above the nuns' heads.

One day a scheme which was thrown from the girls' to the boys' side landed right in the lap of Sister Marietta. Her face lit up with glee as she pocketed the letter, waiting for the perfect moment to pounce on the culprit. By the time she did, the school was buzzing with the news of the person who had been found with a scheme. Most of us were not sure who it was, but we were sympathetic because we knew what this would mean.

I had always suspected Sister Marietta to have a mean streak, but I never thought her capable of doing what she did with Thoko's letter. Of course Thoko's boyfriend denied any association between them, so she had to face the music alone.

Not only was the letter read to the whole school, it was sent home to her parents, with a letter instructing them to arrive at the school to reprimand Thoko 'or else she will be asked to pack her things and go'. I could not understand how a private thing such as a letter could be read to the whole school. That convinced me that Sister Marietta was downright malicious, doing that kind of thing to a nice girl like Thoko. Though remote, the thought of becoming a nun had often crossed my mind. What made me hesitate, however, was my mother's deep and sincere wish that I become a nurse. She would have been disappointed if I had gone the way of celibacy. Old Marie made the decision for me. Her reaction to Thoko's letter dashed my wish of ever becoming a nun. I was disgusted.

Tasi teased Thoko for having allowed herself to be caught with the letter. To her it was a big joke, and her friends laughed heartily when she described how foolish Thoko had been. 'There are only two rules,' Tasi said jokingly, 'it is either you keep away from trouble, or get involved, but be smart enough not to get caught.'

Tasi always boasted about how she and her boyfriend Michael smooched right under the nose of the Virgin Mary. She was referring to the statue of Mary on the lawn outside the school's courtyard. For those who had guts like Tasi, the grotto was a perfect lovers' nook.

More than once I heard Tasi tell the story of how she and Michael had climbed into one of the church towers. 'We stood there kissing to the chime of the bells next to us, while the priests heard confessions in the church below. Old Marie herself was playing the organ!' Tasi boasted. 'We did not get caught. What fool has any business to be caught?'

The stigma of being a boy's love followed Thoko until she left The Little Flower. She was banned from going to the movies on Fridays, and all the newcomers were warned that she was a bad influence. With the interesting parts censored out of all movies, Thoko didn't miss much, but it was the boring evenings that drove her nuts.

Thoko's every mistake became a big issue. She was ostracised by the rest of the girls who feared reprisals from Old Marie. As punishment for an offence Thoko was made to clean the local graveyard. It was not so much the hard work which caused grave-cleaning to be regarded as the most severe form of punishment. According to African culture graves are sacred ground where children are not allowed unless they are there to bury a very close relative such as a brother, a sister, or a parent. When Old Marie sent Thoko to dig round the graves for the second time, Tasi suggested we send a delegation to her to protest, and to make it clear what our tradition was regarding being in the cemetery.

'It is a bad omen, and shows no regard for our culture,' Tasi had protested. Although the delegation was given a hearing, their arguments were dismissed as primitive and unchristian, and Thoko was sent to clean up the graves a third and a fourth time. Such punishment was meted out to various other people, but Tasi vowed she would rather pack her bags and leave The Little Flower than dig round the graves. As if to avoid a confrontation, Old Marie never gave her the grave-digging punishment, robbing the girls of a chance to witness a showdown.

Once Sister Marietta embarrassed Thoko by pulling out the hem of her dress, saying that her dress was too short. As a rule, dresses had to be an inch above the knee. Thoko's must have been slightly more than an inch. The poor girl had to walk around with a funny dress the whole day because Sister would not let her change into another. It was her way of punishing her for, according to her mind, trying to be attractive to the opposite sex. But trying to make Thoko unattractive was an impossible task. Besides her God-given beauty, Thoko had natural style which made her look good with or without a torn hem. She looked elegant even in her gym slip, and Sister Marietta hated her for that. So intense was her hatred that she was forever looking for a reason for her to be expelled from school. 'You will dig the graves for a week, or pack your things and leave The Little Flower,' became the nun's familiar cry whenever Thoko did something wrong.

Tosh and I were both eighteen when we left The Little Flower. As we hugged and said goodbye, we renewed the vow we had made so many times before. If we ever slept with a boy, we would write or telephone to say we had finally fallen. I do not know exactly what motivated Tosh to make that vow. But for me, it was Thoko's experience that pushed me and forced me to make that decision. If a love letter could elicit so much hatred and anger, I thought to myself, then surely boys must be a real threat to girls. I sincerely believed that there would be no place for me in the world if I ever fell into the trap which every man around had set to catch me. As Old Marie said, 'The world will spit at you.'

Twenty years have passed since I last saw Tosh. I did not try to find her after my first encounter with a man.

I did not feel the urge to write to her and tell her that I had finally fallen. To my mind, it had not happened. I remember the incident very clearly. It was on the couch in my mother's own lounge, not even in the bush as Sister Marietta had wamed. Because he was Catholic like me, I trusted Sipho more than I would have trusted an ordinary boy. Somehow, I thought he knew the same rules that I knew.

He pleaded with me and told me it would not take long. He fondled my breasts and kissed me all over. I still cannot say whether the feeling was pleasurable. It was as though a cold and a warm shiver went through my body at the same time. I heard two voices, that of Sipho in one ear pleading with me that 'it won't be long', and Sister Marietta in another, warning 'it will take two minutes'. I saw myself being discarded like an empty shell and the whole world spitting at me.

Suddenly I fought like a little monster to push Sipho away. It was too late. I heard him take one deep breath and the act was over. It was exactly two minutes. I pulled myself together and walked out of the door, leaving Sipho sitting on the couch. When I walked away from him, I also walked away from the fact that he had made love to me. As far as I was concerned the incident had not happened. How could I admit that I had been used?

I have had a lot of sexual encounters since that day on my mother's couch. I am married now with two children; still I have not made love to a man. Sister Marietta never told me that there would come a time when being in a lonely place with a boy would be a right and a safe thing to do. So every private moment I have spent with a man has been wrong, and something I have to be ashamed of. Even as I go to bed with my husband every night, Sister Marietta's voice rings in my mind. 'He will take you and use you and throw you away like an empty shell.' When she drummed those words into my innocent mind, she tied a knot that I am now unable to undo.

How can I give myself on a platter to a person — a man — who will con me and leave me spent and useless? As I pull myself away from each sexual act, I feel used and unclean. A sense of guilt and emptiness comes over me. Often I have felt the urge to go back to The Little Flower, lock myself into a confessional with my priest, and say, 'Father, I have sinned. I have slept with a boy.'

I have not gone back to Tosh to tell her that I have broken the vow we made so many years ago. I have slept with none of the men I have made love to, none of the men I have met over the past twenty years. Maybe one day I will be able to untangle the knot in my heart and mind. I will be able to say to a man, 'Let us eat together from the sexual pot, let us share the pleasure equally.' I will not write to Tosh. No, not until I reach equality with my men. Tosh has not written either. Could it be that she is plagued by the same anguish, or is she still pure?

Deena Padayachee

THE FINISHING TOUCH

The shebeen was full of raucous people having a great old time. But Satha noticed that his friend Muthu didn't look too happy. The old man had come into the shebeen a few minutes before and simply plopped down into a chair. He had taken his first drink in one gulp and was now staring at his empty glass like a zombie. That wasn't like Muthu, ruminated Satha, not like Muthu at all. Satha went over to Muthu and focused bleary eyes glassily on his friend. He asked him why he was looking so depressed.

'That Trishen's robbing me blind, man.'

'He's running your Shakas hardware shop for you, eh, Muthu?' 'Ja, and the money he's bringing in isn't 'nough to pay the bleddy rent!' 'But why for you renting that small shop when you own a nice, big hardware store next to your house?' 'It's for the licence — I run my big business on that small business' licence.'

'Ja,' Satha nodded sympathetically, 'I suppose it's difficult for our people to get a licence for a business?'

'Ja, man. Where a coolie like me's gonna get a licence from the Wurropean man?'

'Ja, that's true . . . white people don't like giving us

business licences, pity, man.' 'Ja,' commented Muthu, 'Europeans don't like competition from us Indians.'

Satha contemplated Muthu's morose face for a while. Then he said, 'Why you don't change your name? You know, to white people's name?'

'What! Can't do dat!'

'But can, man. Look my cousin-brother, his name's Jaybalan . . . white people call him Jesse. He change his surname from Appadu to Appolos. That's a Greek name. When he write letter now to white man, the white man think him foreign-white man. He now getting top-class foreign-white treatment! You know foreign-whites getting best treatment in our country?'

'But he can only do this when he's writing to somebody?'

'Ja, but man, he getting lot privileges with letters . . . because they thinking him one witou, not a bloody coolie!'

'But that must have been long ago?'

'No man, it's happening now. Yay! You go, change name from Coopoosamy to something important sounding. Now what I heard that Major Tate calling you? What was it . . . Cooper, that's it, COOPER!'

'Go 'way man, you mad!'

'How then you gonna get licence? That Trishen's getting fat. You wasting time, money on that Shakas shop. You can't be two places one time. You got to look after one shop, man.'

'Ja, but the white man will never let me get a white man's name. Besides I'm not Christian.'

'Look, you Tamil, you always Tamil. This white name's just to bluff the witous. White name don't make you Christian. My cousin Jaybalan, he not Christian just because white people call him Jesse.'

'Ja, but I don't know, my family always had Indian

name. What are my relatives gonna think?'

'Your relatives, they not clever like you. If they had half your brains they'd make money like you, and they too would have English names. What use our Indian names? Only get us into trouble.'

Muthu suddenly looked serious and sober, 'Ja, but it's like spitting on our ancestors, our culture; our names are symbolic of everything that gives us a rich heritage, our identity ....'

'Addah, man, what you talking? What's in a name? One name's as good as another. And you know for the white man we're nothing. We just non-whites. He know nutting 'bout our culture, 'bout us. We nothing for him. At least when we use his name we might get somewhere ... you not cross when the white customers call you Michael or Cooper?'

'No I'm not cross. But I donno, Satha, fifty years I been Muthusamy Coopoosamy, now suddenly you want me to be become Michael Cooper ... I don't know whether I can adjust to it.'

'For more than twenty years the white people kept name Michael for you. All you doing is making the thing legal, that's all.'

'Hell, I don't know ...'

'You'll adjust, man, we Indians know lot 'bout 'dapting. We good at it. The white man, he always closing the front door and we always finding the back door, the side door ...'

'Heck, Satha, I feel lousy 'bout this; these damn white people ... they name us like they name their cats and dogs and now we add insult to injury by going one step farther and making their "pet-names" legal ...'

Satha was not to be put off, 'Well, you might feel bad about it, but man, it serves a higher purpose. It's gonna help your upliftment.'

Muthu looked away from Satha. For a few moments he became oblivious to the noise around him. He stared into space, much as he did when he played chess, and pondered what Satha had said. In a crazy way it made sense. It was not the first time he had been forced to eat humble pie in order to get ahead. And it was the kind of tactic that had helped people like him to survive.

'We make it by using the opportunity, seizing the initiative, not by sitting on our backsides and letting events overwhelm us! Sometimes it paid to sacrifice the Bishop and gain the Queen,' he reflected to himself. A gleam came into his eyes.

Satha noticed the change in Muthu's face, 'Look,' he said, 'I got one lawyer friend. He tell you.'

The lawyer confirmed Satha's story. Muthu thought about the matter for a few more weeks but there was no hope of getting his hardware licence through a normal application. It was a big thing changing his name, yet he had got used to being called Michael and Cooper. Even his friends and most of the Africans and Indians were calling him by these names. His wife didn't object and he had no children. He thought she actually liked the white name and often called him Michael. It was becoming the vogue for Indians to have shortened English names like 'Pat' for Pathmanandan or 'Terence' for Thenageran. Muthu felt very afraid and nervous, but he decided to put his faith in God and do what was necessary. He has very little land — certainly not enough to farm and survive on. So he set up a hardware store in a *bundu* when other people thought that he was mad to do so. But he had stocked what the farmers had wanted and his prices were keen. He had behaved with humility and the white farmers had not felt threatened. It was to their advantage to buy from him rather than go to the distant town and buy hardware.

So Muthu made the long journey to the Department of Indian Affairs in Tegwhite to change his name. He was directed through a maze of offices (and was often given wrong directions by irritable clerks) till he finally arrived at the section that handled many things, including name-changes. The waiting area was empty. The only person in the front office was an Indian clerk who was busy writing at his desk. The man noticed the sheepish-looking, badly dressed Indian come into the office but he continued writing. There were no seats in the reception area and there was just the one solitary desk behind the counter. A plastic name-plate on the desk proclaimed, 'Ahmed Mayet'. Muthu could see a closed door at the back of Ahmed's open office. The fancy brass name-plate had emblazoned on it: SENIOR SUPERVISOR and below it in elegant capitals: MR BALLARD. Muthu stood respectfully for a minute thinking that the important-looking clerk had noticed him. After another minute Muthu gave a discreet cough. Ahmed ignored the lone, dark man. Then a white man entered the office. Ahmed put on a warm, welcoming, obsequious smile and said, as he stood up: 'Good afternoon, Mr Nicholson, sir! Can I help you, sir?'

'Hello, Ahmed! Yes, I'm just going to see Mr Ballard.' The white man was already entering Ahmed's office through the swing-door. Ahmed's smile widened and Mr Nicholson urbanely breezed through into Mr Ballard's office after barely a knock and a calling out of his name.

'Eh, excuse me, sir,' Muthu asked.

But Ahmed acted as if Muthu was not there. The old man didn't know what to do. He needed help from the clerk, and he couldn't afford to get upset, so he waited meekly. Finally, after a further two minutes Ahmed stopped writing and deigned to cast an imperial glance at what looked to him to be a country bumpkin.

'Ja?' he barked, his hand still holding his pen.

'Please, sir,' said Muthu in a plaintive tone as if he was back at school, 'I want to change . . . to change my name.' Muthu was hunched forward in his shabby clothes clenching his hat in his hands.

He looked thoroughly servile. Ahmed grinned to himself. This was going to be an amusing day after all!

'Ja, well, what is your name now?'

'Muthu, sir, Muthusamy Coopoosamy.'

'So, what are you going to change yow name to? Poo-poo or Coo-poo?' Ahmed grinned.

'No sir.' Years of bureaucratic rudeness and insults had largely inured Muthu to any minor attacks launched by second-rate front office clerks. With great dignity, as if he was already a white man, Muthu said, 'I want to become . . . eh . . . I want to be called . . . I mean . . .'

'Yes man, out with it. What's going to be your new name?'

'Michael, sir. Michael Cooper!' Even Muthu couldn't believe he had so much effrontery.

'What?' Ahmed exclaimed, his eyes bulging. His pale face turned a shade of pink and he pushed his glasses back. This coal-black coolie wanted a white man's name. Everybody knew that lots of coolies were crazy but this . . . ! Ahmed had some white blood in him and he felt that he was more entitled to take on a white man's name than this, this . . . But he had stuck to his own name. Now here was a coolie with the gall . . .

He struggled to maintain his composure and asked, 'Why do you want a white man's name?'

'Oh no sir, it's not that, it's not that at all; it's just that

I got a business and my European customers, they always call me Mike or Michael. My name Muthusamy . . . well, it's difficult for white people to say. Then, all the white people, they calling me Cooper instead of Coopoosamy. Me, I'm thinking, Michael Cooper is a nice-sounding name . . . and it's not wrong, because the clever white people . . . they're already calling me like that. So I thought nice to make it legal on the pass-book.' Muthu had spoken earnestly and respectfully and Ahmed had listened attentively.

'Really? Well, I don't know about this. Why aren't you proud to be an Indian and have a nice Indian name? You can change your name if you want, but change it to an Indian name. Otherwise the white people, they might get suspicious.'

'Begging pardon, sir, but this way I make things easy for the white man . . . and this is the white man's country . . .' Ahmed shook his head . . . the tricks the coolies got up to . . . they were too much. He had heard the Europeans say that you couldn't keep them down no matter what you did. They were too cunning, that was the trouble, said the Europeans.

And he knew that the new laws allowed people to change their names to just about anything. That was bad. Soon you'd have a whole lot of subversives changing their names to that of seditious people like Mandela or Gandhi. This reform business was really getting out of hand. The non-whites didn't seem to know their place anymore and 'elevated' non-whites like himself who were so indispensable to the white baas were coming increasingly under pressure.

Reluctantly, he pushed the necessary forms across to Muthu and told him to advertise the name change in the white daily newspaper three times in three weeks.

Muthu felt as if he was walking on air when he left

the office. 1969 might be a lucky year after all.

Two months after the advertisements appeared in the paper and after he had personally handed the application forms to Ahmed, Muthu had still not been given official notification of the name change. He went in to see Ahmed. Ahmed found it difficult to ignore the bumbling old man completely and after only two minutes he spoke to him.

'Yes?'

'Please sir, when will I be informed of my name change? It's gone more than two months now. There haven't been any objections to my name change, have there, sir?'

'No, there haven't been any objections but you must be patient, Coo-poo-sammy, these things take time. Many important Government Departments must be notified of this thing you want to do. My supervisor, Mr Ballard, is a very busy man. The government can't be hurried, you know. You must be very grateful that we allowed you to do this thing.' Ahmed didn't think it was right that a grand thing like a white man's name should come easily to a coolie

But Muthu was getting a bit irritated now. (Almost like a white man, he reflected to himself with mild surprise.) 'But sir,' he remonstrated, 'I have filled in all the forms and I have advertised as you instructed at great personal expense and nothing's happened.'

Ahmed looked at the Indian with astonishment. Was the fellow completely barmy? Did he think that a white man's name made him even slightly into a white man? The old man was even speaking with a degree of confidence that was not there before and he stood a lot straighter. He was actually looking Ahmed in the eye. This was a coolie who needed to be kept in his place!

He had not passed the Cooper file across to Mr Ballard. Now he wondered idly whether he ever should.

'You must go home and wait, Mr Coo-poo-sammy,' he said sternly.

'Patience. Patience is a virtue that certain races will do well to imbibe,' he added in the same tone of voice that he had heard the Europeans use when they said that sort of thing. The blank bureaucratic wall was impenetrable. Muthu left.

However, three weeks later, Muthu was finally summoned to appear before Supervisor Ballard. Dressed impeccably (after all, he was going to see a white man this time) by Satha in a new three-piece suit and tie, old man Muthu presented himself at the Indian Affairs office. Nowadays he brought a book along that he was studying, so that he could keep himself busy while Ahmed made him wait. The book was *Learn To Speak English Properly.*

He arrived ten minutes early for his appointment but Ahmed only allowed him to see the European half an hour later.

Trying to look as harmless as possible, Muthu entered the office and stood respectfully at attention till the white man decided to look at him. It was a very large, very untidy office full of files and books all thrown higgardly-piggedly all over the place. After about a minute the official cast a scalding look at Muthu as if he was a horrible filthy mess and curtly addressed him from his sitting position.

'Now what's all this about you wanting to change your name to a . . . ?' Ballard couldn't bring himself to say it.

He was a big, hairy, fat man with a huge beer belly that made him look many months pregnant. His brown safari suit bulged in an unseemly manner over his abdomen. His hair was an unruly brown thatch. Ballard was not yet fifty and had lived the good life in what had been a model colony. But now things were changing . . . as was personified by this ebony, cringing little toad. The awful expression on the pink man's face was thoroughly intimidating. This was a cold, hostile wall that Muthu was facing, somehow worse than Ahmed outside. At least with Ahmed you felt that beyond all the crude harassment was a fellow-being with at least some feeling, that the silly superciliousness was in a sense childish playfulness. But this . . . this was a cruel monster. Muthu thought that the of ficial could quite easily issue a decree for him to lose his business or be kicked out of his home without so much as a twinge of his Christian conscience.

He waited for the supervisor to complete the sentence, but then he finally said, 'Sir, I'm not trying to be difficult. I serve the white people, sir. They call me Cooper. Mr Tate is a rich farmer, sir, he told me Cooper is a nice name for me, sir. With respect, sir, I'm not trying to be a cheeky coolie, sir.' Muthu had rehearsed his defence many times at home and he felt quite pleased with his delivery. Even Mr Stevenson, the author of the English book, might have been satisfied, reflected Muthu.

'Well, I don't know about that . . .' Ballard glared at the uncomfortable-looking coolie and remembered that he had named his dog, Bond. Well, what was wrong with the name Cooper for a coolie? It was a good Anglo-Saxon name and perhaps it was all part of the march of Western Culture. The American Negroes had all lost their own names and languages. Perhaps that was the destiny of the Indians too. Besides whatever name the coolies used, they were still coolies. Muthu had known that he would be treated provocatively, but as he had planned, he kept cool.

With a great deal of effort he suppressed the anger welling up within him and continued in an even voice, 'I beg your pardon, sir, but I have a letter from Major Tate, sir.'

'Really?' Ballard was surprised. The Indian handed the Supervisor the letter. Ballard opened the sealed envelope. It was neatly typed and stated:

TO WHOM IT MAY CONCERN

I have known Muthusamy Coopoosamy for the last thirty years. During that time he has rendered valuable service to the local European farming community through his hardware and poultry businesses. He has often served us even on Sundays. During that time he has become known to the local farmers as Michael and at times has been referred to as Michael Cooper. He has always been of a cooperative disposition and I am sure that a name change will merely legalise what has become a statement of fact.

It was signed with a large flourish by the Major. Ballard was impressed. This was the right sort of coolie, then; not one of your agitators. And it seemed the ape was serious about this name-change thing. Ballard played with his little beard, enjoying the feeling of the fur and the sense of sexual power he always revelled in when he tormented a non-white, much like a cat playing with a cockroach. Suddenly he transfixed the Indian with his cold 'white man' look and said imperiously 'You may go.'

Muthu slid out of the office feeling very inferior, very stupid and a real nuisance. Why had he let Satha talk him into this crazy thing?

After another month, Muthu came into Ahmed's waiting room. This time after only a minute, Ahmed said, with just a touch of irritation, 'Yes?' Muthu was tired of everything: coming here, being treated like a pest, everything. But he had spent good money on this thing and it was only right that he got what he had paid for. After all, what he was doing was not against the white man's law. Muthu didn't say anything. He just looked with a haggard expression on his face at the clerk.

Ahmed stood up, threw his pen down on his desk and said, 'Ah, Mr Coo-poo-samy! We've got to know you well!' He grinned at the old man and came over to the counter. He leaned over and said in a confidential, conspiratorial tone, 'You know, old man, the trouble with us Indians (Ahmed's heart almost gave a lurch when he said this. He didn't really think of himself as an Indian, well not the ordinary kind of Indian anyway) is that we tend to work very hard on doing something like building a fine temple, but we lack the finishing touch. What the white people call *finesse*. You know, an Indian will sweat blood to build a house, but he won't spend a rand on getting his grass verge cut . . . Indians will build a magnificent Temple but they'll pay the priest peanuts. An Indian will study hard and qualify as a doctor but he'll talk like a motor-mechanic. Now people like us, you know what I mean,' Ahmed winked a few times at the old man and gave a conspiratorial grin, 'who try for something better with our lives . . .' Muthu's face feigned ignorance. Ahmed continued, 'Oh, come on now, you know what I mean. We are birds of a feather, you and I. You trying to take on a white man's name like Cooper of all things, and me here . . . well if you want a white man's name, you better learn to be a little like him . . .'

'You mean this *finesse* thing?'

'Precisely, old man, precisely!' Who said you couldn't teach an old dog new tricks, thought Ahmed. 'Look here Muthu,' he growled, 'you don't look stupid to me. (Well not completely stupid, cogitated Ahmed.) But things haven't come right for you, because you haven't put the "finishing touch" to this thing!'

'Finishing touch, sir?'

'Yes, man; the "finishing touch" — a bit of gravy; you know what I mean, some butter on the toast, a bit of grease on the . . .'

Ahmed looked knowingly at the Indian. For a few moments Muthu was puzzled but then suddenly the devious expression on the clerk's face made sense . . . 'have to learn to be a little like the white man,' thought Muthu. 'Is there anything in particular you would like, sir, I mean in the way of gravy?'

'Well, I happen to know that Mr Ballard likes Chicken *Biryani* . . . and his mouth absolutely waters for *Dhall-roti* . . . Now if you could see your way clear to . . .'

'Oh, certainly sir, most stupid of me sir! I have a little poultry-farm I run on the side, sir, do you think Mr Ballard and you, would like some eggs too, sir?' Ahmed's face was one big wolfish grin.

Satha and his friend were drinking, and why not? This time they had good reason: they had something to celebrate! 'Mr Cooper, sir, now that you have Trishen in your big shop and under your thumb, are you going to squeeze?'

'Like a white man, Satha, like a white man! With *finesse*, Satha, with loads of ice-cold, decorous *finesse*!'

'Ice-cold *what*?'

'Decorous finesse, Satha, decorous finesse. It means to

handle something carefully . . . with a fine, delicate touch. I'm reading all the books the white people read, Satha. They can't stop us doing that.'

'Really, Mu, I mean Michael.' Satha's eyes were blood-shot and bulging. He was really impressed. He gripped his drink tightly in his left hand and stared at Mr Cooper.

'Yes, man, and I listen to them very carefully when they talk, the white people. Don't you think that I am beginning to sound like them now?'

'Mr Cooper, sir, I think you are.'

'And I've enrolled in a Speech and Drama class . . . you just wait and see; soon, when I talk to you on the phone you won't be able to make out that Mr Cooper is anything but a dyed-in-the-wool Englishman.'

'Died in the *what*?'

Michael grinned. 'A puckah Englishman, Satha. A real, honest-to-goodness English bull-dog!'

'Ja man, that's true; that's how you sound.' Michael gave his friend a benign look of self-assured superiority much like that he had so often seen the whites give the non-whites.

'Well let's celebrate now, eh, Mike. These days you even drinking like a witou!' He held up his drink with a flourish, 'Here's to your new name, Michael, here's to your hardware licence, to the Licensing Bureau, to Capitalism, here's to . . .'

Michael clicked glasses with Satha: 'To the Indian Affairs bums. To Western Civilisation, to Free Enterprise, and Satha . . . ?'

'Yes, my friend?'

'Here's to the Finishing Touch!'

Bheki Maseko

THE WEDDING

I was only ten years old when the wedding took place. Being the youngest member of the family, it was Aunty Lizzy who readily suggested that I accompany my eldest brother as a page boy. Aunty Lizzy, who was my father's eldest sister, was the self-appointed organiser of the wedding.

One Saturday morning Aunty Lizzy dragged me and mama to a shop in Kliptown where she had seen a very beautiful suit for me. She was so excited over the coming wedding that she was going to pay for everything that I needed for the occasion.

The suit she pointed to in the window was a yellow three-piece affair that would have saved a very good purpose in winter. Before I could tell my aunt that I preferred the one next to the yellow one she took me by the hand and dragged me into the shop.

Aunty was feverish with joy when the Indian shopkeeper agreed with her that the suit was nice and added that it was imported from America

'Didn't I tell you, Trifina. I knew from the beginning that it was from America.' Aunty chuckled excitedly holding up the jacket for mama to have a good look.

There and then I was stripped to my skin and forced into that suit before mama or I could say anything. I was then hauled before the mirror. I could not believe my eyes. What I saw in that mirror was a strange looking, dwarf-like creature in a bright yellow suit!

To my relief mama protested that the suit was a little too big for me.

'The boy will grow into it,' the shopkeeper argued. 'And he looks like a young English gentleman.' He fastened the buttons of the jacket and turned me to face mama. I could feel his hand discreetly pinching the back of the jacket to give it the appearance of being the right size.

I was miserable. If young English gentlemen looked like dwarves I really did not wish to look like one of them.

But worse was to come! The shopkeeper brought a hat which he suggested would go very well with the suit. Without giving it a second thought Aunty Lizzy took the hat and slammed it on to my head with such force that, if it were open on top it would have slipped right through to my shoulders. It was so tight that it pinched my eyebrows as she pushed it further down. Then she spun me around to face the mirror once more. What I saw there was beyond description!

On our arrival back home the family piled into the dining room to view my new clothes.

Daniel was there too. He was my elder brother who could laugh so easily that father once said of him that he could laugh at a passing fly. My brother stood behind mama, waiting anxiously. I knew I was in trouble.

When aunty unwrapped the suit and held it up for all to see Daniel began to giggle. But when aunty put me into the suit and smashed my hat on Daniel went into a fit of laughter.

'Get out, you silly fool!' cried aunty, glaring at Daniel and pointing at the door. 'One day you will laugh at death itself. Silly fool!'

Daniel's chest shook as he tried to contain his laughter. He hurried out of the room, keeping a safe distance from aunty. But once out of the room he burst into a hearty cackle once more.

I don't think aunty knew why Daniel was laughing because she again began to praise the suit with the same fervour she had shown at the shop.

Pitched in front of our four-roomed house was a tent into which all the wedding guests squeezed on a hot December Sunday.

The bridal entourage was seated at the far end of the tent, away from the entrance that was blocked by people trying to steal a glimpse of the couple — especially the bride.

The service was conducted by a priest from the Lion Gospel Church of Zion of Nazareth, of which my family, including Aunty Lizzy, were members.

All members of the Church wore blue-and-white uniforms that boasted a very large cross on the back. Women wore hats that were starched to stand upright on their heads like a bristle. This made aunty look like a cock. The heat in the tent was unbearable and I felt as if I were in an oven in my woollen suit that was buttoned upfront and a bowtie strangling me. I protested at this discomfort, sweat streaming down my face and into my neck, but aunty would not allow me to even unbutton the jacket.

The Church members didn't seem to mind the heat though and seemed to be having a good time. They danced vigorously each time the priest started a song.

Aunty Lizzy, who stood right behind me, would scream out the first notes of the song even almost before it left the priest's lips. Then she swayed her huge body rhythmically from side to side so that her big breasts brushed against my ears. I leaned forward to avoid this unnecessary beating and ended up crouched in a very uncomfortable position. Aunt Lizzy was far too spirited then to realise what discomfort she was causing me.

She bellowed like a cow when the wind entered her — bellowing right into my ears. She made me think of the cow that father had slaughtered the previous day for the wedding feast.

Fortunately Daniel was too busy to come into the tent. The silly fool would not have spared me. From the day he saw me in the thing he called me 'Yellow Suit'. But there was some compassion in my brother for he did promise not to tell any of our friends about it.

One guy I did not wish to bump into in my suit was Sipho. Like Daniel he enjoyed poking fun at anything ridiculous, not caring a damn how his victims felt. My eyes kept searching the tent for him but he was thankfully not there.

Not that I was scared of Sipho, mind you; I was physically far stronger than him . The problem was that he was the type of guy who was prepared to fight anywhere, anytime. And if you beat him it meant that the grudge would be borne forever and another fight could break out anytime. Losing meant that you had to dance to Sipho's tune.

And suddenly Sipho was there in the tent, right in front of me! He was sandwiched by two burly women who were too preoccupied by the sermon to notice him.

Our eyes met. And his lips parted into a mischievous smile that exposed two missing front teeth. I was the first to look away.

This day wasn't turning out right for me, I thought. Now all it needed was for Christina to be around as well.

Christina was my classmate who lived a few streets away from us. There was nothing between us. But I was aware of a feeling of emptiness whenever she was absent from class. I felt very uncomfortable in her presence. And I felt jealous whenever I saw guys playing with her or chasing her during break or after school. But I was pretty scared to talk to her. Fortunately she didn't turn up for the wedding.

The priest had been talking for an hour and still had much more to offer. He had a big bald patch on his head that sweated profusely. A moustache that extended about three inches from his face gave him a fierce look. His ballooned cheeks and round spectacles made me think of an owl.

One of the many messages of his sermon was that people should become devoted members of the Church if they wanted to go to heaven and become angels. Aunty Lizzy was a devoted member of the Church and was always in the forefront of fundraising and other Church activities. If Aunty Lizzy ever became an angel she would surely be a very militant one.

The reason why I thought so was because she threw her weight around quite a lot on this earth of ours.

I remember one Sunday our neighbour's dog soiled our lawn after aunty had given the yard a thorough cleaning. Indignantly she called our neighbour across the fence to come and clean up the mess. She didn't have dogs in her yard, she reminded the bewildered neighbour.

It was mama who intervened and begged aunty to cool down. The next day, after aunty had left for the kitchens where she worked and stayed, mama apologised to the neighbour.

'Only those people who are serving the Lord shall inherit everlasting life!' warned the priest hoarsely.

'Amen! Hallelujah! Praise the Lord!' cried the congregation and aunty's voice could be heard clearly above everybody else's.

'All those who are not devoted to the work of the Lord know that they will spend everlasting life in fire in the hereafter. Praise the name of the Lord!'

'Amen, hallelujah!'

The dreaded thought of going to hell after death really gave me butterflies in my tummy. The priest had emphasised countless times that 'thou shall not steal' if you wanted to be assured of a place in heaven. I was stealing sugar and condensed milk every day! Not to speak of the peaches and apricots from people's yards to and from school!

After the priest's long and fiery sermon, the sick were called to the front and knelt in a semi-circle. The priest placed a hand on each of them and called on the power of God to rid them of their ailments and their suffering.

Our overzealous priest was not content with merely laying his hands on the invalids and often resorted to slapping and beating the sick congregants. The believers would squirm and flinch in pain. And the more they reacted in this manner the more they would be slapped, the assumption being that they had a demon in them that could be beaten out.

I remember a middle-aged woman who used to come to Church accompanied by relatives. She was mentally disturbed and a regular victim of our priest's enthusiastic blessing. She was heavily built and squirmed and kicked a great deal under the priest's hand. Aunty was the only one who could pin down the poor woman until the blessing was over.

Others would help by holding the woman's hands and feet to prevent her from booting or smacking the priest or his helpers. This exercise usually took a long time because the woman was unusually strong and energetic and did not tire quickly. The priest and his helpers were satisfied only when the demon was slapped into submission.

After the 'panel beating' — as we called it when the adults were not listening — the participants would pant and wipe their sweaty faces with their handkerchiefs. But not aunty. She always looked ready to take on Muhamed Ali in a fifteen rounder!

After the service aunty would encourage the relatives of the sick woman to bring her as often as possible as the demon was getting softer. She argued that the devil was using the woman to show his strength.

I often thought that, should the devil dare show his ugly face at our church aunty would knock him stone cold.

I used to wish that old bald head should become so sick that his helpers would have to lay their blessed hands on him! I would have loved to see him writhe and kick while aunty pinned him to the floor.

I always stood as far away from that semi-circle of sufferers as possible. But sometimes aunty, for whatever reason, ordered me to enter the fray. Then I would also be jabbed and slapped until I convulsed in agony.

I soon realised that the writhing encouraged the jabbing and slapping and so I remained dead still, teeth clenched, eyes closed and praying to hear the word 'amen'.

The sermons usually took forever. No song sounded better in my ears than the one we sang just before closing prayers. The priest, or one of his helpers, was always long-winded and this was another time I would wait for 'amen'.

Our denomination did not have a church building so the services were held in turn at the homes of the congregants. We would gather in the tiny dining rooms where the furniture would be removed to leave space for the drama. The door would be shut to prevent curious children from jamming the doorway and staring at our wild dances and other antics. In summer my worshipping became unbearable; a wild song and dance accompanied by the beat of a drum tha pierced my ears with its

Gudum! Gudum! Gudum! Gudum! Gudum! the drum continued ceaselessly as we shuffled barefoot in a circle around the room. Nobayeni, a girl about my age, knelt in the centre of the room beating the hell out of that drum as she swayed from side to side to the rhythm of the song.

Nobayeni had a long, thin face and wore a white doek that hung to her shoulders. She was said to have a gift of foretelling future events. Every service sent Nobayeni into a rapture. The elders loved Nobayeni but I loathed her. Aunty, unaware of my resentment for the girl, called her my makoti.

It was customary and respectful to remove our shoes before entering the house of prayer as it were. And the shoes were locked up in a coal box or somewhere safe after one Sunday when we went out to find that all our shoes had been stolen — including my brand new takkies!

It had taken me more than six months of cajoling and begging before father bought me those takkies. And that Sunday had been the first time I had stepped out in them. I would not like to repeat the names aunty called the thief who had taken my footwear as we walked home from Church that Sunday. She must surely have forgotten my presence for, when she came to her senses, she brushed a consoling hand through my hair and told me to forgive and forget.

But what of the wedding!

Many of the guests — and the bride — had begun to doze. Aunty had revived me a hundred times with a few gentle slaps on the cheek — sometimes not so gentle, mind you. She then wiped my face with a damp handkerchief before turning my head upright to face the priest. The strong garlic that whooshed from her mouth was what revived me more than anything!

Thankfully our custom does not allow men to wear hats indoors. What would have happened to me with that hat smashed down to my eyebrows in that furnace?

I was so annoyed that I felt like throttling aunty until she gave a guttural sound instead of bellowing like a beast as she had been joyfully doing throughout the sermon. I also would have liked to take Owl Face and smash his face into the cake that had pride of place on a table near him.

On either side of the wedding cake, covered by a transparent white 'veil', was a colourful array of sweets, peanuts, cold drinks, salads and other delights. How would Owl react if I pulled the tablecloth and sent all these goodies flying?

Slowly I screwed two ends of the table-cloth into tight balls in my damp hands while Owl continued to enrapture his flock with his pompous talk and while Aunty Lizzy continued to sing at the top of her voice and bellow like a beast every time the wind entered her.

I plucked up my courage, clenched my teeth and gave one almighty pull.

People near the table jumped back in fright. My sister, the bride, leapt for safety — but was too slow and a bowl of beetroot salad plopped face down into her lap. The three-tier wedding cake flew in different directions, the smallest tier landing in my lap.

Silence reigned in the room as bewildered guests tried to remove stains from their immaculate clothes. Some tried to remove the stains from the bride's dress but it was crimson from the waist down.

Owl just stood and stared, his mouth wide open. I had messed up his jam session.

Aunty was so enraged I was convinced she would strangle me. But instead she took me by the hand and led me out of the tent and into mama's bedroom where mama sat with other old ladies. Aunty ordered me to sit on a grass mat on the floor.

Mama and her friends were not just seated there purposelessly. Our custom demands that at a wedding the groom's mother-in-law sits in a hut or bedroom during the ceremony. They sit in a dignified manner with rugs or shawls draped over their shoulders.

I found myself in an embarrassing situation as I became the centre of attraction sitting opposite mama and other old grannies who shook their heads sadly after hearing what I had done.

'Poor boy,' commented one of the grannies sympathetically, 'he must have been hungry.'

'What?' sneered aunty. 'He might've been hungry but it was not that which caused him to do what he did. This was simply the devil who worked through the boy to spoil the wedding.'

I felt relieved to hear the devil being blamed for my mischief. Presently aunty left the room and I heard her in the kitchen issuing instructions to feed the guests. I wished she would order someone to bring me a plate of food.

Then Daniel appeared with a mouthwatering plate of food which he placed on the floor before me. He had a smile on his face and I knew that he was dying to tell me something.

'Baba Ndlela (the priest) is very angry,' Daniel whispered in my ear. 'He says he is going to send the devil to take you tonight!'

'Liar!' I cried, sneering boldly at my brother.

But Daniel knew I was frightened.

A thought crossed my mind. Perhaps the devil was angry because Aunt Lizzy had blamed him for my sins.

'The devil will first lick your face to lull you before he takes you away.' He put a hand to his mouth to smother a laughing fit. He knew he had me where he wanted me.

'Liar! Liar!' I screamed, tearing at Daniel's shirt.

A vision of the devil with his horns towering over me filled me wild horror. At the movies I had seen Dracula suck the blood of his victims. It frightened me and whenever I thought of it I dreaded going to bed at night. Now here was Daniel telling me about the devil whom aunty said turned all sinners on a spit as he roasted them forever in hell.

'Get out of this room, Daniel!' mama yelled, slapping the floor angrily with the palm of her hand.

'What did he say to you?' mama asked after my brother had fled from the room.

'He wanted to eat my food,' I lied.

The last thing I remember on my sister' s wedding day was mama waking me to relieve myself before carrying me to my bed. It was dark and most of the guests had left. But fortunately there were many other children in the bedroom. As I drifted back into sleep I saw a picture of Owl advancing on me, the devil's fork in his hand.

Es'kia Mphahlele
CROSSING OVER

I have come to tell you my husband that they are taking us away, this today. I have told you many times, have I not, that they are talking about it in the villages. The cloud that has been hanging over us is at last raining whiteman's urine and excrement upon us. These are bad times for us my husband hard times. Now the chief says he cannot do anything about it did you ever hear of a thing like that! The chief not able to do anything —

hm — mehlolo*! In the old days there was nothing a king could not do — when kings were men — today all chiefs are mere maggots. They have men's pants on but let lightning strike me down if I know what they have got hanging in those pants — truly the ancestors forgive me. Now they are coming with their lorries my man let me tell you they are not playing these white people — it is not small things they are planning. What did you say husband of mine? Oh, whiteman Fatamabele?*[1] *— he is still here. But since you left my good man no one goes to work for him any more. Only that mad Rameetse looks after his pigs. Fatamabele has sold and lost all his other animals. The field lies waste and has become a good home for rabbits and snakes. People say this. We hear tell that Fatamabele goes to Manganeng for strong magic herbs from* *those great mountain doctors and that Rameetse's head has been shaken up by them. You remember how he always complained that an ant once entered his nostril while he was sleeping and now it is travelling up and down and feeding on his brains and mucus. Else why should a grown man still be working for Fatamabele, why should he be taking the pigs out only to chase after them back to the sty when the boerman has gone to Mashishing?*[2] *But you wait, just you watch, Fatamabele's day is coming — this land will stink from a single dead rat, you will see, let me tell you.*

Where are we going? Do I know? Only they know, the men with big fat heads and hearts like rocks. We hear tell it is very far far, away from here towards the mountains of the setting sun. Have I what husband of mine? Oh no, do not worry about him, I will talk to him myself. How can I forget, eh? Forgetting him will mean forgetting the pain you carried to your grave. Sleep in peace son of the ancestors. And our two sons the other end of the burial ground — I cannot go to them because the lorries are coming soon. But tell them I am not forsaking you or else I am not the daughter of Tudumo and my totem is not kubu.[3] *Tell them I am coming to lie here with you all when the long endless night closes my eyes at last. Oh why does this man* Goromente[4] *keep us apart — does he not know that we want to be buried where the Shades will see us — who wants to die away from where they sleep!*

You wait, I will come back. Let me whisper in your ear — no one else knows my secret. Just you wait my man you hear! Something tells me I shall not be long coming to you. Eh? No, I feel no pain anywhere my heart is strong and even stronger when I talk with you like this. But something tells me my days will not stretch out any more. Now I must go my man. Did I tell you also that police — many many — are waiting at Mashishing so that they drive us like cattle if we refuse to move, or did I not? Ahhhh, being here with you husband of mine is a cure for my aching bones. Like the gentle winter sun that eases the body for the blood to flow and give you new strength. Being with you also reminds me each time that I should be tying up my little bundles to come home and join you. But spare my life, badimo[5] *spare it until I shall have done the last duty. Did you call? How can you call me when I am here at your side? Now listen husband of mine, I have hidden the firemaker in a corner that I cannot forget. He will never think there is something like it so close to the farm.*

"It is me calling you, Mama, you will have to stand up; we hear the lorries are just over the hill so we must be ready. Look the sun is already bright. Everyone is ready with their things." The voice came from a woman approaching with her son.

'Ma-Selepe turned round. "*Hao, ngwana'ka*, it is you!" she said, "and my little husband too!"

The older woman took the 11-year-old grandson, Lefanyana, by the hand and drew him closer to the grave. "Here is your namesake husband of mine and here also is your daughter-in-law. Pray for us to the Mighty One and ask *badimo* to bless us and lead the way out of this home ground."

After a few moments of silence 'Ma-Selepe, daughter-in-law Baile, and her grandson began the walk into sunrise, towards the village.

The trucks came.

The chief and his council were ready to take orders from the whiteman Van Rensburg, who led the convoy of authority. He was in charge of the move. The trucks set aside for personal effects, such as linen, furniture and others, lined up for the people to load. Then the vehicles set aside to carry the people of the three villages moved in — some fifty-two thousand heads all told, the officials said. A few families that had a buggy here, a trolley there, and a wagon with four oxen or donkeys used their own transport. Like Motau and his wife, who lived alone. They had a trolley and four oxen. The wife sat upright with her hands crossed on her lap.

"Hei, Koffie!" Motau yelled, "*mosela'mmago*! Go where the others are going, *jou bliksem se donder! Wena* Josefa, move, move it *bliksem*! It is me in charge here. Whiteman is in charge of me I am in charge of you goddammet. Hei you, Tring-Tring, *sewerenoto*, trek! Pull — where are you heading, if you had any balls at all you would understand what is happening to us who have come out of the black womb. Moving us, moving us — they think we are mere rocks they can roll from here to there . . . My parents and their parents and those before them lie buried here at Marulaneng . . . *Ke maloko feela*, I can tell you, just cow dung, this whole business . . . I never thought I would see the day when my body would lie on the ground so far away from our people's home dear woman of mine, *never*. The ancestors are weeping for us I know . . . What does the government man in Tshwane take us for — pieces of furniture?"

"They have been weeping so long, oh, so long." It was Motau's wife to say something, and yet she spoke so calmly, with all the weight of the moment pressing on her shoulders. "We are too old to fight, my old man, death is our only saviour now. I just know it. Every time this *leburu*[6] they call Goromente carries our people away from their burial ground, from the soil whose dust they have tasted all their lives, the older ones simply die as soon as they set foot in the new place. You remember our friends who have been to those far-away lands have told us these things."

Motau's wife wept silently.

To suppress his own urge to bawl out into the pastoral silence, Motau sniffed and with a rapid gesture brushed his nose with the left wrist.

The rest of the journey of some three hundred kilometres was a time of sniffles, expletives, banter, praise songs to the oxen and to the Motau ancestors. 'Ma-Motau sat bolt upright, her eyes fixed straight ahead as if her man's monologue were mere noises that did not touch her. Over fifty years she had learned to absorb grief so that it became part of her whole being instead of reacting to the minute-to-minute ticking of its clock, as if it were an invasion from outside. This way she was able to encompass its pain, deal with it philosophically but without any consciously devised strategy. To encompass grief was to feel its walls, its roof, its floor, its nooks and crannies, its chemistry, to comprehend it in relation to the time and place that contained it, and then to life time, life place.

Somewhere Motau said, "Do nuttin', do nuttin', cannot do anything, dammet."

"What is it you said?" as if to grab the opportunity for a brief diversion, to shift the weight burning its way into her shoulders, ever so slightly so that it presses on another point in the body.

"The chief says he can do nuttin', just plain nuttin', niks, hm!" Motau threw in the word "nuttin'", "niks" into his native speech to sum up the contempt they had for the language in which orders always came to him and his people, whether directly from the whiteman or through the chief, who was a government agent.

"Do nuttin'," Motau kept repeating, "*ka modimo* — by God! He got nuttin' between his thighs — that is what the fool means . . . fokawl! No balls but fat hanging belly, that's all . . ."

"I must go, Mama, I must go."

"You are only sixteen, what do you think you can do without a piece of paper to show you can count and read and write?"

The boy Ramushu looks away, then his eyes rove round in the truck, registering one face after another: old, wrinkled, young, smooth. The pretty face of Mantwa. About his age, he'd say. Her own eyes spell bewilderment. He wonders if his eyes are like hers, seeming to cry out for help; like the young dove she now reminds him of that struggles to disentangle itself from birdlime he has laid to catch meat for the family, and only tying itself up more and more. All a silent struggle, except for the flap-flap-flap-frrrr-frrrr of the feathers as the bird thrashes about. And then he will release it from its misery and its fear by wringing its neck with one decisive movement of the hand.

Then the boy shakes his head vigorously, as if to shake himself back to consciousness. As the truck rocks the passengers over potholes and ditches the girl's face seems to Ramushu to change moods: bewilderment, fear, expectation . . .

Suddenly he comes back to what he was telling his mother. "So many of my age group have gone to the whiteman's town."

"Stop this foolish talk," the mother says impatiently,

"you don't know what you are saying. Your father left, your elder brother, and now *you* want to leave me. Who is going to look after me and your sisters? Besides, do you want to grow up ignorant, your brains nothing but darkness in such a cruel world. Just look at me you boy, just look at me. Your father, myself, your brothers are all ignorant. This is why white people do us such evil as eclipses the sun, we are just plain ignorant, stupid. What do we understand about this journey, just you *tell* me, tell me boy? All we know is that we are face to face with the kind of evil — that is what *leburu* is — we have never known before in this world. If our children and grandchildren of their own free will refuse to allow some light to enter their brains, then the ancestors help us Almighty Spirit."

Her last words sound desperate. Like one who suspects that her son has a defective mind.

"I do not know, Mama, I do not know. But I know I want to go. There is nothing for me here. I can read and write, what more do I need?"

"You need to know more which you cannot get outside school. People are not meant to grow like trees — just because they get water and food out from the ground. People have to grow in the brain and in the heart. We had only three years of school ourselves but our people, no matter they were your parents or not — our people helped us to know how to live, how to raise you. You will have nobody out there, and a person needs people."

Silence follows as mother and son think more about preventing excessive rocking in the truck, the wheels grinding stone and earth over a rugged patch.

"Your father will not like this Ramushu. You must wait for him to come home and talk to him. I cannot let you go unless your father tells me to." She knows that she is clinging to a straw in the sweep of events that are overtaking the people, but she keeps pushing her argument anyhow. Also, there is that fear in her right now, the realization that her son may not be entirely misguided.

"The only reason he is not here is that his white people refused to release him. You heard the son of Ledimo give us the message, from his own lips. You heard it with your own ears. And your brothers are too far away for me to let them know your intentions."

Ramushu is half listening, half engrossed in his own thoughts.

Clouds of dust are swirling all over and every passenger has a hand over the mouth, which opens only to cough. Women look at one another over garments wrapped round them up to the eyes. The people on the vehicle look like cargo that has neither say nor enthusiasm over the purpose of the journey or destination. Mute Fate is in charge here, whose high priest is the Pretoria government, who in turn delegates authority to the likes of Van Rensburg. These holy messengers' response to Pretoria's deity is always swift and sure. A fierce devotion propels them across their areas of jurisdiction. They seldom if ever feel that they owe anyone any courtesy, any kindness, any understanding in return for understanding. If someone accuses them of excesses on the side of cruelty, their stock response is, "I'm only doing my duty." Motau's interpretation is, "They always say that these *maburu*,[7] they always come up with donkey manure when they are being mean, which is always, the man means I am only doing what I love."

Even when the dust has settled, 'Ma-Selepe is silent throughout much of the trip. She nods or shakes her head in reply to daughter-in-law Baile's questions.

"You must not be so sad Mama. What must your grandchildren feel then? You ought to be thankful through the ancestors that you still have a good son who looks after us all, who cares."

"Where is he now, this today? Why has he not come when these *maburu* have turned our lives into dead and worthless toys, carried to a place that does not even have a name? — hm — *babinatau*!"[8]

"*Hao* Mama, the place is called Marakong, did you not hear?"

"Wherever my people do not lie buried has no name. Wherever my afterbirth does not lie buried in a homestead has no name. What name they call it by is not something I can feel."

She begins to weep. Quietly. Like a well yielding up its water. But she says while wiping her eyes with the corner of her shawl, "I will not cry, no I will not, Selepe, I am not crying, you hear me, just you wait, I am not weeping." She shakes her head to emphasize her statement.

Baile lays her hand gently on the older woman's shoulder, while her 14-year-old daughter and 11-year-old Lefanyana (named for Grandpa Selepe) look on. They comprehend nothing in all this, but are buoyed up by their own childlike sense of adventure.

"The children's father will come, Mama, I know, Monope will come. Perhaps his white people would not let him off today. Has he not always come, has he not always brought us money and food and sometimes sent it through some other man!" In the usual affectionate banter in which she uses mother-in-law's pet-name, Baile concludes, "Let us not hear you complain again Ngwana'Tabane, you hear."

'Ma-Selepe continues to sniffle. Then she mumbles some words Baile cannot make out. Lefanyana fidgets and tries to crane his neck to get the full view of the landscape that seems to glide in the opposite direction. But from where he is sitting he can only see the sky and what is defined by the rear opening of the truck. His elder sister looks steadily at her grandmother. Her face is a picture of simple, bewildered compassion.

The old woman mumbles on, "Tell the spirits I did not want to leave you behind at Marulaneng, son-of-Selepe. It is the pain of the times — father leaves wife and children, brother forsakes sister, sister leaves brother, children leave parents . . . How are these old feet of mine going to walk on new ground . . . Marakong, Marakong, let it go fart in the wind — where have you ever heard such a name for a place!"

Her granddaughter's contemplative eyes stay on the old woman, as if she were observing her for the first time. Shadows play on the child's face where innocence and bewilderment alternate with something that flashes an anticipation of adult concern and insight.

'Ma-Selepe looks at the sky and says, "I smell rain. It is coming, I know it." No-one responds aloud, except Baile who remarks almost irrelevantly, "We are all exhausted, the sun beating down on us like this . . ."

At sunset the next day they arrived at Marakong. All covered, it seemed, with 300 kilometres plus hours of red dust.

The rain came.

It was almost as if it had been programmed to fall just when they were laying out the tents brought by Van Rensburg's people. The rain lashed about and in no time the veld was water-logged. Wherever the veld sagged under the fury of the storm it made small dams where the rain danced mercilessly. The water seemed to dally, not knowing where to go. Dallying was short-lived. For gashes appeared that made rivulets, which in turn cut across to provide channels for the water's escape.

The confusion that reigned among the newcomers was of another order. Screams, yells, shouts, arms flailing in the night; lanterns, shadows darting back and forth to find shelter that was not taking shape fast enough. Van Rensburg himself, if he was there, was invisible. But his people were trying frantically to strike the tents, several of the male newcomers themselves hauling pole and canvas this way and that under the lashing rain.

Soon after the downpour had started, Father O'Brien's name was passed from mouth to mouth among the people. "He has come . . . he is here . . . Father O'Brien has come with his people . . ."

He had been following hard on the caravan's trail. With trucks carrying canned and bagged and packaged food, a van carrying medicines and first aid kits. His people struck a huge tent to contain them and the priest.

This Catholic priest had become a notorious name among all white officials engaged in forced removals. He had been speaking out for human rights in general and the African victims' rights in particular since 1964. Now he was embroiled in this Marulaneng-Marakong resettlement process. The officials always emphasized "resettlement", which rang kinder in the critics' ears than "forced removals" — the blunt truth. All African political movements had been banned. The State sent Nelson Mandela and some of his associates to Robben Island for life on charges of treason. Most other leaders, big and small, fled into exile, following those before them.

Whites had barricaded themselves with iron laws in fear of a black revolution. So they told themselves and one another, the propaganda machine of their government reinforcing their tribal myths, their image of themselves as the superior people. What they didn't tell themselves was the deeper truth: fear of themselves. Conscience seemed to have gone dead. Like a torch whose battery's life has run out as a result of its own acid ooze. But in reality this death had always been the warp and weft of the white man's history in this country.

Most other clergy who knew these removals were happening chose to leave at that. They witnessed army trucks thundering past with loads and loads of humans for dumping in some location planned for the resettlement. The authorities knew that Father O'Brien was exploiting the privilege of being born white: he was not so vulnerable to the swift reflexes of a police state. The fact that he was priest-in-charge in the Jesuit mission of St Augustine, some 10 kilometres east of

Marulaneng was but a secondary deterrent against police action. But all this infuriated the officials endlessly. This vast area of sprawling villages that constituted Marulaneng made it one of the most spectacular in the northern region of the old Transvaal Province. Its hills and valleys, its vegetation, were the perpetual envy of the whiteman, provoking the rhetorical question, "What was it that prevented the whites from settling here all these generations past?"

Delegation after delegation, Father O'Brien in each one of them, failed to move Pretoria to change its attitude. He travelled the length and breadth of the country recording forced resettlements wherever they occurred. In all the delegations he joined, he tried to talk reason into the authorities from Pretoria down to the local minions. He produced sheafs and sheafs of paper documenting the soul-shattering state of the areas where people were being moved to. And now Fr O'Brien found himself embroiled in the Marulaneng-Marakong process in an attempt to stall it. He had a faint hope that he might rally financial support and employ legal means to obtain a court interdict. He argued, pleaded, tried to appeal to reason, cautioned with subdued demeanour. His efforts were like trying to strike wet matchsticks on a wet box. How tone-deaf bureaucrats can be! O'Brien mused.

Government said, "There will eventually be 700,000 residents in Marakong . . . . In time the water situation there will improve . . . . People will own plots where they can make vegetable gardens . . . . Eventually there will be no Bantu left in the Republic of South Africa when the homelands have been consolidated, and all will be happy in their separate homelands . . ."

The law and the State's proclamations were irreversible. The juggernaut was set to go.

The delegations despaired. His Archbishop consented to join him in this crusade, but with the propriety befitting his office. They tried to bring home to the officials the brutal truth of Marakong's wretched state. The landscape bore the characteristic scars of soil erosion; a garment of sick grey covered the district, broken by a few hills, abundant thorn bush, cactus. It was drought-prone: for six years running there might be no rain. A smile of half-acknowledgement on the mouth of one of the audience reminded O'Brien of so many other times when he was face to face with inscrutable bureaucracy.

On one of these occasions the Deputy Minister called the Archbishop and his priest instigators, rebels who did not have the support of their congregations. His parting shot was, "And I don't see why you should bring God into this!"

The Pretoria masters moved the pieces on their giant draughtboard at will. Every time they had to account for their policies in Parliament in response to some feeble voices in the opposition ranks, the Minister in charge of the African population or his deputy gave the same explanation in different word order over and over. And Government rode the waves of protest, the honourable members sat back and cheered and guffawed and rested their case with the usual litany of self-congratulatory utterances. The Grand Design was working, they assured their public . . .

As if the Furies were providing an answer, bang! The

territory was declared a "black spot". The authorities, using the jargon of the day, described a black spot as one that contained "surplus people", "redundant, non-productive people". And the military trucks started to roll.

It had rained all that night, pelting and lashing against ill-clad bodies. Stopping for people to relieve themselves merely gave the water more time to drench them, but degrees of wetness were merely an academic matter. The next day the whole landscape was covered with clothes and blankets set out to dry on the baking surface. For the sun had come out in all its renewed fury.

"And now he's here again," Van Rensburg was to say with a smirk, two days after the people had arrived, "he's here again to try to prove how much cruel the white peeples is from this kuntry. Do he thinks my government cannot give this peeples food and medicines? Let him just somaar stomp my toe, poppets they will dance todays — that days. Let him keep out of my ways."

Nothing of the sort happened, on either side. Father O'Brien stayed with the people until they were dried out, the tents had been set up. "Temporary measures" in officialese. Government was soon going to be building three-roomed tin-and-timber structures, the publicity flyer announced.

On the third day Mulder the builder arrived with a huge squad, white technicians and foremen and African manual labourers. Materials arrived shortly afterwards. Pretoria had given him the contract to build 20,000 homes. Individual residents could obtain a permit to build their own homes, with their own materials and hands. Government inspectors would need to approve a house for occupation at the beginning of the operation, in the middle of it and at the end.

Monope, 'Ma-Selepe's son, came with a truck full of building materials. He had taken two weeks from his 21 days' annual leave to come and pitch up a shack for his folks. There were scores of other males who were migrant workers and came at staggered times to build for their families. One of the lasting ravages wrought by the system of migrant labour: the break-up of the family unit, the long intervals between the visits by the male head or other breadwinner. Monope helped one or two families to pitch up theirs and they in turn came to help him with his.

'Ma-Selepe is walking out of the shack in the soft red glow of sunrise. Autumn is in the air. The patches of grass are losing the only little green this part of the land can boast.

Monope and his team have long been up and hammering away to make a habitable structure. These days he does not have time to spend with his mother, as he must finish his project before the two weeks are up. His wife, Baile, is more intimately acquainted with the old woman's anxieties and fears and other moods.

"Did you sleep well, Ngwana'Tabane, you are up so early?" The voice is Baile's. She is sweeping what would have been a yard if the ground around the shack had been fenced.

The older woman does not answer. She simply sits

on a nearby log of wood Monope has hewn out of a tree for her to sit on outside the dwelling-in-the-making. Baile goes to stand by her side, broom still in her hand.

"It is going to be hard, Mother, but things will straighten out, do not cry, I do not want Monope coming here and thinking that I am not treating you well, you hear me Ngwana'Tabane?"

'Ma-Selepe chuckles. "Cry, my child? Women my age do not cry any more. We do not know the meaning of that word any more."

"*Aowa*, Ngwana'Tabane, I do not believe you, there must be things that make you want to cry, things that make you want to laugh. Is it not good life goes on? Surely life is worth the effort to live."

"Wait till you get to my age, my child, and then you will have to ask: 'Is the struggle worth the life?' Take your man, Monope — what is he but a migrant worker — gone for four weeks and home for two days. Is the struggle worth the life?"

"The sun rises for all of us, Mama, it has no spite for anyone, anything."

A low chuckle again. "The whiteman takes it all even before it shows its head in the east — the whiteman — he is in charge of the sun and his god approves. Hear me tell you, my child, even as I say so sitting here, I know the ancestors who sleep awake in those hills we left behind and who roam about in the wind and water and move through the soil and trees — they will also be our strength. Because they have passed through other valleys as painful as ours and they know. But human beings must always have a place to go to where their forefathers lie buried, not so?

"The ground that holds them is holy and now the whiteman has dragged us out and away from them. And now in my old age I feel I have no strength to support me — like a river whose mountain source has been blasted by dynamite and now must choke on its own silt and rocks and who knows what else. I already feel like a mere echo even while I still breathe, and this should not be. It should not be like this. Because either you live in a place and you and the earth give out an echo, or you are an ancestor who is in an echo out of a certain place and a certain time. Do you hear me child?

"Do you hear me child? This is no place — where we are now — the dead hand of the whiteman has fouled it up; this is no time, the dead hand of the whiteman has poisoned it and frozen it. So I should not be sounding like an echo . . . yet I do feel like it: because things are wrong, an evil thing bestrides this land and the sun will be blinded and there will be no night, no day. This is what the whiteman will never understand, never can. When you say to him this ground contains my ancestors, my husband, my children and other beloved ones and I cannot leave them I want to go to their graves so many times to talk to them, to listen to them, whiteman laughs, and then bulges with anger and impatience and he makes long tiresome speeches about somebody in Pitoria they call Goromente, and this man is the father of us all and looks after us. And you know why the whiteman will never understand — not once? Because his big stone head cannot take in anything we tell him — you cannot teach him anything, do what you like. In all my eighty years on this earth I have never known a single whiteman who learned anything or even tried to learn something from us how to live and die. And hear me tell you, child, he could not, so he decided that he did not want to learn, for the reason that he is some god, and a god must not be seen to be stupid, ignorant."

Government brought raw goods to Marakong. Staple food such as maize meal, sorghum meal, flour, sugar, bread, salt, dehydrated milk powder, tinned milk and so on. The people had to buy. Again Father O'Brien was there to provide money to buy food to be rationed. Government trucks brought water in huge drums.

Put a human being anywhere, under the most desolate conditions, and he will instinctively lift himself up to put up a shelter, or hunt for one, gather food and clothing. Van Rensburg knew this. He was cynical enough to lecture his juniors on it — newcomers in the game of processing black people's lives and programming them. Whoever might have had doubts about the agony of removal and resettlement was bound, after the lecture, to feel that the hardships were ultimately neutralized by the human instinct to survive. In other words, you possess the instinct to survive, so what's the problem?

Once a week trucks come and carry people to the town only 100 kilometres away to buy bigger things. They pay but it is not too heavy for them. We allow small traders to come in and sell smaller necessities. We are starting to build a school and a police station for them. What do you find so painful? Van Rensburg would ask, for he was sure he knew all about this instinctive urge. But there was a lot more he didn't know, didn't care to know, couldn't *ever* know. He was aware of this ignorance, but was not prepared to spend sleepless nights over it.

The old woman shivers slightly and adjusts her shawl tighter over the shoulders with unsteady sinewy fingers.

Standing up she says, "Me I am going out to walk about and stretch these old knees. It is also time to find out which way the whiteman's sun is coming from and going, because I can feel that my sun rises and sets elsewhere.

"It is all right, Ngwana'Tabane."

She chooses a direction at random without giving it much thought. Not so long ago she would be walking along a beaten path sure of where she was going. There would be Madinko, Tebora, Santlo, for instance. The four would sit for hours and hours talking and taking snuff, exchanging banter and jokes and woeful stories. Now here she is among strangers from other villages. "Ah," 'Ma-Selepe sighs heavily.

The earth she walks on is grassy and resists her bare feet. Even the bare patches of red soil. The toes begin to tingle and curl inwards, twitching with fear of every step she is taking; twitching as if they had a life of their own, apart from the rest of the body. She turns the feet sideways to feel for softer ground. The undulations she has to negotiate are strange to her, almost hostile, and she nearly falls forward, but for the staff she immediately leans on. For a few crazy seconds she feels as if she has stopped at the lip of a bottomless hole. When she regains her balance and rests both hands on the upright staff there is no hole, the terrain of grass and shrub lies there in front of her, unfriendly, frightfully alien, but there. The breeze comes at her from the wrong side and it chills her bones. An unholy solitude floods 'Ma-Selepe's whole being. She feels as if she can taste, smell, hear and touch something hideous inside and around her.

And as she stands there on the open barren stretch of land, she screams at a quivering pitch, screams to her husband to come and rescue her from the coils of this unholy crushing loneliness.

It is then that she knows for certain it must be done. If she ever doubted that she still had the strength, the revelation of this morning exercise has confirmed her will to do it. This moment when she feels she can hold out her hand and actually touch the pulsating emptiness that hurts so.

In less than the two weeks before her son's departure, 'Ma-Selepe told the family that she had found a friend on the east rim of the new village. She wanted to spend the weekend with her. "I want your father-in-law here to come with me," she announced, referring to Lefanyana her grandson who bore the diminutive form of her late husband's name "Lefa". "Come, come with me my little husband and protect me."

"Wooo-wooh!" Baile exclaimed, "Just look at you Ngwana'Tabane! See there Monope! Her German print blouse and skirt will freeze lions and leopards and antelopes just where they are standing, just to admire her beauty."

"Oh, go away," she said good-humouredly with a gesture of self-deprecation. Baile was still laughing and full of cheer, too, as her mother-in-law and her "little husband" were leaving.

"Wait, wait you two!" Baile called out, remembering something. She ran into the shelter and brought back an extra shirt and pants for Lefanyana.

'Ma-Selepe tugged at the fringes of her colourful shawl to adjust it with an air of finality and finesse that seemed to suggest she was ready, for now, forever. Monope waved as he said, "Go well. Greet them all where you are going." Calling out to his son he said, "I hope you have not forgotten your books I brought you, boy, remember you have some reading to do, eh!"

On the way, not far from home, 'Ma-Selepe stopped by a cluster of trees and pulled out a small bundle of clothing, two blankets, a basket containing a large bowl of porridge, a bag of cooked dehydrated spinach, a small bag of maize meal. Questions from the boy followed in quick succession. "Makgolo, what is in there?. . Why did you hide them here Grandma?. . Do they not have food where we are going Makgolo?. . Are they stingy? Are we coming back Grandma? . . ." Grandma merely said, "Do not be afraid *ngwana'ngwanaka*, do not fear child of my son."

On the road, a donkey-drawn gig stopped abreast of the two.

The reins were in the hands of a middle-aged man, who asked if he might cut short their journey? 'Ma-Selepe's nervous movements as she stepped closer to the gig indicated how much she welcomed the offer. The gigman held out his hand to help the woman up. Soon she and Lefanyana following close behind were comfortably seated behind their host.

"Where is our mother going?"

"Marulaneng," 'Ma-Selepe replied. "If my brother takes us as far as he is going towards Marulaneng — or is he even going that far?"

"Marulaneng?" the gigman enquired. "Did the people not move here?"

"Yes, but does that mean there is nobody at all left in Marulaneng?" She was thinking also, *do not ask any searching questions about me, old man, let us keep things quiet, I pray . . . not when I have such an awesome mission . . .*

The man shrugged his shoulders, saying, "*aretse* — do I know?"

"And you, father, where are you going?"

"*Nna* I am going to Dilokong, still some way before you get to Marulaneng, only I have to leave this road at some point and go west."

After a brief spell, the old woman passed her knotted unsteady fingers over her waist a few times before they disappeared under the cloth belt she wore. She unmade its many folds on her lap. Then she said. "I have fifty shillings here. It is yours, my brother if you take us as far as Marulaneng." She held out five one-rand coins in her hand.

"I will take you to Marulaneng, my sister," the gigman said, taking the money from her hand. "We shall sleep the night at Mogale's village. They will give us food there to eat and to take for the road. Tomorrow we shall continue. As we say, you do not hunt for lice at night, sunrise grudges no-one, it will tell us all we want to know."

As he looked at his passenger she nodded, then

brushed the heel of her hand against the tip of her nose to clear mucus. Something about 'Ma-Selepe's profile — her well defined jaw, her largely unwrinkled face, the taut muscles of her neck — compelled him to keep throwing a glance towards her. In addition to his goodness of heart, the gigman felt a certain aura that commanded acquiescence; some mysterious force radiating from her.

As the donkey cart chewed the road, eating the kilometres, 'Ma-Selepe felt as if it were slowly chewing up the palpable emptiness that was weighing on her. Her shoulders were literally feeling light and at ease. Self-confidence had found anchor, her destination was assured.

The day was silent except for the call of some faraway bird and the jingling of the harness and unrhythmic fall of eight hooves. Here was all shrubland, where the mimosa tree dominates. Far away in the distant haze tall mountains beckoned them. Somewhere in those blue mountains lay Marulaneng. A land from which 'Ma-Selepe's people had been violently uprooted. Because it was surrounded by white people's land and was labelled "black spot".

She knew too that even this land she was travelling through, this vast stretch of brooding thornbush, had once been good grazing land. It fed thousands of cattle and goats and people. Scenes of her childhood and young womanhood replayed themselves before her . . .

The donkey cart ground the miles, bumping over stone and gravel. It only needed her, she realized, to allow her body to hang loose, droop her shoulders, relax the thigh muscles, generally go with the rocking instead of resisting it. The scenes of her life continued to unfold, sometimes seeming to press against her very face and her whole body by turns. Moments of fitful slumber induced by the rocking of the gig kept interfering with the sequence of the scenes.

The rattle of calabashes in earthen pots as she and her peers jogtrotted to the river to fetch water, sunup and sundown . . . the echo of the noise in the valley . . . the loud full-throated laughter of the girls. . . The sounds came alive to her again, travelling some seventy years to remind her of the times of nature's abundance, of innocence . . . She recaptured the *khuui-uuui* in the fields as they chased away the birds from the ripening corn and maize. The afternoon sound of steel pounding on millstones came back to her. This way the stone was made rough for more effective grinding . . . The mind conjured up a picture of columns of smoke from the afternoon's wood fires, shooting up from the homesteads. Girls her age would be preparing the evening meal . . .

She recalled vividly how Lefa Selepe had picked her out of a bunch of maidens who were out wood gathering. Winter time. Just came straight up to her and told her he wanted to show her something. The maiden was puzzled, a little afraid, it seemed her heart had been dislodged from its natural position. Did he beat round the bush? Oh no, not Selepe. She chuckled softly at his forthright manner. Like his name — "axe". He just hacked away at the bush in his way, made a clearing, told her that he wanted her to become his woman. "I want you to be my wife, what do you say?" Her heart did a crazy dance up and down inside her and she was seized by a burning urge to run away. Just as if he had said, "the river is in flood, get out of the way!"

She had bolted out of the clearing, back to her companions. But not before she had observed a lump dart up and down along his throat. That night, oh that night, "What things is this man telling me!" she kept whispering to herself as she lay on her mat. And she felt an ache inside the likes of which she had never known before. Not physical, but an ache in a part of her being that was full of joy and apprehension and was afire — all at once.

'Ma-Selepe had borne him three sons. She and Lefa had known the parental bliss of raising children and seeing one of them, Monope, make his own family and home. Strange, she now thought on the journey back to Marulaneng, how it was that the simple joys of married life merged with larger life and its struggles, to be retrieved years after by the memory and so savoured and cherished even more. Joys that now took on a clearly defined face, like shining pebbles on the bed of a clear stream . . .

It seemed she was never going to stop crying, when the remains of her two elder sons were brought home from the train wreckage. They had been returning home at the end of a mine-work contract that summer, intending both to marry on the same day. The stunning news of the collision: a passenger train and a freight train, one of them on the wrong track. Passengers thrown out as the train, now off its rails for the most part, rolled down the steep slope below . . .

Then Selepe had joined his sons years later.

Every so often tears, which 'Ma-Selepe tried to conceal by inhaling her snuff, stood in tiny points of moisture in the inner corners of her eyes. She wiped her eyes and nose with the back of her hand. The gigman by her side looked stolidly ahead of him. He was not much of a talker, much to the relief of her passenger who had settled for an untalkative journey during which she could collect her thoughts for the ordeal ahead. The man's long silences made 'Ma-Selepe flippantly wonder if he was eavesdropping after her muted rebuke about his long tongue . . . The boy sat or slept behind the couple.

And the cart chewed up the miles of kilometres . . . That stifling and chocking emptiness she had felt before she left was diffused, thanks to her preoccupation with the anticipated conclusion of her odyssey. A conclusion that must end all conclusions. Not long now, she would be on the turf where kith and kin awaited her at the cemetery. What had to be done immediately on her arrival, in itself a task that would claim every nerve and muscle of her being, did not really possess her entire field of consciousness. For there was nothing to cause her anxiety and forebodings.

Nor did she pause to ask why it didn't. She had simply appropriated some corner of a future realm, where she was not accountable for things accomplished or undone. This intervening encounter — this task she had to perform at the end of the journey — she considered to be merely an imperative. It was too important for her to skip if she wanted to lay the matter to rest and then be ready to get on the Major Road to the happier realm. The task would also be an act of self-vindication. A reaffirmation of her state of being and its bond with the rest of nature's mysteries. From the very bowels of her soul she would cry out softly, "Oh Supreme Guide to whom I am joined by the spirits of my ancestors!" An articulation of the very mystery of Nature's continuum. An order by and in which things simply must be done, no matter what. What is more, *we* are the inevitable agents.

'Ma-Selepe noticed that her grandson was in one of the many rounds of deep sleep, interrupted only when he asked to be let down to relieve himself, or when she wanted him to eat something. So she could say certain things with greater ease.

"Old man," she began, "I am going to ask you to do something for us. This child you see here with me, I took with me to protect me. He is a child but with eleven years of day and night in his blood and bones he is a brave man. Now that the ancestors brought you to our help, he can return to his parents. He is my own blood. I would ask you to come back with him on your return. As you tell us you often go to the villages beyond Marakong, you can carry him, he will know where his mother is. I say this because my ancestors are whispering in my ear to tell me that I may not make the journey back to Marakong right away."

The gigman looked at her steadily but her eyes stayed on the course. Perhaps, aware that no amount of scanning would elicit any clue to her meaning, his eyes returned to the road ahead of him.

"Here is the last bit of money I have on me to repay your kindness, child of God, messenger of the ancestors." As she said this she reached for her belt of cloth again to unwrap the money. Ten rands. Another reason for the benefactor to give her a look of amazement.

Lefa, old man, son of Selepe, good husband and father but stubborn, oh, so stone-headed . . . Strong hands, a good farmer . . . Such strength it seems no other person could possess . . . I remember my good man . . . Those months when government forced women to carry passes like our men . . . Then the months of storms when whiteman told us to obey the chief at all times but remember always that there was the great white father in the city of Tshwane who made all the laws . . . The chief was now to be that great chief's eyes and ears . . . I remember all my good man . . . Strange man is that one they call Goromente . . . strange beyond belief . . . strange man . . . A long time ago he took away the chief's manhood, cut off his arms and legs and used him just like a paid policeman . . . He crawled up and down the spine of the chief like a worm sucking on his marrow till the back must break like a twig in the winter time and leave the head dangling like an empty gourd you cannot even use for water to rinse your mouth with . . . My good man how can I forget these things that changed the days of plenty into the desert sands of our present time . . . Today you see the chief dressed in whiteman's cast-offs and canvas shoes without soles and laces, toes sticking out . . . You see him sit before his court of councillors hearing cases of stock thefts and rogues who beat their wives . . . No more than that . . . nothing more . . .

Oh, ancestors that watch over us and ask for nothing in return we have seen things that blind the sun in our time . . . Mabena, Ditau, Matime, Serumula, Makuru — what did they leave behind them but these tiny men who have the time and spirit to quarrel among themselves like crows and chew each other's buttocks off while the other is not looking . . . selling out and betraying each other to please the great father . . . Mabena and Ditau carried away by the great chief's messengers to faraway lands for their disobedience — to Natal, to the Cape . . . I remember how they were first arrested for encouraging us to rise against passes for women . . . The days we were driven to jail for the first time in our lives . . . I chuckle now to think that we should have felt the insult like a spear hanging from the breast . . . that being arrested and pushed this way and that by special police from Tshwane young enough to be still wetting their pants . . . that we should have thought the sun was going to rise in the west or a cow was going to give birth to a pig so much it seemed like woman was no longer woman, neither man, a cow no longer a cow, mountains no longer what we knew them . . . Then, you remember after fourteen days in jail we all said things were never going to be the same again. Funny thing, husband of mine, is it not? From day to day things change in front of our eyes and we never take notice until you are thrown into jail and insulted in a way that shakes you up and throws you bodily against the wall . . .

And now they tell us those big fat red men in Tshwane that this chief is our little father . . . he is filled with the spirit of the white father when he tells us they are moving us to a place of plenty and happiness . . .

My old man you have seen for yourself the earlier time when the people burned down the houses of chiefs and headmen who were speaking to us with whiteman's tongue . . . like Selati and Matime . . . This man they call government simply sent us a useless wet-nose of a nephew of blind old Serumula to rule in his place . . . a young man who has nothing but mud in his head when you put him beside his uncle . . . because his uncle was on our side and said no to the wickedness of Goromente . . .

The anger in the people's hearts . . . think of that, old man . . . because we love Serumula . . . This young iguana his nephew knows no more about our life than he can see the tip of his own nose. Just went to Gauteng and dug the iguana out of the rubble and threw him on our lap . . .

And 'Ma-Selepe's memory reeled off the events of her life, her husband's, her people's. The turbulent times and the quieter times; times of plenty and times of drought. The passes, land hunger, forced removals, all flashpoints of the people's anger, the consequent public stoning of Serumula's nephew to a bundle of mangled flesh and bones, reports of which were noised abroad from mouth to ear to mouth. The chase from the village to village in broad daylight when mother rat is suckling its babies, as the common saying goes . . . yet more stoning . . . and the final blow on the temple: indeed the way boys stoned an iguana because of the common knowledge that you never found it on the killing ground if you returned later . . . What was his name again? Do you think I still remember?

Peculiar man, is *Goromente*. He simply left off . . . did not again try to bring someone else. But how deceptive, too! Just when people are savouring victory the police come, batch after batch. Power show . . . They leave, almost like a dog that has urinated on a tree or vehicle in order to remember where to come next time . . .

Van Rensburg arrives. He is in charge of this whole removal drama. Peculiar. Lays out his net like a spider . . . because Van Rensburg looks all reasonable. Does not usually curse blue fire like so many other State officials. Speaks to the people as if he were actually going to advise Pretoria not to enforce the removal order. But comes the day of reckoning, he is the whiteman people in rural country are accustomed to, white to the marrow: bulging with power borrowed from Pretoria.

Certainly not the farmer type, bloated to the roots of

the ginger hair on his weather-beaten arms; not stomping up and down and spuming off obscenities, generally feeling insecure. No, not that type at all. Even speaks to the chiefs with a show of respect. But when he comes back brandishing the law like a sjambok Van Rensburg will brook nothing that he does not consider to be obedience.

A number of farmers in the district were telling their labourers not to fear removal. Their place on their land was secure. But they ordered their labourers to take the news round among the villages — on weekends — that they were being moved to better land, like the Promised Land in the Bible; that they should not resist the great father's order. They should not listen to those chiefs who, the farmers alleged, were being visited in the dead of night by terrorists. These were also communists, the farmers emphasized.

Selepe was "cheeky" enough to ask what a terrorist was, what a *komunisi* was, and a *terorisi.* For all the labourers cared, the farmer might just as well have been warning them against fireflies.

You want to know what is terorisi, komunisi? I will tell you because I can see that your understanding, your eyes, are still plastered over with black and red mud. They mean trouble-makers, thieves, killers, destroyers, Satan worshippers. That is what the whiteman tells my husband Selepe. When I ask my man whether these trouble-makers we never see, whether they are humans or white people, he laughs and laughs and laughs . . .

'Ma-Selepe, he replies, he says, my wife, you can be so raw like the trees and the grass! They are humans like you and me and many others are white people. I ask where they come from

and my man says Fatamabele told him they come riding on crocodile backs across Lepelle River. But from where? I want to know. Selepe tells me, he says, just close your mouth, God's woman, your tongue is too long.

Selepe my good man, I say to him one night before we fall asleep. It is late, and I can hear the first cocks crow for people to leave their night fireplaces. I say to him this Fatamabele worries me. Like all these farmers to tell the truth. Why are they saying we should not say No to him, I mean Goromente? What have the farmers to do with whether we go or whether we stay? What is it to Fatamabele? Why are they not sorry to lose the people who are like donkeys to them to keep in harness if we all have to move? And still they say we can stay on their land if we choose to — why? tell me Selepe.

And Selepe makes a sound like a yawning lion and he says the white man is always full of mathaithai — just wants to trick us all the time. You see my good woman, he wants it to appear that the choice is ours to stay or to go. But the truth is that they do not mind losing us now that machines and engines do most of the work. See already how Fatamabele is shrinking into a mere pig-keeper. Of course he is plain lazy, drunk most of his waking life. He cannot farm crops any longer, you wait and see. You see the trick, good woman — these farmers must not support us and thus go against their own Goromente, and yet they do not want to lose us all. Now, we shall go and meet — we from Fatamabele and those from the other farms and we shall talk there and give one another advice and hope we can agree not to tell anybody to leave to the new place.

'Ma-Selepe smelled treachery in Van der Merwe's exhortation to the labourers to leave together with the villagers. Why should he say they may leave when he cannot do anything without us, twenty of us?

The land is too big for him, she mused. Especially since his wife and three sons left home, more years ago than she can remember — likely four. *Have you ever seen them again? Remember how leburu went on fire when you first asked him where his family had gone? And then what does leburu decide? — to make you Selepe foreman. Just when tempers were blazing in the villages.*

Yes, Selepe affirms. Foreman on a dying farm. And just when the new orders to move have poisoned village life and people are sharpening knives and axes and government is loading guns. One heart says we should leave Fatamabele, my old man says, the other heart says let the sky rain fire or water we stay here. Then my man breathes fast and loud and he says I am a habit of Fatamabele's, so he cannot throw me out.

What are you saying, my man? I ask, fixing my eyes on his. I do not hear you well. Sometimes my man spoke a language I believed only his own secret heart could understand. And when I wanted to know more he simply kept silent and then ran his hand over his face down from the forehead. As if to say if you do not read my meaning on my face then there is no other way I can explain. Or perhaps, perhaps did he himself know full well what he meant deep down? I do not know.

Then there was no talk in the villages about moving anymore. No more noisy talk about it. It was quiet, like when a hailstorm has been chattering on the roof with a deafening noise and suddenly the rain stops. But the sound of thunder continued to hang in the air. We all knew the storm was not gone. The all-wise Supreme Spirit alone knew when . . .

Fatamabele was constantly in a drunken stupor. He

grew noisier and more boorish by the day, his temper on a short fuse. Some people of his own tribe carried away his tractors and other hardware. He threw his labourers off his farm, one by one. Not in the save-yourself spirit but rather in a mood that said to them, "Get off my land, if I must drown in the raging river of brandy let it be now but not naked before staring mocking eyes of *kaffers*."

Selepe was right, the farm was dying, under stinkweed and coarse grass. Only the oversize pigs rooting in front of the main house gave some indication that there was still human life there.

How could 'Ma-Selepe fail to remember the awful night? How can I ever forget it? she kept saying to herself weeks after the event. The sunset party a few metres from the house . . . tall and burly men on the stoep, some standing, some sitting, all hee-hee-hawing with drunken abandon, their colour a deep brownish red, arms covered with brown and ginger hair . . . Padi and another of Selepe's friends carrying her husband into their shack not far from where the red men are, indeed in full view of them. Selepe bloody all over, a tall lanky body sprawling on the earth floor, cut up as if some unknown creature of the night has mauled him . . .

I can still hear my man groaning and choking on the words that were struggling to come out: they have killed me . . . Fatamabele, F-ata-m-ma-b-ele and his drunken friends . . . they have killed me . . . hear me tell you.

We wash his face, remove his clothing and wrap him up in a blanket.

Padi my son, what happened? Padi tells me. He is not one to speak carelessly on such a serious matter. I was there, he says, I saw everything, our mother . . . One of the men calls Selepe when we pass the house . . . he shouts, "Hei you, what do they call you? I mean you the tall kaffer." It is clear he means Selepe. "You tall kaffer," leburu repeats . . . come and fetch me water to drink . . . Selepe turns round and shouts, "You are not my baas, I do not work for you." The man comes straight to us, takes his fist and hammers Selepe on the side of the head — ta!

Padi continues his account. Selepe holds him, shakes him and throws him hard on the ground. Another leburu and still another one, they throw themselves on top of Selepe pounding him with fists and kicking him. Fatamabele comes with his heavy kubu and gives Selepe a number of savage blows on the body and in the face — vu vu vu! Our mother! We plead to Fatamabele to let us carry Selepe away. Only then do they stop. Our mother! Where are the ancestors to give us strength against these beasts!

In the flickering light of the fire at the corner of our shack we try to stretch and rub Selepe's body. I try to speak to him but he only groans. I cry and cry and through the night from time to time we hear the hee-hee-hawing from Fatamabele, as if the night itself were laughing.

Selepe tries to raise his head and . . . then he gasps . . . the last thing I was ever going to hear my man say. He turns his back on us and the world forever . . .

Padi and his friend report the matter to the chief and the police come from Mashishing far away . . . We never hear of the matter again after this. My son comes and buries his father in the village cemetery. He brings his wife and son to Serumula's village and I go and live with them . . . A woman with a beautiful heart, my daughter-in-law . . .

We always hear stories about maburu beating black people to death with kubu but I never imagined something like this would visit my family, even though we knew it was always possible . . .

After a good night's rest the gigman had anticipated, the cart and beasts proceeded to plough and chew up the last few kilometres with asinine endurance. Enquiries from passersby brought out the information that Rameetse, Fatamabele's swineherd, was the only man left on the farm. Past the deserted villages the gigman, 'Ma-Selepe and grandson went straight to Rameetse's shack on the eastern fringe of the farm.

He stared incredulously at them out of his bleary eyes, as if he had the fright of his life. Must be brewing his own beer, the sot, 'Ma-Selepe deduced.

"It is me, Rameetse," she said, "I have not risen from the grave. I am passing on and ask for shelter for a few nights, son of the people." Gradually things seemed to fall into place in the swineherd's mind. He smiled to show consent, although the whole situation was too complicated for him to comprehend. He seemed to be quite contented to let it be.

Next morning, after a breakfast of porridge and *morogo*, 'Ma-Selepe drew her grandson to her bosom and said gravely but affectionately, "Child of my son, you are a man now. You are grown up, see how you have protected your grandmother all this way. I am so happy you will be able to look after your mother and the little ones who will come after you, not so? Yes. This father who has been so good to us will take you to his home and he will find someone to take you back to Marakong if he himself does not. Say to Mama that I borrowed you and am returning you, you hear? And greet them at home, you hear?"

"When are you coming back, *makgolo*?" He asked the question without showing any anxiety whatever.

"Soon, my child, soon. When I have finished my work here."

Gigman, donkeys and grandson were released, after profuse words and gestures of gratitude and mutual regard between the grownups.

"Rameetse son of the people," 'Ma-Selepe said, "you go about your work, do not bother yourself about this old woman. I do not have many days left on this earth, and I am readier for the moment now than I shall ever be."

He was accustomed to hear old people ramble in this manner, audience or none. A thin shaft of light managed to pierce through the thick layer of his beer-sodden brain. The light brought it home to him that it would be folly for him to stand in the way of the inevitable that he divined was already on its course. Rameetse knew that he was hearing the words of someone whose age and faith entitle him or her to catch a breeze from the ancestral valleys.

At her man's grave she merely said to him, *"I have come my good man, I have arrived. I will be talking to you as soon as I have accomplished what I have to do, which you know very well. All I pray is that you and the whole company of our ancestors with whom you live should ask the*

Supreme Being to give me the courage, the strength , to accomplish this. So be it husband of mine." And she left.

Nothing happened for three consequent nights and days. On the fourth night a befuddled Van der Merwe made it known to Rameetse that he would be gone all of the next day and night and would be back the following day. He also gave the cook a day and night off.

Rameetse having gone out to seek companionship among his beasts, as the villagers used to say, 'Ma-Selepe disappeared in a nearby bush. She came out with a rusted can in her hand. Her gait indicated that the 5-litre can contained something. This was the time for it. A few splashes and the house would be a sure inferno. As long as no one would die. She just had to try to make sure that neither Rameetse nor the cook would do the human but foolish thing of trying to put out the flames. She gave Rameetse a few coins to buy himself beer and to give the cook for the same purpose. She charged him with a threatening look in her eyes not to breathe a word to the cook about her presence and made him swear by his late mother. She wouldn't need to worry about the cook, Rameetse told her, because he had already gone to visit his people a long distance away.

The old woman carried the fuel can to Fatamabele's house. She placed it in a concealed place under the creeper at the back. She walked back to Rameetse's house. She needed to calculate the necessary steps and reinforce her resolve. Although she was sure Selepe and the other ancestors would give her the strength to execute this thing, she was aware of the strain of the last few days on her body and inner resources: all that intensive, almost minute-to-minute awareness of self and purpose . . .

'Ma-Selepe sees the sun climbing towards the meridian and goes to sit down in the shade of the shack, leaning against its wall. A picture of apparent serenity and firm purpose. Why am I not getting up to splash the petrol in every room of that beast? she dares to ask herself. Each time she wants to stand up some force seems to hold her down. She does not feel it physically, she tells herself. It is in another zone of her being. It is not even a change of purpose determined by any moral self-restraint. Because she believes she still feels the hate for Van der Merwe that has become something like a monument over the years, a bitter tribute to the man. She almost knew right after her husband's death just what she wanted to do, had to do, and how to do it. She never conceived for one moment that she needed any extra propulsion for the deed. Now, at this moment, it seems to her that she does need it. Why? Why?

Rameetse returns. He wears that perpetual smile on his face that is not connected with anything one can perceive. They exchange a few words. By all appearances he is sober. He sits in front of her, his knees raised fireside style. He fixes a steady look on the woman. She returns it. There are questions they are asking of each other in this silence.

After a spell Rameetse says, "I am not a halfwit as many people think, you know mother."

"What gives you the idea that I am one of the many?"

"All right mother. Your secrets are safe in this heart,

no living soul can unlock them. You have something terrible to do, I feel it in my bones."

The look on his face makes 'Ma-Selepe feel there is nothing she needs to conceal from the swineherd. "How did you know?"

"My ancestors tell me things. Let me ask you: will it be with a gun or a knife or will you burn the house down, or will it be both death and fire?"

Silence.

"I cannot tell you that," she replies, in spite of what her instinct tells her.

"Let me say this mother of the people, if you want to remove the man from this earth, then do it if you have the heart. Now he is away for the day, so the reason you have not done it must mean that you are hesitating, right? If you cannot do it when he is asleep or awake in his house then what is the use burning down the house? It can only mean that you are afraid, because taking a life or more is truly a terrifying thing. He will not suffer if you choose to destroy the house, because there are many homes where trash like him find refuge. And he is not going to thank you for sparing his life, and he is not going to repent. Have you ever asked yourself daughter of the people if your heart can carry the weight of such a deed? Can you carry the weight across that river we all must come to first before we proceed to the land of the ancestors? For we must all cross over, and the beauty is that we have no choices to confuse us."

Silence.

"Think on it, good mother, think on it. I have brought some meat and will make us fire to cook porridge and pumpkin as well." He leaves her sitting against the wall. She unfolds her legs from under her body and stretches them, enjoying the sensuous uncoiling of the body.

Suddenly 'Ma-Selepe seems to wake up from a dream into a bright new dawn and open skies. The knot that she has felt all along inside loosens. She feels liberated by Rameetse's words. Through his voice, it seems, her own ancestors are coming to her rescue, the kind she would not have dreamed of . . .

Something about the swineherd's face, in its own inarticulate way, was conveying to her some unspeakable terrible truths. She is not sure exactly what they are. She must cross over without a load on her back. Her instinct tells her: let the wind blow trash, like chaff, any way it wants. Me and my husband are together again . . .

After a delicious supper, 'Ma-Selepe says slowly, "Son of the people, night is here, and I must go and speak to my husband at the cemetery. The ancestors, like the Almighty Spirit, do not give any one by hand. They send someone, some event, some moment. So they will repay you for your kindness. Me I have only been given the tongue to thank you."

Again Rameetse knows better than to try to stall the inevitable. He merely helps her up and gives her her staff, and says, "may the ancestors light the way ahead for you, good mother".

His eyes follow her until she disappears in the dark.

She walks slowly until she reaches the graves. She goes to her man's, sits down and lies on the warm earth of the mound. She is sure her people will find her in quick time — here, her last resting place . . .

Notes

1. Sesotho adulteration of Van der Merwe.
2. Sesotho for Lydenburg.
3. Hippopotamus.
4. Government.
5. Ancestors.
6. Sesotho for boer.
7. Plural of leburu.
8. *Tau* = lion: *babinatau* is an exclamation by one whose totem is the lion.